Golf in the Kingdom

An Esalen Book

The Esalen Publishing Program is edited by Stuart Miller

"Hell," from *The Garden of Earthly Delights* by Hieronymus
Bosch. Shivas Irons claimed that Bosch played an early form
of golf called *kolven*. This painting, he said, depicts the
agonies the painter saw on those early golf courses.

Golf in the Kingdom

Michael Murphy

For my parents,
John and Marie Murphy

"The game was invented a billion years ago—
don't you remember?"

—Old Scottish golf saying

Contents

Golf in the Kingdom

PART I

Shivas Irons

In Scotland, between the Firth of Forth and the Firth of Tay, lies the Kingdom of Fife—known to certain lovers of that land simply as "The Kingdom." There, on the shore of the North Sea, lies a golfing links that shimmers in my memory— an innocent stretch of heather and grassy dunes that cradled the unlikely events which grew into this book. For reasons political and arcane I cannot tell you its real name, so will call it instead the Links of Burningbush. Maybe you have played it yourself and will recognize it from my description. But I must warn you that even its terrain and the name of the town in which it is located are veiled, for the members of the venerable golf club that governs those links are strangely threatened by the story I will tell.

There I met Shivas Irons, introduced to me simply as a golf professional, by accident one day in June 1956. I played a round of golf with him then, joined him in a gathering of friends that evening, followed him into a ravine at midnight looking for his mysterious teacher, watched him go into ecstatic trance as the sun came up, and left for London the following afternoon—just twenty-four hours after we had met—shaken, exalted, my perception of things permanently altered.

The first part of this book is about that incredible day, seen again through fifteen years in which my memory of our meeting passed through unaccountable changes. How did he and his teacher carry on their experiments with consciousness and the structure of space during all those rounds of golf on the Burningbush Links without the players or green-keepers ever knowing? Did he actually change shape and size as I seem to remember him doing, or was that a result of the traumas I went through then? Did he drive the eighteenth green some 320 yards away? I'm fairly certain he did that. During the years since our meeting I have been haunted by questions like these. Our day together has gotten into my inner life, shaping and reshaping my memories, my attitudes, my perceptions. At times I almost think he is here in the flesh, his presence is so vivid, especially when I play a round of golf. Then I could swear he is striding down the fairways with me, admonishing or consoling me with that resonant Scottish burr or suggesting some subtle readjust-ment of my swing. His haunting presence leads me back to the game, in spite of all my prejudice against its apparent inanities. On a golf course I can begin to recreate that day in 1956.

Part two of this book is my attempt to make sense of some passages which I was fortunate enough to copy from his journals. For the man was a philosopher-poet and an historian of sorts. His sayings have stuck in my mind as well as the memory of his prodigious golf shots. Whatever led me to copy those sentences escapes me now. Like my meeting with him, I must put it down to unbelievably good luck. Or perhaps I knew, in some precognitive way, that I was not to see him again. For I have tried without success these several years to re-establish contact with him. In the town of Burningbush no one knows where he is or what he is doing. He is simply—as the barman at the ancient golf club said—at large in the world.

When I left Scotland after that memorable visit, I was on my way to India, to study philosophy and practice meditation at the ashram of the Indian seer Aurobindo. When I reached my destination, I became absorbed in the discipline I found there and the memory of my time in Burningbush began to recede. In that austere and devoted place adventures on golf courses seemed a frivolous waste of time. My rhetoric and interior dialogues then were clothed in the words of Aurobindo and Saint John of the Cross, Plotinus and Meister Eckhart. Hardly a notion or phrase from my conversations in Scotland crept in.

After a year and a half in India, I returned to California, It was then that Shivas Irons began to haunt me. I began to hear his voice, making the same suggestions he had made to me during our day together. "Aye one fiedle afore ye e'er swung," the sentence came like a litany. Sometimes I would hear him as I was falling asleep.

In the summer of 1961 Richard Price, a classmate from Stanford who had become fascinated with the latent possibilities of the mind, heard that I was living in San Francisco and came to see me. Before long we had conceived a plan for an institute in Big Sur, on my family's old estate there, and our dream soon became a reality of sorts—not the one we had talked about exactly, but something like it, something recognizably in the direction of an ashram and forum where East and West could meet. About that time memories of Shivas took an even stronger hold on me. That someone so mystically gifted should be a golf professional— and such a proficient one—filled me with increasing wonder. For the difficulties of remembering and embodying the higher life while laboring in the lower were becoming ever more apparent as our little institute took shape. Psychiatrists, hippies, and swingers, learned men from universities and research centers, wounded devoted couples and gurus from the end of the world were descending upon us in answer to our letters and brochures. We were caught in a social movement we hardly knew existed. New adventures of the spirit were beginning, of the spirit and the body, of the spirit and the bedroom, of encounter groups and endless therapies—a vast exploration of what my teacher Aurobindo had called "the vital nature." Swept along in the heady river of The Human Potential, as we called it then, I came to admire what Shivas Irons had so firmly joined in his life—all those worlds above and below that met in his remarkable golf swing, in the way he greeted friends at the bar of the Burningbush club.

One night in Big Sur, after a particularly rousing and exhausting session of something called "psychological karate," I was drawn to the box of papers I had collected during my trip to India. I found the notes I had copied from his journals. Seeing them again in Big Sur, so far from the Kingdom of Fife, brought back the experience like a flood. Suddenly the feeling of it all, the smell of heather and those evanescent vistas of purple and green were there again in all their original intensity. For an hour or so I was in Scotland again, walking the cobblestone streets of that little town, smelling the salt air, looking out in some kind of satori from the hill above hole thirteen. The thrill of it was so deep, so full of blazing awareness that I wondered how I had forgotten. I was dumfounded, as I read through those notes, at my genius for repression.

I decided that the time had come to reestablish contact. The next day I wrote him a letter. Months passed without a reply. But my desire to hear from him continued to grow. I wrote a second letter sometime during the summer of 1964, but still there was no reply. I wrote a third to his friends the McNaughtons, but it was returned without a forwarding address. By then it was well into 1965 and I was caught up in the full tide of those utopian days at our institute. We were becoming famous, at least in certain circles, and for a while it seemed that we were on the verge of some immense discovery. We were planning a Residential Program with a huge array of disciplines for stretching the human potential; the idea behind it was to develop "astronauts of inner space" who would break through to dimensions of consciousness not yet explored by the human race. At times we talked in terms of a "Manhattan Project" of the psyche. But it soon became evident that breakthroughs could be in the wrong direction, that we were in for a longer haul than some of us had thought. Our more ambitious programs began to founder as some of our astronauts came crashing back to earth, and we began to learn that the programing of consciousness was an unpredictable venture. This sobering change in perspective was reinforced by what we saw happening in the Big Sur country around us. Thousands of young people from all over the United States were coming down the coast highway looking for some final Mecca of the counter-culture, and during the summer of 1967, the "Summer of Love," it seemed that most of them wanted to camp on our grounds. They came with dazed and loving looks, with drugs and fires, swarming into the redwood canyons and up over the great coast ridges, many of them polluting and stealing along the way. The air was filled with a drunken mysticism that undermined every discipline we set for the place. Late that summer I got hepatitis.

Convalescing, I resolved that I would visit Burningbush again and find the man who embodied so much of the life I was aspiring for, so much that was lacking in that summer of chaos. But a slow recovery and the adventures and problems of our institute kept me from the journey for another three years. I was not able to arrange a visit until the summer of 1970.

I had come to England with a group of friends, and as soon as I could I rented a car and drove to Edinburgh, and thence to the Kingdom of Fife. But what disappointment! Shivas was long gone, where he was no one knew. His old landlady rolled back her eyes when I asked about him, gave a wistful shrug, and said that letters sent to his forwarding address in London were now returned. He had left sometime in the fall of 1963. "Oh, he was a wild one," she said in that fondly reproving way I remembered all his friends doing. I could tell she still missed him terribly.

The Burningbush golf club was rich with the smells of leather and burning logs, with quiet good cheer and mementos of a treasured past—crossed swords and tartans, enormous trophies and pictures of ancient captains staring down from the walls. The bartender, my one link with that day in 1956, fondly reminisced about his extraordinary friend. I learned then that Shivas had never actually worked for the golf club itself. He had been a teaching professional in his own employ; he had wanted it that way to "preserve his peculiar teaching ways."

"Oh, there was no one else like 'im, that's for sure," the barman said and smiled wistfully. " 'Cept for Seamus, and he's gone, too." Seamus MacDuff, whom Shivas called his teacher, had died a few years before. So had Julian Laing, the town's remarkable doctor, who was another of Shivas's special friends. Evan Tyree, the well-known golf champion and his most famous pupil, had gone to New Zealand in some mysterious land deal. And the McNaughton family had moved to Africa. All the people I had met fourteen years before had vanished, except for this good-natured rotund barman, red-faced and grayer than when I had seen him last.

I introduced myself, suddenly aware of how important he was, my last link with Shivas Irons conceivably.

"Liston's my name," he said, reaching out a hand, "just call me Liston. Christian name's Sonny, but the men here call me Liston." He slipped me a glass of Scotch—and then another—and we spent the afternoon reminiscing about our departed friend while he served the club members and kept the fire, which I remembered so well, burning brightly.

"It was amazin' to watch him come on to the people here," he said, "he was so different with each and every one, if ye watched him close. So I can see wha' ye mean when ye say he changed his shape. I watched him for so many years, watched him grow up, ye know. He was more fascinatin' the more ye watched him. My wife used to say she could tell when we'd been togither—said I picked up his way o' talkin' and gesturin'. Funny thing about that, she liked it when I'd been around 'im, said I seemed to like *her* more afterwards." He shook his head with the knowing smile of a husband who has been through the marital wars. "He was a vivid one awright. Ye know another peculiar thing? I've been thinkin' about 'im lately, been thinkin' o' the way he hit his practice shots out there," he pointed out a window to a deserted tee. "There was somethin' about the way he hit those shots tha' used to get to me—and still does—somethin' funny. I still think about that swing o' his . . . and the look on his face." I asked him if he and Shivas ever talked about the philosophical side of the game. "Very seldom," he said, "hardly ever, come to think of it. I never understood his talk about the inner mind and such, but he never talked much like tha', just now and then wi' someone like yersel', someone on to philosophical things. But with everyone he talked—never knew 'im to be lost for words. Course most o' the men here wanted his advice from time to time, and he was quick to give it."

I asked him if he had any idea about where Shivas might be. "No idea at all," he said. "Somethin' was gettin' to him though, toward the end. He talked a lot about the need to move on, heard him say that to the people here before he left. Sometimes too he talked about his needin' to help the poor." He shook his head as if he were puzzled. "And then there was quite a bit o' talk about his galavantin'. 'Twas said he had some problems wi' the women. 'Twas even said he was a little off when it came to the ladies." He pointed a finger at his head as he said this. "But of coorse 'twas said about him generally from time tae time—just a little off." Again the finger was pointed at the head. "But he was aye guid to me, and a great one for singin' and enjoyin'. No one else could sing a ballad like 'im."

After more conversation, it became apparent that Liston still missed his friend keenly, and was telling the truth when he said Shivas had left no traces. No one in Burningbush, it seemed, knew how I could find him.

I left Scotland in a heavy depression. I had waited so long

to see him again, a place in my consciousness had been prepared for our eventual meeting. The depression lasted until I decided to write this book. Writing it would summon his presence, I thought, and indeed it has. Digging into my memory for clues to his character and state of mind has yielded unexpected insights. Once I began to write, I realized that that one day in 1956 had enough in it to last me a lifetime, especially if I put some of his admonitions to work.

Having completed this book, I realize there was far more to Shivas Irons than I have been able to capture. Some of his enigmatic remarks, all those journals of his I never opened, and the unexplained events of that day in 1956 constantly remind me of that. There is much about our meeting that is still obscure. I have decided to put forth what I have, however, rather than wait for the day of final clarity, which may yet be a long way off.

And also—I must admit it—a hope lurks that this slender volume will lure its real author out of hiding.

A Footnote Regarding His Name

As I have said, "Burningbush" is a fanciful name for the actual golfing links in Fife upon which my adventures took place. The same is true for the names of three or four characters in the story. But I have left the name of my protagonist intact: Shivas Irons was the appellation he had carried all his life. It is so unusual that I have looked up its etymology; and indeed there are records of its origins and history. Shivas or Shives is a Scottish family name, which was known in East Aberdeenshire as early as the fourteenth century; a district there has sometimes been known as Shivas. *Chivas Regal* is a famous Scotch whisky. In Scots dialect there is a verb "shiv" or "shive," which means to push or shove; perhaps the family took its name from some early conquest in which it pushed the older peoples out. There is also a noun "shive," which means a slice of bread; I would prefer to think that his name derived from that, since he offered me the very bread of life in his presence and wisdom. There is also the noun "shivereens," which has approximately the same meaning as the word "smithereens," namely fragments, atoms, shivers ("he was blown to smithereens"); that relationship is apropos, seeing what he did to certain people's perceptions. I could find no connection though with the ancient Hindu name for the God of Destruction and Redemption, perhaps the oldest of all living words for Deity (icons of Shiva date back to the second or possibly the third millennium B. C.). That was a disappointment, but I have consoled myself by remembering that direct etymologies are not the only sign of inner connection.

The name "Irons" was known in the region of Angus as early as the fifteenth century. I have not been able to trace a clan connection for it, however (or for Shivas). Every bit of knowledge regarding his ancestry holds great fascination, I find, increasingly so as my hopes of seeing him again continue to fade, for perhaps the family history will give me some clue to his character. The Scots word "iron" (or "irne") is interesting in this regard, for it means a sword. That it came to mean a golf club suggests an important turn in the Scottish character. Indeed, it also came to mean a part of the plow. Turning swords to plowshares is, as I like to see it, one of the chief promises the game holds out for us.

Shivas Irons: it is such an appropriate name for the man. What did his parents have in mind when they laid it on him? Another Scottish philosopher, Thomas Carlyle, said a name surrounds us all our life like a cloak and ". . . what mystic influence does it not send inwards, even to the centre; especially in those plastic first-times, when the whole soul is yet infantine, soft, and the invisible seedgrain will grow to be an all overshadowing tree!" A name can shape a life, and if his soul took birth to do the work I found him doing, how well his parents sensed it and named him for the task.

Golf in the Kingdom

Personal charm is a physical thing. It also carries elements of endless surprise. Physical and surprising, matter and something new, bodying forth what you would never expect. From the very beginning that is what my encounter with Shivas Irons was like.

The pro shop at Burningbush stands behind the first tee, some 30 yards from the imposing clubhouse. The little building seemed familiar as I entered, for I had read about it in a book of memoirs by a famous Scots golf professional. There was even a sense of *déjà vu* as I looked around the place; I could have sworn I had seen the little man behind the starter's desk before. He showed me the clubs and shoes he had to rent, studying me, as he did, with a sly curiosity. I could tell he was watching as I waggled some of the woods and irons.

"Are ye lookin' for a game?" he asked. I said that I was. Having heard so much about the difficulties of Burningbush Links and its well-known obstacles, I felt I could use some support and guidance going around it.

"Are ye an American?" he asked as he fussed with his equipment display.

"Yes, I am," I replied.

"A toorist heer?"

"I'm a student. I've heard a lot about Burningbush and always wanted to play it. I had a dream once I played it."

"Wha' ye studyin'?"

"Philosophy. I'm on my way to India." I was a little embarrassed saying it. I usually was in those days, especially around men. Indian philosophy was neither practical nor completely manly.

He watched me put on a pair of golf shoes and choose the set of clubs I wanted.

"Well, I think I can get ye a game," he said after a moment's silence. "There's a professional here takin' someone for a teachin' round. Maybe ye'd like to play along wi' them?"

I was delighted. A pro could help me out there on Lucifer's Rug, I said, referring to one of the links' famous hazards.

"Oh, he may help ye now, and then again he may na'. There they are, out there." He pointed through the pro shop window to a pair of men talking on the first tee.

I gathered up the paraphernalia I had rented and carried it outside to a little bench, then took out the driver for some practice swings. The two figures were conversing about 30 feet away. They stood with their backs to me, looking down the first fairway. The taller of the two, obviously the teacher, was pointing to a distant object and explaining something with a voice that conveyed a strong sense of authority. I walked toward them and hesitantly cleared my throat to announce my arrival. They continued talking, apparently unaware that I was there. I cleared my throat again and ventured a small "Hello." The taller one, the teacher, turned to face me. That penetrating, disconcerting look—I realized at once that we had already met!

About an hour before, I had taken a wrong turn on my way to the clubhouse. By mistake I had gone down a path behind the caddies' shelter and had come to a dark, narrow corridor between the shelter and a high embankment. About 15 feet away from me, a figure was jumping grotesquely and kicking at an overhanging beam some 10 feet above the ground. With each kick the jumping figure would twist and fall back, breaking the fall with outstretched arms. The performance was repeated several times. He was apparently trying to kick the beam, trying to reach a point as high as a basketball hoop with his foot instead of his hand! Not knowing whether to intrude or retreat, I stood transfixed in the shadows of the passageway as this strange performance continued in silence. The only sound the jumper made was a weightlifter's explosive exhalation before each effort. He was totally unaware of my presence. After five or six arabesques in midair, he finally grazed the beam above him with the toe of his shoe—I realized it was a golf shoe!—and landed on his chest and stomach. For a moment he lay with his face to the ground, breathing deeply. Then he looked up and saw me staring down at him with embarrassed fascination.

He stood up without a word, pulling himself to his full height, some six feet two or three, and I met that uncanny look for the first time. It was ever so slightly cross-eyed—perhaps from the jumping—something wild and serene, for a second the space between us wavered.

Then, suddenly, he grinned and a second face appeared, an entirely different emanation, a look that was immensely warm and engaging with a big, slightly bucktoothed grin. He winked and wagged his head with an ironic gleam—as if to say, "Hang in there, boy"—and walked past me without a word. As he went past, I could smell him. It was the smell of eucalyptus and baking bread, a powerful and distinctive odor.

Now here we were face to face again. A shock of untamed reddish hair fell across his forehead and his blue unsettling eyes looked straight into mine. I introduced myself. He smiled his bucktoothed smile again and said in his resonant Scots dialect, "Shivas Irons ma nemme, and this gentleman is Mr. Balie MacIver." He pointed to his playing partner, then turned abruptly to look down the fairway. I brought my golf clubs up to the tee blocks and took a few practice swings, relieved that he was preoccupied with the lesson he was giving.

While I practiced swinging, I watched them. It was hard to follow their Scottish idiom, but I got an idea that he was giving MacIver a kind of game plan for the entire round. "Noo, we'll play six holes for the centered swing, six tae feel gravity, and six tae scoor," he said—or something to that effect. Then they stood for a moment with their eyes closed, as if they were praying. Maybe they were saying the Lord's Prayer, I thought, like professional football teams do before a game.

After their brief meditation they started taking their practice swings. MacIver took his with a long iron. "Nae. Use yer play club noo," said the professional, pointing to his pupil's driver. As I would learn eventually, he believed that "driving" was a term that by its very connotation threw some golfers off their truest swing. He preferred to say that he was "playing" the ball on a drive, and called a driver a "play club," as golfers had done in centuries past.

As I watched him I could see he was not your ordinary golf professional. His look was an important part of his teaching. To emphasize a point he would impale MacIver with it, then flash his big engaging smile when a point had been conveyed. As I moved closer I saw that his left eye was slightly off focus—not enough to be readily perceptible, but enough to be disconcerting. It was focused ever so slightly to the center, giving his steady blue eyes a penetrating quality, almost as if he were looking at you from two vantage points at once. "Murphy," he said turning to me, "ye swing at the grass real purty, hav' a try at the ball"—a challenging invitation. He smiled as he said it and gestured toward the tee.

As I teed up my ball I looked down the gently rolling fairway. It was serenely inviting in the afternoon sun, but I knew from my reading that hazards lurked along its course all the way to the green. I could hear the pounding of ocean waves beyond the rough and see them breaking over boulders within range of an errant drive. The anticipation of playing Burningbush and this unusual golf professional's commanding presence had thrown me off—I remember wishing we could stop to pray again. As I addressed the ball I knocked it off the tee with the club face. Shivas Irons seemed to be seven feet tall as I glanced back. He looked down at me with compassionate good humor, as if he were rooting me on. He made one small gesture, a brief movement of his hand in front of his hips, palm held downward. I instantly knew what he meant. As I teed the ball up again I settled into a feeling of stomach and hips, making a center there for my swing. And then a vivid image appeared in my mind's eye, of a turquoise ball traveling down the right side of the fairway with a tail hook toward the green. I took my stance and waggled the club carefully, aware that the image of the shot was incredibly vivid. Then I swung and the ball followed the path laid down in my mind.

"Guid shot," he said loudly, "ha' did ye ken tae hit it thair? 'Tis the best lie tae the green."

"Just luck," I mumbled and stood aside, relieved that I had gotten past the first obstacles so well.

MacIver swung with what seemed to be a mere half-effort and his drive traveled 180 yards or so down the middle of the fairway. "That's it, that's it," the professional's voice rumbled with its heavy brogue. MacIver was dressed in white shoes and pants and a black cardigan sweater. It was a striking costume, all the more so because he seemed so modest. He was completely devoted to his teacher's admonitions, listening carefully to every word of instruction, concentrating utterly upon the game. He mumbled something and quickly stepped aside, smiling proudly in spite of himself.

It was the professional's turn now. He stooped down gracefully to tee his ball, balancing for a moment on one leg as if to test his balance and spring. It was a kind of ritual dance he was to repeat on several holes. Then he stood addressing the ball for a few seconds, a brief address, but during that moment all his attention came to awesome focus. Like Ben Hogan, he seemed to peer into the very center of the ball and summon a secret strength. I could feel the energy gathering, feel it in my solar plexus, a powerful magnetic field drawing everything into itself—and then his swing unfurled, slower than I had anticipated after that awesome address but impacting with immense power and following through with utter grace and balance. I held my breath as the ball flew, stretching as if to hold it in the sky. It sailed 280 yards or more down the middle of the fairway—hovering there longer than any shot I had ever seen—then it landed, bouncing high toward the green. He picked up his tee, winked, and gave a little kick to suggest the performance I had watched behind the clubhouse. "Someday perhaps the ba' will na' come down again," he said with a smile. "Have ye e'er had tha' feelin'?" He was obviously pleased. It had been an awesome shot.

He walked ahead of us down the fairway with a long rhythmic stride, a russet sweater tapering from broad shoulders to a pair of hips as well formed and contoured as a football player's. He wore a pair of golden-brown corduroy pants and ordinary brown golf shoes. I found it hard to take my eyes off him. He stopped by MacIver's ball and watched his pupil make the next shot, another half-effort that landed in front of the green.

By now MacIver was totally preoccupied with his game. His swing was neither graceful nor powerful, but it was impressive to see his concentration and total devotion to the discipline his teacher had set for him. I felt a twinge of envy for their collusion.

I hit a seven iron onto the green—the example they were setting was having its effect. Shivas hit a wedge 3 feet from the cup, with the same grace and power he had shown with his drive. I was beginning to feel a sense of awe as I watched him, something I have always felt around consummate athletes. He birdied, I parred, MacIver bogeyed the hole. I wrote a four on my scorecard; MacIver was keeping score for them.

"Ah like yer swing, Michael," he said as we walked to the

second tee, giving me that sudden smile. The remark startled me. I was touched that he called me Michael, that he had noticed my shot.

"Any chance of getting a lesson?" I answered, blurting out the thought that was running through my mind.

He looked directly into my eyes. "Oh, but ye may na' ken tha' that is a solemn and serious matter, a serious matter indeed." He smiled good-naturedly, but I could see that he meant it. Then he grinned and reached out to shake my hand. "Just call me Shivas," he said.

"Do you teach here all summer?"

"It depends," he replied, then turned away without further explanation.

The second green could be seen from the tee, some 353 yards away according to the scorecard, down a straight, gently rolling fairway. The rough on the right was full of stones and gorse, or "whin" as it is sometimes called, the small spiny bush that grows on Scottish links-land. An incoming fairway ran down the left side. Not a very difficult hole, I said to myself as I surveyed it. MacIver hit another short, unpretentious shot down the middle, conscientiously following the game plan. It was my turn now. Once again an image came of the ball in flight—a turquoise ball down the middle —and so it flew. I had somehow developed the knack of seeing the shot in my mind's eye as I addressed the ball. On both drives it had appeared spontaneously, a bright, compelling image. Was I learning something just being around them? Shivas was next. Again the ritual dance as he teed the ball, and again the awesomely concentrated address. He split the fairway with a lower drive this time, something more like a rifle shot. As I was to learn later, he never used the same swing twice—or so he said—though it was difficult for me to see the changes.

As we walked up the fairway, I took the scorecard out and looked at the yardage figures. The course was about 6800 yards long, not too long to play in par. To shoot a par round at Burningbush, that would be something to remember! I began calculating how many birdies I would need, maybe two or three on the par fives, maybe one or two more on the other holes, that would give me a chance for a 72 or better with the bogies I was bound to make. I hurried my steps to see what kind of lie I had for my second shot. The ball was near the center of the fairway, about an eight-iron shot from the green. Maybe I could get a birdie on this one, I thought. Then images of veering shots started to form in my mind. Images of the gorse, of the bunkers in front of the green, of the rocks behind it. I began adjusting my swing as I addressed the ball. The poise I had felt on the drive had disappeared; excitement, anticipation, and bobbing images of disaster had taken its place. I backed away, and approached the ball again—and then as I began to swing, a picture came of the gorse to the right. I pulled the shot to the left, into the adjoining fairway. I slammed the club into the bag and hurried toward my ball, not waiting for the others.

"Now, hold there, Michael," Shivas's authoritative voice came booming across the fairway. "Just wait yer toorn." He was suddenly stern as he looked at me.

I stopped in mid-stride and waited for them to play. As I stood watching Shivas make his shot—another lovely approach onto the green—my fantasies of an exceptional score continued. I pulled out the scorecard again to see which holes were par fives.

When I got to the ball, I saw that a bunker stood between it and the green. The pin was about 100 feet away, just a pitch and run for a par. I pulled a nine iron from my bag and took a few practice swings, adjusting them for distance and roll. With each practice swing the bunker got larger. I backed away twice from the ball—but to no avail. As I swung, I looked up and the ball landed in the sand. I lifted back my head and stared up at the sky, hovering somewhere between a curse and a prayer. Shivas and MacIver watched in silence. As I disappeared into the bunker they waved and shouted some words of encouragement, but that was the only sound until I blasted onto the green and two-putted for a double bogey. My fantasies of a 72 at Burningbush had been dealt a blow.

A little bench stood behind the third tee. MacIver sat down on it and began writing scores on his card. To my surprise he wanted to know what I had shot on the two holes we had played. "I'll keep my own score," I said. "You have your lesson. Don't bother." I didn't want to say it out loud, that I had shot a six. We all knew, but saying it out loud was harder. But MacIver insisted that he keep all our scores. "Four on the first, and a six on the second," I finally said. "That damn bunker, and I should have sunk the putt. . . ."

"Ye had a five oon the first," Shivas interrupted me sternly.

I turned to face him. He was looking straight at me, with that steady cross-eyed gaze. "Ye must count that one ye knocked off the tee when ye took yer waggle," he said solemnly.

Have you ever felt as you talked to someone that everything was turning unreal? That is exactly how I felt then, as I realized what he was saying. The shock of this all-seeing scrutiny, the small-mindedness of it, and the embarrassment I felt for violating their code of honor drew the blood to my stomach.

"So, a five and a six?" MacIver asked.

Shivas could see I was having a hard time answering. "Now, Michael," he said, raising a long finger and shaking it at me, "ye must rimember that ye're in the land where all these rools were invented. 'Tis the only way ye can play in the kingdom." Then the big grin appeared, his second face. I can't remember what I said in reply, but I submitted to the discipline.

I have thought of that line many times, "the only way you can play in the kingdom." I didn't fully appreciate it at first. Not until I realized that for him the Kingdom of Fife was very nearly the Kingdom of Heaven.

But I was not ready to appreciate it then. Even though he

had reached out to me, I could feel his scrutiny. I felt a growing edge of resentment as we got ready for our drives—it was going to be hard to shoot a 72.

But my hopes did not die easily. The upcoming hole was a par five, a possible birdie—I could get a stroke back there, one or two more on the other par fives, shoot even on the rest, and still get a 72. I made my own game plan as I watched MacIver get ready to drive. Go all out on the drive, I thought, but keep it smooth—I formed an image of Snead's strong, rhythmic backswing and combined it with a picture of Shivas's concentration as he stood up to the ball. Or just swing like Shivas himself; that is what I resolved to do as I teed up and took my stance. I waggled the club carefully, remembering the first tee, picturing Shivas as he took his stance, thinking also of Snead as I had seen him once during a driving contest at Pebble Beach. I peered fiercely into the ball and swung. It sailed in a long sweeping hook, an impressive sailing carry across fairway and rough, far out into the gorse. It was perhaps the longest shot I had ever hit.

I began to grit my teeth as if I were biting some invisible opponent. Exhilaration over this sudden power was mixed with the utter frustration of my deteriorating score. I asked Shivas if I could hit another in case the ball was lost.

"No, not heer," he said forbiddingly, "ye can aye find it in tha' particular ruif."

Again there was a sense of unreality about our exchange. As he got ready to shoot I slammed my club into the bag and swore out loud. It didn't seem to faze him though; he hit another amazing drive down the middle of the fairway.

The rough along the third hole at Burningbush is full of rocks and gorse. Gorse, a low brambly shrub of the genus *Ulex*, is common to Scottish wastelands and golfing links. It is said by some to grow as well in the fields of Hell. Occasionally, a ball will come to rest upon its top branches a foot or two above the ground. In that case one is required to play out, since the shot is possible—barely. That was my good fortune then. I could see my ball as I approached, nestling on its thorny cushion awaiting deliverance.

In playing a shot like this you must be careful not to jostle the bush in any way, for the ball may sink deeper into its branches. Knowing this, I carried my bag of clubs in a wide arc around the ball and stepped toward it slowly, seven iron in hand, determined to hit my approach within range of the green. An image of par still danced in my head, in spite of all the omens. I held the iron away from the yellow blossoms as I took my stance, as one does in a sand trap, and lined up my feet. I started the club back a few times to see that my swing would not be impeded by rocks or gorse—there was plenty of room. I eyed the flag, still so far way. Then as I began to swing in earnest, the ball sank gently out of sight among the flowers on that innocent bush. I looked up to the sky and shook my head. "This fucking game," I said, "this fucking game."

"How does it lie?" Shivas's stentorian voice suddenly reverberated across the gorse. He stood watching me from the edge of the fairway some thirty yards away.

"It fell into the middle of a whin," I yelled back. "Should I play it, or drop out?" Perhaps he would show me some mercy.

"No, play it like it lies," he yelled. "It'll come out."

I cursed him silently. Since the ball was invisible now I had to guess how deep my seven iron should cut into the shrub. I lined up again, eyeing the distant flag, testing my backswing for potential obstacles. Then I chopped down viciously. Yellow flowers flew in all directions, a veritable shower of gold, but no ball was forthcoming.

"Bring me a bouquet when ye come oot," he bellowed. I looked at him standing there. I couldn't believe it, it must have been the Scottish sense of humor.

"I can't even see the ball," I shouted back. "I think I should drop out."

"It'll come out," he answered. "Keep choppin'."

I swung again, even harder than I had the first time, and hit a rock as I hit the ball. Sparks flew in all directions, a second shower of gold. The ball flew about 30 feet, into another patch of gorse.

"Fucking bastard," I said, chopping furiously at the devastated bush. "Fuck the score." Shivas had turned away and was walking toward his ball. I felt an urge to give him the finger.

I hit a wedge shot onto the fairway and joined MacIver. I was lying four and hadn't even reached his modest drive yet.

At about this point I began to feel like revenge—against Shivas, the course, even MacIver for his plodding game. I would hit a 250-yard three wood onto the green and hole the putt for a bogey, a prodigious recovery; that would show them. I thought of Snead again as I lined up, of Hogan, Jimmy Thompson, George Bayer, a whole array of potent images to summon my strength. I threw everything into the shot—and topped it badly. It bounced straight up and landed about 20 or 30 feet away. Poor MacIver, he was trying to give me room, trying not to interfere with my struggle while concentrating in his own methodical way. Still he could not suppress the urge to give me some advice. He was a middle-aged, kindly-looking man, with a trim mustache and crisp manners, perhaps an Army officer judging from his bearing. "Now, Murphy," he said, "just try usin' yer short irons tae finish the hole." It was the most galling remark of all.

I mumbled something in reply, and watched him hit another inexorable shot down the middle.

Shivas was standing near his ball, ahead of us to our right.

"The twa o' ye remind me o' the tortoise and the hare," he said. I gritted my teeth and shook my head to acknowledge the fact that I had heard him.

My ball now had large gashes in it, and when I hit my next shot—with a five iron, dejectedly following MacIver's advice—it wobbled in flight as a ball will do after being so badly treated. It veered in two directions like a wounded bird.

"Guid man!" cried our professional. " 'Tis the first time Ah e'er saw a hook and a slice on one shot." I was beginning to think I was his straight man.

He put his three wood on the green, hitting the very shot I had visualized for myself.

When we got to the green Shivas lay two and was putting for an eagle; MacIver lay four, just 3 feet from the pin; and I lay seven. I was tempted to pick up, but sensed what they would say. In spite of my growing resentment, Shivas's authoritative presence was enough to keep me quiet. I marked my ball and started to clean it. The gashes I had given it smiled hideously, it would be impossible to putt. "May I put down another ball?" I asked meekly. Neither of them answered. Perhaps they were too sorry for me to say no. But they were not sorry enough to say yes. I put the mutilated ball back on the putting surface. As I bent down to make the putt I had the impression—I can remember it to this day— that one of the gashes winked at me. It's only a game after all, it seemed to say, only a game. When I putted, the point was made more vividly. The ball veered to the left like one of those trick balls that are sold for practical jokes. The thought occurred that I would never get it into the hole.

MacIver sunk his putt for a par, his first of the round. Shivas narrowly missed his, ending up with another birdie. I tried again. This time the ball veered to the right, stopping about 3 feet from the cup. Then Shivas, who had been looking away during the entire performance, turned and said, "Noo try willin' it in, it'll never get there in the regular coorse o' things." He meant to be helpful, I suppose. I glowered back at him, my first act of overt defiance. I hit the putt without lining it up, not caring where it went. It rolled straight at last, hit the back of the cup, bounced high and came to rest on the other side. Seeing it lying there, I remembered something I had seen my brother Dennis do back in our high school days. Following his example, I leaned back and looked at the sky, then raised my arm to God and gave Him the finger. My two playing partners laughed and turned away. I tapped the ball into the hole and we walked off the green in silence.

On the next tee, MacIver, methodical again after my display, took out his score card and wrote down their scores. "How many, Murphy?" he asked crisply, peering at the card. I stared at him for a moment. He peered at the scorecard, waiting for my reply. How many! They were going to count them! "Just give me an X," I said.

"A what?" He looked at me as if he did not comprehend.

"I'm not counting that hole," I said.

"Noo, Michael," said Shivas, "put doon yer score, it'll do ye good."

I could tell he was trying to reassure me, but I also sensed their incredible sense of honor about keeping score. My dropping out offended their whole sense of things.

"An X?" asked MacIver, as if he hadn't heard me right.

"Oh, put down a ten," I finally said with exasperation.

For a moment there was silence. MacIver stared at the scorecard, pursing his lips, somehow reluctant to write it down. Shivas cocked his head to one side as if he were thinking. It was a silence full of unspoken thoughts. Finally, MacIver lifted a hand to scratch his ear and looked at his teacher for advice. Shivas looked solemnly at me.

"Michael, Ah think 'twas eliven," he said.

MacIver looked at me, waiting for my assent. "An eleven," I said, nodding with resignation, and he carefully wrote it down.

Shivas came over to me then and put a big hand on my shoulder. "Dona' worry aboot the score so much," he said, "it's not the important thing." He squeezed my shoulder and turned back to MacIver with more instructions. Not the important thing, I thought as he walked away, not the important thing! I was touched by his reaching out—and dumfounded.

Scoring not the important thing! While they watched me like hawks! I thought about it all the way to the fourth tee.

When frustration grew to the breaking point during a round of golf I would do either one of two things—get ostentatiously slaphappy and hit my shots in any direction as if it were the outing that was important, or play with concentrated fury. I went into the latter mode on hole number four— I would show them. Playing that way, I would think of Ben Hogan, his Indian profile cutting through every obstacle, and squint my eyes like a prairie scout. I would begin an interior conversation, or rather a stream of incantations that had as their goal the willing of the ball to its target. It was a kind of black magic, whereby the mind forced itself upon the ball and steered it right in spite of all the errors my body committed. I sometimes tried it at baseball and football games. I had even developed a whammy which, when used properly, could bring a man down.

I gathered myself for the attack as we got ready to tee off. I summoned images of fierce swingers like Hogan and Bayer, with something of Shivas's own concentration thrown in, and glowered down the fairway. When I stood up to the ball I held my stance for a long time, eyes squinting, showing them that I really meant business now, and imagined the ball rocketing toward the green. I hit an exceptionally long drive.

It was a 400-yard par four, curving to the left. The drive cut across the corner of the dog-leg, leaving me a seven iron to the green. I hit my second with the same concentrated anger, a low shot that sailed true—and sailed over the green into some unknown hazard. I had willed it with all my might, and had willed it too well: I had hit the shot some 20 yards farther than I ordinarily did with a seven iron from that kind of lie.

We never found the ball. It had disappeared into a rocky draw that led down to the ocean. Perhaps it had bounced into the waves. So I dropped a second ball and shot a double bogey.

When we finished the hole, I sat on a rock and looked at the waves. Shivas came over and laid a hand on my shoulder I suppose he could tell I was losing heart. "Ye try too hard and ye think too much," he said with the authority that Scots golf professionals often assume. "Why don't ye go wi' yer pretty swing? Let the nothingness into yer shots." His words made me feel better. It did seem silly to ruin all the beautiful scenery with the fuss I was making.

The next hole was a kind of purgatory after the hell I had put myself through. Perhaps it was the influence of his advice and its apparent success with MacIver, perhaps it was the resignation I felt about my score. In any case I managed to get a bogey five, playing each shot as carefully as MacIver had been doing. The tortoise was teaching the hare.

I had overheard Shivas telling his pupil to think of the ball and "sweet spot" belonging together. The "sweet spot" is the place on the clubface where the ball should be struck; one might hit a decent shot, even a very good one, and not hit it exactly, but when you do there is no mistaking it—to hit it is the very essence of golfing pleasure. Shivas had told MacIver that the ball and the sweet spot were "already joined." "Just see it that way," he had said, "they're aye joined afore ye started playin'." The advice helped. I began to imagine them fitting together as I laid the clubhead behind the ball. It helped settle me down. I had—almost in spite of myself— joined MacIver to form a small procession following in our teacher's impressive wake.

For the next few holes our game was relatively uneventful. MacIver continued keeping my score—he was probably incapable of doing otherwise—and I continued thinking that the clubface and the ball were one. I watched Shivas whenever I could, and slowly his example began to influence me in a peculiar way. I became more and more aware of the *feeling* of the game, of how it was to walk from shot to shot, how it was to feel the energy gathering as I addressed the ball, how the golf links smelled. It was not that he said anything to me, but his example. He was so physical in the way he moved and responded, like a big animal. The only thing he asked me in fact during those middle holes was whether I could smell the heather. "It's growin' way over there," he said, pointing to a distant hill, "but ye can smell it from heer." I could smell it, and though I didn't tell him, I could also smell that powerful odor of eucalyptus and baking bread.

Those middle holes were a lesson in resignation and simple sensing. No more ambitions for prodigious shots and scores, they seemed out of reach; just a decent modest game and enjoyment of the endless charms of Burningbush. It was a new way to play for me; I had always been so focused on the score and the mechanics of my swing. I had always tried for spectacular shots—long drives, approaches stiff to the pin, shots I could talk about and collect like medals in my golfing memory. Now my focus of awareness included other things, like the heather and the waves coming in from the sea.

The holes ran along water, and you could see for miles along the sandy links land, across gently rolling hillocks lavender and yellow in the afternoon sun. Better sights to fill my memory with than mutilated golf balls and careening shots.

MacIver now had gone into the second phase of his game plan. He was working on something called "true gravity"— something, as far as I could make out, that involved an awareness of "energy-dimensions" and the relations of things. Following Shivas's instruction, he was trying to "see" the subtle fields of energy that were supposed to surround the ball, the club, and his very own body. Although they kept me out of their conversations, I overheard them discussing it from time to time and began to see if I could understand what it was all about. I had heard other strange theories during my golfing travels—golfers keep coming up with amazing things along this line—but nothing quite so organized as this. Mac-Iver was now trying to see the one energy field that enveloped his body, ball, and club. For the first holes he had been focusing exclusively on the ball and clubface, he was extending it now to include the rest.

I tried it for three or four shots but nothing seemed to happen. I did keep my eye on the ball, however, and that was a gain. Maybe that is what these things are all about, I thought, ways to keep a person looking at the ball—anything to help concentration. Plenty of other things had been tried, God knows, why not metaphysics? Though I failed to see the auras MacIver was looking for I felt a new elasticity in my swing. Then on the ninth hole I did see something. It wasn't much, just the tiniest glimpse, but I did seem to see a yellow light around a sea gull swooping in from the sea. Then as I was driving on the tenth it happened again, a tiny aura around the ball, a violet one this time. When I hit the ball I hit the sweet spot.

"That's the sound we want," said Shivas, as if he had been waiting to hear it. The drive was not particularly impressive, but it felt good.

As I walked toward the ball, I wondered if seeing those auras could be tricks of the retina. I told him what had happened and stated my doubts.

"Noo, Michael," he said firmly, "when ye think tha' maybe it's yer retina, ye'r just one step awa' from really seein' things." On my approach shot I hit the sweet spot again, after watching the "aura" expand and contract, and the ball landed 20 feet from the pin. I told him what had happened after we finished the hole. "Keep swingin'," he said. Just the two words, nothing more.

I parred ten and eleven, fascinated with what I would see and feel on each shot. This was a new kind of game for me, a series of strange sensations and intuitions, my first exposure to that order of things called "true gravity." But I could only sustain it for a while. On the twelfth hole our drive was into the wind, down a narrow fairway that dog-legged to the right. Familiar images of disaster came back to haunt me as I took my stance. I sliced the drive and the sea breeze carried it into the rough. Shivas walked along beside me up the fairway, and asked me what I was thinking. I told him about the awful thoughts. "They'll pass," he said, "if ye daena' fight 'em. Come back to where'er ye were a minute ago. Wait 'em oot." Those words were a great help—not only for the rest of the round but for my life ever since. The admonition to "wait

'em oot" was one of those sayings of his that came back
to haunt me.

I managed the hole in bogey, by hitting a conservative
wedge from the rough and approaching the green with a five
iron. When MacIver asked my score there was pleasure in
saying that I had made a five—such a different reaction from
the one I had felt on the third tee! Even a bogey seemed
good, everything was beginning to carry some unexpected
satisfaction.

We had now come to the thirteenth hole, which is famous
in golfing circles. It is a par three up a hill, to a pin that
stands silhouetted between a pair of twisted cypress trees.
Between the tee and the green lies Lucifer's Rug, a field of
clotted gorse, 200 yards of it to catch any shot that is
less than perfection. Along the left runs a steep ravine, from
which several boulders rise. It was fortunate, I thought as I
looked to the pin, that I had come to this concentrated state
of mind by now. Every Monday the caddies of Burningbush
and other links came here to hunt for lost golf balls, some
trained their dogs for the task. At various points in the history
of the club there had been efforts by members to have the
hole enshrined as a golf museum, thus prohibiting further
play upon it. It was even said that a body had once been
found "under the rug."

The tee shot had to carry to the green but not roll down
the other side, for another ravine dropped off there. Few
players could reach it with an iron, so in effect a wood was
required to do the work of a pitching wedge. To make matters worse, there was usually a wind across the rise—
witness the twisted cypress trees—so the shot had to be
played to the left, to the ravine side. It was a hole in all
respects suited to test the powers of "true gravity."

The wind was now blowing from left to right, hard enough
to lift the distant flag. I took out a two iron and gazed at its
sweet spot, as if it were an icon. MacIver seemed to be in a
trance as he stared dumbly up the hill. But Shivas went into
the oddest ritual of all. First he stood on his left leg, then on

his right, once with eyes open, once with them closed. Then he cupped his hands to his mouth and gave an incredible cry toward the ravine. It was a long wavering wail, something between a yodel and a cry for the departed dead. It sent a shiver up my back. We could hear its echo from the ravine, bouncing off the rocks. Then he turned and nodded gravely, indicating that we should proceed.

MacIver, apparently unfazed by this unexpected performance, took his driver and stood like a statue before his ball, a figure of total dedication. All dressed in white and black, he contrasted vividly with the ascending vista of yellow gorse. A tiny figure there, I had an image of him flying like Chagall in the wake of his shot. He stood motionless for a very long time, plumbing the depths of "true gravity," I suppose, and then he swung. It sailed straight and high—and landed in the gorse some 20 feet short of the summit. He grimaced as he turned toward his golf bag. I slowly marched to the firing line, praying to my golf club icon and looking intently for that mystical joining with the ball. I teed up. As I did there was another bloodcurdling cry, Shivas was wailing again behind my back. I was so startled I jumped. He shook his head apologetically, but said nothing—his attention seemed to be focused somewhere else.

Whether from the many holes of high concentration or from this incredible performance my mind seemed blasted empty. It was impossible to summon any image. I swung without thinking and the ball flew like a bullet on a low trajectory, a white streak against yellow, rising into the sky before it fell to the green. The picture of it is still painted brightly in my memory.

Shivas was smiling at me as I turned around. He winked as he went past, but his glance was wilder and more unsettling than ever. I walked over to my golf bag and slipped the iron into it, thinking as I did that maybe I should always pray to the club I was using. I was beginning to feel an exaltation about this round of golf. Then I turned to watch him make his shot. For a fleeting moment there was an odd distortion:

he seemed blurred as he stood there. To this day I do not know whether there were tears in my eyes from the wind or whether there was something else that caused it. He seemed smaller. And when he swung I could not see the ball in flight. I blinked as I looked up the hill, but it had disappeared. I asked MacIver as we walked to the green if he had seen it. He nodded vaguely; I could tell from his manner, though, that something odd had happened to him as well. That distortion seemed strange, however, only upon reflection later that day. The growing exaltation I was feeling possessed me then, crowded out questions, problems, anything that seemed not to fit. I felt the land as we climbed the hill, the sea breeze, the grass beneath my feet. A film had dropped from my eyes, from my hearing, from all my senses. The smell of the sea and the grass, of leather and perspiration filled the air. I could hear a cry of delight in the distance, then tiny cheers. Something had broken loose inside me, something large and free.

We found MacIver's ball and watched him play a little wedge shot to the green. And there upon the smooth green summit lay Shivas's ball and mine, just a foot apart near the pin. We played out in silence, a pair of birdies to go with MacIver's bogey, Shivas solemn and centered, not giving a hint of what was going through his mind.

I looked out from our vantage point; we could see for miles now. The sun was dipping behind the western hills, while purple shadows spread across the water and arabesques of grass below. The curving fairways and tiny sounds arising from them, the fields of heather, the distant seacaps were all inside my skin. A presence was brooding through it all, one presence interfusing the ball, the green, MacIver, Shivas, everything.

I played the remaining holes in this state of grace. Specters of former attitudes passed through me, familiar curses and excuses, memories of old shots, all the flotsam and jetsam of my golfing unconscious—but a quiet field of energy held me and washed them away. I can think of no better way to say it—those final holes played me.

There were moments when the thought occurred, "maybe this will disappear." The new-found strength, that too was questioned. But there was another thought, "wait 'em out," and eventually I did.

The incoming holes of Burningbush unfolded before us, wild and gentle by turns. I could see why they were so loved and famous. They are so much more than you can see at first, fierce as Lucifer's Rug and familiar as the old town that beckons from the surrounding hills. From the thunders of the North Sea to the gray stone houses and cobblestone streets, Burningbush shimmers in my memory.

As if to show us that virtue will be rewarded, the occult Powers and Dominions gave us a grand finale. Shivas hit a drive on the eighteenth hole that carried all the way home— to the green 320 yards away. He was hitting with a wind to his back, and he took it to full advantage, sailing the ball toward the ancient clubhouse with a fade along the fairway to the green. I hit a wedge to the pin for a birdie, following MacIver, who had done the same. One eagle and two birdies closed out the round.

Shivas put an arm around my shoulder. "Ye deseruv' a drink," he said, "come j'in me and ma friends." So we headed for the clubhouse bar. MacIver said good-by, dutifully setting a time for his next lesson. Before he left he announced our scores, so faithfully recorded, a 67 for his teacher, an 84 for him, and an 86 for me. "And, Murphy," he said with an admiration that surprised me, "ye shot a 34 comin' in, the same as Mr. Irons, which only proves"—he raised a finger for emphasis—"that true gravity works on this plane too." I shook his hand and followed Shivas into the famous Burningbush clubhouse.

Singing the Praises of Golf

Liston the barman was lighting a fire in the clubhouse bar as
we entered. A few moments later I was sitting in front of the
blazing logs, whisky glass in hand, listening to Shivas and his
friends sing Scottish golfing songs. The fire in front of me and
the subtle fire of Shivas's presence were warming me inside
and out. I listened to them singing in their rich Fife accents,

> ". . . among the heather and the gorse,
> ye must remember of course,
> not tae lose yer balls at ol' Sin Tondress. . . ."

listened to their laughter and raillery, to the sounds of golfers
stomping grass from their cleats, then a cheer from the eighteenth green—sounds that reminded me of a special Christ-
mas when I was a child. I was filled with gratitude, my eyes
filled with tears as I looked around that glowing room. The
mood that had come over me out on the course, that sense of
an enormous presence suffusing the world, was with me still.
I could feel the wild and mysterious terrain of the Burningbush Links, those immense worlds waiting, but this warm
place was at the center of my feelings now, the convivial
faces and friendly words, the songs, the walls covered with
dancing firelight. I felt as if I had found my way home at
last.

For more than an hour I watched the clubmembers come
and go, and gazed into the fire as I savored that incredible
round. Shivas was greeting friends at the bar. I could hear his

34

voice above the rest from time to time, giving encouragement or answering a friendly gibe; his presence seemed as important to them as it was to me.

During that hour no problems existed. But then questions began to form, began intruding themselves as they inevitably do. The aura of utter well-being was fading, and I began the return to my ordinary state of mind.

What was this strangely impressive man really up to? What was he doing on the thirteenth tee? There had been something uncanny about that hole, something I could not quite bring into consciousness. What had the bartender meant when he taunted him about "defiling the old men of Burningbush"? Later that evening some of these questions would be answered and others would be compounded.

He had invited me to dinner, interrupting my ruminations with a sudden shout from the bar. "Michael, ma good lad," he said, coming over and putting his hand on my shoulder, " 'tis time ye're exposed to the true complexities o' the gemme." I would soon find that the thoughts which had begun to disturb me were being developed at length by others.

The meal was to be at the home of the McNaughtons', he said as we left the clubhouse. I was surprised and flattered at the sudden invitation, and sensed his excitement about the gathering that was soon to take place. He had changed into a white crew-necked sweater, and either because of the clothes or a change of mood had a different look about him. He seemed less massive and concentrated, even a little smaller in size. His wind-burned face contrasted sharply with the sweater's whiteness, making him more handsome than ever. He hummed a tune as we walked along, some old Scotch ballad, I think, with a vaguely Oriental air, that mysterious longing and joy you catch sometimes in the wailing of the pipes.

The strange melody trailed off as we approached our destination; he seemed to be distracted. When we arrived at the McNaughtons' house, he touched my shoulder vaguely and murmured something about needing to be alone for a moment. "Ye go ahaid, Michael, they'll understand," he almost whispered the words, then wandered off down the street. Startled and embarrased, I explained to the handsome woman who answered the door that Shivas Irons had invited me to dinner and that now he had gone off down the street. She asked me to come in. As I stepped through the doorway, I looked back and saw him sitting on a window ledge looking up into the evening sky. He seemed to be lost in thought.

"Did ye play gowf with him today?" the handsome lady asked as she ushered me in. "He sometimes brings his playin' partners here afterwards." She introduced herself as Agatha McNaughton. Following her up the narrow staircase, I couldn't help noticing what a great figure she had—she moved ahead of me up the steep passageway with slow pleasurable steps.

The other guests had arrived and were sitting with their drinks around a stone hearth that framed an inviting fire. Above the mantel an ancient-looking pair of crossed swords gleamed in the firelight. The men stood to greet me. Peter McNaughton, Agatha's husband, was a vigorous-looking red-faced man in his fifties, perhaps twenty years Agatha's senior. He shook my hand, pulling me toward him with two muscular jerks. "Welcome to our guid café," he said with gusto. "What did ye do with our unpredictable friend?"

"He went for a walk. . . ."

"Waitin' for the moon to rise perhaps," he said and smiled, cutting me off in midsentence as if to save me embarrassment. "He may stay out thair for an hour or more. But here . . ." he introduced me around to the others—an imposing craggy-faced old Scotsman named Julian Laing, an English couple named Greene, and Peter's sixteen-year-old son, Kelly. Laing, it was explained to me, was the town's "main doctor"; he had delivered five thousand of the town's ten thousand inhabitants. He was also, I was to discover, a psychiatrist of sorts with remarkable, highly eccentric theories. As he shook my hand he winked enigmatically and asked if Shivas had brought me "through the eye of the needle." I wasn't exactly sure what he meant.

The Greenes were visiting from Cornwall, up to study the ecology of the Firth of Forth and tell Shivas their new theories about golfing links. Spirited, bouncy little people not much taller than five feet, they reminded me of a pair of elves from Tolkien's trilogy. His name was Adam and hers was Eve, they were meant for each other, they said. Everyone laughed at the familiar joke, which must have been trotted out for the hundredth time. Adam Greene taught "cosmic ecology" at a London "Free University." God knows how he supported himself. I think he had been an engineer or inventor before his turn to philosophy.

Peter McNaughton acted as master of ceremonies with enormous zest and a sense that this was a special gathering indeed. It was obvious that he was very proud of his friends. His son, Kelly, was over six feet tall, had a kind of sardonic whisky brogue, and blushed whenever he smiled. He smiled and blushed when he shook my hand.

"Did ye git the traitment today?" he asked. The remark carried all sorts of insinuations. I mumbled something like "Yes, I did have quite a round, how did you know?" evoking a laugh from everyone.

"How do we know!" exclaimed Agatha, with a warm, richly textured brogue. "Why, that bad man wouldna' just let ye play an ordinary round of golf!" I felt like I'd been taken into the clan.

We sat around the fire drinking whisky and trading pleasantries. I couldn't stop thinking about Shivas down there on that window ledge, but no one else seemed concerned. There was excitement underlying the hospitable remarks, a sense of anticipation about this gathering. "And what do ye do to keep the body alive, Mr. Murphy?" Agatha asked. She wore a light brown woolen blouse that showed the contour of her breasts. I said something about being a student and aspiring writer. They wanted to know what school I went to and I told them. Old Laing then got the conversation going in earnest.

"Well, Murphy," he intoned with his gnarled burr, "as an aspiring man of words, will ye tell me whether words have a future? They've had a dismal past." He raised his brambly eyebrows and peered over his glass at me. He then looked around at everyone else and came on with another conversation opener. "Wuidna' all of ye agree tha' all logic, all human history, all our experience compel us to recognize tha' the only thing in life worth doin' is the will of God?" I hadn't expected that kind of statement. I thought of some people in my home town, Salinas, from the First Church of God of Prophecy.

No one seemed disposed to reply. Any further remarks would have to carry some metaphysical force. There was a long silence as we drank our Scotch and looked into the fire.

"Well, Shivas would agree with ye," Kelly said at last with his sardonic inflection.

"Aye, we've discussed the matter for years," the old doctor replied, "but ye ken how he is. Tomorra' he'll be tellin' Murphy heer that believin' in God is dangerous. He's the dangerous one, o' course." He repeated the words with affectionate irony, "He's the dangerous one." There was affection in the old man's voice as he invoked his friend's presence, but with it there was an unmistakable sense that Shivas Irons was indeed dangerous.

"As long as we're talking about him, shouldn't we tell him it's time to eat?" Eve Greene broke in. The McNaughtons replied, almost in unison, that there was no use disturbing him now, that he would come in good time. "Ye know how he is," they said protectively, and ushered us into their dining room. It was a long, low candlelit room with latticed windows and wood beams across the ceiling. The dining table was some 20 feet long, and 4 feet wide, a table for a banquet. Seated around it we seemed yards apart.

The McNaughtons' hospitality, the happy anticipation I

felt among this group of friends, the whisky, and the winds of Burningbush had all had their effect upon me. I was warmed and lifted high. Peering down the table at those faces in the candlelight I began to smile. It must have been an idiot smile. "Ye look so happy, Michael," Agatha said, "a round of golf with Shivas will do tha' to ye."

"Oh, where is he, where *is* he?" Eve Greene persisted, looking hopefully about the room over her attractive upturned nose. Her head barely made it over the edge of the table. Both she and Adam needed cushions to reach their dinner. "We've been looking forward to seeing him for weeks. Our theories about golf and evolution are growing larger every day."

"Aye, ma guid Greenes, yer theories were enormous awready," said Peter, lifting his glass high. "Let us drink a toast to all theories round, let us sing the praises of gowf." His always ruddy face was red with pleasure. "To gowf!" he exclaimed, and we all raised our glasses—of water, milk, or whisky, a makeshift but inspired toast to golf and the good life.

Agatha then brought in a large tureen of broth, full of dumplings. For a moment we ate in silence, savoring the aroma of that ancient Scottish potion. It smelled to me like heather and the breeze above the thirteenth hole, warmed with bullion and flour dumplings.

Suddenly, there was a loud knocking at the front door and Shivas's stentorian voice shouting, "Open up in the name o' the law." Peter hurried down the stairs and we could hear them talking below. Then Shivas appeared at the dining-room door. He was flushed and radiant.

"Ah, ma guid cronies, Ah see ye've waited for me. Is thair anything *at a'* left to eat?" He embraced Agatha with a bone-crunching hug and held her for a moment while she tried to squirm away. "Adam and Eve, love birds still," he grasped their hands, "what new theories have ye now? Julian Laing, protector o' Burningbush and ma very own soul!" He went round the table as he greeted everyone. "And *you*." He squeezed the back of Kelly's neck and the tall boy punched him playfully in the stomach. "What d'ye think o' this group, Michael? A motley lot, wouldn't ye say?"

He was strikingly handsome, tanned and ruddy in his white sweater and golden pants. Something had given his spirits a tremendous lift.

"I see that I've gotten here at the right moment. Lay on, Mrs. McNaughton," he said in his booming voice. And we all began eating the impressive meal that Agatha laid in front of us. What a wife she was, I thought, lucky Peter. Shivas obviously appreciated her too. "Agatha, Agatha, ye remind me o' what I'm missin'," he said as he demolished a plate of stew.

It was somewhere between the stew and the dessert that the conversation we had all been secretly waiting for finally began. Peter proposed that we all take our turn describing the game of golf. Since the Greenes were here with their new theories and as this was a gathering that was not likely to recur for a while, if ever, he said, we should each in turn tell what the endlessly mysterious sport was really about. The Greenes were by now virtually standing on their chairs, which seemed so much lower than the rest, to talk about their discoveries. They had been waiting for weeks for the occasion. Shivas was enthusiastic too. " 'Tis time tha' we did justice to the subject," he said, "and this is just the group tae do it. But I want tae hear yer ideas first. I shall speak last, plagiarist that I am, and, Michael, I want ye tae remember it all for posterity. Now, Peter, begin. Ye're the host."

"No, Agatha is," protested the good husband, "this is her party."

"Then Agatha, *begin*," boomed Shivas.

"No, Peter is the one with ideas," said our handsome hostess, and everyone began talking at once.

Eventually Peter began. "All right, my friends," he said, leaning forward and looking round at us all, his graying temples reflecting the candlelight. "I'm not an intellectual sort like the rest o' ye, so ye're not goin' tae get any fancy theories from me. And I'm goin' to keep this speech very

short, for I'm sayin' my farewell to the game. I've suffered
enough with it."

Peter's seemingly decisive statement was met with a round
of hoots and gibes. Apparently he had made such renuncia-
tions before. "Let us drink a toast to Peter's imminent departure," said Shivas, lifting up his glass, "and to his pre-
dictable retoorn." There was a round of laughter as we all
lifted glasses toward our host.

Kelly got up from the table and went into the sitting room.
He returned with an old wooden-shafted club that was taped
together with wads of black binding tape. "Break it noo," he
said, offering the golfing stick to his father, "it'll bring
everyone luck."

Peter smiled and took the club with both his hands. His
face was bright red now from drink and what seemed to be a
sudden embarrassment, "Ye see, ma friends," he said, holding
up the stick, "we call this our wishbone. Ye can each make a
wish." Then he stood up and broke it with an enormous crack
across his knee. He stood at the end of the table, sheepishly
holding up a broken piece in each hand. "We do this, ye see,
whenever I give up the gemme. Did ye make yer wishes?"
There was another round of laughter and our host sat
down.

The surprising performance had happened so swiftly that I
had not had a chance to make a wish. But the first thought
that had flashed in my mind, I can still remember it, was an
image of a golf pro at the Salinas club who had come from
Oklahoma, a colorful man with gigantic temper, throwing a
sand wedge at me by mistake. It whirled like a vicious
helicopter blade as it came right for my face—I ducked and
it grazed my scalp. It was the closest I had come to being
killed or maimed and now the image had surfaced as Peter
broke his club.

"What did ye wish, Mr. Murphy?" Kelly asked in his
whisky brogue from the other end of the table.

"That no one kills me with a golf club," my reply popped
out. Everyone thought it was a great wish.

"Ye see, that is why I *break* my club." Peter grinned. "To save ye all from disaster."

"Oh, McNaughton, ye'll be back," Shivas's voice resounded above the rest, "but finish yer speech." The rest of the group urged Peter to continue.

"Awright, I'll tell ye what I think, for through my sufferin's a certain understandin' has developed." He looked with sad eyes around the table and winked at Julian. "If I've learned one thing about the game it is that 'tis many things to many people, includin' the many ones in my very own head." He tapped his temple. "We've certainly seen them come and go through Burnin'bush. Tall ones, short ones, scratch players, and duffers from the end o' the wardle. Intellectual sorts and workin' men, pleasant tempraments and mean ones, the MacGillicudys and the Balfours, the Leviases, the St. Clairs, the Van Blocks, the gentlemen from Pakistan— in terms of origin and character and ideas, a most diverse and complex lot. For each has his peculiar understandin', his peculiar theory, his peculiar view o' the world, his peculiar swing, God knows. Get them here on the links, and all their parts fall oot." He smiled sadly again and shook his head. "Gowf is a way o' makin' a man naked. I would say tha' nowhere does a man go so naked as he does before a discernin' eye dressed for gowf. Ye talk about yer body language, Julian, yer style o' projectin', yer rationalizashin', yer excuses, lies, cheatin' roonds, incredible stories, failures of character—why, there's no other place to match it. Ye take auld Judge Hobbes, my God, the lies he told last week about that round o' his in the tournament, 'tis enough to make ye wonder about our courts o' law. So I ask ye first, why does gowf bring out so much in a man, so many sides o' his personality? Why is the game such an X-ray o' the soul?

"Now let's take this thing ye call projection," he looked again at Dr. Laing. "One man sees the Burnin'bush Links as a beautiful thing, the next sees it a menacin' monster. Or one man'll see it friendly one day and unfriendly the next. Or the same hole will change before his very eyes, within minutes. What d'ye call that ink-blot test, Julian?"

"A Rorrshock, Peter, that's what ye're talkin' aboot."

"Yes, a Rorrshock, that's what a golf links is. On some days I love these links of ours, on others I hate them. And it *looks* different, by God, it *looks* different dependin' on my mood. Agatha heer says I go through the same kind o' trouble with her, guid woman." He reached toward his wife. "Like marriage it is, like marriage!" The idea seemed to have struck him for the first time. He and Agatha looked at each other in silence for a moment. The sounds of silverware striking plates and the slurping of broth quieted as the two of them exchanged secret knowings. All heads turned up from the dinner and looked to the end of the table. Peter and Agatha were sharing untold numbers of insights and feelings regarding the relationship of golf and marriage, and the group seemed to be awed by the sight. Six faces waited expectantly in the candlelight.

"Just like marriage," Peter said at last, in a quiet solemn voice. Then he turned toward us with a small boy's smile of discovery. "Why, Agatha's like a Rorrshock too." There seemed to be a dozen "r's" in the word Rorschach. "Just like a Rorrshock," he said again, turning back to look at her with his child-like smile. "Marriage is a test of my devotion and my memory that things will be all right."

Words of approval and congratulations sprang from all sides of the table. We all wanted to cheer them on. I could see that Agatha was his mother and young lover and God knew what other incarnations in the Rorschach he saw. The same complexity seemed to be true for her.

"A good marriage is as rare and complex and fragile as the world itself," said Shivas, "and very like the game o' gowf. Ye're right, Peter, ye're right." I remembered that he was a bachelor and wondered if he had ever been married.

Then our host and devoted husband broke into an impassioned speech comparing marriage to golf. The connection had sprung some trapdoor of insight and lyricism in his heart, and all his sufferings and enthusiasms poured forth. Like golf, marriage required many skills, he said, "steadiness of purpose and imagination, a persistent will and willingness to change, long shots and delicate strokes, strength and a deft touch," the metaphors were tumbling in all directions now, "good sense and the occasional gamble, steady nerves and a certain wild streak. And ye've got to have it *all* goin' or the whole thing goes kaflooey." He clenched his fist and turned his thumb down. "Any part o' the game can ruin the whole. Ye've got to have all yer parts and all yer skills, yer lovin' heart, yer manhood, and all yer subtleties. Not only are ye naked to yerself and to yer partner, but ye've got to contend with yer entire self, all yoor *many* selves. Nowhere have I seen the Hindoo law of Karma work so clearly as in marriage and in golf. Character is destiny, my friends, on the links and with yer beloved wife." He took Agatha's hand and they exchanged unspoken thoughts again. "Get me another glass o' whisky, darlin'," he said, "this clarity is frightenin'."

Perhaps the insight regarding marriage or perhaps the whisky Agatha brought him cast another light on the game for Peter. Like a barometer of his mood, his complexion had become bright red again with pleasure.

"There is somethin' benign about the game after all," he said expansively, "we can read it in our history. It's recorded that after the Treaty of Glasgow in 1502, which ended our worst wars wi' the English, James the Fourth bought himself a set o' clubs and balls. The prohibitin' laws against the game, which he had renewed because the fields were needed for war practice, were dropped tha' year since there would be nae mair fightin'. Then he married Margaret Tudor the followin' year—bought himsel' some clubs and married the daughter of the English king—wha' d'ye think o' that! Marriage and golf again, both recorded for posterity! 'Tis curious, ye'll have to admit, that all o' this has been remembered in our history books."

Some of us asked how he knew all that. "He reads all he

can about the game," said Kelly, "thinks he'll finally read the secret."

"Now I've often thought about James the Fourth," Peter went on undeterred, "how he signed that treaty and bought himself those clubs. Reminds me o' President Eisenhower." He looked at me. "It's not a warlike man that loves the game so much." I felt constrained to say that Ike was getting a lot of criticism for all the time he was spending on the course. "Well, I'll admit that a man like that could get more done, but at least he probably willna' get ye into wars or silly ventures, seein' how much time he needs for his leisure. I think the very *thought* o' liftin' that prohibitin' law led James the Fourth to sign the Glasgow treaty. He couldna' have played unless the war was over, since they needed all that links-land for practicin' their bows and arrows." Julian Laing and Shivas both laughed at this proposal.

"Yer history's a Rorrshock," the old doctor rumbled with a smile that revealed several golden teeth. "O' course history aye has been."

But the challenge only seemed to fuel our host's passion for his subject. He claimed that men who loved games "did not have to use other human beings for their sport"—or lord it over private lives and morals. After the union of the Scottish and English crowns James Six and One proclaimed that Sunday sports were to be permitted in Scotland. Peter recited a declaration by the king, which he had memorized, something to the effect that on Sunday "our good people be not disturbed or discouraged from any lawful recreation such as dancing, leaping, or vaulting." Those good Presbyterians could now leap about the streets after divine service. "And, moreover, that was the year the featherie ball was invented!" he exclaimed. "A ball that could fly further than any before it." The coincidence of those two events—the discovery of the "featherie ball" and the relaxation of the sabbath prohibition against sport—was significant, for every improvement in leisure got into laws and treaties and politics generally. The first international golf match, between the Duke of York (later James the Second of England and Scotland) and John Patersone, the shoemaker, against two English noblemen, "a match much remembered and in the spirit of the Restoration," was held at the Leith Links sometime later in the century; its importance as a public event showed how games encouraged the meeting of men in a peaceful manner. He said that the house John Patersone built with his winnings from the match still stood in Edinburgh, that we could all see it for ourselves. Then he talked about the first golfing societies, the competition for the silver club at Edinburgh, and "the banding together of the brothers." With the English wars lessening, Scotsmen could now join to fight the elements and the "demons of their souls" at the Royal Aberdeen Club, the Royal and Ancient Club, the Honorable Company of Edinburgh Golfers, or the Musselburgh Club. All these fraternities made their rules, started their competitions, adopted their emblems and uniforms. Black jackets, red jackets, tartan jackets, and even more colorful outfits became obligatory for club festivities and play on the various golfing links. "Ye were fined if ye didna' wear the uniform—and why was that?" he asked. "To form a band o' brithers, that's why. *It was a way for men to join in peace and mak' it vivid to themselves.*" He pounded fiercely on the table for emphasis, rattling the dishes. "About the time o' the first clubs even the English and Scottish parliaments joined together, completin' what the Treaty o' Glasgow started two hundred years before. So ye see, at every important joinin' o' the English and the Scots golf played a part. At the very least, the memory of these great events of golf and politics were joined in our memories and imaginations and history books. Now extend this to all the history o' games and leisure. In golf our spears —and my friends, the Scots have had some fierce ones—get beaten into gowfin' sticks. Now we would beat the good earth instead of our fellow man."

At about this point in the conversation, I told the group about my friend Joe K. Adams' proposing a Gymnasium for the Production of Dionysian Rites and other Health-Giving

Rituals. Adams claimed that body chemistry was altered during wild dancing and other emotional sports. He claimed that dancing helped the bodily functions in general and opened up the mind. Julian thought it was a good idea. He had developed a theory that certain kinds of psychosis came from a lack of proper exercise.

"Better games would empty entire wings o' oor mental 'ospitals," he said in his broad Scots burr. His wispy silver hair glowed like a halo in the candlelight, giving his face an iridescent quality. "I've cured several myself with nothin' mair than games and dancin'. And listenin' to the pipes can blow the mind free, too." He then described the "perfect golf links." It would include music on certain holes. All sports, he said, are improved when you can hear the right music, with the inner ear if possible, or with bagpipes and bands if you couldn't. Ecstasy produced beneficial vitamins, it seemed.

"Oor brain is a distillery, pumpin' strange whiskys into the bloodstream to produce a permanent intoxication. Ye've got to feed the right things to the distillery, or ye get some bad green whisky." He made a retching sound and spit into his plate to emphasize the point. Eve Greene flinched and Adam pretended not to notice.

"But not gowf, Julian," Peter broke into the old doctor's speech, "not gowf. Gowf is for quietin' the mind, not stirrin' it. Look what happened when ye sent poor Campbell aroond the links with that dancin' step ye showed him. The members wanted to lock him up." Apparently Julian had prescribed an eighteen-hole Highland Fling for one of his patients.

"Oh, oh, oh." Julian leaned away from the table and his voice rose, "but look wha' happened to the man. 'Twas a cure, wouldna' ye say?"

Peter and the others agreed it had been a cure. Campbell had eventually gone off to the South Seas to write a book. But the argument continued. Peter and the Greenes took sides against Julian, maintaining that the beauty of the game lay in its poise and decorum, in its Apollonian virtues. The fierce old doctor took the Dionysian line; the game was meant for dancing, he said. "Noo look at ye, Peter, ye play against yer emotions, with yer emotions, through yer emotions. Wha' about the names ye have for yer different selves?" It was true. Peter McNaughton, like many others, had different names for his different golfing selves. I cannot remember them exactly, but they went something like "Old Red," for a mean and choleric one that broke clubs and swore viciously at his wife; "Divot," for a spastic one dangerous to onlookers; "Palsy," for another with floating anxiety, tremors of the hands and huge nervousness on the first tee. He seemed to have a certain detachment about them, referring to them as if they were familiar presences. He talked to them apparently. Agatha and Kelly knew who they were. Dialogues were held with them at dinner. Peter was a foursome all by himself.

"Tae me," said Julian, "yer a livin' example o' what the game is all about. What is it but the comin' together of our separate parts? Ye said it yerself, Peter, just a little while ago when ye compared the game to marriage. Our inner parts want to marry too."

I looked at Agatha. She was nodding in agreement, like many wives I have seen who pray for their husband's integration. Her hands involuntarily formed a prayerful attitude.

"Well, 'Naught' has taken ower now," said Peter with sudden vehemence. I think he sensed the group was ganging up on him. "There is nae mair gowf while 'Naught' is in command." He had rejected these uncontrollable sub-personalities, along with golf and the whole business. Julian asked him what was left. "Oh, my friends, this lovely family, my sanity, my peace o' mind," he said with unconvincing gusto.

"Now, Peter 'Naught,' I think yer many sel's will return ere long over another game, over another dinner, in the midst o' this very family. There is nae banishin' them," said Julian with a sinister smile.

Peter was getting angry. He rose from the table. "Here, poor gowfin' addicts," he said, "drink up and arm yersel's against yer madness. I've said my piece. Ye can see I love the game, have my theories just like you, even my historical understandin's. But I'm leavin' it all behind. We will heer nae mair o' 'Palsy' and 'Divot.'" There was a finality in his voice that none of us wanted to question. It was someone else's turn to speak.

Agatha proposed that we go into the sitting room; perhaps she sensed that we needed a respite from so much talk. We found seats for ourselves while Peter stoked the burning logs. For a moment there was silence. There was a hint of embarrassment as we looked around at each other. Shivas spoke up first. "Now, Adam," he said, "ye've been tellin' us about yer theories the night, heer's yer chance. I ken they're goin' tae be guid ones." We all looked at the little man, who was almost invisible now in the shadows of the couch. I remember hoping that he would make a long speech that would give me some ideas for my own. But his enthusiasm and bouncy spirit seemed to have left him; he looked at us shyly as if he were afraid to say anything. We all sensed his discomfort. When he finally spoke his voice was so low none of us could hear what he said. Julian leaned forward with a hand cupped to his ear. "Wha' was that, Adam," he asked, "wha' was that ye said, did ye say the supermind?"

Adam nodded. It was painful to watch his embarrassment but we still wondered what he had mumbled. The entire group turned toward Julian. "What did he say?" someone asked.

"I think he said that golf is the *supermind*," the old man answered, scratching the back of his head. We all turned back to Adam. The bashful little figure whispered another inaudible sentence. We all turned to Julian again, as if he were our interpreter. The old man shook his head and leaned toward Adam. "Adam, ye'll have tae speak up," he said. "Did ye say the *supermind*?"

The little man raised himself an inch or two on the couch and spoke again. We could barely hear him. "Golf is the new yoga of the supermind," the bashful voice said.

"Good man!" Shivas exclaimed. "I can see that I'll enjoy this." Apparently he was the only one who understood. Everyone else looked puzzled. Then Adam sank back into the shadows of the couch. It was going to take more encouragement to get him going in earnest. Eve reached over and put a reassuring hand on his arm.

"Well, now, that's certainly an interestin' beginnin'," said Julian. The rest of us nodded in agreement. There was still no response from the declivity in the couch.

"The yoga of the supermind," someone said as if he were just comprehending the meaning of the phrase, "yes, I see what he means."

I felt myself nodding in agreement. Yes, the yoga of the supermind, ye . . . es, I see.

Then Adam spoke again. The only words I could hear distinctly were "the next manifesting plane." I closed my eyes to ponder the gnomic phrases. There must be something to them, Shivas certainly seemed to think so. Supermind, a term from Aurobindo, but golf being "the yoga of the supermind," that was a little hard to follow. And "the next manifesting plane," what was that? As I pondered thus I heard a small commotion across the room. I opened my eyes and lo!—there was Adam standing on the couch. He stood in the flickering shadows bouncing gently on the cushions of his seat. Then he began to speak. "Golf recapitulates evolution," he said in a melodious voice, "it is a microcosm of the world, a projection of all our hopes and fears." I cannot remember all the phrases, but his words were an ecstatic hymn to golf, not golf the game I knew, but golf as it might appear in the Platonic World of Ideas, the archetypal game of games. As he talked I wondered what his course in "cosmic ecology" must be like. No professor of mine at Stanford had ever talked like this.

He told about the technological changes in the game and how they brought new powers and awarenesses into play for those who pursued it with a passion. With its improved clubs and balls and courses, golf reflected man's ever-increasing complexity. It was becoming a better vehicle for training the higher capacities. And so it was becoming the yoga of the supermind, the discipline for transcendence.

As he gave this incredible speech I wondered if he played the game himself. Being no taller than five feet four, he must have had a difficult time if he did. I wondered how far he could hit the ball, if he could reach a green in regulation figures.

"Golf is played at many levels," he was almost chanting now as he swayed in the firelight. "Take our love of the ball's flight, the thrill of seeing it hang in the sky." He made a sweeping gesture with his arm, tracing an imaginary trajectory against the fire's glow. "How many games depend upon that thrill—archery, football, golf—the thrill of a ball flying to a target, have you felt it? The ball flying *into* the target; it's a symbol, of course. And here, friends, my theory leads . . .", he stepped down from the couch and crossed the room to the fireplace, ". . . my theory leads to the simultaneity of past and future. For everything has a past *and* future reason for being. Projectiles for example, our urge to see them fly is derived from our paleolithic past, from the hunt, we love to see the spear or stone in flight. But," he stood on tiptoes and his voice rose, "it is also an anticipation. The flight of the ball, the sight of it hanging there in space, anticipates our desire for transcendence. We love to see it curve in flight as if it is free—why else do we hit a fade or draw? We love to see it hang there, that is why we love to hit our drives so far. The ball in flight brings dim memories of our ancestral past *and* premonitions of the next manifesting plane."

He rocked slowly back and forth, occasionally making a wide, sweeping gesture with an arm. We were all staring at him now with amazement. "The thrill of seeing a ball fly over the countryside, over obstacles—especially over a stretch of water—and then onto the green and into the hole has a mystic quality. Something in us *loves* that flight. What is it but the flight of the alone to the alone?"

He was tilting back his head and his black eyes were dancing. One sensed that his shyness had given way to a passion tinged with madness. A few moments before I had wanted to draw him out and give him support, now I was beginning to think we should try to slow him down. He was not the first person I had seen grow strangely intense while attempting to account for the game's mystery.

"The theory of golf," he continued, "which Eve and I have evolved, is the most elaborate and complete one ever invented to account for the game. I think it explains *everything*."

I was suddenly aware of Julian. He was frowning and glancing from time to time at Shivas. I wondered what he saw in Adam's behavior. He had said that he was generally in favor of madness, but now he looked concerned. Though I was fascinated by the speech emanating from the fireplace I was glad we had a doctor around.

"Have you ever pondered the mystery of the hole?" the swaying figure asked. "What are its past and future connotations? Think about that one. And a *hole-in-one*, have you ever thought about that!" He looked around at us with a wide-eyed look full of portent. "A *hole-in-one*," he intoned the term as if it were the holy of holies, "the flight of the alone to the alone."

Julian turned in his armchair to look at Shivas. "Ye incourage 'im in this kind o' thinkin' now and ye see where it leads 'im." Shivas did not answer; he only looked at Julian with a grave inscrutable look. The old man turned back to Adam. "The flight o' the alone to the alone, do ye equate the average gowfer wi' Plotinus noo? It's a dim connection, Adam."

"But it's *so real*," the little man answered solemnly, with a glint in his eye. He stood on the hearth as if to get more height into his words. "All of our experience is full of anticipations, we love what we might be. That is why we love a low-sailing two-iron or a three-hundred-yard drive."

I wondered if he had ever hit a two-iron shot like the one he described—or a 300-yard drive. He was indeed describing the Platonic Game of Golf. "We know in our bones what we are meant to be, so we are attracted by any glimpse of greater possibilities. There are moments in every golfer's game when he gets off a Promethean shot or when he feels a marvelous state of mind. Do you know what I mean?" he asked, suddenly looking down at me.

I thought of my shots on the back nine that day and nodded, in spite of my fears for him. Yes, I knew what he meant, how could I forget? There was logic in his madness.

"Some players embody that feeling," he said in his melodious voice. "Bobby Jones did. If someone else does, we will love him too. So . . ." he paused in mid-sentence as if pondering the next turn of his thought ". . . so because evolution is always at work, golf is becoming a better and better vehicle for it all."

This last generalization was all Julian could take. "Humbug, it's all humbug," he growled. "There is nothin' awtaematic about evolution or gowf or any other thing. Adam, it's you that's awtaematic when ye talk like that."

I was surprised at the old doctor's anger and direct confrontation to Adam's logic: my impulse had been to listen and hope for the best. But Adam now had too much passion to be deterred. He launched into another line of reasoning about the inevitability of life's unfoldment, arguing that any human activity that received the investment golf did was bound to reflect more and more of the human situation with all its hopes, fears, loves, ways of coping, struggles for survival, aspirations for God—the works. Therefore, it had to reflect the always upward tendency of life. "Golf is a microcosm of the world," he said. "When you invent new clubs, you get new attitudes. Replacing divots only began when courses were built from scratch instead of being marked off across links-land. Replacing the divot means a change in consciousness. . . ."

"Now, Adam," Julian broke in, "ye dinna' mean tae tell me tha' the replacin' o' the divot shows an improvement o' the spirit. It only shows *me* that the herds o' public gowfers realize they're about to overrun wha's left o' the green." Peter nodded in agreement. The two of them were a dour contrast to Adam's incredible optimism.

But Adam Greene sailed on. "I look for signals of transcendence in golf as in everything else." He smiled triumphantly and stepped down off the hearth. "I ask you to think about your own experience. If you are honest—even you, Julian, you—will have to admit that I'm right."

"If I'm goin' to be honest, Adam Greene," Julian replied, "then I've got to talk about the signals o' the damned along wi' the signals o' transcendence. Ye can see any signals ye want in the game."

"Well, Julian, if you had eyes to see . . ." Adam threw his hands up.

"But there is more to it," Eve Greene interrupted, coming to her husband's rescue. They had talked so much about these things, these speculations were so important to them. Their eyes shone in the firelight. "The environment is so crucial," she said. "Our playing partners, the course, our state of mind, our whole life affect our game so much. Whenever we play Burningbush we feel something special, the kind of thing Shivas and Seamus talk about. We think the thirteenth hole is haunted."

Haunted? I thought of my own experience there. "Who is Seamus?" I asked.

"We'll not be bringin' Seamus MacDuff into this," said Peter vehemently. "I can't stand the man."

"Now, Peter," said Shivas, "now, Peter—Seamus is our great good friend." He smiled at our host and reached over to squeeze his arm.

"Who is Seamus MacDuff?" I asked the question louder this time.

"Seamus MacDuff," said Eve Greene, "is the local madman, or a very *wise* man, depending upon your point of view. He and Shivas are very special friends."

"Who is he?" I persisted. There seemed to be no end of strange characters in this innocent-seeming town.

"Well, Ah'll tell ye, Michael, if ye promise to keep it a secret noo," Shivas fixed me with a solemn look. "Seamus

MacDuff is the man who invented the game so long ago. He's workin' on it still, perfectin' it ye might say. And blessin' our town here by choosin' our links to do his special work." He leaned toward me. "And Seamus it is who teaches me most o' what Ah ken about the game."

There was a long silence. The ghost of Seamus was with us. I began to wonder if I had seen him on the course. I seemed to remember a seedy-looking character walking back and forth along the far edge of that treacherous ravine on the thirteenth hole. Then—weird sensation—I realized I *had* seen him! The glimpse I had gotten had not been important then, absorbed as I was with our play. But now I remembered him vividly. I could have sworn he was wearing a tattered black tail coat! "Did we see him on the thirteenth?" I whispered to Shivas.

"Noo did ye see him there!" he answered loudly, pulling back from me with a wide-eyed look. "Did he speak?"

"Well, he did seem to be saying something," I answered. To my amazement I now remembered that he *had* spoken. "But I can't remember what he said," I went on vaguely.

Had he been talking to us? How could I repress such a vivid perception? I had been totally preoccupied with my game after Shivas's strange performance and my own extraordinary shot. But to have my recognition of Seamus Mac-Duff totally obscured. . . . At that point I asked Agatha to get me another glass of whisky. There was a long silence. Finally Shivas spoke.

"I like yer theories, Greenes," he said. "Speakin' o' environments, I've aye wanted to play at the Tuctu gowf course in Peroo. 'Tis the highest in the world, they say. 'Tis said tha' the game is played there from mountain top to mountain top. There wid be yer environmental effect, now widn't? The ball wid fly a mile."

"I thought ye wanted to play in Tibet," said Kelly.

"Well, Tibet [he pronounced it Ti'but] wid be a place a'right, but this is the worst yeer in their history and I dinna' think we'll have much o' a chance tae do it," he said gravely. That was 1956, the year the Chinese overran Tibet. I learned that this had affected him deeply. "But gowf has been played there, o' that we can be shair noo." He said this last with great conviction.

"I always said ye shoulda' played wi' the Sodom and Gomorra' Gowfin Society on the Dead Sea," rumbled Julian from the depths of his armchair. "Noo there yer ba' would nae 'ave gone very farr," he rolled his r's as if he were savoring them. "Nae verry farr at a'. Twelve hundred feet below the sea, their li'l coorse was. Played the thing maself before the war. Like playin' in the inferno. The inferno itself. Only the English woulda' thought of doin' a thing like tha'."

"The Sodom and Gomorrah Golfing Society!" Eve exclaimed. "There was such a place?"

"Indeed there was, in a town called Kallia, upon the Dead Sea," Julian said.

"Now, Julian, you must admit that playing such a course affected your game," said the pixilated lady, ever hopeful for her husband's theories.

"Well, I'll tell ye, Eve," he replied, "it left an indelible impression on me that the English could stick it out in hell and niver know the difference."

The whisky now was having its effect, and the conversation bobbed along as if we were shooting the rapids of the Colorado. Adam and Eve continued to elaborate their sweeping theory of evolution. They talked about successive levels of mind, the opening up of supramental powers and awarenesses, and somehow came around to gardens. "The history of golf and the history of gardens are interlocked," they said. "The golf links here in Burningbush are an exploded garden." Then they explained the relationships between gardens and certain states of mind, how the English made the formal European gardens more like nature, made them gentler and more random. I said that nothing in England or Scotland could rival Pebble Beach for sheer grandeur, that the famous

California golf course should certainly produce some wonderful states of mind, though I had never heard of any actually occurring there. Then the conversation came round again to Seamus MacDuff.

"He's an embarrassment to the city and a royal pain in the ass," said Peter abruptly. "Why they let him live out in that ravine, I'll niver know."

"Does he actually live out there?" I asked.

"Let us say he spends a good deal o' his precious time there," said Shivas. "He's studyin' the game at all times, workin' on his theories o' the wardle."

It was uncanny how much I could remember now about that scroungy-looking character. I seemed to remember him gesticulating in our direction as he walked along the far edge of the gully.

"It's reputed that he's writing a book which will be published after his death," said Eve. "But no one knows for sure."

"Oh, he's mad as a loon and why d'ye all pretend to take him so serious?" said Peter. "Ye're makin' fun o' him just like everybody else. That's what ye're really doin', just makin' fun of him."

"I niver make fun o' the man," said Shivas gravely. "And he has a book indeed, a great book. *The Logarithms of the Just*, it's called, bein' first notes for a physics o' the spirit. I've seen it twice. So dinna' tell me that I'm makin' fun of 'im, Peter. He's my truest teacher."

"What kind of theories does he have?" I asked, my curiosity growing with each statement.

"Apparently he's studying gravity," someone said. "His theory explains the alignment of human consciousness with the physical forces of the universe."

"Is he a mathematician?" I asked.

"In the Pythagorean tradition," said Shivas. "Ye see, Michael, he's had to tip the balance of his mind to study gravity. He's floatin' free now to get a better fix upon this world of ours." In a few hours I would discover Shivas's own formulations relating gravity to the subtle forces of the human soul.

"Seamus MacDuff is the one sane man among us," Julian slapped the arm of his chair. "The only sane man among us. In a world gone completely off the target he's readjustin' his sights. What if it takes a lifetime, are any o' us here doin' any better?" He scowled at us all. "The whole o' our world is gone off target. Now, I would like to say my piece about the game of gowf." He cleared his throat and spat into the fire. Then he began to speak in his richly cadenced, rumbling brogue, and summoned a vision of hell on earth. In attempting to recreate his monologue I have become aware once again that a vision can be communicated only by the person who has it. His words went something like this.

"Now see how spellbound we are by the wardle around us. Hypnotized from mornin' to night by every influence, human or otherwise, that impinges on our senses. Adam, ye talk about the grand evolution but despair yerself about our times. For every theory ye propose about the improvement o' the game, I'll show ye how the game is fadin' away, losin' its old charm, becomin' mechanized by the Americans and the rest o' the world that blindly follows them. Look at the crowded links, the lack o' leisure, the hurried startin' times, the ruination o' the old clubs where ye could gather with your friends and enjoy some good conversation. Where's the evolution in all o' that now, I ask ye? Show me where it is. Now my special angle on life is bein' a doctor, lookin' at people's ailments these fifty years. And I want to tell ye tha' the language o' the body says, help! help! help! There is no apparent increase o' longevity, health, happiness, or digestin' in the world as far as I can see. A chance for more to live all right, an elimination o' the plagues and epidemics, an end to infant deaths. But with all o' that nae increase in the higher goods o' life. We are all o' us hypnotized, I tell ye, and you're just refusin' to look at the facts if ye say it otherwise. Now gowf reflects all this, yer right, Adam. It does indeed reflect all this. But what an awful reflection! What an *awful* reflection," he shook his head sadly as he repeated the words. "I see the distorted swings, the hurried rounds, and now the electric carts tae ruin the courses and rob us of our exercise. And the configuration o' physique that shows me how our twisted lives twist our bodies. I don't think evolution is goin' ahead so much as just goin' along breedin' more unfitness every day. We have got off the mark, gone for the wrong things, forgotten what it's all about, gotten oursel's hypnotized by silly people. If it weren't for Shivas here, and Seamus MacDuff, I would say there's nae hope left at all." He then went around the room pointing to each person's foibles and source of unhappiness. He asked the Greenes about their constant hypochondriacal complaints—Adam's bad back, Eve's migraine headaches—all the complaining which punctuated their grand theories of the universe. And Peter McNaughton about his endless rushing—at work, at home, at play, his irritability over tiny frustrations, his compulsive avoidance of pleasure through most of the day. Even Shivas was not spared. Why, asked the forbidding doctor, did he have to rush about the streets in the early morning hours provoking theories that he was some kind of sexual offender? He ended with a horrendous blast at me. He could tell just by looking at me that there wasn't a fiber of dedication in my character, that I was a good American boy "pluckin' the fruits of an easy life." The line he ended with, the last twist of his conversational dagger, was an admonition that each of us compare our complainings and frustrations now with our sufferings ten years before. "It is interestin' to see how persistent the patterns are," he said. "And then we sit here, gettin' high on whisky, paintin' glorious pictures o' the higher life, while the world outside grows ever darker."

As the old doctor's black and eloquent harangue developed I became aware of Agatha McNaughton. She smiled at each person as their turn came for Julian's roasting. She had seen him do this before, I suspected, and would help carry her friends through it as she would a child who cried in the night.

She gave Shivas a long and affectionate look when his turn came. Then she winked at me. When Julian was finished she quietly rose and brought us each a cup of tea. It was a time for silent thought, so many of the old man's words had hit the mark. Eve Greene was furious, I thought, and had a difficult time returning Agatha's understanding look. Adam looked dumbly into the fire. Agatha permitted the silence, but was seeing to it that we were comforted through our dark reflections. Dr. Laing spit into the fire again and muttered a few inaudible curses.

Shivas was the first to speak. "Julian," he said solemnly, "ye've made it difficult for me to sing the praises o' gowf. There is somethin' like the final word about yer speech. I think we need Agatha's blessin' now if we are to proceed." He leaned toward her. "Now Agatha, lassie, tell us what ye think. Ye're the fairest one here, and the only one to break the spell tha' Julian has put upon us." His sentiment was echoed by the rest of the group. We all wanted her warmth after the pounding Laing had given us. So Agatha spoke about golf and about the love men have for one another.

"It's the only reason ye play at all," she said. "It's a way ye've found to get togither and yet maintain a proper distance. I know you men. Yer not like women or Italians huggin' and embracin' each other. Ye need tae feel yer separate love. Just look—ye winna' come home on time if yer with the boys, I've learned that o'er the years. The love ye feel for your friends is too strong for that. All those gentlemanly rools, why, they're the proper rools of affection—all the waitin' and oohin' and ahin' o'er yer shots, all the talk o' this one's drive and that one's putt and the other one's gorgeous swing—what is it all but love? Men lovin' men, that's what golf is." The strong lines of her face were softened by the fire's glow. "I think the loss o' love is Julian's real despair, whate'er his philosophizen' tells him. He misses the leisurely pace when there was time for more affection. Now don't ye, Julian? I miss it too. Most of the women miss it, the ones I know. We hurry through our days." She looked at

Peter and took his hand. Then she lifted back her head. "Oh, golf is for smellin' heather and cut grass and walkin' fast across the countryside and feelin' the wind and watchin' the sun go down and seein' yer friends hit good shots' and hittin' some yerself. It's love and it's feelin' the splendor o' this good world." There was music in her gentle Scottish burr, a fullness in her feeling for us. It was becoming obvious by now that each of us had a different song to sing in praise of the mysterious game.

"Oh, Agatha, Agatha," said Shivas, "how can I say anything more after that? Yer eloquence leaves me dumb. It would be embarrassin' for me tae say anythin' at all, so I'll not speak. Good friends, let me be now. I'll just look into the fire and roominate about what ye've all said."

But his friends would not have it. They all urged him on. He protested again, but was drowned out by their urgings and derisions. "Humbug," rumbled Julian, "enough now o' yer habitual laziness. We willna' let ye git away wi' that." It was apparent that they knew what a put-on artist he could be.

"Well, now, what d'ye make o' that?" Shivas said. "Ye really value my poor views on the subject, it almost makes me want to weep." He smiled though as he said it.

And so his talk about golf began. He first asked Agatha some questions about what she had said, getting her to admit the game had its foul aspects as well as its noble and beautiful ones. He gave Julian credit for having stated so well the dark and tragic side, man's "hamartia" in golf and everything else. He got her to agree that people were usually hypnotized by the game, just as they were by most of the other activities in their lives, that Julian had been eloquent on that subject too. "But we must remember that hypnosis is first cousin to fascination," he said, "and all art and love depend on fascination. Ye can hear Beethoven playin' on the radio and not recognize it nor feel it at all if ye're preoccupied wi' somethin' else. But once ye turn to hear it, down ye go into his world, into his deep and stormy world. Or a poem bein' read by a friend, or a lovely face—if ye're not fascinated by it, it goes right by unnoticed. So it is with golf. There's no use playin' if the fascination doesna' take ye." He was silent for a while. "Now ye've brought in Seamus MacDuff, so I must tell ye what he tells me, him bein' my main teacher about the game. Accordin' to him, life is nothin' but a series of fascinations, an odyssey from world to world. And so with golf. An odyssey it is—from hole to hole, adventure after adventure, comic and tragic, spellin' out the human drama. Fascination holds us there, makes us believe 'tis all-important. Now, and this is the point Seamus makes so often and which I love so much, fascination has a gravity of its own. It can draw upon the subtle forces, draw them round us lik' a cloak, and create new worlds." He looked at me as he said this. Suddenly his face began to shimmer. I felt the same presence I had felt on the course with him. "Worlds of subtle energy when the fascination takes us," he said, drawing us into his spell. "Now this happens all the time, every day, and we go like Ulysses from place to place, hardly knowin' what we're about. But— and this is the second point from old Seamus's book—we can begin to look around and ken these many worlds, what they are and what they make us. World upon world, all the heavens and hells of our daily lives. 'Man the great amphibian,'" he began reciting from the *Religio Medici*, "'whose nature is disposed to live, not only like other creatures in divers elements, but in divided and distinguished worlds.' And his odyssey does not end here or there or any place we've seen yet." He paused again, gazing across the room as if waiting for the next inspiration. "So as we ken these many worlds, see them with a clearer eye, we learn to move more freely—and learn o' worlds tha' lie beyond." He raised a long finger and held it in front of his nose. "Yes, worlds within worlds right in front o' our nose. Think about the times ye really concentrated upon a thing, did ye see it change in front o' your very eyes? Now, did it not? The lovely face tha' grew lovelier still, the new music in the old tunes, the new meanin's in the familiar poem, the new energies in the old swing? Yes, worlds within worlds here, with new shapes, new powers.

Now did ye e'er make a ball curve in the air just by willin' it? New powers there, will ye na' say? So this is the first point o' my speech, my friends, namely that fascination frees our journey through the worlds and opens the doors to where we want to go. In this I think—when I get into my metaphysical mind—I think we're like the great God, who lost Himself in this dark unconscious universe and wends His way back toward light and fullest knowin'. Forgettin' and rememberin', losin' and findin' our original face—the great God and all of us are in the game togither. We're all o' us joined to the growin' world, with God we're wakin' up." There was total silence in the room now, except for the sound of logs snapping in the fire. Then a smile appeared on his face, it broadened to a grin, he began to laugh. "Oh, we forget and remember every day, forget and remember what we're all about. And so, my friends, we come to discipline and the loveliness o' rools, the very loveliness of the game o' gowf. Fascination is the true and proper mother of discipline. And gowf is a place to practice fascination. 'Tis slow enough to concentrate the mind and complex enough to require our many parts. In that 'tis a microcosm of the world's larger discipline. Our feelin's, fantasies, thoughts and muscles, all must join to play. In gowf ye see the essence of what the world itself demands. Inclusion of all our parts, alignment o' them all with one another and with the clubs and with the ball, with all the land we play on and with our playin' partners. The game requires us to join ourselves to the weather, to know the subtle energies that change each day upon the links and the subtle feelin's of those around us. It rewards us when we bring them all together, our bodies and our minds, our feelin's and our fantasies—rewards us when we do and treats us badly when we don't. The game is a mighty teacher —never deviatin' from its sacred rools, always ready to lead us on. In all o' that 'tis a microcosm o' the world, a good stage for the drama of our self-discovery. And I say to ye all, good friends, that as ye grow in gowf, ye come to see the things ye learn there in every other place. The grace that comes from such a discipline, the extra feel in the hands, the extra strength and knowin', all those special powers ye've felt from time to time, begin to enter our lives."

I thought of our round that afternoon. "Those special powers and knowings," I knew what he meant. That drive on the first hole, curving gently to follow the path I had seen. The crystalline view from the thirteenth green, yes, I knew what he meant.

"My friends," he said, "devoted discipline and grace will bring ye knowin's and powers everywhere, in all your life, in all your works if they're good works, in all your loves if they're good loves. Ye'll come away from the links with a new hold on life, that is certain if ye play the game with all your heart."

Evanescent corridors of memory intervene between my writing and his talk, so there are gaps in this brief account. I remember well, however, the applause and hurrahs that followed and the magical presence he left in the room.

But this was not to be a gathering for contemplation. We were soon embarked on a lively discussion of shanking and the problem of evil; Peter, well influenced now by drink, maintained that in terms of body language it was the clearest example of the game's diabolical nature. Then suddenly there was a loud banging at the front door and raucous shouts from the street below. Someone was trying to get in. A large, ebullient man who looked to be in his late twenties came bursting into the room. He was dressed in an orange sweater and enormous red Tam O'Shanter. He demanded loudly that we join him in his revels. "Come on, ye sober logs," he bellowed, grabbing Peter's shoulders, "come to Clancy's house to celebrate my victory." He wrestled Peter around the room knocking over a chair. I was alarmed, he was so enormous. He must have been six feet five or so. He caught Agatha in a bear hug, then Kelly with a hammerlock around the neck. Then he saw Shivas sitting in a corner. "My God, look there," he cried, "who let him in, the hound of hiven, the bastard. He hounds me e'erywhere, the terrible man hounds me e'ery-where." He took off his Tam O'Shanter and sailed it across the room onto Shivas's lap. "A hole-in-one," he bellowed.

Shivas put the Tam on his own head and pointed a menacing finger at the intruder. "Ye'll na' disrupt our higher talk, Evan Tyree. We'er onto better things and will na' be led by you nor any man to celebrate mere victories o' the flesh."

Evan Tyree was the local golf champion, one of the best amateur players in British history, they said. When it came to scoring, he was the most proficient and famous of Shivas's pupils. He had just won a notable British tournament.

"My good friends, I've celebrated about the town wi' all the sober judges and potentates and will na' leave ye, the very arcane priests o' gowf. And ye'll na' tell me, Shivas Irons, to sober up—for God or any other one."

"Nae, nae, Evan, ye canna' end our party here," said Peter. "We've been singin' the praises o' gowf the night, each sayin' what it is that makes its mystery and allure, so now ye do the same. Tell us what the game means to you, great champion."

The rest of the group joined to urge the colorful intruder on. "Let's get the genuine word from a genuine champion," said Shivas. "Now we'll hear what it's really all about. Evan will put our poor talks to shame."

Evan Tyree walked across the room, grabbed the enormous Tam from his teacher's head and placed it on his own. "Let me wear my champion's crown if I must speak," he said. He drew himself to his full height and looked up at the ceiling. "But I winna' speak o' gowf, oh, no. I can only tell ye about my teacher, for 'twas he wha showed me the way." He bowed deeply, doffing his Tam to Shivas. " 'Twas he wha taught me a' the graces o' the gemme, to hold my temper when retreatin' from par and bogey, to use the inner eye to make the game a very prayer."

He held his hand to his chest. "When I was young and he was first a legend, I had the privilege o' playin' with him on many a day. And I wid throw my clubs and shak' my fist at God and scream across the links like a banshee. 'Twas he wha showed me self-control. For he would miss his shots, deliberately I later learned, and stay so cool to embarrass me. One day he shot a ninety, yes, a ninety, my friends, and laughed and complimented me all the way. Had a grand time, he did, never lookin' back at par, never panickin' or cursin', just steady through it a', the same as he always is. And that I say is the mark o' a brave and holy man, that he can retreat like that from par without a whimper. I've never forgotten that holy round, the memory o' it haunts me still and settles me after many a rotten hole.

"And morower, 'twas he wha showed me the religion o' the game. I'll ne'er forget the time he stood there on ol' thirteen upoon the hill, for hours lost in contemplation, doin' his meditatin' while standin' up. Jist a boy I came to watch him there at sunset, and he stood into the wee hours, waitin' for his inspiration. I learned a thing or two about the higher laws tha' night watchin' him there lookin' out tae sea.

"And all the times I've tried to lead the man astray, a hundred times, wi' bets and drinkin' and fornicatin', but there he stands like the Rock o' Gibraltar, givin' in to his prayers and contemplations but niver once tae me. Oh, we've gone out on the town so many nights and howled at the moon together and laft until the sun come up, but ne'er once did he j'in me in my wretched time wi' the men and women o' the town here. When we went to London I thought I would corrupt him then, for once and for all. So I took him to the greatest place in Mayfair, full o' the finest lassies o' England and the Continent. I thought that night I would see him fall but what d'ye think happened? He was the sensation o' the house, regalin' fower or five o' the lassies wi' his stories and winnin' smile, a regular satyer on the face o't. And disappear, he did, upstairs wi' a few o' them. But he winna' tell me to this day what he did. Oh, he is a hard man when it comes to deviatin'. Only in the upward direction will he go astray."

"Enough now, Evan," Shivas broke in, "ye're only tryin' tae rooin my reputation among the lassies, makin' me out tae be some kind o' churchmoose. But we winna' be fooled by all o' that. It's my very own wildness that has so influenced you, just look at yer wild ways." Evan Tyree, I learned, was vastly erratic in tournament play and private life. Contemplation did not seem to be his calling. He picked Agatha up and fell with her in his lap onto the floor. "Now, Agatha darlin', ye're my true love, let's rin awa' frae Peter," he said and smiled drunkenly.

Agatha pushed him away. "Shivas is the only man I'd run away with," she said demurely.

"Oh, Peter, see that," Evan bellowed, "d'ye see that? The man steals the women too. Beats us on the course, steals the women, shows us up at philosophizen', a man to be contended with at every turn."

And so the party turned to raucous repartee. Evan and Shivas joined in a Highland Fling, while the rest of us sang "Munlochy Bridge" and "Devil in the Kitchen." They danced between the old crossed swords, which Agatha had taken from the mantel. They danced like two gazelles, locking arms, their heads almost hitting the ceiling as they jumped across the blades, their footwork flawless in spite of all the whisky. Then Peter emerged blowing his bagpipes, skirling "Scotland the Brave" with all its surging power, and we marched around the room, Julian leading the way, until Peter could blow no more.

Seamus MacDuff's Baffing Spoon

Around midnight we started slowing down. Julian slumped happily in his armchair, regarding us all with a benign look that betrayed the dark views of life he had been propounding. Agatha was urging him to go home, it being hours past his customary bedtime. No, he wanted just one more turn around the room, the old doctor said, but Peter's lungs had reached their limit. Gradually the party came to an end, and with hugs in all directions we tumbled out into the night. The McNaughton lights were the only ones on along the darkened street, and our voices—especially Evan's—bounced off the neighbors' houses until a shutter flew open and someone yelled at us to stop. The leader of our revel held his Tam in front of his mouth and waved good-by, as he swayed off down the hill toward Clancy's. Kelly managed to get Julian into the Mc-Naughtons' car to drive him home. Shivas and I were left alone in front of the house. "I'll walk ye to the Inn," he said, and we started off down the cobblestone street.

We walked along in silence, simmering in our alcoholic happiness. I was warmed by these new-found friends. I thought of Agatha and Peter asking me to return, their smiles as I looked up the stairs to say my last good-by, then Julian shaking my hand and asking me to forget some of the things he had said, and the Greenes insisting that I have their address in Cornwall. I knew I would remember that gathering for the rest of my life.

But then through the good feeling and warmth of friendship, through the alcoholic vapors, one thought intruded, one piece of unfinished business. How had I repressed that glimpse of Seamus MacDuff? I tried to remember whether he had said something, whether he had actually worn a tattered black tail coat as I seemed to remember. It was disturbing to think my memory and perception could be so unreliable. Something exceedingly strange had happened, yet I had forgotten it completely. I told Shivas what I was thinking.

" 'Tis nervous-makin' when yer mind does tricks like tha'," he said, "I know wha' ye mean." The more I let the memory develop the more certain I became that something very strange indeed had taken place on the thirteenth tee. Bolder now with camaraderie and whisky, I asked him why he had loosed that blood-curdling scream.

"Oh, that," he said quickly with a little smile and shrug, "I do that a lot on the thirteenth, tae scair away the divil." He turned and looked at me. "Did it disturb ye?" he asked innocently.

I said that it hadn't, seeing how I hit my approach. But he must have sensed that I wanted more explanation. He gave me a quick intense look, that sudden X-ray glance of his, then turned away. We walked along for another block or two until we turned into the street that led to The Druids' Inn, an old hotel I had found. He stopped and put a hand on my arm.

"Michael, have ye got a bottle in yer room or a cup o' tea?" he asked. "I feel like talkin'."

I said that I did and we went up to the little room I had taken for the night. To this day I can remember the excitement and sense of anticipation I felt then. I was sure he was about to take me into his confidence. But when we got to the room he simply stretched out on the bed and stared at the ceiling. I broke out a bottle of Perrier Water, something I carried with me all the way through Europe on that trip. I suddenly felt awkward being alone with him. After a few painful moments he broke the quiet.

"Tell me about yer trip heer," he said. He seemed utterly distracted, I could sense that he felt as awkward as I did.

And then one of those abrupt changes in my perception occurred. He suddenly seemed much smaller in stature. His face looked green and wizened in the room's dim light. I began telling him about my trip but the words were mechanical; I seemed to be watching the entire conversation from a distance. I told him about my interest in Eastern thought and contemplative practice, about Sri Aurobindo and the ashram in Pondicherry. I had a sense he was listening with half his mind.

"Do ye think ye'll stay at the ashram?" he interrupted. I said that I didn't know, that I might or might not depending upon what I found there. He studied me as I said it.

"Aurobindo believes in the earth—is that true?" he asked. The question surprised me. Apparently he knew something about the Indian seer, who was unknown in the Western world except to the most ardent students of Eastern thought. He jabbed his finger toward the floor for emphasis. "Is tha' true?" he repeated the question.

"Yes, he does," I replied, touched by the crude grasp he seemed to have of Aurobindo's thought.

"Well, how would ye like to meet Seamus MacDuff?" he asked. The rapid sequence startled me. Aurobindo, believing in the earth, Seamus MacDuff—I must have looked perplexed. He stood, regaining his expansive manner.

"Come, let us call upon Seamus in the midnight hour," he said. "And bring the Perrier Water." I hurried after him, a bottle of mineral water under each arm, wondering what adventure was coming next.

We found his car, a little Morris Minor, in front of his apartment a few blocks from the Inn. His head almost touched the roof as he got behind the steering wheel. With considerable coughing and sputtering the engine started and we shot off through the deserted streets. Burningbush locks up early, like most Scottish towns.

"The sound o' this machine is much discussed," he said as we careened around a corner. "Word o' this will certainly get out." He seemed excited. "Gi' me a slug o' tha' Perrier Water," he said as we roared through the night.

The oldest part of Burningbush Town adjoins the first and last holes of the links. One of the cobblestone streets in this section runs into a narrow grass-covered road that leads out into the golf course and then to the sea. We turned onto it and he shifted gears. "There are animals heer," he said, "all sorts o' animals." And indeed a pair of eyes gleamed in our headlight, then disappeared into the gorse.

"What was that?" I asked.

"Tha' was a banshee," he said decisively, as if he believed it.

We drove out slowly toward the thirteenth hole, bumping over the little-used road, both of our heads hitting the roof of the car. "Have you ever come out here before at night?" I asked. He did not reply as he concentrated on the potholes and gullies around us. He turned the little car off the road and stopped under a tree.

"From heer on, we walk," he said as he jerked the emergency brake. It was a windy night and I pulled the collar of my windbreaker up as we got out of the car, hunching my shoulders for warmth. Shivas spread his arms toward the sky and slapped his chest. "Hah, wha' a good idea," he said with gusto, "wha' a good idea." Still dressed in his white sweater, he seemed oblivious to the cold. He set out for Seamus's ravine at a half run, as if he knew every step of the way.

The golf course had a different look about it now. It seemed much more precipitous and full of jagged edges. Another pair of eyes appeared and hurried away. The wind made an eerie sound coming through the fields of gorse and sharp ravines, shrill, then deep like the sound of a drum. I could hear the surf booming in the distance.

We were descending into a gully and a small rock-slide started under my feet. I called out, asking him to slow his pace, but he had disappeared and there was no answer. Then as I started up the other side of the draw, something grasped my shoulder. It felt like a hand; to this day I could swear it was a hand. But as I jumped away there was nothing except an enormous boulder, a huge rock outcrop looming over my head. I sat on the rocky slope to get my breath. The impression of being grabbed had been so definite, I stared at the boulder until my heart stopped pounding. Then I heard Shivas calling down.

"Michael, where 'n the hell are ye?" his stentorian voice echoed through the howling wind.

I shouted back and started up the gully wall. He was standing at the top. "Something grabbed me down there, I could swear," I said as I joined him.

"Now, Michael," he said, "now, Michael, have another Perrier Water." I was still carrying one of the bottles. He squeezed my shoulder to reassure me. I jumped back. "That's just how it felt," I said.

He laughed at my fright. " 'Twas a banshee," he said with his big-kid grin. "They're harmless, completely harmless." He squeezed my shoulder again and started off toward the ravine. After he had taken a few steps he stopped, then split the air as he had done that day with a bloodcurdling scream. And then a second time—that eerie yodeling wail.

"God dammit, what are you doing?" I gasped.

"Gettin' rid o' the stale aiyer in my lungs," he shouted back at me through the wind.

"Jesus, can we slow down?" I gasped again. The rapid pace he was setting and the increasing weirdness of the situation had me shaking and out of breath. "Can we please slow down a minute?" I was almost pleading.

He stopped without looking back, put a hand to his forehead as if he were shielding his eyes against some invisible sun and peered into the darkness. I stood a few yards away from him and held my sides to get my breath back. The wind was howling and snapping the collar of my windbreaker around my ears. He turned in a semicircle as he scanned the inscrutable night.

"What are you looking for?" I shouted.

"Wha' do ya think?" he shouted back without turning to look at me.

Then, just as he uttered the words, the most God-awful sound began to rise from what I took to be the ravine. It sounded like a single high note from a gigantic organ, rising steadily in volume until it shivered the night. Then around it like sunrise came a massive chord of lower register, swelling to encompass the original note and spreading until it seemed to come from all sides at once. I ran up to Shivas's side and grabbed his arm.

"Jesus Christ!" I shouted.

He drew back and stared at me with what seemed to be astonishment. "What in hell's wrong now?" His voice had an edge of reprimand.

"That sound!" I cried. "That sound!"

"Oh tha'," he said loudly, pulling his arm away. " 'Tis the wind from the ravine. It means the comin' o' the northern lights."

As he said those words, the sound began to fade away, leaving the original high note wavering in the wind, as if it were echoing off the walls of some immense cathedral.

He glanced back to check my state, then started off again for the ravine at a half-run. My heart was beating wildly and I was still out of breath, but I stayed as close to him as I could, not knowing what would happen next.

Though we could see no more than 20 or 30 feet in any direction, I could tell from the bench and bag stand I had seen that afternoon that we were crossing the thirteenth tee. He slowed his steps and turned left toward the ravine. I shuffled along after him, feeling the ground cautiously with my feet.

Sensing the place again, I tried to summon my memory of where I had seen the strange old man. Where had I been standing? It might have been from the hill after we reached the green, or perhaps from this tee? The failure of my memory was unnerving. My shin hit a rock and I swore again— somehow the curses kept down my fear.

Shivas shouted one last time, then started down a rock fall into the ravine. It was pitch black below us. There was not the slightest sign of life.

We inched our way down the jagged incline, sliding at times in loose rock. The floor of the ravine was, I would estimate, some 40 feet below: it took us several minutes to reach it. As we climbed and slid through the rocks and dirt I could feel a growing stillness; the place was completely protected from the wind. When we got to the bottom I looked up at the boulders looming over us and wondered if we would ever get out.

"Seamus may not be heer," he said. "He woulda' answered us by now." He groped his way through the darkness up the gentle incline of the canyon floor. I stayed as close to him as I could in case another hand might reach out for me, swearing steadily as we inched along. We were coming to a wider place and the going was easier. I began to feel sand under my feet instead of gravel and dirt. He sat down on a rock. "Let's rest a minute heer," he said. "If he's around, he'll soon let us know."

We waited in silence for several minutes. My hard breathing and anxiety were subsiding and I began to discern the outlines of the cliff edge some 40 feet above us and the shape of the declivity we were in. As I grew accustomed to the darkness, I could see that there was a large open space around us. I ran my feet through the sandy dirt and wondered if anyone had played a golf shot from here to the thirteenth green. What would Seamus do if someone descended into his lair? I had an image of him scampering away like a frightened animal, like dirty old Ben Gunn in *Treasure Island*.

"Does he actually sleep out here?" I asked.

"In his cave over there," he nodded toward the wall of the ravine.

I peered through the darkness, but could see nothing, no cave opening or shelter of any sort.

"I can't see it," I said as I peered at the inscrutable rocks.

"Right there." He nodded toward the cliff again. Still I could see nothing. It occurred to me that Seamus might enter through some tiny hole.

There was a protected feeling under the looming canyon walls, a heavy feel to the air. We sat for several minutes savoring the stillness of the place. Shivas seemed abstracted, in a state like the one he went into before dinner. He sat looking at the sky, as he had on that window ledge. Watching him, I remembered Evan Tyree's story about the night-long trance so many years before.

He gazed at the starry sky for several minutes, then he pointed upward and asked if I saw a constellation of the zodiac (I cannot remember which it was). I said that I didn't; that the only things I could recognize were the Milky Way, the North Star, and the Big Dipper.

"I'm sorry," he said, "for I'd like to show ye somethin' ye've probably niver seen. It's the real zodiac, the true one. That there is Hogan." He pointed at a constellation he had named after the famous golfer and then at another named "Swilcan Burn." He traced the outlines he saw in the sparkling sky, but I could only see an amorphous mass of stars. "Too bad ye canna' see it," he shook his head, "it's too bad. Ye'll see it though if ye look a while."

Apparently he had discovered a new zodiac. He gazed up at it and began to hum a plaintive Irish melody. As I looked at the sky I saw an outline of Ben Hogan's Indian profile appear amidst the other constellations. It was the only one I could recognize besides the Big Dipper.

Shivas was silent again, then his resonant voice broke the stillness. "He's na' heer," he said decisively, "but let's wait a while in case he retoorns." He began rummaging about in the rocks around him, and in a moment had gathered some twigs and branches. He took a match from his pants pocket and ignited the little pile he had made. It took flame immediately. "I've aye been good at startin' fires." He smiled proudly. "Now find me some bigger pieces."

We built ourselves a rousing fire and settled down to wait

for Seamus. The towering cliffs were alive in the firelight. "Gi' me some o' that Perrier Water," he said.

He leaned back against a rock and gazed reflectively into the flames, as if he were willing to wait indefinitely. "Do you think he might be asleep?" I asked. "Why don't we go look?"

"Oh, no"—he raised his hand in warning—"niver do tha'—it would distoorb him somethin' awful. I ken his ways. He's na' heer, I tell ye, he's na' heer."

I asked him where Seamus might have gone, seeing what an ungodly hour it was.

"He has another place he goes to upon occasion. But he loves to work at night—that's when he can feel the things he's studyin'."

"*Feel* them?"

"Feel them, tha' is what I sayed." He cocked his head and looked at me gravely. "Ye're interested in 'im, aren't ye? How would ye like to see his weapon?" Without waiting for my answer he got up and went over to the rocks he had said were Seamus's cave. In a moment he returned with a long black gnarled stick that looked like a gigantic Irish shillelagh. He was waggling it as if it were a golf stick. "This heer is Seamus's club," he said, gazing at it fondly. He swung it at an imaginary golf ball. "Would ye lik' to see it?"

He handed it to me carefully, holding it gently with both hands as if it were carried on a velvet cushion. It was the meanest-looking stick I had ever seen. Black and gnarled and hard as a rock, it was about the length of a driver. On one end there protruded a heavy burl with a flat face. It was a golf club fit for a caveman. I waggled it as he had done and swung it carefully to avoid hitting the ground. It swung easily. I swung it again. It zipped through the air as if it were perfectly weighted. I swung it three or four times more, it seemed to swing by itself.

"Tha's enough," he said, abruptly taking it back. "Tha's enough," and started swinging the thing himself, half a dozen times as if he could not stop. "We must na' damage it on the rocks heer," he said as he swung, "or Seamus 'll gi' me dreadful hell. But ye must see this." He put the club down and went over to Seamus's hiding place. In a moment he returned with two white objects about the size of golf balls. He carried them as he had the stick, as if they were on a cushion. "These are his balls," he said with a fond wry smile. "Look at them."

They had hard leather surfaces and felt lighter than ordinary golf balls. "They're featheries," he said, "real featheries from the ol' days."

"Featheries," I learned later, were the balls used until the middle of the nineteenth century when gutta-percha balls were introduced into play. They were made of feathers and leather and hardened by being soaked in brine. "Seamus uses them in his research," he said. "Found them heer in the ravine, he claims."

He stepped over to an open space with a sandy surface and put them on the ground. Then he pointed with Seamus's shillelagh down the ravine. "See tha' target there?" he said. I looked in the direction he was indicating and indeed there was a target, a white circle some 3 or 4 feet in diameter painted on the ravine wall. It was about 40 feet away from him, barely discernible in the wavering firelight. It reminded me of a photograph I had seen in the *National Geographic* of a paleolithic cave symbol used for magic hunting rites. "Now watch this," he said.

He placed one ball in front of him and took a stance with the shillelagh as if it were his driver. He waggled it carefully, holding it an inch or two above the ground, gathering his concentration as he had done through our round that afternoon. I felt the same suck of energy as he centered his attention on the ball, then his swing unfurled. The ball exploded from the club and flew into the shadows, hitting the target with a loud pop. He took his stance in front of the second ball and swung again, hitting the target right in the middle.

"Ye see that?" he said, turning to face me. "Ye can do it with a stick if ye concentrate." Then he paused and looked thoughtfully at the gnarled club. "O' course, this is not yer ordinary stick," he murmured.

He retrieved the balls and hit them into the target again. I sat by the fire and watched him. I had the impression he was somehow compelled to repeat the performance, almost as if he were in the grip of the club. It went on for fifteen minutes or more. He may have hit twenty or thirty shots, a strange figure in the shadows, like some ancient shaman firing his darts at the approaching buffalo.

At one point he turned and held up the shillelagh. "He calls this his baffin' spoon—the name he rimembers from his chile'ood. Says one club's all ye need to play the game."

I leaned back with my feet toward the fire and looked up the cliff. The rock formations above me curved and receded into grotesque shapes and seemed to move in the flickering shadows. I saw two horned birds flying upward, a row of human heads in profile staring dumbly at one another, and the crenelated cliff edge like the wall of our fort. I tried to imagine other shapes as the jagged rocks moved in the firelight. At the very top, between the crenels in my fortress wall, I saw a face staring down at me. It was the face of an old man with a large frizzy beard, motionless like the imaginary faces below it. As I looked at it, I could make out other features—tiny squinting eyes, a look bright with curiosity, and a mad, gay little smile that seemed to relish what it was seeing. I cocked my head to one side to get another angle on it. Then I started back.

It *was* a face. It was Seamus MacDuff!

I jumped up and shouted at Shivas. "There he is!" I cried. "There he is!"

He was picking up his balls at the target. "Now, Michael, now, Michael," he said loudly, "calm yerself. Seamus'll niver come if ye carry on like that." He came over to me and looked up the cliff. "Now, where is he?" he asked. I pointed at the cliff edge, the face was still there. "See it?" I said loudly, jabbing my finger toward it. "Look where I'm pointing."

"I canna' see anything at all," he said impatiently, "where ye lookin' now?" He looked back and forth along the edge of the ravine. "I dinna' see a thing. The place is gettin' to ye."

The face was still there, staring down at me, I was amazed that he couldn't see it. "Look," I shouted, grabbing him by the shoulder and pointing so that he could see down the line of my arm.

"I dinna' see a thing," he said again. "I dinna' see a thing." Then he turned away and stood in front of the fire, rubbing his hands for warmth. "Michael, come heer," he said firmly. I turned away from the cliff. "Look at the fire," he said, "it'll calm ye doon." I raised my hands to feel the fire's warmth, shaken and still certain that Seamus was watching.

"How'd ye lik' to hit a few wi' Seamus's club?" he said quietly. He walked over to the open space where he had been hitting his shots and held up the shillelagh. "Come," he said, waving me toward him with an abrupt decisive gesture. I looked back at the cliff edge. The face was gone. I peered intently at the place where it had been, then scanned the entire perimeter of the ravine wall. There was no face to be seen.

"It's gone," I said.

"Ye see," he answered, "the fire plays tricks there on the rocks. Come hit a few."

I was relieved—and disappointed. I wanted to see the mysterious figure of Seamus MacDuff in the worst way by now.

He handed me the gnarled stick, cradling it on its imaginary cushion as if it were a scepter. I waggled the stick carefully, gradually lowering it into the arc of my golf swing until I was swinging it with a full sweep. It had amazing balance. "It's incredible how easily it swings," I said. "Did he make it himself?"

"Claims he made it from an old shillelagh." He was watching me with amusement. "Do ye want to hit one now?" Without waiting for an answer he teed up a featherie on the sandy ground. "Now, Michael," he said as he put the ball on a tiny mound of earth, "try to hit it clean without hittin' any rocks. Seamus'll gi' me royal hell if we hurt his baffin' spoon."

I eyed the primitive target and swung. The ball exploded from the club and I looked up to follow its flight. I could not see where it had landed in the dancing shadows.

"Ye missed the taraget," he said with a broad smile, "but ye hit it good. Seamus woulda' been proud o' ye. Heer, hit another one." He teed up the other ball.

I swung and hit it squarely. "Where did it go this time?" I asked, peering into the shadows.

"Ye hit it on the other side o' the taraget this time, but yer swingin' good." He was grinning broadly now. "Ye're the first person I've e'er seen wi' Seamus's club beside maself. Ye make a funny sight."

I held the shillelagh up in the light. "I feel funny holding it. I swear it wants to swing itself."

"Come, let's find the featheries," he said, walking off toward the target. I followed him down to the white circle. It was painted with some kind of whitewash. I could see that it had been painted over many times.

"Has he repainted this?" I asked, pointing to the crusty markings.

"Been usin' it for yeers. It washes off each winter in the rains." He picked up the balls and led me back to our imaginary tee. "Michael, come heer," he said, "I want to show ye somethin'." He had me take my customary golf stance in front of a ball he had put on the ground. "Now, I want ye to try somethin' slightly different this time, will ye do it?" He looked at me hopefully, cocking his head to one side. His large blue eyes caught the flickering firelight. I could see my reflection in them, he was standing so close, a distorted image of my entire body wavering like a flame. "Would ye like to try it?" he repeated the question, fixing me with that slightly cross-eyed double-angled look. I could now see two images of myself in the mirror of his eyes, each one slightly different from the other. I nodded that I was willing. "Awright, now," he said quietly, raising a long finger. "When ye swing, put all yer attention on the feelin' o' yer inner body—*yer inner body.*" He whispered these last words as if he were telling me a secret.

I looked at the shifting reflections in his eyes. To this day I can vividly remember my reaction. It was as if an immediate split occurred in my mind. A part of me instantly knew what he meant; another part began to question and puzzle. I looked at him dumbly, without answering, as the two attitudes formed themselves.

He leaned toward me and took my arms in his hands. "Close yer eyes," he said soothingly. Then he lifted my arms, I was still holding the shillelagh like a golf club, and moved them through the arc of an imaginary swing as a golf professional does with a student, whispering again the words, "feel yer inner body." My questions and puzzlement quieted and I fell into the rhythm of his movements, slowly swinging the club and sensing what he meant. It was like the state I had discovered that afternoon during our round of golf—a growing power, rhythm, and grace, a pleasure that had no apparent cause. Yes—perhaps you have had that sense of it—a body within a body sustained by its own energies and delight, a body with a life of its own waiting to blossom.

"Do ye see what I mean?" he murmured as he swung my arms back and forth. I nodded and he backed away. "Now try to hit the ball tha' way," he said.

I adjusted my stance and waggled the club, focusing my attention on the sense of an inner body. When I swung I topped the ball and it bounced high in the air.

He nodded with approval. "Good, good," he said loudly, "ye stayed right in it, now try another."

I took my stance and swung again. This time the ball flew toward the target but fell short. "Ye did it again. Good!" he said decisively. "Now stay wi' tha' feelin'." We found the balls and repeated the exercise. He seemed oblivious to the results as he studied my attitude and "energy." He claimed that my state of mind was reflected in an aura around me which he could sense. "Yer *energy* was good that time," he would say, or "it wavered on that one." He was as definite about these statements as he was about my physical form.

Our lesson continued for half an hour or more, some twenty or thirty shots, while I practiced that indubitable awareness of my "inner body."

The experience went through stages. At first there was a vague yet tangible sense that there was indeed a body closer to me than my skin, with its own weight and shape. It seemed to waver and bounce and subtly change its form, as if it were elastic. Then—I can still remember the feeling so clearly—it changed to an hourglass: my head and feet were enormous and my waist was as small as a fist. This sensation lasted while we looked for the balls and returned to our tee, then it changed again. My body felt enormously tall, I seemed to look down from a point several feet above my head. I told him what I was feeling. "Now come down heer," he said, calmly putting a finger on my breastbone. "Just come down heer." I returned to my ordinary size and shape, and continued swinging.

I was aware that part of my mind had suspended judgment, that many questions were simmering still. But it felt marvelous to swing that way, so absorbed in the pleasure and feel of it. And it was a relief not to worry about the results. I could have gone on for hours.

But he ended the lesson abruptly. "Enough for now," he said, putting a finger on my chest, "rimember the feelin'. Yer inner body is aye waitin' for yer attention." We added some branches to the fire, which had almost died out, and leaned back against a pair of rocks. I glanced up the cliff, but no face was there, just the writhing shadows on the canyon walls. I felt marvelously alive, as if I were floating in some new field of force, but the questions that had been suspended began rising like vapors. This state I was in was too good to be true, too easily come by, I began to wonder how soon it would fade after Shivas and his colorful admonitions were gone. Anyone would feel good around him, getting so much attention, being led into adventures like these. Dark and true premonitions, I felt an edge of sadness.

He must have sensed what was going through my mind. "Wha' ye thinkin' there?" he asked with a fatherly tone in his voice. "Tell me wha' ye're thinkin'." I told him some of my doubts. I especially remember asking him if all his talk of inner bodies and subtle energies wasn't a mere device for helping concentration. I told him about the Hawthorne experiment in which a group of social psychologists had found that workers in a factory had improved their output every time a change was made in their routine, no matter what that change might be. I asked him if he was running a Hawthorne experiment on me.

He leaned back with his genial grin and shook his head in mock exasperation. "They're two Michaels, I can see; Michael the plunger and Michael the doubter," he chided. "Wha' a shame it is tha' ye canna' even go five minutes heer without yer good skeptical mind intrudin'. Yer good skeptical mind, tha's a problem for ye." He raised his finger like a wand and shook it at me. "Watch out for yer good mind," he said.

I gave him some kind of argument, I am not sure of its exact content, but felt as I was doing it that some monotonous tape loop was running in my brain. I felt the excitement of our adventure, but the tape loop kept running. I asked him if Seamus MacDuff was insane, living in this ungodly ravine.

He gazed into the fire with melancholy amusement and began shaking his head. "Wha' yer sayin' tells me again tha' the world is na' ready yet for Seamus. To swing his *baffin' spoon* and still question the man . . ." He shook his head sadly. I felt chagrined. I was the first person to swing that stick besides Seamus and himself and now I was questioning it all. He was more vulnerable about this hidden world than I thought; I could tell he was hurt.

We were suddenly shy with one another. I was too much in awe of him to be reassuring; he was intimidated by my doubts and questions. I mumbled something about how good it felt to swing from the inner body, that it didn't matter what I thought as long as I could feel that way. But that line of reasoning didn't help. I said that the experience was far more important than our ideas about it, that Seamus was obviously an incredible figure whether he was mad or not.

He turned and glowered at me. "Wha' do ye mean, whether he's mad or na'?" he snarled. I could feel the blood rushing to my stomach. "Yer world is mad, young man," he spit the words at me and rose abruptly. "Let's go. This has been a mistake, I can see." His totally unexpected sensitivity had broken some unspoken code we had adopted with each other. I began pleading with him to stay and wait for Seamus, confessing my stupidity about the strange things he was showing me, my timidity, my lack of experience. I remember being on my knees through most of it looking up at him as I pleaded for another chance, like a pathetic lover. My unexpected performance must have startled him as much as his had startled me. He frowned as he looked down at me. There was a long silence as he studied my face, then suddenly he smiled. "Git off yer knees," he said, wagging his head, "ye look lik' yer askin' me to marry ye." I pleaded with him to stay and after a reflective pause he sat down again. I quickly added some branches to the fire. I was determined by now to wait all night if necessary for Seamus's appearance. Still confessing my total ignorance of things mystical and occult, I managed to get him talking about his teacher.

"Ye see the world is na' ready for someone lik' 'im, ye can see tha' from yer own reactions. The world was na' ready for Pythagoras either." The name of the Greek philosopher was intoned as if we both understood that he was one of the keys to history. He pronounced it Pith-uh-gor'-us. "The wardle was na' ready for Pith-uh-gor'-us either," he repeated the statement with a melancholy look. "Ye see Pith-uh-gor'-us had *the clue*." This was said with solemn emphasis. I was touched and amused by his quaint self-educated assurance. I had studied the pre-Socratic Greek philosophers that spring at

Stanford and knew something about Pythagoras. I wondered what the clue might be.

"Now there are some things I could tell ye, if I thought ye'd tak' 'em seriously," he went on, eying me suspiciously. I urged him to tell me, promising that all my doubts had subsided. "Well, I'd lik' to tell ye . . ." His voice trailed off as he studied my expression. "Well, I'll *do* it," he said quietly. "The world should o' followed the lead of Pith-uh-gor'-us." He almost whispered the words. "And 'tis this—*to ken the world from the inside*, not the outside as we've done. Like I showed ye wi' yer gowf shots there." He gestured toward the open space we had used for our practice. "Tha' is how Pith-uh-gor'-us heered the music o' the spheres—and started all our science." My mind raced back over the passages I had read about the famous philosopher. I remembered that he had invented the word "philosophy," that he had discovered certain relationships between musical intervals, that the Pythagorean theorem had been named after him, that he had founded a school in Crotona for the practice of philosophy, mathematics, and the good life.

"After Pith-uh-gor'-us science turned to magic, naethin' but superficial powers," he continued. "And so we rely upon our instruments instead o' oursel's. Tha' is why Seamus says we only need a baffin' spoon like his to play a round o' gowf—if we would e'er *ken the world from the inside*." He stood and kicked the embers into new flame. Then he picked up Seamus's "baffing spoon" and fondled it. "Do ye ken what Seamus is really doin' heer?" he asked. "He's makin' himself into a livin' laboratory to right the balance o' our Western science, to show us how to know true gravity." He lapsed into silence, and for several minutes we stared into the fire.

"True gravity, 'tis Seamus's term for the deeper lines o' force, the deeper structure of the universe. But this is the thing," he raised his hand and shook a finger at me, "ye can only know wha' it is by livin' into it yersel'—not through squeezin' it and shovin' it the way they do in the universities and laboratories. Ye must go into the heart o' it, through yer own body and senses and livin' experience, level after level *right to the heart o' it*. Ye see, Michael, merely shootin' par is second best. Goin' for results like that leads men and cultures and entire worlds astray. But if ye do it from the inside ye get the results eventually and *everythin' else along with it*. So ye will na' see me givin' people many tips about the gowf swings lik' they do in all the 'how-to' books. I will na' do it. Ye must start from the inside, lik' I showed ye there." He pointed again to our sandy practice area. "And tha' is wha' Seamus is doin'!" He shook his head slowly. "But no one understands, and poor Seamus runs away."

He lapsed into silence once more. My memory of the conversation blurs at this point but I remember asking him about Seamus's shillelagh. I wondered if it had taken on the old wizard's presence, like the seamless robe of Christ in Lloyd Douglas's book. Of course that was just a story, I said, while this was real, but it was the same idea.

"It gave ye a good swing there, Ah could see," he said with a sly smile, "but tha' is just another kind o' magic—Seamus's magic. 'Tis no different from the magic o' science and steel-shafted clubs, just another kind. Tha' is why he will na' let me try it on the links heer. Says it's just another diversion. O' coorse, the members might na' let me use it either."

In the midst of these ruminations about Seamus MacDuff and true gravity he suddenly exclaimed (I cannot recall the exact context of the remark), "Or Western science'll run into a stalemate and then," he raised a doubled fist for emphasis, "and then thair'll be no more answers for us until we ken this world from within."

As we gazed at the dying fire a small rock-slide started down the fairway side of the ravine. We looked up into the shadows but could see nothing above us, just the rocks receding into utter darkness. "Ye know, Michael," he said, "I've of'en wondered what it'd be like to play the coorse wi' the baffin' spoon." Apparently his earlier remarks were still on his mind. "I've of'en been tempted tae do it when he's na' around." He poked a stick into the embers. Then he turned to me. "Why don't we try it now?" he said with a gleam in his eyes.

"You mean now—in the dark?" I wasn't sure if I had heard him right.

"Right now, wi' one o' the featheries." He stood as he answered and picked up the shillelagh. I asked him what would happen if we lost them.

"Tha' is what scairs me about it," he seemed to lose his zest for the idea as he considered the dire consequences of our losing Seamus's precious featheries. Research into the structure of the universe would be impeded, I imagined, if they were lost in Lucifer's Rug. But then to my utter surprise he picked up the two old balls and the club and gestured for me to follow. He walked 20 or 30 yards up the ravine, then started climbing upward toward the fairway. I stumbled along after him. We had come to a precipitous stairway carved into the cliff, with steps about a foot wide and four inches deep. He scrambled up this dangerous path like a sailor going up a rigging, holding the club and balls in one hand, and grasping the tiny ledges with his other. I inched my way after him, expecting to slide back at any moment.

It was a frightening climb. Near the top I started to look down, but thought better of it and pressed my nose to the cliff. After a five-minute climb I finally came out on level ground, back into the windy night. It was the thirteenth tee. He reached down to help me up the final steps.

"Do ye think we should do it?" he asked with an edge of doubt in his voice. "I wonder if this is a good idea."

I said that he wasn't going to get me to hit one of the balls, seeing that I was almost bound to lose it in the Rug. I could hardly breathe after the strenuous climb. "I think ye're right," he said. He was having second thoughts about the whole thing.

He walked over to the tee and put the balls on the ground. It was pitch black and the wind was still blowing, though not as hard as it had been when we arrived an hour before. You could see the silhouette of the cypress trees on the hill. The flag was lost in the darkness though, so he would have to judge where it was from the position of the trees. "What do ye think?" he asked again.

We stood there in the windy dark staring up the forbidding hill. "What would Seamus do if you lost his balls?" I asked.

"I don't know," he answered. "I don't know. It would be somethin' awful." I wondered what was compelling him to try it. "What do ye think?" he asked, almost pathetic now in his indecision.

"Do you think you could reach it, especially in this wind?" I wondered, surveying what must have been one of the world's most difficult golf holes. How he ever thought he could hit a ball made of feathers 200 yards on a windy night with an Irish shillelagh was beyond me.

"Oh, I think I can do that awright," he answered softly. "It's hittin' it straight in the wind that makes me wonder. But wha' would Seamus do if we lost his balls?"

"I'm not hitting any," I made the point again with stronger emphasis.

Apparently he hadn't heard me. "Heer," he said, "you hit first. I'll get my line from *yer* shot."

"Oh, no, not me." I backed away from the proffered club, as if it were a dangerous snake.

"Now, Michael lad"—he was suddenly composed and re-assuring—"it'll do ye a world o' good. Come try. Just one shot."

I was dumfounded at his insistence. I began to wonder if something had gone wrong with him. He must have seen that I was not going to play the hole, however. He turned abruptly and put a featherie on the tee. Then he lined up toward the invisible flag and waggled the ancient shillelagh. He waggled it slowly, and then he swung. There was a hissing sound as the ball took flight. I could not follow it, but then, above the hill, we could see where it was. It was gleaming against the sky, a luminous white point hanging like a tiny moon before it dropped toward the green.

"Aha, aha," he cried. "The old spoon did it, it did it!" He

did a little jig around the tee. I hadn't seen him so excited all day. "The old spoon did it!" he cried as he jumped and clicked his heels.

He started up the incline to the green, deciding apparently that one shot was enough, and I ran after him. Our anticipation was high as we approached the top, for we knew the ball might be lost. I had seen MacIver put a good shot into the Rug that afternoon, and there were drop-offs on all sides. We also knew that it might be very close to the pin.

But when we reached the crest of the hill there was an awful sight. Though the green was visible enough, no ball was there to be seen. Moreover, there was no pin, no flag.

"Where is the flag?" I asked. I was afraid to ask about the ball.

"Hiven knows," was the only answer he gave, in a barely audible voice. He went to the back edge of the green and peered into the darkness below. There was no ball there. I looked over the edge of the green on the ravine side.

"Maybe it fell in the gorse," I said with growing anxiety. I started back down the hill and began running my foot through the grass between the green and Lucifer's Rug.

"It's na' there," he said impatiently. "I hit it over the green if I hit it anywhere. I'll be damned," he said as if he could not believe his eyes. "I'll be damned." He whistled between his teeth, as if he could feel the impending wrath of Seamus MacDuff.

"Well, what'll we do?" I asked.

"Hiven knows," was his only answer.

I was crossing again toward the back edge of the little hill when I had a sudden idea. Then, as if I were drawn by the first flash of the premonition, I looked down as I crossed the middle of the green. There in a dark declivity, in the hidden cave of the pinless hole, lay Seamus's featherie. It was faintly luminescent as it peered at me from its dark resting place, an eye peering out of the deep.

"Shivas, here it is!" I cried and picked it up. "It's here in the hole!"

"I'll be damned," he said, his eyes more crosseyed than ever. " 'Tis the first time I e'er shot a hole-in-one on the thirteenth." He looked at the shillelagh, and kissed its meanlooking burl. "Ye saved my life, ol' spoon," he said with enormous relief. "Thank ye kindly."

We Are All Kites in That Wind

We crawled back down the rocky stairway, both of us relieved that we had come through unscathed. God knows
what might have happened if that ball had been lost.

When we got to the bottom of the ravine we threw some
last sticks on the fire and resumed our conversation. I think
we talked mainly about English and American football, seeking respite from the strenuous adventure we had embarked
upon.

The sky was turning gray now along the edge of the
canyon. Summer dawn comes early in Scotland, it must have
been around 2:30 or 3:00. Our fire had burned itself out and
I was beginning to realize that Seamus was not to make an
appearance. We both stood and stretched. Birds were singing
in the cliff wall above us; they too were getting ready for the
day. As the contours of the ravine gradually appeared, I
could see that this was a redoubtable fortress indeed from
which to conduct research subversive to the Western world.
Shivas put the featherie balls and shillelagh back in their
hiding place and said no to my final request to see
Seamus's cave. " 'Tis as cursed to strangers as King Tut's
toomb," he said. "Ye might na' survive it." He gave that
abrupt decisive gesture for me to follow which he had given
several times that night and we started back along the ravine
floor. When we got to the rock-slide down which we had
originally come he turned and looked me straight in the eye.
"Michael," he said, "I want ye to do one more thing, since

I've let ye in on all these mysteries. Will ye do it?" I asked him what it was. "I want ye tae yell lik' I do, like this . . ." and he let out that bloodcurdling scream. I started back.

"Now just try it once," he said. I looked around the canyon, as if someone might be watching, cleared my throat and gave a choked little yell. It was a pathetic attempt, a constipated bleat after his bellowing warrior cry. "Try again," he urged. The second one was better, but I realized how deficient I was at yelling. He wagged his head at me with a sly smile, and we started up the rocky path.

Birds were singing in the growing light as we walked through the damp and deserted golf links. I followed the trail of footprints Shivas left in the grass, kicking up drops of water and pondering these strange events. We found his car and drove back into town. Neither of us felt like sleeping. "Since ye dinna' have anythin' fit to drink, come to my place," he said and I jumped at the invitation. I was curious to see how he lived and it would be good to get a drink of something warm or warming.

He parked where we had found his car near The Druids' Inn and led me to the gray stone house in which he had an apartment. We went up through a narrow staircase that was separate from the main entrance to the house and ducked through a tiny door into his sitting room. It was not the kind of place I had expected, but I could see at once that it was all his. The wooden ceiling was no more than eight feet high, maybe less, and latticed windows stood two feet off the floor. Shelves of books lined two of the walls and another was covered with long sheets of brown wrapping paper, hanging from wooden cornices near the ceiling. These paper tapestries were covered with lists and odd diagrams. A wood-burning stove stood in a corner near a roll-top desk; old bags of golf clubs were stacked in another. A threadbare rug covered most of the floor; it had a faded blue line sewn into it which he apparently used to practice his putting alignment. It was a small place for so large a spirit, I thought; no wonder he spent so much time roaming the streets of Burningbush and the spaces of his inner life.

He built a fire in the iron stove and put a kettle of water on to boil. "Sit," he said, pointing to a battered leather couch that had stuffing coming out of it at some of the seams. He made a pot of powerful tea, a recipe he had learned from an officer of the Black Watch who had been a student of his, a recipe they had discovered in Afghanistan or some such place that was supposed to light up the mind. The bittersweet taste of it sent a shiver up my back. He settled into a big stuffed armchair (he called it his "meditation chair"), and turned on a creaky-looking reading lamp against the gray morning light. We sipped our mind-warming tea in silence. We were awkward with each other again, as we had been at the Inn. The compression of the little room perhaps took an edge off his freedom; it occurred to me that he always seemed more subdued indoors. As we sipped our tea he leaned back against the armchair to gaze at the ceiling. Cupping my hands for warmth around the cup, I studied the paper hanging against the wall behind me. It had lists of philosophers neatly printed in a vertical column down one side and a list of inventions printed in a column down the other. Lines connected some of the philosophers with some of the inventions. At the very top of one chart there was printed in large block letters the title DANGEROUS CONNECTIONS. Scanning the lists again, I saw that some of the connecting lines were red and some were green.

The room was getting warmer as the stove gave forth its heat. I took off my jacket and we sat sipping our tea in silence. His eyes were closed now, he seemed to be dozing or resting. I got up and tiptoed over to the bookshelves. He had gathered an impressive library, several hundred books at least. The first one my eyes settled on was a copy of *Sartor Resartus* in a long row of leather-and-gold volumes by Thomas Carlyle. Max Müller's entire *Sacred Books of the East* was there and the complete works of Coleridge. An extraordinary collection for an obscure golf professional. On one shelf a large book of photographs depicting Sam Snead's swing in all its phases was sandwiched between the *Enneads* of Plotinus and a musty old copy of the Koran.

He was still leaning back against his comfortable armchair. I took a volume that was familiar to me, *The Gospel of Sri Ramakrishna,* and sat down again on the decrepit leather couch. So many of the books he had gathered around him were familiar; it was almost the library I would like to have. I leafed through the Ramakrishna volume, a large, handsome edition containing the conversations of India's greatest nineteenth-century mystic lovingly recorded by his disciple "M." Thinking that I would visit Dakshineswar, where Ramakrishna had undergone his incredible search for God, I found some pictures of the famous temple there. As I leafed through the photographs, my head began to nod—I jerked up with a start and reached down for my cup of tea. I sipped it slowly, feeling the warmth spread out in my chest. Shivas was sitting erect now, facing away from me at an angle, I could see that his eyes were open. He stared straight ahead as if he were concentrating on something across the room. I put the cup down on the floor and continued leafing through the book. I read a page or two of Ramakrishna's sayings, marvelous passages I had read before, and looked at the pictures. I reached down for the tea and looked at Shivas again; he was still sitting erect as he stared across the room. He was absolutely motionless. I cleared my throat to catch his attention but he did not respond. There was something odd about his posture; I could feel it, something had happened. I stood up and tiptoed around in front of him—and suddenly felt faint. His eyeballs were rolled back leaving nothing but white. He was totally unconscious. I felt his pulse, my heart pounding, and bent over to smell his breath. He was still alive. Epilepsy? Heart attack? Stroke? I looked wildly around the room fighting off the first sense of panic, my mind a complete blank. Then, as if by reflex, I stumbled down the narrow staircase and knocked at the main entrance to the house. No one answered. I knocked again more insistently, but there was still no answer. The street in front of the house was deserted. It was still early, probably around four o'clock, every window on the block was shuttered. I ran back up the stairs and fumbled around the apartment looking for a telephone book—under the desk, on the shelves, apparently he didn't have one. I picked up the phone and dialed o, and got a buzzing sound, then remembered that 999 was the emergency number. A voice answered as soon as I dialed, a man's voice. I remember how eerie it seemed having a man answer. I told him someone was dying, glancing back at Shivas. "I know someone who might come down," the voice said calmly, then I could hear a clicking as connections were made. A long moment passed while the clicking continued. Shivas sat rigid as a corpse, his eyes rolled back, without moving or falling forward as well he might have from his sitting position. He couldn't have been drunk, I thought, after everything we had been through. Still no answer on the other end of the line. "We're having a little trouble, but hold on," the man's voice reassured me. Finally someone answered, an irritable rasping old voice, "Yes, what is it?" I told him that someone was dying. "What's he dyin' of?" the old voice asked, intoning the word "dyin" in a kind of sing-song. I said that I didn't know. He asked if there was some way I could describe what was happening, some symptom, anything. "Tell me *how* he's dyin'," the old voice rasped. I began fumbling for words, but as I did Shivas spoke quietly behind me. "I'm all right, Michael. Tell him I'm all right." There he sat fixing me with those crystal blue eyes.

"Good God, you scared me," I said, then turned and apologized to the voice on the other end of the line and hung up the receiver. At that moment I could have sworn I saw an aura around him. For a moment he was sitting in a pool of turquoise light—just for a second—then I could feel some quick shutter close in my brain. He looked slowly around the room and flexed his hands. "Have I been gone long?" he asked quietly.

"Around fifteen minutes maybe."

"I almost disappeared," he said softly. "Almost disappeared."

"Shit, you scared me to death."

A smile began to form on his face, spreading slowly as if the muscles around his mouth had grown stiff. His eyes looked straight into mine, they were not crossed at all. "Do ye na' ken ye're flyin' heer like a kite—wi' nae mair than a threid holdin' ye?" He raised his muscular hands and snapped an imaginary string between them. "We're all kites in that wind," he said. And off he went into trance again.

For another half hour or so he sat there erect, looking like a corpse more than anything else but soaring within to regions I could only guess at. I was frightened, angry, and spellbound by turns. In the Ramakrishna book there is a picture of the saint's disciples staring up at him with bulging eyes as he stands in ecstatic trance. I must have looked like that as I watched the incredible corpse in front of me.

I closed a banging shutter and huddled at one end of the couch with my knees drawn up. I finally roused myself, stoked the fire, and made another cup of tea, circling carefully around the corpse which had grown enormous now with its mysterious presence. I sat watching him, wondering if I could ever brave the skies he was exploring. After all, that was what I was going to India for. The lamp shade glowed like an ember against the cold winds of those inner spaces, winds that could snap the thread that held me there.

But there is some inexorable density in the brain. Fear and awe gave way to sleep and my head began to sink. I was beginning to drowse, in front of the first ecstatic trance I had ever seen. I do not know how long I napped, for in sleep experience is transposed to another order of time: some barely tangible presence was entering my body, locking my joints, reassuring me—while a parade of images drifted past, memories of childhood, odd dreamlike shapes floating through the stillness of the room. His presence was entering mine by some osmosis, drawing me toward it by gentle steps.

I was cradled in a pleasurable field, held in a stillness carrying premonitions of vaster realms and tiny hints of music, music I might have heard if my brain were more open and finely tuned—distant horns, shudders of ecstatic voices just an eyelash flick away. Something in me was reaching toward those close yet distant realms but the weight of sleep pulled me back.

It was hard to tell how long it lasted. He broke the silence in a voice so faint that I thought at first I was imagining it, some words, then he cleared his throat. I looked around the room savoring the earthy familiarity of everything in it, interfused now with stillness and pleasure. " 'Tis amazin' to me how these forms, these bodies, these ideas float in this emptiness . . . strange gravity," he whispered the words in a soft hoarse voice. We looked at each other through the subtle presence that filled the room. "Just kites in that wind," he said with that bucktoothed grin and slowly stretched as he rose from his chair.

He disappeared into another room and I slowly looked around me. Everything sparkled with a new clarity as the morning brightened. I felt a freshness and pleasure as if I had slept well, and a calm poise that seemed to hold me. I was curious to know more about this amazing room.

Long brown scrolls of wrapping paper covered one entire wall. Each had a title at the top: DANGEROUS CONNECTIONS and GOD IS WAKING UP are two I remember. Another was entitled HISTORY OF THE BODY, with lists of historic events joined by red and green lines to names of political leaders, philosophers, and artists, to organs of the body including the heart, liver, kidney, and lungs, and to certain psychic centers like the Indian chakras. It was a complex chart depicting, I think, his own notions of how consciousness has unfolded in the world during historical times and how the body, or the general human awareness of the body, has developed along with it. He found me studying it when he came back into the room.

"Wha' d'ye think o' that?" he asked matter-of-factly.

"Well, I've never seen anything like it. I don't understand it really."

"Not many people have seen them, and no one yet has understood, 'sept Seamus." He had begun fixing us breakfast. As I studied the charts he fried some eggs, sliced a loaf of brown bread, and set some plates on a table near the stove. The food tasted marvelous, I felt exhilarated now. My admiration of him was growing every hour we were together. I asked him if he had ever written down his thoughts, that he should, seeing how deeply he had gone into things.

"Well, Michael, I'm against writin', seein' how many books there are in the world. It's the livin' of these things that counts. The livin' of them." Then after a long pause, "But I do have some writin's, would ye like to see them?" He looked at me bashfully. "They're funny writin's."

I said that I would be fascinated to see anything he had written. We finished eating and he cleared the table. Then he turned and regarded me with his solemn look. "Michael," he said, "I'm goin' to show ye my writin's. Yer only the third person to see them, after Seamus and Julian. Come heer." He led me into the other room. It was small and low-ceilinged with a bed and dresser and latticed windows. He stood in front of what was apparently a closet door and hesitated. Then he opened it and motioned for me to follow. It was a linen closet some ten feet deep, lined on one side with books, on the other with shelves of clothes. As I followed him into it he said gravely, "Rimember, ye must not tell anybody about this." This hidden library, this collection within a collection, seemed to center around occult lore of various kinds. Madame Blavatsky's *The Secret Doctrine* and *Isis Unveiled* were there, Bishop Leadbeater's books on the chakras, Aurobindo's *Life Divine*, and a copy of Ben Hogan's *Power Golf*! There were two or three more books about golf by authors I had never heard of. At the end of the narrow closet hung another brown chart, entitled THE BASIC STRUCTURE OF THE UNIVERSE. On it was drawn the figure of a man some three feet high, like the figures you see on anatomical charts except that it was divided into various centers and levels of consciousness instead of the usual bodily organs. Crisscrossing the entire chart were lines of psychic latitude and longitude: apparently it represented the entire human race. Behind the chart there was a small door, perhaps a laundry chute. It occurred to me that it might lead to yet another library or secret chamber.

He kneeled down and lifted a small stack of notebooks from the lowest shelf. "Heer they are," he said, looking up at me bashfully. "What d'ye think?" I said that I would have to read them before delivering any judgment. He stood and let me out, pausing once more to lift a warning finger. "Rimember, ye must na' tell anybody about this," he said.

He laid the notebooks on the table in his sitting room. They were a ragged collection, some of them obviously dating back twenty years or more. One was a ledger book with narrowly spaced writing lines, filled with what I learned was his recent handwriting. Another was a ringed binder with a yellowed label on its cover, full of handwriting that was quite different, with large looping letters, a fancier, more flowery style. His thought and expression had changed, I discovered later, from an extravagant romantic style reminiscent of Thomas Carlyle to rough, pithy sentences more like Heraclitus and the *Upanishads*. He watched me suspiciously as I leafed through the pages, scanning the titles and sayings that struck my eye. I can still remember the very first words I saw: "*Shiva* without *Shakti* is *Shava*," a gnomic phrase that turned out to be an old Hindu saying.*

"Some o' this may not make sense to ye, because they refer to my charts," he said after I had scanned all the notebooks. He seemed ill at ease, almost apologetic. "I think ye should see some other things I have, if ye're goin' to put it all

---

* Dr. Haridas Chaudhuri, of San Francisco's California Institute of Asian Studies, my authority on Sanskrit and Indian philosophy, explained that *shava* is the Sanskrit word for corpse. *Shakti* is the creative, female, time-involving, world-manifesting aspect of the Supreme Being. *Shiva* is the God of Destruction, Redemption, and Liberation.

together," he said abruptly. I had the feeling he was sorely conflicted about letting me read further.

He went over to a huge trunk standing under the brown wall-charts and opened it. As he pulled up the lid the first rays of sunlight broke through the latticed windows. I looked outside. The golden edge of sunrise framed the gray houses across the street from his study window.

"Michael, lad," he enunciated my name, "how much of our conversation have ye forgotten?" He was facing me from across the room as he stood in front of the open trunk. The question surprised me. I gave some self-effacing response, mumbled something about how vivid it was to me. "Come on, come on now," he said, his broad Scots dialect full of authority. "I can see ye dinna' ken the limits o' yer memory." I was too surprised and embarrassed at his sudden change of attitude toward me to muster a reply. Showing me his charts and notebooks had affected him, I said to myself.

"Ye see, Michael, I'm afraid ye'll forget all this," he continued. "I've learned my best students and friends forget. Or e'en worse"—he shrugged—"they rimember it wrong when I tell 'em. Sometimes I think I need to start a monastery. Which leads me round to this," he pointed down into the trunk. "But first, I must ask ye, who can teach us about rimemberin'? Think now, who can teach us?" He looked across the room at me with eyebrows raised. I said that I didn't know. "Well, I'll tell ye," he said emphatically, "the advertisers, that's who."

I was dumbfounded by this turn of the conversation. "The advertisers!" I exclaimed. "Even here in Burningbush?"

"Yes, sometimes they do it like masters," he said with a triumphant gleam. "With heraldry and pageants and cunning toorns. I've been usin' their methods."

"Their methods! Good God!"

"Some o' them have stumbled right into the first principles of occultism," he said with a look of great portent. "Put a symbol into the mind and it takes on a life of its own. Just think about it." I thought about a tune I often remembered from a television ad for Hamms Beer, and a bear beating time with its tail to a tom-tom. I had often wondered why the image was so indelible.

"Strong images are like seeds in our soul," he went on. "When they're planted there they grow, start havin' a powerful effect. Propagandists know that." I wondered who the "propagandists" were. They seemed to form a clear category in his thinking.

"But now," he said emphatically, "and this is the point, ye can make' the principle work for you. The symbols and images yer soul needs are all around ye. Tak' the hidden meanin's o' golf—a lot o' it is in those notes ye have there. I use them to remind myself." He turned and reached into the trunk. Fascinated, I moved closer. He took out a stack of picture frames and placed it on the floor, then closed the trunk. Then he carefully arranged the frames on the trunk and along the wall. "Look at these," he said as he arranged them. I can remember the images within those frames as if I had seen them yesterday.

They were all photographs, some in vivid color, some in black and white. They all had immense detail and a fine-grained clarity reminiscent of Edward Weston. The most startling thing about them was the perspective they brought to familiar places on a golf course. One showed a putting green from above, it must have been taken from a tree. At first I could not comprehend the small point in the picture's center. Then I gradually realized it was the flag and pin—the camera must have been held directly above them, directed straight down into the hole! Another, in colors shading through turquoise and green, showed a putting green and flag taken from about a foot above ground level, perhaps 25 feet from the pin. On a level with the green stood the tee, on the tee stood a player hitting his shot with a driver, apparently some 350 yards or more away. The uncanny thing about the picture again was the perspective: the player seemed exactly as tall as he would have been on the green itself. He was obviously driving toward the hole, but he already seemed to be on the green!

A third photograph showed a ball in flight about 3 feet away, coming out of the setting sun into the eye of the camera. A black ball, coming with terrific velocity! When I recall that image at times I see it exploding out of the light into my face. Sometimes when I am falling asleep the memory of it brings me awake with a start.

A fourth picture was a color portrait of Shivas himself looking directly into the camera. The immense detail of the photograph gave prominence to each pore and piece of stubble on his face. His face in fact was like a field; indeed, there was no apparent boundary between it and the brownish-green fairway around him. Then I realized the picture was a double exposure, that his own full figure appeared in his left eye, holing out a putt. The double exposure had given his face a second aspect: it was the green he was putting on!

Another picture, the most incandescent and prismatic of them all, was a high-speed shot of a golf swing, the kind you see in studies of Palmer or Snead. The remarkable thing about it was the spectrum of color and brilliant lighting. Shivas said the effect came from sunlight "through the prism of the swing." In his notes there was an obscure sentence about "a feathered body of revolving shafts, a propeller of moons, a symbol of the original emanation . . ." that possibly referred to this dazzling image.

On the floor, in the corner, as if it were hidden, stood a frame with an elaborate drawing instead of a photograph. It resembled the figure hanging at the back of his closet, a kind of medical chart depicting the human race with undecipherable lines of psychic latitude and longitude running through it. The chief difference between it and the figure in the closet was that this Representative Man held a golf club.

There was a profound silence as we pondered this extraordinary gallery. Shivas seemed totally absorbed, as if he were seeing it all for the first time. I looked at the picture which stood on the floor directly in front of me. It had apparently been taken from within the hole itself. Through a perfectly round aperture you could see Shivas's face looking down into the camera while appearing over one rim of the circle was a golf ball, beginning its descent into the hole.

Perhaps it was the lack of sleep or the series of shocks to my ordinary frames of reference, but the pictures now began to waver; I felt an edge of nausea as one of them went completely out of focus. I lay back and looked at the ceiling, letting my attention settle on a point there. I stared at it for several minutes, and gradually felt a sense of relief. I sat up slowly. Sunlight was streaming through the latticed windows. Shivas was still gazing into the pictures, which had begun to sparkle in the slanting beams of light.

"Well, Michael, what d'ye see?" his resonant voice cut through the morning chill. He was looking straight ahead as he asked the question, at a picture he had placed on top of the chest. Holding up a hand to shield my eyes, I squinted into the brightness to see what he was looking at. And there it was. A portrait of Ben Hogan, staring directly into the camera. No double exposures, no strange perspectives, just Hogan himself, big as life!

"Well, what d'ye mak' of it?" he asked again. I could only mumble some formless reply.

For the next hour or so he seemed unsure of himself. He was showing me things he had hidden from the world, and was as uncertain about it as a struggling young writer might be about his first novel. But he grew more confident as the morning wore on, seeing that I was awed by it all. Indeed, awe is not the only word I could use. I was dumbfounded, fascinated, and finally dazed from all the blows to my usual perception. His little gallery of pictures, charts, and writings was more confounding than the *Koran* or *Finnegans Wake*.

As he grew more confident he began making more explicit hints. What he was gingerly working up to—what he had been working up to, I think, from his first invitation to visit his apartment—became more apparent. He wanted me to be some kind of link with the outside world, a Boswell, an editor, an agent, or some other role, I don't think he knew which, as long as I was a translator of any kind to the world at large.

He was shyly coaxing and prodding me to explore his work. "Why don't ye read these through," he said, arranging all the notebooks in chronological order, "and I'll get us somethin' to eat. Now come spend the day and we'll play more golf."

It was hard to resist his proposal. Though I was feeling the fatigue of our adventures, the tantalizing promise of his odd paragraphs and incredible gallery of charts drew me on. I pored over them for several hours, all that morning, through lunch, until I left that afternoon. He went out for a while to get us something to eat.

He returned an hour later in high spirits. As he put away the groceries he softly sang a lilting Irish ballad about someone named "Peter Putter" and his adventures in the wheels of time, and did a little jig around the room. He came over to me. "I'm glad ye're heer," he said, looking down at me with great warmth. "Stay the night and we'll plumb the depths o' true gravity. And who can tell, maybe we'll e'en find Seamus." He winked and squeezed my shoulder, then turned back to his groceries and started making us a meal. He seemed enormously pleased to have me there. Encouraged by his growing affection, I began asking him about his past, especially about certain events he described in his journals. And then I had the good sense to walk over to The Druids' Inn, get my camera, and photograph a letter he had just written. I even persuaded him to sit for a portrait in his meditation chair. He posed with great solemnity, eyeballs down this time. What a loss when that photograph disappeared!

He was, I discovered, half Irish and half Scottish, O'Faolin on his mother's side, born of a dour, prosperous father and a mother "who made God's eyes while she sang old Catholic hymns and bawdy songs." His parents and his birth signs, he said, had conspired to make him "a veritable saloon of conflicting impulses." Indeed, when he read in the *Religio Medici* about man the "great and true amphibian" he instantly recognized that exciting and painful truth, for he was full of urges in many directions. His teen-age years had been a torment, until the stormy events of his nineteenth summer.

He was a gifted player in his teens and members of the Burningbush club had wanted to send him to America to play on a tour, as a reminder that Scotland could still produce champions. But another destiny had been growing in him, he said. In those days he often played 45 or 54 holes of golf at a stretch through the Northern summer evenings, a kind of sensory deprivation, and while he walked those endless miles around the links strange states began to steal over him. He had an image of countless lives one day as he circled round the course and then a vastness settled in his mind, a sense which would remain with him for the rest of his life—that everything transpired in the bottomless void. (His sense that each round of golf was a new incarnation was heightened, he said, by the fact that the eighteenth green at Burningbush was built on the remains of a graveyard.) This experience had led him to philosophy and Eastern wisdom and he began to collect the books and thoughts I found in his apartment some twenty years later. He had resolved to become a priest of the church—and start a revolution of the mind. Every winter through those years he wanted to be a priest, but then summer would come again and with it all those marvelous days to walk the links and flex his skills. By August he would decide to be a golf professional.

A second conflict was developing then, around people, between "the shy one" and "the brave one" in his soul. He was often "a rabbit quiverin' under a granite face"; maybe it was the split between his mother's and his father's influence. He was a stickler for rules and proper conduct, but also a "mass of awful thoughts and perceptions about people and things in general, thoughts I couldn't account for." These conflicts had come to a head during his nineteenth summer, leading him into a series of psychic upheavals.

"Tha' simmer a strange fear began creepin' into me—in the night as I was fallin' asleep sometimes, or out on the links, or sometimes in a crowd o' people. I began to think about epilepsy, that maybe a fit was comin' on. The thought got worse and worse 'til I had to do things to forget it, busy things, or runnin' to find someone to talk to, sometimes just whistlin' to distract myself. I was in a state as the simmer woor on, it got to be the curse o' my life. At times I thought it wid niver leave me, that it was burnt into my brain. Then I read some o' those books," he gestured around the room, indicating the shelves of mysticism and philosophy, "and found out about Ramakrishna and Plotinus and people lik' that, how Ramakrishna passed out cold for the love o' God. Knowin' that must have given me some courage, for one day after 45 holes o' gowf or moor I was walkin' home and I began to shake. The thought o' the fit and the fear was comin' back and I started swearin' and makin' my mind busy to fight it off. And then I rimembered the ol' mystics and the thought came, 'go into it, go right into it.' And I did. I started imaginin' what it would be to have a fit and then I began to shake all over. Weird images started comin' into my mind. Pictures o' my body breakin' tae pieces, arms and legs flyin' apart, things like that"—he began to tremble as he recalled that shattering experience—"and then I saw the stars above me and felt a joy. Oh, I'll niver forget it—it was my first journey into *the one*." He said this last in a voice so low I could barely hear him. "Ah dinna' ken how long it lasted, maybe ten or fifteen minutes, I really dinna' ken. But howe'er long it was it changed my life. It was the first step in findin' my way."

This overwhelming experience had converted him forever away from church and school. He dropped out of the college he was attending, and made a living by caddying and giving occasional golf lessons. But people were a torment to him.

Like some monstrous tree his psyche was throwing enormous roots into the depths of inner experience but reaching out toward his fellows with tiny branches. When he caddied that summer he hardly talked. It became almost impossible for him to be in crowds. He was embarrassed to enter the bar or dressing rooms of the club. Then the opportunity came for him to compete in the British Amateur.

The older members at Burningbush would put up the money for his expenses. Some even wanted to send him to America for the glory of their ancient club. At times he wanted to do it. But he knew that his growing phobia about people would make competition virtually impossible, what with the crowds and dinners and awards and official cere-monies. As the summer wore on and his alienation from others became more intense he began to see the world as a vast illusion, "a play of shadows against the immensity" he had seen. During those months he saw the truth in the Indian view of the world as *maya*, pure illusion; he knew what the old mystics had meant. Why return to this brawling pit when other worlds held such promise of peace and delight? He thought of going to India to join an ashram, as I was doing, or of holing up in the Outer Hebrides, in order to live entirely in the mystic state. He had "fallen into Nirvana" and now he was tempted to stay there for the rest of his life.

(As I give this brief account of what he said I realize how inadequate it is to explain such sea-changes in his character. I would need to know more, far more, to tell the full story and to fully understand him. I know from my own experience in India that great energies come into play in the mystic life, that one needs a sturdy ego from which to explore the realms of transcendence. One needs help when navigating there, for any personal weakness may become inflated with the hidden energies of the soul. Of course, help in these areas is hard to come by, at least in the Western World, and certainly there in Burningbush in the late 1930s.)

The members became impatient as the summer wore on. They finally summoned him to a meeting in the clubhouse, in the very rooms I visited decades later, under those imposing portraits of the club's heroes and captains. He had to decide now whether to play in the tournament or not. "It was the most frightenin' thing I had ever been put to," he said as he recounted the story. "I was on the verge o' faintin' all through the meetin', thought I'd faint dead away, everything seemed so unreal. No one had e'er put me on such a spot before in my entire life, or cared so much about me, or challenged my worst weakness straight on." Then, from some depth of his soul, from some region down deep where his strange roots had grown, came the response. It was a sudden burst of uncoordinated thoughts, wild talk, some of it in the Latin he had learned in school. About the pretensions of the club and all its prejudices, about its sense of privilege and lack of religion, with ramblings about God and Demons and the Mystic State. Then he launched into the members themselves, how each of them was hiding something just like he was.

The assembled group was not prepared for such an event. This early attempt at group therapy ended in total silence. No one responded as his diatribe continued, in a kind of sing-song toward the end, "something like speaking in tongues or Baptist prayer meetings." The poor members were caught between their fondness for him and their outrage. As the rant went on they began to slip out of the room with a "whole array of looks." Only one friend remained, Julian Laing, the town's doctor and psychiatrist, who had begun to formulate his eccentric theories about mental health. They stayed up most of the night together and talked about his fears and hidden thoughts. The next day he woke to a cold demand: he would have to go around to all the members and talk to them man to man. Julian had helped him see that the only way to hold his mystic high was to do his human duty. As they talked that night they had concluded that all the "messages" were telling him to follow the destiny that was being laid out for him, not to fight it like temptation. He had the talent, the members wanted to support him, everyone who knew him sensed that he had a mighty work to do. "Let God show the way," Julian had said, "even if He uses other people."

So he began to go the rounds of all the men who had been there that night, telling them about his shyness and dishonesty and fear. Some of them listened and forgave him, some backed away, out of embarrassment or "their own shyness and dishonesty." Having made the decision to build a new life, he went those rounds with all the thoroughness he was to show in compiling his endless lists of philosophers and historic events. He began to grow a fuller self, one closer to the strong, good-humored Shivas Irons I was to meet. And then he went out to face the crowds and reporters at the British Amateur.

It was another difficult initiation. At first he thought his nervousness would disappear after his brave encounters with the members of the club. But the quivering rabbit was there as usual, "like a second self, floating right there next to all my willpower." He was given a prime starting time for the opening round, and when the moment came he was pitted against one of America's most famous players in front of the tournament's largest gallery. When he stepped out on the tee and saw the crowd lining the fairway he felt as if he were in a dream—the old fear was on him again. But then he knew that "the decision to go ahead had been made far deeper than my fears and ordinary reflexes," for without stopping to consider the consequences he began a short speech to the gallery. It was a shorter version of his speech to the members, a brief pithy sermon about fear and courage, dishonesty and true fellowship, with a brief confession of his own sins and a homily about the need for a new religion. The spectators listened attentively, many of them American tourists who apparently believed this was the Scottish custom, some of them the same poor members from Burningbush. His performance did not dispel all his fear, but at least made it possible for him to hit the ball off the tee. Walking down the fairway in the crowding gallery, he ventured a handshake or two and told a couple of jokes. By the time he addressed his second shot his strength was back.

"There's nae better way to kill a dragon," he said as he told me the story, "than to charge right up to it and shove a spear down its throat. That was the day I began to look at people's faces. I was so grateful to all that gallery. One young laddie came up to me and said that speech was the greatest thing he had e'er heard, never expected it at a gowf toornament. One old woman had tears in her eyes. O' course the toornament officials were mad as hell and there was some talk, I heard later, about kickin' me out awtigither. But they couldn't, ye see, because I won my first round from the American player and broke the course record doin' it." He made a cat's cradle with his fingers. "Me and the gallery got to be like this. They thought I was somethin' special and I knew they were rootin' for me. My drives were sailin' 10 yards longer than usual—psychic force can add 10 yards to yer drives, ye know. God bless them. I never would have made it back to the world o' people if they hadn't been so good to me—they and the members here. Their help and a few risks —what a time!" He shook his head and whistled through closed teeth. "I slew the dragon awright. With one blow. Sometimes that's the only way ye can do it."

He looked at me as he told the story, as if he were deciding whether I believed him. "D'ye want to hear what happened next?" he asked. He could see that I did. "Well, we all went out together and broke the course record, that's what we did. We went out and broke the course record. After that first drive I was feelin' all that separation *gone.* I wanted to cry, I was so relieved and free o' fear. There was nae mair fear at all. I was feelin' so good I didna' look at the ball and I hit to the rough. And then things began to happen. I hit a little wedge out to the fairway. And then I knew, Holy Jesus, that the Lord had broken through again. The ball hit a hard spot and kept bouncin', about a hundred yards, almost down to the green! Just kept bouncin' along, I couldna' believe it.

Looked like a Mexican jumpin' bean. I thought I was at one
o' those old *Topper* movies where things move by themsel's.
So help me God, that ball just kept goin' by itself. I knew
then that somethin' was goin' on wi' that gallery. They
'wanted me to *win*.'

"Well, it went on like that," he said slowly, as if he were
deciding what I was ready to hear. He studied my face.
"Then everything turned to Technicolor," he said at last.

"Technicolor?"

"Technicolor, full-blown Technicolor. And I could heer
the insects too." He paused again. "And music."

"Music?"

"A choir way in the distance. A great choir and drums.
Some o' the gallery heard it too. They heard it awright. I
could tell by the way they looked at me. That laddie who
came up to me at the very beginnin', he knew what was goin'
on the whole eighteen holes."

A round of golf in technicolor to the accompaniment of
drums—all because he overcame his shyness! As you can see,
there are enormous gaps in the story. I have often wondered
how much he might have doctored his tales. If I hadn't seen
Seamus's shillelagh and that fantastic gallery of charts and
pictures stacked up around me, I might have thought it was
all fabrication.

After the tournament he could see that golf and his inner
life were one destiny. He would be a golf professional *and* a
philosopher, using the game to body forth the truths he was
discovering within.

Once he made the decision to accept these disparate leadings he was no longer "a chameleon on a tartan plaid" responding to every situation and impulse that came his way.
He had a center, at last, albeit one that would keep unfolding. He was finally growing into the self which God had
intended. For several years after that Julian Laing had
helped him understand these regions of the soul, had listened
to him for hours and confirmed his new resolution.

But there were still some things he did not ken. To help him understand them he needed another mentor. In August 1945, two weeks after Hiroshima, he met him.

Shivas had spent the war years on a Scottish island in the North Sea as a lookout for enemy bombers, an assignment that "fit his talent for brooding." He was on a team of four men who worked alternating three-week shifts on the island with another team. Between his tours of duty he played golf on the mainland. Those five years had confirmed his calling, for during the eighteen-hour winter nights he had perfected the contemplative part of his discipline as he watched the skies for attacking planes. The constant anticipation of enemy bombers had gradually turned into a vision that God himself would descend to earth one day. This vision possessed his mind that week in August 1945.

He was on leave in Burningbush when the meeting occurred. He had gone to pray in the old cathedral, something he had always done even after he left the church. After his prayers he walked into the adjoining burial ground, "as if he were drawn there." In front of a tomb commemorating a famous golfer stood Seamus MacDuff. Shivas had seen the old man when he was a child, going around the local course on a white Shetland pony. He was one of the great characters of the town in the twenties, a prosperous eccentric inventor, who had discovered certain engineering principles that led to the development of missiles and supersonic flight. His aloof and imperious ways endeared him to many in Burningbush and outraged others, especially because his African ancestry was so at odds with the traditions of membership in the club. He was the son of a wealthy Scottish merchant, who had made a fortune in the Africa trade, and a Voodoo priestess from the Gold Coast. His father had imagined himself a kind of Richard Burton bringing back the lore of the primitive mind, and in the course of his travels had met the clairvoyantly gifted black woman who eventually gave birth to Seamus. The youngster had been raised in his mother's tribe, and tutored in British ways by teachers his father sent to the Gold Coast. He was then sent to Oxford when he was seventeen. His eventual fascination with the dark underside of modern science undoubtedly derived from his African roots. He sometimes compared himself to Amenhotep the Fourth, the monotheistic Pharaoh known as Ikhnaton, who was also a combination of Northern and Southern genes. In any case, Seamus's swarthy face and white bristling beard confounded many of the people of Burningbush who had never seen anyone like him. His habit of riding around the links on a Shetland pony only heightened the impact of his startling presence.

He had gone into seclusion sometime before 1930, no one knew why. Some thought he was mad; others said he had gone bankrupt while developing a new scheme for harnessing power.

Now he stood gazing at the statue as Shivas approached. Without turning, he said, "You and I have much to do, for these are our final days." If I correctly remember Shivas's account, their collaboration started immediately, Seamus following his new protégé around the Burningbush links as they had their first seminar on true gravity. During that round, I believe, Shivas hit his first hole-in-one across Lucifer's Rug.

In the years that followed, they worked on the relations between consciousness and physical laws, Seamus being the theorist and Shivas his practitioner in the world of golf. He hinted that the old wizard had other areas in which he was trying his theories, that many other human activities would be transformed one day in the knowledge of true gravity and the "luminous body."

Hiroshima was the beginning of the end, according to Seamus MacDuff; it was the final sign that man must discover the secrets of his soul or go the way of dying species. The discovery of atomic weapons had come too soon, before the deeper revelations of science that were ultimately meant to be. Evolution had taken an awful turn and there was not much time to right the balance. He was studying the golfer's tomb that day in the cathedral burial ground because he and Shivas had to make golf a matter of life and death. It was an appropriate place for them to meet.

Shivas Irons and Seamus MacDuff, what a pair! I don't know if I will ever live down the fact that I ran away from their incredible world.

That afternoon I abruptly decided to return to London. I have always been a sucker for exact schedules; a psychoanalyst once said I had a "completion complex." The afternoon was slipping away and the time for my train approached. Shivas had never said I should stay. He had only hinted and held out tiny blandishments. We had never really discussed what I was going to do with all the notes I was making. I had come a long way and had made elaborate plans for the trip. I had a ride to Dover and Calais from London, with a young lady I had met on the *Île de France*. I had planned my trip to India for over a year. All of this propelled me onward. At about 3:30 I said I was going to leave.

He stood and looked out a window. Then he turned and gave me a withering look that said I was unworthy of everything he had shown me. I hurriedly gathered up my notes and asked him to come with me to my room and then to the train. He reluctantly consented, and we walked over to The Druids' Inn in silence—two awkward figures, one embarrassed and nervous, the other smoldering with unspoken thoughts. I cannot remember what we said to each other then, just the feeling of it.

I can still see him waving as my train pulled away from the station, an angry figure growing smaller against the shimmering perspective of that marvelous little town.

What is repression? How does it work so insidiously in our lives? Why can't I recall what was going through my mind as I raced away from Burningbush? I only remember consoling myself during the trip to London that most of his other students must have done what I was doing.

Epilogue

But the story did not quite end there (indeed in many respects it is not over yet). During the following week a remarkable incident occurred in the cathedral of Rheims, one which seemed related to my adventures in Burningbush.

In London I met my companion of the *Île de France*, who was surrendering herself to the surprises of a European summer. She had rented a Morris Minor and was a jaunty chauffeur for a merry ride to Canterbury. We had not been together for more than fifteen minutes before I began to relate my story of the previous two days. Perhaps it was the shock of those events to my nervous system or the lack of sleep but I told the story in two or three different versions. Her woman's eye for the absurd and her general good spirits cast a warm spell around me and I began to sort out the deceptive complexity of that brief visit to Scotland.

While she drove, I fell into a reverie. Pleasant and seemingly random thoughts softened by the green English countryside, then vivid scenes from my past forming and reforming, sorting themselves out, leading me back to childhood like hypnotic regression. I was in warm, unaccountable spirits, anticipation spreading in my cells as if I knew this reverie would bring some marvelous secret. Both of us felt that sense of zero gravity that comes when you are traveling without an immediate or particular goal. In Canterbury we got into the old cathedral sometime after midnight because the wizened caretaker liked the gleam emanating from this loosening of my brain.

The next day we drove to Dover and crossed the channel to Calais. I still remember the smell of a store there, a smell that was familiar at once for it was the one I grew up with in my grandparents' laundry and kitchen—salamis and parsleys and spices and consommés, a combination of ingredients I could never forget. The store in Calais brought memories of vacations in San Francisco when I was a child, with my fun-loving, pleasure-loving Grand'mère and Grand'père and all their children and cousins (many of them gourmet cooks); a peasant world, a breath of air from the Pyrenees, full of the very same smells I found in this store in Calais. These smells from the past gave body to my reverie as we drove toward Rheims, absorbing me all that day until we arrived at the great cathedral and I saw the banner and figure of Saint Jeanne d'Arc.

The memories began in earliest infancy, feelings with no graspable image or event to hold them: feelings of cradling and rocking and my mother's pleasure, a time of membranes' sensuous stretching, with textures of reassuring blankets and diapers like warm water-beds, adventures of water and air, a trip well begun; then an image of a kindergarten class, watching all the others on the merry-go-round but too uneasy to get on myself, the shy one standing near the teacher while most of the kids screamed and laughed and fell on the whirling frame; and a third-grade teacher with a wall of bugs and spiders in bottles filled with formaldehyde, my peering through protective glass at those mysterious many-legged creepy-crawlies, knowing at once what they felt like and curious thereafter about other beings, teeming worlds of them appearing in books I could find on my parents' shelves and in fortunate classrooms; then books about stars and planets and finally the mystery underlying. I became an early philosopher—late into puberty, early into God—wandering into bookstores and feeling my way to the right shelf, the opening in the mystery: somewhere in that store was a word, it never failed, I would tell my friends that I could dowse for books, for the Word—the trip began into those reachings of the mind when I was still five feet four. And then the memory of that shattering day in a class I came to by mistake, the class of Frederic Spiegelberg, known to many of the students in those nonphilosophical nonapocalyptic days of 1950 as the best teacher on the Stanford campus, remembered him rolling the Sanskrit words, intoning the *Brahman* and the Vedic Hymns and knowing that I could never be the same again, that all the dowsing for books in my teen-age years was coming into focus—at Stanford, the fun-loving school, Spiegelberg rolling out the Vedic Hymns, bringing a few of us home to the beginning of things; and then our little group of dropouts in 1951, led by Walter Page, older than we with his streak of white hair running Mohawk-style down the middle of his head; Walt Page and his closet full of books—a forerunner of Shivas Irons. The memory of all my teachers and conversions rolled through me that sunny summer day in 1956.

We drove into Rheims and circled round the great cathedral, viewing it first from our car before we found our room. I had read a long shelf of history books before this trip, for I had decided to recapitulate the march of Western History on my way to India: I wanted to get my bearings, perhaps, on my way out to sea. The cathedral of Rheims and the armor of Jeanne d'Arc were special places on that journey back. I had read Shaw's play and preface and two or three books about her, for her life was one of those intersections I needed to comprehend if I was going to find the link between this world and the ones I was about to explore. She was a *pitha*, as the Indians say, a place where something breaks into our workaday world and bothers us forevermore with the hints it gives.

We found the small hotel we had heard about and asked for a room. Then I caused a scene by asking for *two* rooms. My companion, first of several good women confounded by sudden turnings of the erratic compass needle of asceticism and sensuality in my soul, was angry and hurt, and the innkeeper—well, I had never encountered one so jealous of his rooms; he thought I had asked for another because I didn't like the one we saw first, so came like a gallant Frenchman to my companion's defense. After much argument he said that this was the very last room in his inn, that, moreover, there was not another left in the entire town. So I said we would go on to Paris that night. In spite of all the trouble I was making, I had to make the renunciation, there was no resisting it; I had to prepare for whatever was emerging in these days of reverie and catharsis.

Jeanne d'Arc. I remembered seeing sailors from a French warship with her name on their caps while I was stationed in Puerto Rico, remembered my uncle's joke about being captain of the ship since he had been aboard it once in San Francisco; he had joked about it during every party at the Frenchmen's gatherings when I was a child, never tired of getting us to salute, my brother and I and all our cousins, whenever he announced he was "Captain Pierre" of the French fleet, captain of the *Jeanne d'Arc.** As we walked toward the Gothic spires looming now above the town I remembered these and other associations to her name, an arc joining this world to the others, the charts on Shivas's wall with lines joining vertical columns, one entitled DANGEROUS CONNNECTIONS, another GOD IS WAKING UP, and his notion that God gives us a million clues but because we are so dense he must shove some of them right in our face.

Then we came to the cathedral façade. There was con-

---

* I have only to turn my head as I write to see the *Jeanne d'Arc* moored at a pier on the San Francisco waterfront.

I wrote this epilogue in Big Sur (in the spring of 1971) and returned to find a ship glowing in the water beneath me like an illuminated cathedral. At first I did not know its name. Then an announcement came over a local radio station that the *Jeanne d'Arc* was receiving visitors at pier 39—the pier beneath my window! I focused my binoculars on it, and there were the words spelled on its bow; there was no mistaking them. As a friend remarked, my ship had come in.

struction under way inside and you could see at once that much of it was newly built. The ravages of bombardment during the war were still being repaired, we were told, that was why this rear part of the towering nave looked so clean, so free of soot and all the centuries' calefactions, almost as if it had shed a skin. It was not at all as I had anticipated it, not dark and libidinous and full of mystery; it reminded me in fact of a gigantic bower, full of springtime leaves and sunbeams streaming through the unstained glass. On all sides there bustled children from some French school, whispering and giggling as they scampered after their brisk and upright teachers: their chirping voices echoed off the tall, empty windows and airy vaults, receding into waves of formless sound and the beginnings of music. The cathedral of Rheims was for all the world like an airy bower, its power and mystery was in the sound it gave back.

The sound. I was struck by the amazing swirl of it through the towering vaults: giggling children, hollow footsteps, the occasional shout of a workman rising above a quiet roar like distant surf.

The sound and then the tiny figure at the end of the nave. For there she was as I had hoped, the figure of the Maid in the original armor, carrying a banner of white that seemed four times her size.

I circled away from my friend and walked alone toward the statue, poised at last on insight's very edge. Memories recalled and impulses cleansed, mind empty now, a pious bore to my friend but ready nevertheless for the omens, I came like a sleepwalker to the point of intersections embodied in the relics of Saint Joan.

Then the omens began.

As I walked up the side aisle on the right, a weathered old lady dressed in black rose from her prayers near the aisle and watched me intently. As I passed her she grabbed my arm. Her face had a simian look, with flaring nostrils and flat high cheeks, and her eyes showed white as if they were rolled back permanently from so much prayer. *"Entendez vous les voix sous les voûtes?"* she asked with an urgent voice—did I hear the voices in the vaults? She rolled back her eyes and looked toward the cathedral roof, then repeated the question. I started to pull away but felt drawn to her strangely importuning look, for a moment I was going two ways at once.

She asked the question again with growing agitation —did I hear the voices? What was she driving at? She was mad, I thought, an eccentric old peasant woman centering her delusions in her prayers. But I followed her gestures and looked up into the cathedral vault. As I did, the echoes of the place engulfed me.

Distant ocean waves, elusive whispers were forming in the sibilant echoes. Yes, I could hear them, I could hear the voices. I sat down next to her and listened. The memories and catharsis of the last few days had prepared me perhaps for this unlikely event. I looked into the Gothic arches, up into the overturned keel of the nave. What were they saying? What were the old lady's voices saying? If I let some door in my brain swing open, there would be a voice and a word, I had learned how to do that during long hours of meditation. There was a resistance though, for the voice invariably left me with nausea—something was threatened by such interventions and reacted with an automatic visceral no. But now I was in a mood to let it come, the last few days had given me a taste for abandon, yes, whatever had begun at Burningbush was carrying me to this cathedral bench. I closed my eyes, let the swirl of sound congeal round that elusive door in my head, and sure enough the arches spoke. A tiny voice coming as if through distant echo chambers said, "Come home"—"Come home," it said again and then like distant choirs came the beginnings of music, emblazoning those words on my brain forever. Come home, come home, I was breaking through to another realm: come home, it said, follow the music home at last.

I will never know what happened next, for when I opened my eyes the old lady was gone and in her stead there sat my companion of recent days. I stretched my arms and reached out to touch her. Her hair in the sunlight was like a halo and her eyes and mouth curled upward with fond amusement. We looked at each other for a moment and I could see that she understood something of what I had seen. She leaned toward me and kissed my cheek and whispered that she would meet me outside when I was ready, then rose with a little wave and slipped away.

Perhaps an hour or two had passed, judging from the change of light. It seemed to be late afternoon and there was a hush in the cathedral now. The armor on Saint Joan's statue caught a ray of sunshine and flashed it back down the lengthening nave—perhaps the Maid was sending me signals. I felt a faint impulse to rise and explore the place, but the afterglow of trance held me in its blissful field: in the heavy stillness there was the subtlest suggestion of the fairy dust Shivas had mentioned filtering through the membranes of the inner body, as if my ordinary frame were being transformed by the explosion of light and sound triggered by the strange old lady. I sat for several minutes savoring the quiet and the process of change going on inside me and thought again of Shivas. This was the kind of thing he was into—what a pleasure and what a privilege! The thought occurred that he had passed the secret of it on to me. For it was said in most of the ancient books that *darshan*, as the Indians called it, the passing of the light, could only come directly from teacher to student, that it was rarely mediated in any other way. I said a little prayer of thanks to my Scottish golfing teacher.

The beams of light shaped by the tapering walls of glass were softening now and casting longer shadows among the branches and spreading trees on the walls of the church. I looked around the enormous space, at Saint Joan, at the people filing out the great rear doors, at the figures kneeling in prayer, then up to the Gothic columns, and the catwalks high above. High in the shadows of the nave, some 90 or 100 feet above me, a tiny figure was looking down, perhaps a workman looking for his helper. As I watched him I realized he wasn't moving, that he was looking in my direction. I could not discern his features but could see he was dressed in black with a frizzy beard, that he seemed to have a smile on his face, a mad, gay little smile.

I looked around the nave, then up at the ceiling again: the bearded face was staring down at me still, with the same little smile.

The relentless scrutiny of the distant figure was obscene. I stood up and started down the aisle toward the cathedral sanctuary to get another angle from which to see him. His head turned to follow my movement. There was no doubt about it, he was watching me intently. An old lady was sweeping at the edge of the choir; I pointed toward the figure in the rafters and asked her who it was. She shrugged her shoulders and said she did not speak English. "*Qui est-ce?*" I asked insistently, pointing again at the peering face. "*Mais de qui parlez vous? Je ne vois rien,*" she said in a rasping voice as she looked toward the distant ceiling, "I don't understand."

I jabbed my finger at the smiling face. "There, right there, don't you see it?"

"I don't understand," she answered with a shrug and turned back to her sweeping.

For a moment the lights grew dim. I looked for someone to help me, but there was no one else in this part of the cathedral. Then I noticed a figure walking toward me up the center aisle, a tall man with a dark beard and priestly suit of black, a rabbi perhaps. He seemed to be looking at the figure of Saint Joan, for as he approached his head turned slowly to keep the statue in sight. As he passed I cleared my throat and touched his arm.

"Excuse me, sir, but would you do me a favor?" As I asked the question I glanced up to check on the figure above. It was in exactly the same position, peering down at me with a clearly discernible smile.

"Yes?" the stranger paused and looked at me with a kind and curious expression. He seemed strangely familiar.

"Forgive me for this," I asked, "but I think someone is

watching me from the roof. Would you please see if you can see him?"

The stranger in black smiled through his bushy beard with a wide, slightly bucktoothed smile and said in what seemed to be a British accent, "I don't think one can get into those arches."

"But look, would you please look?" I asked again, an edge of pleading in my voice now.

"Well, then, show me where he is," he said and turned to follow my pointing finger. "I don't think there is anyone there," he said after he had scanned the long sweep of arches in the cathedral vault.

"But look, look there," I insisted, holding my arm so he could look down the line of my finger. I could see the face as clearly as ever.

"I'm sorry, I'm very sorry," he turned to face me. "I simply cannot see him. Perhaps you've mistaken a gargoyle for a living face." He smiled another bucktoothed smile and put an arm around my shoulder. "Young man," he said, "let me show you the banner of Saint Joan. That is far more interesting than a face in the roof."

I glanced again at the staring figure. But I followed the stranger, for his presence reassured me.

He led me to the base of the little statue. I could see when we got there that the Maid must have been less than five feet tall. We stood looking up at her in silence for several moments, then the kindly man in black said in his British accent, "That banner, have you ever seen it before?" I said that I had read about it and had seen it on a postcard. It was surprisingly long and I wondered how the little woman could have carried it; she must have been as strong as an ox. The stranger moved closer and reached over to touch it. Then he stroked it gently and brushed some dust from a fleur-de-lis. "She designed it herself, you know," he said. "Can you imagine the inspiration it must have been?" I was touched by his fond regard for the ancient object. My upset was going away. "Do you think it has some power still?" he murmured, almost as if he were asking himself the question. "I would love to pick it up." He touched the dusty banner now with both his hands, and for a moment I thought he might take it from the statue. I had an image of him holding it above his head and marching around the cathedral. He must have sensed what I was thinking for he turned to me and winked and said, "You be the Dauphin and I'll be the Maid." I was at ease by now and gave a little laugh. Then he smiled through his bushy beard.

The bells were tolling in the cathedral of Rheims and acolytes were lighting candles. It was time for Mass.

"Would you like to join me for the service here?" my new friend asked with an engaging smile. "Then I will tell you some secrets about Jeanne d'Arc." I was about to say yes, but at that very moment I saw him looking skeptically over my shoulder—I remember his look so well. Then I felt a hand on my neck and knew it was Dulce, my good companion come after these many hours to get me. There she was with her golden hair and twinkling eyes, patient to the end with all my dallyings.

"I'm sorry," I said to the stranger, "but we have to drive to Paris tonight. There's not a room left in Rheims."

He seemed to be disappointed. "Well," he said, with a gesture toward the cathedral roof, "at least we got rid of the ghost." I looked up and indeed the figure was gone. "I do that sometimes, see faces like that," my embarrassment must have been plain. "Thanks for your time."

I reached out to shake his hand and he gave me a bone-crunching grip. Then he smiled his bucktoothed smile for the last time and I saw that his gaze was ever so slightly crossed.

"Whenever you feel oppressed," he said, "remember Saint Joan and her angels and remember that she made herself a banner." He raised a large hand in farewell and waved it in front of his face as if he were opening and closing some invisible curtain. We waved good-by, then arm in arm we walked outside into the light of the setting sun.

PART II

The Game's Hidden
but Accessible Meaning

Certain events may reflect the significant dimensions of all
your life, mirroring your entire history in a passing moment.
Have you ever had an experience like that? Have you been
caught by an event that suddenly pulled the curtains back?
Shivas Irons maintained that a round of golf sometimes took
on that special power.

The archetypes of golf are amazingly varied, he said, that
is the reason so many people gravitate to the game.

Golf as a Journey

"A round of golf," he said in his journal notes, "partakes of
the journey, and the journey is one of the central myths and
signs of Western Man. It is built into his thoughts and dreams,
into his genetic code. The Exodus, the Ascension, the Odyssey,
the Crusades, the pilgrimages of Europe and the Voyage of
Columbus, Magellan's Circumnavigation of the Globe, the
Discovery of Evolution and the March of Time, getting
ahead and the ladder of perfection, the exploration of space
and the Inner Trip: from the beginning our Western World
has been on the move. We tend to see everything as part of
the journey. But other men have not been so concerned to get
somewhere else—take the Hindus with their endless cycles of

time or the Chinese Tao. Getting somewhere else is not necessarily central to the human condition."

Perhaps we are so restless because like Moses we can never make it to the promised land. We tell ourselves that It is just over the next hill: just a little more time or a little more money or a little more struggle will get us there; ". . . even our theology depends upon that Final Day, that Eschaton when the journey will finally arrive, to compel our belief in God."

The symbol of the journey reflects our state, for man is surely on the move toward something. Many of us sense that our human race is on a tightrope, that we must keep moving or fall into the abyss. "This world is for dyin'," he said that night. We must die to the old or pay more and more for remaining where we are.

Yes, there is no escaping the long march of our lives: that is part of the reason people re-enact it again and again on the golf course, my golfing teacher said. They are working out something built into their genes.

But there are other myths to govern our lives, other impulses lurking in our soul, "myths of arrival with our myths of the journey, something to tell us we are the target as well as the arrow."

So Shivas Irons would have us learn to enjoy what *is* while seeking our treasure of tomorrow. And—you might have guessed it—a round of golf is good for that, " . . . because if it is a journey, it is also a *round*: it always leads back to the place you started from . . . golf is always a trip back to the first tee, the more you play the more you realize you are staying where you are." By playing golf, he said, "you re-enact that secret of the journey. You may even get to enjoy it."*

---

* I have often thought that his sense of golf as the journey-round was deepened by his memory that the eighteenth green at Burningbush was built on a grave.

The Whiteness of the Ball

What the golf ball was to Shivas has been hinted; what it has come to mean for me remains unsaid. And for a reason. Its power as a symbol is so complex and labyrinthine, so capable of lending itself to the psyche of each and every player, that once an attempt like this has begun to comprehend its "inner meaning," all bearings may be lost. For the golf ball is "an icon of Man the Multiple Amphibian, a smaller waffled version of the crystal ball, a mirror for the inner body; it is a lodestone, an old stone to polarize your psyche with." The more I ponder its ramifications the more I see that each and every bit of this world reflects the whole.

A friend of mine sees it as a satellite revolving around our higher self, thus forming a tiny universe for us to govern—a marvelous image really when you think about it, one I am sure Shivas Irons and Seamus MacDuff would have approved of. Our relation to the ball is like the Highest Self's relation to all its instruments and powers; the paths of its orbits reflect those of the planets and suns. The ball is then a symbol of all our revolving parts, be they mental or physical; for a while we re-enact the primal act of all creation: the One casting worlds in all directions for its extension and delight. Shivas anticipated the image in his notes: "For a while on the links we can lord it over our tiny solar system and pretend we are God: no wonder then that we suffer so deeply when our planet goes astray."

The ball is also a reflection, as Adam Greene said, of projectiles past and future, a reminder of our hunting history and our future powers of astral flight. We can then ponder the relation between projectile and planet, our being as hunter and our being as God; the hunter, the golfer, the astronaut, the yogi, and God all lined up in the symbol of the ball.

"The ball is ubiquitous," say the notes. "It is in flight at this very moment above every continent. Moreover, it is in flight every moment of the day and night. It may take flight one day on the moon, especially when you consider the potential prodigies of mile-long drives and the wonder they would bring to millions. Consider the symbolism inherent in that indubitable fact: a golf ball suspended in air at every moment!" There are so many golfers around the globe.

At rest, it is "like an egg, laid by man," for who can tell what prodigies the next shot will bring? In flight it brings that peculiar suspended pleasure which lies at the heart of the game; it is "a signal that we can fly—and the farther the better!"—it is a symbol of our spirit's flight to the goal. It is perfectly round, for centuries of human ingenuity and labor have made it so, and "the meanings of roundness are easy to see." (Parmenides and other Greek philosophers said that Being itself was a globe, that we must therefore "circulate" our words in order to tell a "round truth.")

So the symbols and meanings are endless. But when all these are said and done, there is a fact about the ball that overpowers all the rest. It is the whiteness of the ball that disturbs me more than anything else. "Though in many natural objects whiteness enhances beauty, as if imparting some special virtue of its own," said Herman Melville in a well-known passage, "and though certain nations have in some way recognized a certain pre-eminence to it, there yet lurks an elusive something in the color which strikes panic to the soul."

Only black so reminds us of the great unknown. Black and white, we throw them together in the old cliché, but somewhere deep in both there lies a hint of powers unforeseen. Do they remind us of the void, since they represent the absence of all ordinary hue? Is it annihilation we fear when we encounter them? "All colors taken together congeal to whiteness, the greatest part of space is black," say the journal notes. "What would happen if someone introduced a golf ball painted black?"

The Mystery of the Hole

In no other game is the ratio of playing field to goal so large. (Think of soccer, American football, lacrosse, basketball, billiards, bowling.) We are spread wide as we play, then brought to a tiny place.

The target then leads into the ground, leads underground. I realized this once reaching into one of the exceptionally deep holes our Salinas greenkeeper was cutting in 1949 (he had procured a new hole-cutter). What a strange sensation reaching so far into the ground. What was down there, underneath the ball?

There was a section in his notes entitled "The Psychology of Passageways," which has a bearing on the hole's mystery. In it there was a list of "holes and doorways in our ordinary life," which included a long paragraph about the significance of looking through windows (something to the effect that windows have a function other than letting us look outside, that we build them to simulate our essentially imprisoned state), another on the subject of toilets and the draining away of our refuse (including some sentences about the need to examine our stool whenever we feel disjointed), an essay on picture frames and other boundaries on art objects, and a list of all the "significant openings" in his own apartment (apparently, he had taken a careful inventory of these). There was also a list of "Extraordinary Openings." This included a constellation in the new zodiac he had made (see "A Golfer's Zodiac," p. 153), various kinds of mystical experience—an entire catalogue in fact of transports and ecstasies; a list of historic figures (including Joan of Arc, Pythagoras, Sri Ramakrishna, Seamus MacDuff, the Egyptian Pharaoh Ikhnaton, and a Dundee cobbler named Typhus Magee); a list of historic events (including the outbreak of philosophy all over the world during the sixth century B.C., the first flights at Kitty Hawk, and a drive he had hit sometime during the summer of

1948); certain places in Burningbush and its environs (I think he compared these to the points on the body which are probed during treatments with acupuncture), a golf course in Peru (perhaps the Tuctu golf course, which he had mentioned during our conversation at the McNaughtons); certain phrases, philosophical terms, and lines of poetry (including the word *Atman*, the *Isha Upanishad*, and a limerick by one of his pupils); a list of coincidences in his life; and the unpublished manuscript of his teacher.

Our first passageways, he said, are the avenues of sense—our eyes, ears, nostrils, and mouth. We build our houses and churches to simulate these, we relate to the earth itself as if it were our body, for "we start as someone looking out, and as soon as we look we think of escape."

"Life is a long obsession with passageways," the notes go on, "we are ever breaking through to the other side—of ignorance, isolation, imprisonment. Memory, catharsis, travel, discovery, ecstasy are all ways of getting outside our original skin."

He thought it significant that an entire fairway, with its green, rough, hazards, and traps was called a "hole," that the tiny target was used to characterize all the rest of the playing field. " 'How many holes have you played?' is the way the question is asked, not 'how many fairways?' or 'how many tees?' " He thought it had something to do with the fact that after all our adventures, all our trials and triumphs on the journey-round we are left with that final passage through; that the hole and what it leads to is really what the game is all about.

As it turns out some of the most original thinking on the subject has been done by Jean-Paul Sartre, who ends Part Four of *Being and Nothingness* with a short essay on the hole and its implications. I don't recall Shivas quoting Sartre but their thinking on the subject has some extraordinary similarities. The French philosopher, admittedly, is not an accomplished golfer, but his apparent grasp of the hole's mystery suggests that he has had his problems and triumphs on the links. "Thus to plug up a hole," he says, "means originally to make a sacrifice of my body in order that the plenitude of being may exist." (How we golfers can sympathize with that.) "Here at its origin we grasp one of the most fundamental tendencies of human reality—the tendency to fill. . . . A good part of our life is passed in plugging up holes, in filling empty places, in realizing and symbolically establishing a plenitude." In establishing a plenitude! Perhaps this is the most fundamental clue. And the comprehension of that essential act of sacrifice involved in every disappearance of the ball into the hole (sacrifice and inevitable rebirth)! For the journal notes say, "In golf we throw ourselves away and find ourselves again and again. . . . A ball is in flight somewhere at every moment. . . ." What are all these but glimpses of plenitude! To fill the hole with our ball is to reaffirm that fullness.

Replacing the Divot

Our green-loving philosopher claimed there was no better way to deal with our existential guilt than replacing a divot or repairing a friendship. "We act on friendship every moment: with our fellows, our land, our tools, with the unseen spirits and the Lord whose world we are tending."

"Golf is a game of blows and weapons. In order that the game continue we must make amends for every single act of destruction. In a golf club everyone knows the player who does not replace his divot. One can guess how he leads the rest of his life."

Replacing the divot is "an exercise for the public good." It is also a reminder that "we are all one golfer." There would simply be no game if every golfer turned his back on the damage he did.

A Game for the Multiple Amphibian

Bobby Jones and other lovers of the game have attributed its widespread appeal to the fact that it reflects so much of the human situation: comedy, tragedy, hard work, and miracle; the agony and the ecstasy. There is something in it for almost everyone. Shivas liked to quote the *Religio Medici*, especially the passage that described man as ". . . that great and true Amphibian whose nature is disposed to live, not only like other creatures in divers elements, but in divided and distinguished worlds." He believed that golf was uniquely suited to our multiple amphibious nature. It gives us a chance to exercise so many physical skills and so many aspects of our mind and character.

I need not catalogue the game's complexity to make my point: you know about all the long and the short shots; all the nuance of weather, air, and grass; all the emotion and vast resolution; all the schemes for success and delusions of grandeur, and the tall tales unnumbered; the trials of patience and fiendish frustrations; all the suicidal thoughts and glimpses of the Millennium. We all have a golfing friend we have had to nurse past a possible breakdown or listen to patiently while he expounded his latest theory of the game. How often have we seen a round go from an episode out of the Three Stooges to the agonies of King Lear—perhaps in the space of one hole! I will never forget a friend who declared after his tee shot that he wanted to kill himself but when the hole was finished said with total sincerity that he had never been so happy in his entire life. No other game is more capable of evoking a person's total commitment.*

This immense complexity delighted Shivas. In fact, he would add more complexity to the game, perhaps to satisfy his endlessly adventurous spirit. Running, for example, has been left out, as well as jumping and shouting; so he advocated your exercising these basic functions sometime during the golfing day if you wanted to balance your mind and nerves. We must give these large needs adequate expression, he said, otherwise golf would "imprint too much of its neces-

---

* An insightful book in this regard is *The Mystery of Golf*, by Arnold Haultain, recently reprinted by The Serendipity Press, though out of print now (ca. 1971).

sarily limited nature on us." For ". . . every game must have its limits, simply to exist, just as every form and every culture does, but our bodies and our spirits suffer." So somewhere and somehow we should run and jump and sing and shout. (I don't want to give you any advice about this, especially when I think about some of the trouble I have had on golf courses when I have tried to follow his advice. Perhaps you should confine these more strenuous activities to your local school-yard or gym. But you might find it interesting to see how your game fares when you exercise those muscles and functions that golf neglects.)

This is true for much more than running, jumping, and shouting though. For our golfing teacher maintained in his inexorable way that our "emotional and mental body" needed as much exercise as our physical body did. So "poetry, music, drama, prayer, and love" were essential to the game too. "There is no end to it," he said, "once you begin to take golf seriously."

Of a Golf Shot on the Moon

It can now be argued that golf was the first human game played on another planetary body. Those two shots Alan Shepard hit with a six iron at the "Fra Mauro Country Club" have brought a certain stature and gleam of the eye to golfers the world over. Coming as they did while I was writing this book, they appeared to me as synchronicity: the game has a mighty destiny, the event said; Shivas Irons was right. In the shock I felt when the news appeared (I had not seen the television show) I thought that in some inexplicable way those shots had been engineered by Shivas (from his worldly hiding place) or by Seamus MacDuff (from his hiding place on the other side). But the subsequent news that Shepard and his golf pro, Jack Harden, had planned the thing ruled out Shivas and restored some perspective to my hopeful speculations. Still, the meaning of it continued to loom before me.

Golf on the moon! And the command module named Kitty Hawk! (Shivas had called Kitty Hawk an "extraordinary opening" in this unfolding world and had worked with Seamus all those years on the possibilities of flight with "the luminous body.") The event was a tangle of synchronicities.

I wonder how many other golfers have felt the same way. So many of us are alive to the other edge of possibility (perhaps because the game has tried us so sorely) and ever alert for the cosmic meaning. This event confirms our sense of mighty things ahead.

There are other implications, however, some less promising. A trusted friend of mine, someone with a quick keen eye for injustice and intrigue, saw an ugly side to the whole affair. It was, he said, an imperial Wasp statement, however unconscious, that this here moon is our little old country club for whites, thank you, and here goes a golf shot to prove it. I hated to hear that, for I wanted to dwell on the hopeful meanings. And I hated to think what Seamus would do, being half-black, if he were fiddling around with it all from his powerful vantage point. The Kitty Hawk might not make it back to earth! But the heroes are back and so far so good. Still, I am left wondering what latent imperialism lay behind that six-iron shot.

And I am left with other thoughts about the character of Alan Shepard. What could have led the man to design that faulty club, smuggle it on board with those "heat-resistant" balls and risk some billion-dollar disaster from flying divots or tears in his space suit? What could have led him to such monumental triviality amid the terrors and marvels of the Moon? The madness of the game had surfaced again, I thought, as I pondered his motives.

Had NASA put him up to it for public relations reasons? Maybe they wanted some humor in the enterprise or the backing of certain rich and powerful golfing senators. Perhaps he would collect on some stupendous bet (after all, he was interested in money and had made a pile in his astronaut years). Or could it simply be that all his golfer's passion to hit the ball a mile now had a chance to express itself, indeed the chance of a lifetime, the chance of history! Perhaps the collective unconscious of all the golfing world was delivering itself at last, seizing him as instrument for the release of a million foiled hopes for the shot that would never come down. And indeed the cry came down from space, ". . . it's sailing for miles and miles and miles," Alan Shepard was giving the mad cry of golfers the world over who want to put a ball in orbit and reassume their god-like power.

Yes, indeed, indeed, Shivas was right; the game keeps giving us glimpses.

The Inner Body

A. As Experience

When Shivas gave me that midnight lesson and whispered his instructions to "ken yer inner body" I sensed his meaning at once, even though my "good mind" kept raising questions. Most psychologists would say that he was merely reinforcing my kinesthetic or proprioceptive sense, making me more aware of the messages coming from my muscles and enteroceptors. Or they might say he was making me more sensitive to "the body image," the fluctuating gestalt that emerges from our various bodily sensations. They would thereby reduce it all to proportions which their psychology could manage, for psychologists are generally conscientious people quite concerned to keep man's psyche orderly and comprehensible, and God knows, they have a hard time with the limited tools and maps they have. Concepts like the "inner body" or the "higher self" give most of them enormous difficulty: the Irons-MacDuff Psycho-Cosmology as a whole would give them a very bad time indeed.

But that night Shivas was turning my attention to much more than the kinesthetic sense or the "body image," though these are related to it. For him, the inner body was more than metaphor or "experiential construct." It was a vivid undeniable reality forever impinging on our workaday world. And once you paid attention to it, it was a doorway to marvelous realms.

Psychologies other than our twentieth-century Western model include these dimensions of human experience, and have included them for thousands of years. It has been helpful for me to remember that. Indian psychology, for example, has much to say about the *sukshma sharira*, the so-called "subtle" or "feeling" body; the Upanishads describe various *koshas* or "soul-sheaths"; Hindu-Buddhist contemplative practice has given birth to elaborate systems of inner anatomy, full of *nadis* and *chakras* and *Kundalini* powers. These esoteric anatomies correspond in significant ways to similar systems in the lore of Africa, China, and the American Indian nations. Not only has there been a perennial philosophy, there has also been a *perennial anatomy* of the inner body. Lately, these ancient discoveries have been finding their way into the outskirts of our cautious Western psychology. They were bound to find their way there eventually, given the fundamental and irrepressible power of the realms they point to.

Now let us look more carefully at the term we are dealing with. The first word points to the subjective nature of the phenomena and also to the fact that this other body, this *inner* body, is somehow enclosed or placed within our ordinary physical frame. But here the term can be misleading. For as Shivas described it and as I have experienced it, the inner body is not bound to the physical frame it inhabits. It is far more elastic and free, more like a flame than a rock. The term *body* can also be misleading, since body connotes boundary. In Shivas Irons' sense of the term your inner body has no final boundary, unless it is that final paradoxical line in the "bounded infinite." It is a center to operate from, an indubitable *something*, to be sure, but it wavers and dances like a living flame and stretches at times to alarming proportions. It may hurtle through star-gates and openings in time. It/we may suddenly come out in another place, in another body. It/we may merge into everything at once.

Defining the term is a frustrating job. The intellect is often frustrated when it encounters phenomena like these. You need poetry, mathematics, philosophy, and music to approach them. Then your own fantasy can take on the task, drawing you into the reality itself.

We were coming down one of the final fairways toward Burningbush Town. In the silence and the softening light I felt a quiet exaltation. The golf course was still as a quiet lake and as I walked along I heard a sound—a popping of the inner ear, or a cricket—I could not tell where it came from. As I walked along the sound continued, it was impossible to tell if it was coming from within my head or from a distance. Gentle and rhythmic, it sent tiny waves of pleasure through me.

The experience was a first lesson in boundaries, for when I got to the green Shivas asked if I could hear the evening bells from the cathedral. As he asked the question I heard that sound change place, from somewhere inside me to the old church tower. Explaining its origin had created a boundary between it and me.

A similar thing happened during our midnight lesson. As I fell into the focus Shivas wanted, my body widened until it embraced the ball all the way to the target. He had said that the club and the ball are one. "Aye ane fiedle afore ye e'er swung," I can still remember the way he said it, and sure enough I became that field. The first time it happened, I felt the ball hit my stomach as it hit the wall of the ravine, a solid blow that felt like a child's fist. I told him what had happened and he said that he had felt it too.

Like true gravity, the inner body stands outside our ordinary Western view of things. It is real in a way conventional Western psychology will never admit—until psychologists enter these realms themselves.

Artists and poets have seen it more clearly. El Greco's saints or his "View of Toledo" shudder upwards into the living vortex of the sky. "The gallop of his rhythms runs away with the sense," an eminent art critic says; the energy of the inner body is breaking through, drawing everything with it, including the critic's mind. The German painter Matthias Grünewald was more conscious and deliberate about it. Many of his figures are enveloped in aureoles and glories, you can see their subtle bodies made explicit. When he was alive, in those late medieval years, auras, halos and the occult were accessible to the common culture; the artist had seen them or knew a local witch or saint who did. Either he or someone he knew conversed with angels and demons. But as religion waned and worldly skepticism flourished, this subtle vision turned to artifice and mere convention—halos flattened into golden beanies, angels turned to dumplings. What did you do with your saint's nimbus when he turned sideways, show it in two dimensions or three? No one knew *what* they looked like now.

Our contemporary artist invents his own ways of mirroring the inner man. Picasso's "Guernica" is such a device for rendering the psychic mutilation, agony, and terror of war in the twentieth century. The inner body can be torn and rent, pieces of it can be splattered against the wall. Mental hospitals are full of such carnage, so are broken homes and ghetto streets. Have you ever felt it, a piece of your substance blasted away? Why do we say our heart is *broken* or our personality is *split*? These old clichés point to the mutilation of our very substance, to gaping wounds in the inner body that impress themselves irresistibly on our physical guts. We have all felt it. Picasso holds up a mirror to our battle-twisted souls.

Artists and poets who reveal these things may say they are only making metaphors or symbols, but the pictures they make have power because they suck us toward real shapes and forces, because they bring invisible worlds into this one. I think that is the reason some people grow weary at museums and art shows. Boredom can be a defense against dark intrusions. For:

> The Ghosts, and Monster Spirits, that did presume
> A Bodies Priv'lege to assume,

Vanish again invisibly,
And Bodies gain agen their visibility.

The metaphysical poet was describing the light of day-break—and suggesting dark transferals and passageways from this world to another.

B. As Fact

In the Stanford University library there is an enormous collection of books on mysticism and the occult. The founder's brother, Thomas Walton Stanford, developed an interest in these matters and donated large sums of money to the university for their study. He also sent long shelves of theosophical writings, and a case of apports to his brother's school. (An apport is a materialization of the ectoplasm or subtle substance emanating from a séance with the dead.) Through the years I have explored this towering collection, spending many a day leafing through dusty books hardly opened since they were printed, and have discovered that research into the phenomena of the inner body has been going on incessantly since the founding of the British Psychical Research Society in 1882. I would estimate that several thousand independent inquiries have been conducted to see what reality there is in the ancient reports about auras, telepathy, clairvoyance, survival of bodily death, and related matters. The American and British Psychical Research societies have accumulated, in their journals, annals, and proceedings, reports that are staggering in number and impressive in method. If these people can be trusted—and many of them like William James have been respected in other fields of inquiry—the evidence is compelling that we do indeed possess another body, an *inner* body, a vehicle of consciousness that survives death, travels to far places during sleep and trance, and changes size and shape. It can be seen by certain clairvoyants and be made to appear to unsuspecting persons like an apparition. There is a perennial anatomy of this subtle body, and many attempts have been made to organize the knowledge about its structure and functioning. One such attempt, a kind of *Gray's Anatomy* of the soul entitled *Human Personality and Its Survival of Bodily Death*, was compiled by Frederic Myers, the neglected genius of psychical research who invented the word "telepathy" and other terms used by parapsychologists. And there are other compilations of past research and belief about the occult too numerous to list, but you can explore for yourself by reading any book on ESP with a bibliography and fanning out from there. One book leads to another, and if you go on, you will find yourself wandering in a world of inquiry, speculation, and adventure more vast than you ever would have imagined. You will see the teeming underside of our Western rationalism and science.

C. As Luminous Body

Shivas and his teacher had elaborated a theory that for nearly every major invention in recent times there was a corresponding power man could develop in his own being without needing a mechanical or other external contrivance. For example, we could learn to fly without airplanes once we fell into "true gravity" and learned to breathe properly (or hit fantastic golf shots with Irish shillelaghs when we mastered the secrets of the "inner body"). This, of course, is an ancient idea, going back to alchemy, Gnosticism, and the Vedic Hymns of India which were written thousands of years

"Oh Son of Energy," says the *Rig-Veda* (VIII, 84.4), referring to the primal Consciousness-Force that underlies all things and dwells in the human soul, "other flames are only branches of thy stock." At the heart of human consciousness is the same power that "is in the waters and the forests, in things stable and in things that move, even in the stone. . . ." The Vedic rishis believed that through this basic connection in our soul with Agni (the Primal Fire), man could evoke and assume Its power. As you discovered this profound connection, they said, you would begin to grow into the Being from which everything sprang. And as you did, certain manifestations of that Being would begin to appear in your life. Your body, for example, would begin to glow with the First Light. This assumption of inward powers has been glimpsed by El Greco in his pictures of the saints, in Byzantine mosaics shimmering with golden aureoles. The emanation of light from within, in fact, became a convention for many centuries of Western art, codified in *mandorlas*, nimbuses, and glories, in halos of varying sizes and shapes.

Energy was another sign of the transformation, how else to account for the fact that Shivas Irons and Seamus MacDuff seemed rarely to sleep, starting legends about themselves throughout the Kingdom of Fife? Energy, as relativity theory and other formulations of modern physics say, has something to do with structure: this is how I account for the weird perception I had when Shivas hit his shot that day on the thirteenth tee. Something extraordinary happened there, even though a shutter in my brain snapped shut before I could comprehend it. My impression is that it had to do with the structure of the entire hole and its relation to Shivas's body. Whatever it was that he triggered, there can be no doubt that some incredible energy had manifested itself, without the intervention of atom smashers or other machinery.

The transcendence of ordinary gravity is a privilege of the luminous body, say the journal notes. "If I ever breathe with it, I will fly across the ravine," is an enigmatic saying I found the other day. (I am not sure what the "it" refers to.) There are other references to flying in the notes. Shivas was trying to identify with the ball in flight for several months, to incorporate its trajectory into his inner being; he meditated on sea gulls as they skimmed the waves off Burningbush; he played with all sorts of mathematical formulas concerning gravity and its relation to music. Most of all, he was working to bring the inspiration of the inner freedom directly into his body. He called his trances "the trip up" and his work on the body "the trip down," because his cells were slowly being altered by the primal force he brought from his ecstatic states. (There was a similar emphasis in Aurobindo's work, hence his appreciation of the Indian seer.)

In one passage he speculates about his bodily organs being transmuted into luminous centers that would do the job our ordinary parts were secretly aspiring to do. ". . . heart into warming fire, lungs into wings, sexual organs into flaming swords of love. . . ." The body itself was being turned to gold in his joyous alchemy.

Some Notes on True Gravity

When I began work on this book I was tempted to make a glossary of terms from the Irons-MacDuff cosmology, but soon realized that what they were talking about was too complex for straight-line definitions. What you really need to explain "true gravity," for example, are photographs (such as the ones Shivas had in his room), mathematical demonstrations, music, and inspired chapters of poetic philosophy. But this would still be inadequate: a round of golf with Shivas Irons would finally be needed to comprehend it in depth, or a night in Seamus's ravine with the "baffing spoon."

There are other terms in Shivas's private vocabulary which are roughly synonymous with "true gravity." For example: "feeling-force," "heart power," and the Sanskrit philosophical word *chit*, which is sometimes translated as "consciousness-force." Other related terms and phrases appear less frequently in my notes and memory, e.g., Gravity-with-Loving-Eyes, shimmering Body-Field, a MacDuff-Body, a Pythagorean Unit, a PK Field (or Psychokinetic Field), breathing baffing spoon, Galactic-Ecstatic-Hole-in-One, eighteen holes on the "milky fairway" (Shivas saw golfing figures in the starry heavens), and, of course, all the words having to do with the "inner body."

As you can see from these various phrases, true gravity connotes the joining of awareness, delight, and embracing-force. According to Shivas, these are joined at most levels of existence, but our modern world and its dominant philosophies work to separate them. True gravity is, on the one hand, an experiential reality; it is also a force-at-large in the world, the omnipresent "heart power" or "feeling-force" that permeates all things. It is the dynamic aspect of the one Omnipresent Reality, like the *shakti* of the Tantric school of Hindu and Buddhist philosophy. It is this double nature of the idea that makes it so strange to our Western sensibility, for we have learned to internalize the ordinary scientific notion of force as something separate from consciousness and feeling. We may speak of "personal force," "weight of character," and "the gravity of a situation," but these are generally regarded as mere metaphors.

Gravity as described by Sir Isaac Newton is a concept rendered with mathematical equations which are used to achieve certain feats of prediction and control in the physical sphere. "True gravity" connotes force, but it is also a highly aware entering and joining of those "swarming fields" that make up our universe. It would bring our overcontrolling manipulative ways back into harmony with nature on all its levels, animate and inanimate. It is good for man to assume power, but power joined to consciousness (as Pythagoras had intended), power "in the Will of God."

Which leads to another term in the Irons-MacDuff cosmology, namely, "the next manifesting plane." The world is always tending toward some new and fuller being, and true gravity is a way into it. GOD IS WAKING UP was the title of one of his charts. The mentality of ordinary Western science is ultimately a dead end because it is only in touch with part of that emerging reality; it is only a thin slice of God's Will. "How-to" golf books were part of the tendency of the modern mind to rely solely on technique, hence Shivas's primary reliance on true gravity and the inner body in his golf instruction.

True gravity is a universal force, an ethical imperative, and an overwhelming spiritual experience.

True gravity is intentional. That is, once you enter these realms you cannot will any result arbitrarily; you must learn to join your will to the emerging will of God, or to put it another way, you must place yourself in ecological harmony with the awakening world, not the "old-static-dying-world" but to the "next manifesting plane" as it develops in and around you. Modern science is a kind of black magic that tries to lord it over nature from a limited and inadequate consciousness: like all black magic it produces an "occult backlash" that will bring the world down unless it is tempered and eventually subsumed by the kind of consciousness Shivas was aspiring for. God intends the fullness of His being in the world, not just a thin slice, so "He will bring down the modern mind like a fallen species and clear the way for His greater life." That line sent shivers up my back when I read it. Today it seems more prophetic still.

There are endless symptoms of body, mind, and spirit, he said, when we fail to align ourselves with this beckoning power, "a thousand painful warnings that we are off the path." Once we sense its true intention, ". . . there are always signals enough to steer by." He was working on a "Hamartiology of Golf," a science of our misalignment, to help his students learn the way.

It is an adventure of unimaginable consequence and splendor, this discovery of true gravity, and "we quaver in its presence." Modern technology and hedonism, say my Scottish wizard-teachers, are defenses against its ecstasy and light. They are "hazards where the match might end."

Shivas's journals were full of hints about that adventure: one section described "the streamers of energy that guide any golf shot hit in true gravity." The path I visualized spontaneously for my first shots at Burningbush were anticipations, I now think, of a more deliberate process of visualization he was teaching MacIver; I was picking up on his lessons unconsciously. Many golfers do this, perhaps you do; Shivas was developing it into consummate art. Visualization of the ball's path could lead to actual streamers of energy emanating from the golfer to the target, streamers upon which the golf ball traveled. One reason for the quiet surrounding the game is that players and onlookers alike sense that something occult is under way and that they should not interfere. For, as the notes go on, ". . . they [the energy streamers] can be affected by the player or the gallery."

The notes continue, ". . . suddenly I have new powers and apprehensions, invisible arms like Shiva, everyone senses it. Campbell and MacIver half-sensed that I was swinging with extra legs and arms today, inner body wide as a green. Indian artists showed us . . . not until lately our Western artists who, like science, fit into the Western world. . . . imagine God, how does he hold the world since He *is* the world in all its parts? All our scientists could imagine how God *holds* us, practice it in school, in their laboratories, at least ask for guidance. My golf students can do it, some of them. How did God get this earth-ball rolling? True gravity permeates the universe, He holds it all in Shiva's arms."

". . . Newton divided his work into scientific and occult-religious studies, went along with the European split . . . his good crazy side fell asleep. He and his scientific world held their other voices down, amen, establishing themselves as competent men. Their forgotten murmurings: in finding the way for Western science they were ever in touch with the darker fullness but tailored what they sensed to the culture of their time. Science growing up. Competent men. Seamus says he will study Newton's forgotten papers about the history of the world."

"A True Idea has arms to embrace. True Ideas are a body's and a culture's invisible center. Mathematics are invisible . . . [my writing was indecipherable here] . . . streamers of light."

Occult Backlash

The wisdom of my Scottish teacher suggests that there are lines of intention guiding all our human experience. These ever so gentle "psychokinetic" fields become more apparent as we grow sensitive to life's messages and vibrations. There is sometimes a temptation to manipulate them before we know their full intent, but we can only follow their lead and yield to their unfoldment. When we do not, when we try to turn them to our small advantage (which is our large disadvantage), they come back to claim us for their larger purpose. Their occult principles are yet to be understood, the results of tampering with them are still unpredictable. When they are not approached with love and modesty they lash back.

When I willed my shots with all my might on the early holes at Burningbush I damaged my clubs, my ball, my score, my good humor, my relationship with MacIver and Shivas. A part of me—my scheming imagination—was going faster than my other parts, "faster than the Lord," in the words of an older psychology. In his notes Shivas refers to psychic "carom shots" and "occult backlash." These result when power is applied from inadequate love and awareness. They operate in all dimensions of life.

Something happened to me ten or twelve years ago that brought me back to his thoughts on the subject with a jolt. It happened in the most innocent of circumstances, at a base-ball game.

The San Francisco Giants were playing the Los Angeles Dodgers on a cold and windy night, a typical night at Candlestick Park. I had gone to the game with three friends, in high spirits, determined to root our team to victory and prevail over the bitter weather. Jack Sanford, the Giants' best pitcher then, was going against the nearly unbeatable Sandy Koufax. In those days I had developed a set of whammies to use against opposing teams, a whole array of cries and gestures reminiscent of cartoons about voodoo witch doctors. As cheer-leading devices they often worked to perfection: George Leonard and I had once timed a war cry so well that Bob Gibson fell on his posterior while delivering a pitch, something he had never done before according to the next day's *Sporting Green*. (There was no doubt about his fall being provoked by our well-timed cry.) On occasion I would get the people sitting near us to use these gestures too. Usually they wouldn't, out of either embarrassment or common decency. Once, in fact, a man had been so offended by my performance that he had hit me a karate chop on the back of the head. But on this particular night everyone around joined in. I told some of them that the gestures had been developed by shamans in the Amazon basin to kill their enemies, one in particular in which the two middle fingers were doubled back under the thumb with index finger and little finger extended like evil horns toward the target. Various movements of the hands could sharpen the emanation. It was my most successful night as a cheerleader. By the third inning there were perhaps two hundred rooters practicing this form of Amazon witchcraft on Sandy Koufax and the unsuspecting Dodgers. At two points in the game I grew dizzy from the excitement we were causing.

It soon became obvious that our devil's rooting section was having its effect. The Dodgers began to make weirdly inept plays whenever we got a strong wave of gestures and curses going. Several hundred sets of evil horns pointed toward the diamond. But Koufax, being the phenomenal pitcher he was, was hard to budge. Inning after inning went by and there was still no Giants' run. Toward the middle of the game the Dodgers scored once, in spite of our psychic fire-storm. We were going like fury though, working ourselves into shamanistic possession, all two hundred of us out in section 17. I thought I might faint, the energy was running so high.

Then came the first omen. Jack Sanford was forced to retire from the game in the seventh inning, even though he had held the Dodgers to one run, because "something had happened to his arm." Jack Sanford was ineffective for the rest of the season. In fact, he was never any good again.

But our furious gestures and shouts continued. We had by now helped stimulate the entire crowd to frenzy. Into the ninth inning we went, still behind 1 to 0, riding the excitement we had started like the troops of Genghis Khan. We were getting better and better at timing our shots. Then with a crescendo of awful howls and laughter, we finally broke the Dodgers' hold: in the last of the ninth the Giants scored twice and victory was ours. I staggered out of the stadium suspecting that I had almost given myself a heart attack, a psychically depleted witch doctor.

The next morning I opened the *Chronicle Sporting Green* to read about the game. The first thing I saw was a very small article, a little filler, at the bottom of the page. It said "Michael Murphy dies at Giants' game." The article briefly told how one Michael Murphy, aged seventy-two, had died of a heart attack that night at Candlestick Park.

"Psychic carom shots," "occult backlash"; naturally I remembered Shivas's words. Had I murdered poor old Mike Murphy? You might think about it if something similar happens to you.

A Golfer's Zodiac

One starry night during the war Shivas rediscovered the zodiac. The "true zodiac" he called it, since it bore little resemblance to the one your ordinary astrologer refers to. He did not see it *all* that night, in fact there was still a constellation missing when I met him fifteen years later. But during his lonely nighttime vigils he looked up there and eventually put most of it in place.

It had thirteen signs. An extra one was needed, he said, to fit the stars to our new age. As in other spheres science was badly out of touch here. We were passing now from the age of Shank to the age of MacDuff; he had named the governing constellation of the coming age after his teacher. Reading round the heavenly circle, the signs went like this: Burning-bush (where Aries had been), the first sign of spring, then Porky Oliver, Morris and Morris (after Tommy, Jr., and Old Tom), Vardon, Jones, Slice, one unnamed, Hook, Disappearing Hole, Swilcan Burn (after a famous golf hazard), Hogan, MacDuff, and Shank. These were the configurations marking his "milky fairway." He had been born, I believe, on the cusp between Hogan and MacDuff, hence his enormous regard for them both.

The most interesting sign as far as I am concerned was "Disappearing Hole." I thought about it after I saw the movie *2001: A Space Odyssey,* for it was something like the stargate through which the astronaut plunged toward his shattering transformation. Apparently it was the sign Shivas peered into first during his nocturnal meditations, at least when it was in the sky. For all I know, he was looking for it that night on the window ledge. He related it to the mystery of the hole in golf, our willingness—our passion even—to humble ourselves to that tiny opening after ranging "far and wide across the green world." Star-gate and golf hole, two symbols of Man's crossing through, I wish I could make it out on a clear night. But I have trouble with all the signs he showed me, even though he took great pains to point them out.

It was good to hear that we were passing out of the terrible age of Shank. The past centuries, like the dreadful golf shot after which they were named, were the very worst in civilization's troubled history; we could look forward now to an age of "true gravity" and the apotheosis of his teacher's vision. Hook and Slice had been other bad eras in the world's unfoldment. The Age of Jones had been a good one.

If my memory is correct, he said I had several planets in Swilcan Burn—though my birthdate fell on the cusp between Slice and the unnamed sign. He could tell just by looking at me that the planets were there, and this meant that I was always in danger of ending in the final hazard. Though he pronounced upon the fact with great solemnity and conviction, I have never been able to remember what the "final hazard" was.

I asked him why he didn't name that last sign, seeing that he could always change it later if it didn't seem right. But he shook his head decisively and said that every sign made itself known "when he was ready." Naming a constellation "was nae little thing."

Hogan and Fleck in the 1955 U. S. Open

Many players have a natural sense of their inner body and true gravity, according to Shivas. Nearly everyone has had a glimpse or two. Certain players must have had an especially great sense of it, he thought, especially Ben Hogan. In 1955 he had made his one and only trip abroad, to see about living and teaching in America when Seamus died, and during the trip he had seen the U. S. Open Championship at the Lakeside course in San Francisco. He had followed Hogan through all four rounds, until the final tie with the then unknown Jack Fleck. He said that Hogan was centered in the "fourth and sixth chakras," psychic centers near the heart and between the eyes. He emanated a presence that could be felt by any sensitive observer, in fact it had affected the entire gallery. He was part-way into true gravity, it seems.

Shivas had followed him up the clubhouse steps after the final round, to "experience his presence at close range." He had followed Hogan into the dressing room, pushing his way through guards and officials as if he belonged there. He said that Hogan seemed to recollect himself as if by long habit, "almost like a monk." Reporters and some of the other players had gathered to congratulate him on the first-ever fifth U. S. Open title. But Hogan would not accept the congratulations. He had reluctantly held up five fingers for Gene Sarazen and the television cameras out on the eighteenth green because Sarazen had coaxed him into doing it. But now he would not get his hopes up, no—not until victory was certain. The even attitude never wavered, even now in the moment of victory, his composure was so deeply rooted. Then, according to Shivas, an enormous cheer went up outside and Hogan swore, his equanimity broken for one angry phrase. He knew that Fleck, an entirely unknown professional, had tied his score, that a playoff would be necessary. But then, Shivas said—seeing hidden meanings everywhere—Hogan automatically snapped back to "the fourth *chakra*."

A little later he found himself sitting on a couch upstairs with Hogan's wife—synchronicity having led him there—when the champion appeared, composed as ever, gracious and smiling to his friends, as centered as he was on the course.

Fleck started telling the press he had discovered Hogan's "secret." But he wouldn't tell what the secret was. Some speculated that it was the "pronation" Hogan had introduced into his swing to prevent hooks, but Fleck wouldn't say. Even Hogan couldn't figure it out the next day during the play-off. Shivas, however, as you might expect, knew what it was. It was Hogan's own presence, communicated directly to Fleck: the champion's "inner body" had emanated directly to the younger professional, so much so that Jack Fleck won that U. S. Open title. Hogan was a true teacher but an unconscious one, said Shivas, the mental part of his game had come so naturally. Just as Sam Snead was a natural "physical golfer," Hogan was a natural "in the psychic sphere."

As far as I know, Hogan was Shivas's chief golf hero. He had a theory that the great champion was not meant to win a fifth U. S. Open title, because he had to pass "the secret" on. An occult process was working itself out teacher to teacher—Shivas and Jack Fleck were now part of the circulation of the golfing light. I have often wondered if some of it was passed along to me.

I think it is good to remember that the mental states these unusual methods induce are familiar to golfers the world over. And I thought it might reassure you to know that Ben Hogan has been involved in these occult matters all along.

A Hamartiology of Golf

How the Swing Reflects the Soul

Peter McNaughton had remarked that nowhere does a man go so naked as he does before a discerning eye all dressed for golf. Shivas recalled the remark and asked me if I knew the word "hamartia." (I can hear his broad Scots accent shading at times into the King's English he had learned in his few years of formal schooling.)

"It originally meant bein' off the taraget, in archery or some such," he said, "and then it came to mean bein' off the taraget in general in all yer life—it got to mean a flaw in the character. Now I dinna' have to tell ye that the body and the mind are *both* parts o' the character, so when a man swings he tells us all about himself. Ye take MacIver now. He's a marvelous methodic man, but damn he tries so hard, I dinna' like to ask him out to dinner. He's not much fun. He'll niver be a brilliant one, but he's got that bulldog will and 'll probably learn somethin' about true gravity before he's through." I thought of our playing partner and his absolute devotion to every maxim laid down by his teacher. Images of other people I knew began to parade before me.

"Ye see, the basis for a change in the way a person plays the game must be laid in his entire life. Now take this talk about keepin' yer eye on the ball. Everyone talks about it, it's almost the first rool o' the game. But there's so much more to it than simply lookin' there a' that little thing, yer whole life is there, man, in the way ye do it, ye bring yer entire past into every shot. It's all written there in yer bones and muscles and nerves. Ye take a man who aye looks down the fairway before he's e'en turned into the ball, why I'll show ye how he does it in everything else in his life." He stood to demonstrate the movement of overanticipating during a golf swing, jerking his head and shoulders up as his hands came into the ball. He pretended to stumble back against his chair.

"Now take every other kind o' error." He began to list them. "Lunging; now how does the fellow lunge into things generally? Maybe he disna' have energy enough to get any power, or maybe he hasna' learned that power comes with waitin'." He brought his hands down gracefully into the imaginary ball, as if waiting for the club head.

"Or blowin' up, he disna' ken what to do with excess energy or frustration or fidgetin'. God, I've seen players who fidget get back in the bar and keep jumpin' around—*nae center at a'!*

"Or boastin', God, what bores some o' them are. An enormous ratio o' talk to skill. Compulsive talkers, recallin' every feeble accomplishment, ye think they were heroes parring that one hole. They're usually in bad health, I've noticed. Haven't learned to get the feelin' into their bodies, it's so bottled up in their words.

"Ye can tell a lot by listenin' to the sounds a man makes, all the grunts and breathin's around a green or on the tee. Sometimes I close my eyes to heer my pupils better—ye might try it yersel' sometime, just listenin' to yer foursome as if 'twere a piece o' music. Are they makin' good music or bad, just try listenin'." He then described the varieties of sound he was talking about, various grunts, squeaks, and cries of the golfing world—I was amazed at the wealth of example he gave and its obvious accuracy. A golf course does give off an exhalation of sound that tells a lot about its clientele.

"Yes, a man's style o' play and his swing certainly reflect the state of his soul," he resumed his description of golfing hamartia. "Ye take the ones who always underclub. The man who wants to think he's stronger than he is. D' ye ken anybody like that?" He raised one quizzical eyebrow. "Think about the rest of his habits. Is he always short o' the hole?"

"Then there are the ones who are always owerclubbin' and landin' on the next tee. It's an X-ray of the soul, this game o' gowf. I knew a married fellow from London who kept a girl goin' here in town, a real captain's paradise. Well, damned if he didn't keep two score cards for a round, one for the first nine and one for the second. And changed his balls for the second nine too, just like he did in real life. I wonder which scorecard he showed to his wife?

"I could give ye hundreds o' examples. Someone could put an encyclopedia together about it. Tak' the lads who run around the course with nae ability to enjoy the game or their surroundin's oor their friends. Some o' them have heart attacks on the uphill holes. One man owns a couple of restaurants in Dundee, big promoter, out o' breath all the time. I won't play with him any mair. And he certainly has nae time for me. I've learned these hurryin' types can hardly wait to take their putts, especially the short ones. That's the time to make 'em a bet—ye can win a pile knowin' that." He paused, shaking his head. "There is a right speed for playin' the game, a right speed. And for living all the rest o' the day.

"Then there's the man who can't stand prosperity. One or two good holes and he's beginnin' to imagine the worst. Ah take 'im home and get 'im to act out his catastrophic expectations and practice some meditation.

"If I were to paint a picture o' the gowfin' world, it'd look like the Hell o' Hieronymus Bosch. Ye ken that's what he was really paintin'."

"Bosch!" I exclaimed.

"Bosch," he said, gravely nodding his head. "Toorns out he was a gowfer too, played a game called *kolven*. Ye can see it when ye look at the picture o' Hell in his 'Garden of Earthly Delights.' "

There was not a trace of doubt in his voice that Bosch had

played the game and drawn inspiration from it. I have a copy of the famous triptych and look at it from time to time to comprehend his words more fully. The panel on Hell does seem to reflect the agonies I have seen on many a golf course.

The Rules of the Game

The thought of Shivas Irons playing golf sometimes strikes me as an utter absurdity. Can you imagine other philosophers and mystics out on the course? Saint Francis, for example, laboring over a 3-foot putt, or Plato slinging a bag of clubs over his shoulder and striding happily down the first fairway. How a spirit so mad for the deeper mysteries could devote a life to this frustrating sport is a question that still distracts me. I sometimes grow vague at dinner parties when I think about it. And when I think of his passion for keeping score and following the rules I am sometimes led to ponder the final absurdity. The thought of him counting all eleven strokes I took during that hole at Burningbush still bogles my mind. "Michael, I think 'twas eliven." I will never forget those words and the image of faithful MacIver writing it down as if the number would be engraved on some Rosetta stone.

How a spirit so large would confine itself to things so small is the kind of paradox that gives birth to philosophy. Life in its tormenting wisdom must have given it to me for a reason, I tell myself, perhaps as a koan, delivered by some guardian spirit at the proper moment. It is significant perhaps that I met him on my way to India in search of the Infinite Mind.

Thinking about this paradox, I realize how fascinated he was with the mystery of the hole in golf. "Do ye know any other game where ye roam so far and wide to reach such a tiny goal?" he asked us all that night. "Why do we submit to such a thing?" He was speaking for himself, not us, for no one else at the McNaughtons' that night had so given themselves to the game. But the question is still with me. Why we choose such an anally frustrating outcome for such a wide-ranging game is a puzzler; Hogan for one has sometimes said that putting should be abandoned, that it ruins an otherwise exciting game. Does it reflect some profound constipation in the Scottish and Anglo-Saxon character? One has to wonder. But more basic to golf's paradoxical nature than putting and the spectacle of that tiny hole at the end of all our endeavors is the utter devotion to rules and exact scorekeeping that all true golf lovers maintain. "To cheat is to end the game," say the journal notes.

What is the reason for this scrupulous honesty, I ask myself, having doctored my own scores for years in endlessly ingenious ways. Does it spring from the bottomless need to test and prove oneself which is so apparent in all man's quixotic endeavors on mountain tops and outer space—or in ravines with baffing spoons? That certainly has something to do with it. Is it a way to prove yourself good to the parent within, to the court of law society has planted in your brain, is it a way to alleviate the guilt we feel just being alive? Yes, we nod in agreement, that could well be part of the reason for such scrupulous trials. But these motives, certain as they may be, are not enough to explain my teacher's horror at golfing dishonesty and his total acceptance of the game's confining structure.

Pondering the question, I have come to think that a person grows in his regard for the rules as he improves his game. The best players come to love golf so much they hate to see it violated in any way. In that they are like anyone who is consummately skilled, be it in the arts, science, or loving their wives. A scientist loves the procedures that give birth to discovery, an artist loves the skills that go into his art, the good man loves the moral dimensions in every act. So Shivas loved the rules and skills of golf. It was a mark of his commitment.

And yet all these explanations, compelling as they may be, do not completely satisfy me. Underlying all the other reasons for his devotion to the game's restraints, I think, is the fact that golf is simultaneously a doorway and a prison, the very mirror of life in that regard. It provides us a jail to be broken out of, but a jail we can clearly see rather than the often invisible one that holds us in our daily life. Shivas always seemed subdued to me when he was indoors, but it was then that his spirit soared in conversation or ecstatic trance to spaces far beyond those enclosed by the room he was in. So it was, I think, with his surrender to the game; its constraints dramatized the situation in which he found himself in this bounded world, it was a place from which to effect a marvelous transcendence.

But there is more to it than that, more than escape is involved. I think of his words about "the trip down," that movement of his soul from the mystic heights "bringing fairy dust into the world." On the practice tee and on the links he was opening himself to subtle energy transferals between the inner and the outer worlds, entering by slow steps into the "luminous body." This amazing alchemy, practiced so faithfully for so many years, was leading to a transformation of his very substance, he said, not a mere escape from this painful earth. Golf was a place for the transformation to unfold.

You might know that the beginnings of this mighty work would occur in such unlikely circumstances, this being such an unlikely world.

On Keeping Score

"Keeping score is a koan, a reminder of the dualities."

"Our relation to paradox is a barometer of our enlightenment."

These two sayings from Shivas's journal give the essence of his attitude toward keeping score. He was scrupulous about counting every stroke, but he was just as insistent that his pupils let the awareness of it recede to the "back of their minds." He sometimes instituted a "second scoring system" for pupils who were having a difficult time with this. He would give them points for certain attitudes and behaviors, to reinforce the changes he wanted. This reconstruction of the scoring system was always done with the player's consent, he said, "to preserve his dignity." For example, MacIver was getting points that day for his unflappability; it "was the strength he had to build on." You will remember how inexorable that golfing tortoise was as he showed me the way to a fine equanimity; well, he was being rewarded for that by Shivas's unforgettable smile. Experts in behavior modification and operant conditioning would have been proud of my obscure Scottish professional's grasp of their science.

You might try making your own "second scoring system," giving yourself points for a calm and centered attitude or for sweetness in the rough. Perhaps a smile after a double bogey or a gracious remark to your playing partner when he beats you would be worth a point. If you know an expert in "behavior mod," as it is called in the trade, you might bring him in.

It is important to remember that your handicap is not an exact mirror of your soul. It is your relation to your score that really counts. A gracious acceptance of your place on the golfing ladder might even help the world in unexpected ways. Many of Shivas's pupils were British men of affairs, he said, secretly swallowing their pride as the Empire dwindled, and since the reconciliation of infinite hopes and limited means was at the heart of all his instruction, he conjectured that he had helped Britain through its painful transition to a humbler, more humane role in the world.

The Pleasures of Practice

Sonny Liston in reminiscing about Shivas said that our departed friend often drew a small crowd of caddies and club members around him when he practiced. "There was somethin' hypnotic about the way he hit those shots," he said. "Worked himself into some kind o' trance out there. Sometimes he would hit balls all day, tradin' stories wi' the boys and givin' 'em tips from time to time. A special provision was made for 'im to use the extra fairway, the members liked his practicin' so much." Seven years after Shivas left Burningbush, Liston was still thinking about how he looked on that practice tee, about the look on his face.

I can imagine what an experience it must have been to watch the subtle transformations that were taking place. That magnificent swing being refined even further, a piece of earth being slowly enveloped in the subtle stuff of the inner worlds. Though most of his onlookers had no clear idea about what he was doing, they must have sensed the majesty and artistry involved. It would have been a meditation just to have been near him. Liston said that one of the special pleasures in watching him came when he put on a demonstration of "ball steering" in which he would hit deliberate fades, draws, and other special shots. I wonder how many in his audience realized what experiments were being conducted then!

He loved to practice as much as he loved to play. That night in the ravine he told me there was little difference any more between the two activities, "the pleasures of practice had become so profound."

If I had stayed in Burningbush I might have learned more about "the second art" of golf, as one professional I know has called it. But I have salvaged some wisdom on the subject from Shivas's notes and some discoveries of my own. These I present below, with the hope that I will fulfill at least some of the Boswellian task destiny has given me.

We play the game at many levels. Every golfer knows this, once he begins to examine himself from the point of view of the inner body. To some extent we all go in and out of those extraordinary states I experienced that day in 1956. But how deeply we do depends upon us. We must deliberately cultivate the attitudes and faculties that support such experience; we must practice these things as Shivas did. We need not limit our practice to a golf course, however; we can develop the "inner eye," for example, "at home on a rainy day."

Golf is first a game of seeing and feeling. It can teach you stillness of mind and a sensitivity to the textures of wind and green. The best instructional books have always said this. Golf is also a game to teach you about the messages from within, about the subtle voices of the body-mind. And once you understand them you can more clearly see your "hamartia," the ways in which your approach to the game reflects your entire life. As Peter McNaughton said, "Nowhere does a man go so naked . . ."

Beyond such openings to the immediate worlds inside and around us lie "true gravity" and those "images that become irresistible paths." I have devoted a section to them below. They are powers that bring the most inspired golf and give us hints of what we may eventually be.

And finally, underlying and interfusing all these is the one presence and delight, the "Higher Self" and its transforming power that "we are looking for through all the others."

Golf is "a game for taking off the seven veils," said Shivas.

"Never think yer first glimpse the last, for there are aye another six." When I told him about my experience on the thirteenth hole he spread his arms as if he were opening a curtain and shook his hands to say the World-to-be-Seen was shuddering with glory. "Ye only saw tha' much," he added, holding his thumb and forefinger an inch apart to suggest how small was the rent in the veil I had seen through.

Keeping Your Inner Eye on the Ball

Imagine a golf ball. Make the image of it as vivid as you can. When anything intrudes upon the image, let it pass. If the golf ball disappears, imagine it again. If it wavers, make it steady. Doing this you can practice keeping your eye on the ball. You can practice in your room on a rainy day.

If you cannot keep something out of your mind, some hive of your soul-skin, when you are practicing this inner sight, get to know the intrusion. What does it show you about yourself and your situation in the world? Exploring the invader can be helpful to your game.

These are two paragraphs from his notes. They describe a technique for developing concentration and stillness in the disorderly mind. As soon as I saw the words I stopped to visualize a golf ball: I could see the word "Titleist" printed on it. Then the image turned to a little spot of dancing light, and I felt myself rising gently upward. I told him what I was experiencing. He said that any image might take on one's latent mood, the feeling that wanted to come to the surface. In my case, it was the effect of all our "galavanting" that caused my inner eye to dance, for my organism wanted to turn toward the restful light of the "higher self." He said to follow its impulse for a moment, then recreate the image of the ball and try again. It was a surprisingly restful and pleasurable experience.

Lately, I have begun to practice the method with regularity and find that it has a definite carry-over onto the course. When I practice seeing the club and ball as one, following his first instruction to me, I sometimes experience the kind of intrusions he described. Letting them pass in meditation has helped me let them pass on the golf course when I am addressing the ball. My awareness of them, of the way they sneak in when I least suspect them, has grown more acute. It is easier now to see the ball and the golf course as one unbroken field, "Aye ane fiedle afore ye e'er swung."

Blending

Aikido is a Japanese art of self-defense. Robert Nadeau is a teacher of this subtle art who lives and works near San Francisco, and in recent months he has helped me bring the principles of it into my golf game. Although he has never played the game himself, he has an amazing grasp of its problems and opportunities. "Blending" for example is a way to join yourself with your opponent's strength in order to divert his attack; when used correctly it turns a fight to a dance. He has shown me how to "blend" my strength with club, ball, and terrain on the course, in the same way I join with attackers during an Aikido class. It works surprisingly well. Perhaps the most impressive thing about it has been the way in which it has helped me adapt my swing to every situation. My repertoire of shots has grown because I have learned to go with the dynamics of air, wind, and slope, using the energies of the situation to help rather than hinder me. Shivas had said to find my "original swing" in every situation, claiming that he never swung the same way twice. It was hard for me to see the deviations in his flawless strokes, but he claimed they were there. The "blending" principle has brought that subtle adaptation of method to situation into play for me.

An old letter Shivas had never mailed to some student or friend was among the papers I photographed in his apartment. It is a small essay on blending.

"Can you see the brook that golfers fear and not fearing

– and will be in harmony
with you as the dog to the
flocker, as the crop to the
farmer. Walking the course you can
learn many things from your
new found friends, the tree
rooted deeply to the ground, firm,
the upper branches swaying as
natural as the breeze flowing
through it. So reflect on your
stance as you pass the tree.
Can you do this, can you see
the brook that golfers fear and
not fearing but feeling can
you put that flowing water
into your swing. The green
grass restful to body, soothing
to soul. Is it so many paces
that you put on it or is it
a period of rest and calmness
between you and the ly of
your ball. Be the tree rooted,
be the brook flowing, be
the calmness of the green,

but feeling can you put that flowing water into your swing," what a beautiful way to say it. I think of his swing as I read these words and realize what grace and what strength there is in such blending.

There may also be certain unexpected results from a discipline like this. Shivas for example had learned the art of dowsing while meditating on his union with nature. Burning-bush Links had begun to dry out after the war and for the first time in its history had required a watering system. During all the centuries of play upon it, rain and mist had preserved its subtle textures, but now with the postwar golfing boom players from every continent were wearing its resilient fairways down. There was violent disagreement in the club over the measures required to keep the course green. Then, at the very height of the crisis, Shivas discovered water at several places on the links themselves. The knowledge had come to him, he said, "through the handle of his five iron": he felt his golfing stick twitch whenever he approached a potential well. He prevailed upon one of his rich admirers to finance a drilling at one of the sites he had found, and, sure enough, water was there. The discovery settled the club dispute, for now there was plenty of water for little expense. The members had given him a plaque for his help. He told me that the first twitch of his five iron came when he was practicing the kind of blending I have just described.

Becoming One Sense Organ

There is a psychological phenomenon in which one sense modality is stimulated when an impression is received by another, as for example, when the feel of a well-hit golf shot starts a melody in your inner ear. Poets have written about seeing bird songs or hearing flowers blossom. Last season at the San Francisco Forty-Niners-Atlanta Falcon football game I heard Wagner's "Ride of the Valkyries" as the Forty-Niners rallied to win in the fourth quarter. Religious literature is full of similar reports, like the Italian saint's description of colored lights when he heard songs of worship in the village church. For Shivas Irons this mingling of the senses was one of the pleasures of practice.

In his journals he recommends that you try to cross your senses deliberately, as when he says to see *and* feel "the club and ball as one unbroken field" or to "hear the breaking waves when you hit a bag of practice balls."

Bobby Jones often heard a melody through a round of golf and followed its rhythm when he swung; Shivas recommends something like that when he says to "hear the inner sounds and rhythms and let them enter your play." Sometimes such synesthesias carry an informative message, sometimes they are simply there to be enjoyed. I will never forget that experience on the thirteenth hole at Burningbush, when all my senses joined. For a moment then I was one sense organ: the world was a single field of music, joy, and light.

Some of Shivas's exercises remind me of the centering techniques in Paul Reps's little book *Zen Flesh, Zen Bones.* These are taken from Tantric disciplines which used the natural impulses as pathways to enlightenment: behind each impulse there is a higher possibility, the Tantric philosophers said. For example, the journal notes suggest that "when the fear of failure steals over you imagine the bottom of your mind dropping out as you fall into the Void." The fear of failure may be a premonition of the liberated state.

Or, "sometimes a path appears in your mind's eye for the ball to follow: let it blend with your body." That, of course, is what happened to me on the very first hole I played with him. But my greed for par blotted the image out.

The Value of Negative Thoughts

One night I was ruminating about my adventure in Burningbush, counting the shots I took during our round of golf (only 34 of them on the back nine), recalling the remarks that were made around the McNaughtons' dinner table, visualizing Shivas's room with its butcher-paper charts and arcane books. As the impressions of that crowded day mingled in my memory a clear gestalt began to emerge, taking for its central image the chart on his wall entitled, GOD IS WAKING UP. Remembering it and the photographs and his memorable sayings, one central theme emerged: that everything in life is potentially something more, that every person, every object, every event is waiting for transformation. Or to put it like he sometimes did, "from your deeper mind everything has an aspiring face."

Now, for most of us, this is a difficult truth. Perhaps because we are not in touch with our "deeper mind," most of what we are confronted with on a given day has no special meaning at all. At best it looks like a battlefield between God and the Devil, with the Devil winning at least half of the time; more often it seems like one damned thing after another. The profoundly optimistic vision underlying the phrase "God Is Waking Up" seems to have little basis in fact, at least the facts as we perceive them. Ah, but there is the catch! If we are honest, we have to say "the facts as we perceive them," thus leaving open the possibility that they may be seen *another* way.

For him everything was full of messages. Nowhere was this so apparent, he said, as it was in golf. And nothing is more informative during a round of golf than the so-called negative thought.

There are two attitudes you can take to these, he maintained; one of detachment and disidentification or one of listening to the perverse voice to see what it may tell you. Many thoughts that arise as you are playing must be brushed aside: there are ways to do that, ways to strengthen "the inner eye." But certain ones that will *not* be brushed aside must be understood, otherwise they will haunt you until your golf game and your disposition suffer. Some years ago a thought like that began to torment me.

It began entering my mind when I was putting. It said, "You are not lined up straight, line up again." It occurred to me over and over that the angle of my putter face was slightly askew. I would stand back and try to line up at a better angle, but still the thought was there. It kept coming back through the entire round. When I played again, a week or so later, the same voice began again— "You are not lined up straight, line up again," it said, creeping into my mind on every green and eventually as I was addressing the longer shots. I adjusted and readjusted my stance, waggled the club endlessly, the greens and fairways began to look like cubistic drawings as I surveyed them for a better line. Then it slowly dawned upon me that the thought was coming from some deep recess of my mind, that it was one of those thoughts Shivas had said I should listen to. What did it have to say? I let it run through my mind after that second round, let it play itself out, "You are not lined up straight, line up again." Slowly, inexorably, the meaning came clear: indeed I was not lined up straight, in my work, with my friends, during most of the day. I was sleeping in my office then, rising to telephone calls concerning the Institute, doing business over every meal. I was as disorganized as I had ever been and my unconscious knew it, and now it was speaking to me clearly on the golf course. I needed to realign my life, it said, not just my putt or my drive. Only during a round of golf did I slow down enough for the word to get through.

As I put my days in better working order, with the help of a "Time Analyst" named Alan Lakein and some invaluable help from my friends, the obsession left me out on the course. Golf had been my therapy.

It is hard to protect yourself from a nagging impulse during a four-hour round of golf—your mind is rarely so exposed. When such a voice begins to speak, it is wise to let it deliver its entire message.

There are also happy obsessions. The other day I could not repress a smile each time I addressed the ball. The higher self was smiling down, telling me to swing just the way I wanted to. I shot a tremendous round and grinned like a kid all the way back to the clubhouse.

"All life is yoga," said the Indian seer Aurobindo. "All golf is yoga" might have been a line from the journals of Shivas Irons. Yoga means joining our deepest self. We may be tending that way, he said, but we need to give the process our deliberate assent to get the ball rolling well. We have to go with all our negative and positive urges, wisely following or guiding them in the Godward direction they want to go.

". . . ugly images are like peyote buttons, they turn into vision." Shivas Irons, *curandero*, with his bag of peyote balls, teaching the unsuspecting people of Burningbush the fundaments of visionary golf!

"The psyche never quits. The messages are always coming. Life is taking us on a mighty journey, if we will only go."

"Driving downwind, follow the shot to infinity." Have you had that sense of it, just for a fleeting second?

Or— "Driving directly into the wind, become the calm solid center." That's a tougher one, but haven't you felt it once or twice? (Among professionals there is an expression "turning the wind around" which refers to the possibility of hitting a long ball into any wind.)

"Walking downhill, become weightless. Walking uphill, slowly become your strength."

There are endless ways to turn an impulse into an exercise. Each of us is given the opportunity every day.

"Imagine the golf ball as a hole in space." The memory of that sentence sprang out at me one day at Lincoln Park, a course on a cliff looking down on the entrance to San Francisco Bay. Fog was rising in slow spires around the red towers of the Golden Gate Bridge and rows of pine and cypress trees lined the fairways like monastery walls.

Through half a round I remembered times when things were giving way: when I was a child locked in a closet shouting for help and the question came "Who am I?" then feeling that I would vanish— "Who am I?" the question was overwhelming me and I repeated my name to hold me there; or fighting a psychic duel with a superior in the Army who was out to get me, thinking I would disappear then; and making love with my head growing dizzy and boundaries falling; these and other images passing through as I walked the fairways between those green sentinel walls and listened to the foghorns in the Golden Gate and watched the ships come into the sunlit sea. Remembering Shivas's words, I saw the ball become a porthole into empty space, with memories of all those fearful glimpses of the Void sorting themselves out for my inner eye. Emptiness within emptiness, protected all around by green grass, good friends, and the blue Pacific hundreds of feet below.

It turned to a crystalline day. And that night another sentence of his pulled the curtains back. "Imagine the stars beneath your feet," I could hear his voice in the ravine as we waited for Seamus.

On Breakthroughs

The greatest breakthrough, Shivas said, was taking your own sweet time to reach the goal, be it par or enlightenment, working all the while with the attitude that any sudden opening comes like Grace, that it is given when the time is ripe and not before. ("The greatest breakthrough is taking forever," was the way he put it.) That does not mean you need practice or aspire any less. On the contrary, it means you can work at your game even more because you will work at it in a way you enjoy.

"Ohne Hast, ohne Rast," he quoted Goethe, "without haste, without rest, be ye fulfilling your God-given hest." I can see him now sauntering down that final fairway with a deep and

glowing look, not overly excited by his 320-yard drive to the green, for some new adventure was coming soon.

Against Our Ever Getting Better

But now, before we go any further, let me raise a glass with Shivas as I did that night in Burningbush, and say with all my golfing brothers and sisters, "Fuck our ever getting better."

"Ye'll niver improve yersel', my boy," he roared with glass held high. "How could golf e'er make ye a better person? Just look a' all the ones ye know."

"But that's all you've been talking about," I protested, "our getting better."

"Aw, niver, niver this shitten-gemme," he said with that manly smile. "Just look at Evan thair." He pointed toward the drunken figure across the room, playing an invisible violin. "Do ye ca' tha' self-improvement now! Tae enjoy yersel', tha's the thing," he said, "and beware the quicksands o' perfection." Then he raised his glass of whisky up and shouted, "I say fuck oor e'er gettin' bitter!"

I bring this up because the application of these many exercises in personal growth can lead to a piety and fanaticism he never intended. Crazy for God my teacher may have been, but a gray and lonely one he never was.

As he often said, trying too hard is the surest way to ruin your game.

The Game Is Meant for Walkin'

"Ye're makin' a great mistake if ye think the gemme is meant for the shots," he said with his penetrating look as we sat before Liston's fire in the Burningbush clubhouse. "The gemme is meant for walkin'." He pointed to one of the great Victorian portraits that hung on the wall above us, "And that man there showed us how." The portrait showed an erect, fierce-looking man with a Vandyke beard staring straight ahead like an Indian scout. I imagined him striding down the fairway with that very look, stalking the heathen natives with his shoulders back. He had been a colonel in Queen Victoria's Indian regiments. Shivas could see that I was puzzled.

"Ye see," he continued, "tha' man got to be famous heer for his walkin'. 'Twas said tha' if ye played along wi' him for very long ye'd get the spirit o' it yersel' and learn to enjoy each and every step. 'Twas said tha' he sometimes forgot his shots, the walkin' got to be so good. Had to be reminded by his caddy to hit the ball." He motioned Liston over from the bar and asked him if he had ever known the man in the picture. The jovial barman looked up at the imposing figure and shook his head. He could not remember him; he had come to Burningbush after the old man had died. Shivas went on with his story. "I played with him once when he was ninety yeers old. 'Twas an experience I'll niver firget. He was still walkin' and enjoyin' wi' his clear blue eyes, said he learned to walk like tha' from an Indian yogi back in the 1880s. Went on a walk wi' the yogi into the Himalayas and niver got ower it. Said that a walk like that could be as good for the soul as a day in church, and that was somethin' comin' from him since he was a good Presbyterian. I notice ye hardly pay attention to the walkin' part."

I admitted that I didn't. The next shot usually preoccupied me. Indeed I still have trouble remembering his advice.

"Well, that's too bad," he said as he looked into the fire, "not many people do. 'Tis a shame, 'tis a rotten shame, for if ye can enjoy the walkin', ye can probably enjoy the other times in yer life when ye're *in between*. And that's most o' the time; wouldn't ye say?"

Visualizing the Ball's Flight:
How Images Become Irresistible Paths

When Shivas told me the story of his conversion he said that his obsession with epilepsy and dismemberment was a "prophetic image," a "psychic body" as real as any body we can see. It had emerged from the unconscious, he said, with a power to transform. Such visitations may come to us all at crucial moments of change in our lives. But we do not have to wait passively for their coming; we can deliberately cultivate them to support a discipline, or help us hit a golf shot.

I have already discussed the value of negative thoughts like the one that was telling me to straighten out my life: by letting that voice speak to me clearly, I learned a valuable lesson. Shivas did the same kind of thing when the image of epilepsy exploded in his inner eye and he fell into the ecstatic state that changed his life forever. In both cases the "prophetic image" had to be recognized and accepted before it could do its work.

But images that we *deliberately* foster without any obsessive inward leading can also have a transforming power. Meditation on a golf ball may help you get a sense of life's wholeness, for a sphere is an archetype of perfection (Parmenides thought Being Itself was a globe); or contemplating its diminutive size, the fact that it weighs just an ounce and a half, may lead you to see that in some sense this world is light as a feather, that all life is, as Shivas said, "an earthy nothingness." In his journal he had written that "meditation is an art we need—we lose our way so easily in this teeming world. . . . with eyes open and with eyes closed, on prophetic images and the consequences of our acts, until true gravity takes us up." Along with our inward turnings he would have us stay open to all around us, including the disarray our acts so often bring. On a golf course he was insistent that we follow the flight of every shot to the very end— no matter how bad that shot may be. That is the only way to learn from our mistakes and our successes. It is the only way our unconscious mind can absorb the information it is given; and "we blind ourselves by turning away too soon." (What lessons there for the rest of our life!)

But the most basic kind of meditation during a round of golf is the visualization of our shot as we stand up to the ball.

An image in our mind can become an irresistible path—it happened to me at Burningbush on the very first hole and later in that round after my greed for par had subsided. Many players will tell you they often see their shot before they make it. Many well-known teachers recommend visualization as one of the game's most important secrets.

Shivas said that as you practiced this skill of the inner eye, you would develop a capacity which put forth "streamers of heart power for the ball to fly on." At times it has seemed that my mental picture has changed the direction of a shot after it has left the ground, as if I were steering it from afar.

But these living and tangible images cannot be forced by brute will. Sometimes they form themselves as if guided by a superior intelligence. For example, I saw the path of my ball on the first hole at Burningbush going down the right side of the fairway with a draw, not down the middle as I might have seen it, and so it flew—to the best part of the fairway for an approach to the green. Some invisible radar of my inner body had superseded my ordinary judgment. This has happened to me many times. Through experience you can learn when to stay with your original image and when to yield to the new one.

Whether or not these "streamers" are real remains a question you will have to decide for yourself. They are certainly real in *some* sense. Reality as we ordinarily perceive it is much less rigid than our recent past has taught us.

Shivas Irons' History of the Western World

In the journal notes there was a triple list that went like this:

Inventions	What Could Soon Be	What Will Eventually Be
Airplanes and Automobiles	Ravine Jumps	Full Flight in True Gravity
Telephones	Urgent Telepathic Messages	The Divine Silence
Radio	Sensitive Listening	Universal Clairvoyance and Psychic Mobility
Heating Systems	The Tumo of Tibetan Golfers	The Primal Fire in the Living Soul
Clothes	A Lovely Body	The Power of Emanation and Invisibility
Food Industries	Little Need for Food	Constant Energy Interchange
Newspapers	Intuition of the World's State	Omniscience and Self-Existent Delight
Orchestras	Melodies in the Inner Ear	The Music of the Spheres
Hospitals and Medicine	Bodily Harmony	The Luminous Body
Atom Smashers	Baffing Spoons	Knowledge of the Cracks in Space-Time
Rocket Ships	Astral Flight	Materialization in Another Place
X-Rays	Body Reading	Universal Transparency
Hydrogen Bombs	Psychokinetic Blasts	Explosions of Ecstasy

GOLF IN THE KINGDOM

182

His handwriting wavered across the page, as if he had been drunk when he wrote it. Maybe he had conceived the list after a rousing night at the McNaughtons'. But whatever the case may be in that regard, it was an example of the kind of thinking he and Seamus were likely to indulge in. For they believed that the direction of Western scientific mastery was only one of several our human race could have taken. In a way, their thinking anticipated that of Herman Kahn and others who like to think about alternative futures. Their main idea about our recent history was that as we accumulate extraordinary inventions to do our work and even some of our play, we gradually lose our latent powers of world-mastery and enjoyment. Behind every invention stands a withered human faculty. One of the reasons Western society took this direction, they maintained, was that the shamans of the West directed themselves to magic and manipulative power, becoming the scientists of our day instead of the luminous sages they had often been in former times. Isaac Newton, for example, obviously suppressed his interest in religion and the occult in his later years; Kepler was a mystic to the end, but focused on those aspects of things the new mania for physical discovery was celebrating; Swedenborg gave full play to his shaman-side but was seen as an oddity. Right down to Robert Oppenheimer the greatest scientific minds put aside their dark intuitions about possibilities of inward knowing—or had them put aside by others. All the inner powers were seen "out there."

When such inquiry began in the West, with Pythagoras and other pre-Socratic Greek philosophers, there was a first sense of the inner-outer joining: Pythagoras had enjoined his followers to grow in soul as they grew in world-knowledge, to "ken the world from within." The Greek sage talked about the music of the spheres, meaning that realm of sound the mystics hear, the *Omkar*, the Original Voice, the birth-song of all the world. Hearing that music you comprehend the octaves and rhythms interfusing all the rest. But to hear it you must surrender, giving yourself over to its pulse of ecstatic love. There is no seeing the world as an object then, for you are joined to the ravishing heart of things, with a memory of God burned in your brain.

But our science only sees the edge of that primary fire, hears only the faint reflection of the primary sound, and so its grasp on the world is mixed and muddling, its outcome still in doubt. "It is a poor lover to this trembling world," said Shivas. "Our hearts cry for deliverance and will not be mocked by half-knowledge, however grand."

"The world is a passage back to God, that is the only reason it is here."

"Hardest matter is consciousness going back, breaking all the bonds as it has for a billion years." The story of our science is a story of mutilated vision, say the Burningbush seers. On one of the charts there was a list of "men who knew," a mind-bogling list running from Pythagoras and Plotinus to Einstein and Henry Ford. It was the crooked golden river of true knowledge running fitfully through our Western centuries. Its title was DANGEROUS CONNECTIONS. The impression you got when you looked at it for a while was that the wires joining our world to God were hopelessly tangled. But at the very bottom there was one hopeful sentence, written in tiny letters: "There is still time," it said.

The Crooked Golden River

A List of People Who Knew

The following list of people is taken from the journal notes. It bore the title I have used above. I do not know what it means exactly, though it seems fairly certain that most of the people listed believed in reincarnation and the evolution of the soul. The list resembles the one on his chart entitled DANGEROUS CONNECTIONS.

"Consider: Lao-tzu, Henry Ford, Mark Twain, Plato, Heraclitus, Pythagoras, Thomas Edison, Thomas Wolfe, Aurobindo, Charles Lindbergh, Goethe, Wordsworth, Coleridge, Salvador Dali, Henry Miller, John Woolman, James Joyce, Yeats, AE, George Bernard Shaw, Oscar Wilde, Gen. George Patton, Hermann Hesse, Jack London, Rilke, Klee, Kandinsky, Steiner, Mondrian, Sibelius, Lloyd George, Gustav Mahler, Emerson, Thoreau, Ramakrishna, Walt Whitman, Saint Teresa, Joan of Arc, Saint John of the Cross, Boehme, Eckhart, Tolstoi, Dostoevski, Herman Melville, Richard Grossman, Richard Wagner, Robert Browning, Tennyson, Schopenhauer, Nietzsche, Oliver Wendell Holmes, Beethoven, Balzac, Victor Hugo, Thomas Carlyle, Heinrich Heine, Bishop Isadore Balls, Bronson Alcott, Shelley, Hegel, Fichte, Schiller, Schelling, Schlegel, William Blake, Immanuel Kant, Spinoza, Benjamin Franklin (The body of B. F., Printer, Like the Cover of an Old Book, Its Contents Torn Out and Stripped of its Lettering and Gilding, Lies Here Food for Worms, But the Work shall not be Lost, For it Will as He Believed Appear Once More In a New and

More Elegant Edition Revised and Corrected By the Author), Voltaire, Dante, Swedenborg, Leibnitz, Thomas Vaughan, Thomas Traherne, Henry Moore, Giordano Bruno, Paracelsus, Hippolyta, Proclus, Porphyry, Iamblichus, the late Roman emperor Julian, Ammonius Saccas, Origen, Plotinus, Plutarch, Ovid, Lucretius, the Buddha, the authors of the Upanishads and the Vedic Hymns and the *Bhagavad Gita*, the Druid priests, American Indian tribes, Siberians, Patagonians, Peruvians, Eskimos, Aruntas, Tahitians, Okinawans, the people of Madagascar, Zulus, Bantus, Ibos, Yorubas, Freemasons, Theosophists, William Judge, Socrates, Madame Blavatsky, Mahatma Gandhi, Jalal Rumi, Sufis and World-Poles, Friedrich Schleiermacher, the Essenes, Mozart, Arthur Conan Doyle, Somerset Maugham, Jesus of Nazareth, Vivekananda, Amenhotep IV, Bodhidharma, Milarepa, Marpa, Ramana Maharshi, Averroës, Hermes Trismegistus, Domenikos Theotokopoulos, Houston McOstrich, Alexander the Great, Calanus the Gymnosophist, Picasso, Maimonides, Typhus Magee, Ben Hogan, Richard and Hugh of Saint Victor, Sherlock Holmes. But we forget and we forget. Down through the ages we turn away from light!"

The Higher Self

"The Higher Self," which is neither higher nor lower than anything else, was a term of ultimate reference for Shivas. He used it in the manner of the perennial philosophy, to indicate that reality which has been seen and described by mystics and philosophers for thousands of years. It is the *Atman*, the *Brahman*, the *Jiji mu-ge* of Buddhist Philosophy, the Godhead or Fertile Void. To invoke its presence, he sometimes quoted passages from the *Upanishads*, such as these translations I copied from his notes.

One unmoving that is swifter than Mind, That the Gods reach not, for It progresses ever in front. That, standing, passes beyond others as they run . . .

That moves and That moves not; That is far and the same is near; That is within all this and That also is outside all this.

But he who sees everywhere the Self in all existences and all existences in the Self, shrinks not thereafter from anything.

And this from the *Rig Veda*, the first citation in Sri Aurobindo's *Life Divine*.

She follows to the goal of those that are passing on beyond, she is the first in the eternal succession of the dawns that are coming—Usha widens bringing out that which lives, awakening someone who was dead. . . . What is her scope when she harmonises with the dawns that shone out before and those that now must shine? She desires the ancient mornings and fulfills their light; projecting forwards her illumination she enters into communion with the rest that are to come.

Relativity and the Fertile Void

Shivas was explaining a line in his journal which I had asked him about. It read, "Golf is an exercise in perspective: every shot requires that you estimate where you are in relation to the target. Enough golf springs you free."

"Free from what?" I asked.

"From yer attachment to any point. Some part o' yer mind begins to sense the relativity o' things and the fertile void." The "fertile void" had come upon him, as I have said, when he was nineteen and playing golf through those northern summer evenings. He believed that somehow, by some unconscious process, the constant exercise of the sense of perspective required in golf sends a message through to our higher centers that you can never be in the same place twice in relation to the target. Every moment on the course, like every moment in life, is to some degree unique and unrepeatable. And from that realization the mind begins to grope, perhaps unconsciously, for some secure place that never requires a final standpoint in this always shifting world. The mystics have described such a place, or such a no-place, and have called it by names like the Godhead or the Brahman or the Fertile Void.

Such exercises in perspective are a good thing, he said, "for nothing seems satisfying to us short of that. And this Western world is finally getting the message—just before the game is over." Apparently our entire Western culture is learning the

188

lesson in its journey round the globe. It has been forced to change its perspectives so many times.

Not that he was against a sense of duty and doing our work in the world. Far from it. But "part of our human duty is *to bring Being into higher definition* and not save it any more for the Sabbath or the Judgement Day."

Postponement can get to be a disease.

Universal Transparency and a
Solid Place to Swing From

Tradition has it that contemplative masters, be they yogis, shamans, Sufis, or Neo-Platonic seers, can read another's mind and heart. As cosmic consciousness develops, the hidden side of things becomes transparent. The deepest Self begins to show itself to itself (*Atman* in Sanskrit is a reflexive pronoun). The world becomes the Net of Jewels in which each jewel reflects every other. We need not be mystics to have glimpsed this possibility, however: how many times have you read your friend or lover in a moment of clarity or high careless embrace? You know you cannot gossip about a friend without his somehow knowing.

Shivas confided to me during our final conversation that a few of his pupils had become so open to hidden influences while developing their game under his tutelage that he had to teach them how to close off and shield themselves again. "Ye must have a solid place to swing from, before ye open up so wide," he said, "otherwise ye'll be swept away." He made a big distinction between "Mind-at-Large," which included all the invisible worlds around you, and the Higher Self. He said that it was wise to know the latter before you opened to the former, otherwise you could drown in the sea of forces and impressions forever enveloping you and pressing to enter. That is the reason for discipline in the contemplative life and for monastery walls to protect you. That is the reason nearly every great teacher has stressed the importance of a healthy body. The old explorers knew what dangers lay in wait once the familiar psychic boundaries had been crossed. Nowadays this wisdom is often forgotten. Many a seeker, opened up and made bold perhaps by LSD or some other plunge to the inner depths, has mistaken each new experience for enlightenment, each hot pleasure for the kiss of God. Moral entropy is often mistaken for nirvana.

"Ye need a solid place to swing from," a place above and beyond these teeming worlds. " 'Tis a thin line," he said, " 'tween the madness of God and the madness of the Devil."

Humans Have Two Sides

or

Dualism Is All Right

Shivas was left-handed. I did not consider it an important
fact until I heard about the recent discoveries concerning the
roles of the left and right sides of the brain in mediating
various altered states of consciousness. It now appears that
mystical states and other inspirations involve a special activa-
tion of the right hemisphere, perhaps because the left one is
too preoccupied with the functions of speech. The right
hemisphere is connected in its motor functions, however, to
the left side of the body. So, to take a quick, long leap, all the
legends about lefties being just a little daffier than the rest of
us may have some basis in this differential action of the
brain's two sides: lefties perhaps are more open to the impulses and firings of the mystical half, and inspiration always
has an element of surprise and things you would not predict.
(What implications for the alignments of politics!) Shivas
also had that disconcerting left eye, focused ever so slightly
to the center; I remembered when I heard about this recent
research that it had not been crossed when he came back
from his awesome trance that morning. Was that eye always
watching for messages from the inspired side, content to look
straight ahead only after it had its fill? Then I remembered
that he had originally played the game from the left, changing over to conventional right-handedness about the time he
reached puberty. (In that he was like Ben Hogan, who had
also begun from the deviant side.) Did his muscle memory
and golfing unconscious carry all that left-handed perspective

still? Was his intuition informed by all those thousands of left-handed shots? (I remembered that Hogan had shifted from a tendency to hook to a deliberate fade when he reached the peak of his game: was he still wrestling with the left-hander in his soul?) I don't have the answers to all these questions, but some things he said make more sense now in the light of these recent findings. For example, he commented on the game's asymmetry and said that it reflected our essentially human imbalance. "The Fall was a fall from the Right," I seem to remember him saying with that look of sly and sinister portent he was wont to give me whenever he was making an especially significant remark. "That the game is played from one side always reminds us that we're still lop-sided and incomplete." Indeed, humans are the only animals on the earth whose brain function is asymmetrical: no other creature must wrestle with the angels and demons of speech and elaborate conceptualization.* Mystics have always said that words can be a barrier to enlightenment. The Upanishad says that liberation lies beyond "the golden lid" of thought. Men have long felt this separation from their fuller being as a fall and have told the tragic story in their myths. Golf reflects the Fall, said Shivas, "the fall from the Right."

But the game also shows us a way out. Some of the psychologists studying these things maintain that all contemplative disciplines are "strategies for getting around the left lobe of the brain." They point to the fact that certain gestures used in meditation, the mudras of Hindu-Buddhist practice for example, play on the left-right aspects of life (the "left-hand

---

* Such wisdom of the body is there in our language: the word sinister derives from the Latin word for left, and remember that the left side in action connects to the inspired right brain; the word right has meanings to stretch across an entire page of a modern dictionary, all of them pointing to the structuring and proper aligning of life's many aspects in the linear mode of civilized order, e.g., mathematics' right angles, civil and legal rights, what is fitting and desirable, genuine and authentic, straight or perpendicular, ethical and sound, at the right time and right place, etc. Our language is deeply informed by our ever-present two-sidedness.

path," a "left-handed blessing"), that certain ritual proceedings make a big thing out of which way the devotee turns or faces, that the dances of the dervishes turn to the left and then the right. Shivas had said that each golf shot involves a small turn of the body to the left as one comes into the ball (if one plays right-handed) and that this subtle turn has something to do with inspiration. Once again his largely untutored genius had sensed an important connection—with dervish dancing no less! For in those Sufi whirlings one can open to Mind-at-Large if one turns with attention centered on the heart or inner eye. That is not unlike the centered turnings of golf, or so at least our philosopher of the links suspected.*

The left-right dimension of the game is also involved in the relationship between voluntary and involuntary controls. All skill involves a certain measure of spontaneity and unconscious functioning: no one can create beauty, be it in a work of art or on a golfing links, unless he has both disciplined control and the ability to let go to the sudden glimmer. In following the leadings of the "inner eye" while visualizing a shot or sensing what club to use one must draw upon all the unconscious stores of learning one possesses. We all know that. We all know that we could never plan each shot exactly without that immediate tacit knowing which comes from immersion in the game over years and decades. Every shot has a conscious component and an unconscious one, a voluntary control and one that is involuntary. To know how to strike the balance is the very essence of golfing skill. The greatest champions, while having grooved swings to envy, come up with surprises that astound us. They pull off the unbelievable shot in the midst of contingencies too numerous to calculate ever. How else to account for Shivas's hole-in-one that night on the thirteenth hole? Or, if modesty allows me, my own shot there that afternoon? One of the beauties of

---

* Of course, the golf swing is an incomplete dervish turn. Obviously this aspect of the game needs more research.

sport is the inspirational heart-stopping move that reminds us of possibilities yet unguessed.

Inspiration and spontaneity must be given their place if any game is to be mastered and enjoyed. But, alas, there is a tendency in many golfers to repress all wellings from within and all the delicate leadings in their devotion to some steely program of the will.

Not only must one learn how to strike a fine balance between the disciplined and the inspired, but one must know when to quit, said Shivas, "and even when to collapse. . . . There is a time for lettin' the bottom drop out," he said, "for forgettin' yer score entirely, for forgettin' yer mental tricks and devices, for just swingin' any ol' way ye please." If we don't do this from time to time, he said, "our game goes kaflooey" anyway. Indeed if you were an absolute perfectionist on the links, if you could not stand to see a single bad score on your handicap card, you would never have come as far as you have with the game. When you allow yourself to fail on the links, the golfing unconscious learns the lessons which such unwindings teach. Perhaps the left and right sides of your brain are readjusting their marriage, perhaps some tangle in the nerveways of the autonomic system is shaking itself out; whatever the specifics of this "positive disintegration," renewal may be on the way. "One of the joys of self-knowledge," say the journal notes, "is the increasing sense one gets of the soul's wise rhythms."

The process is trying to work all the time, even when we are unaware or refusing assent. Then collapse may force itself upon us. Gambling, he said, is one unconscious way of tempting collapse, a "positive disintegration" that doesn't renew. It is a way of calling in the inexorable powers of chance to ape the experience of being overwhelmed. To lose a bundle brings secret relief, I know from my own experience and that of certain relatives who carry. the propensity. (My brother, for example, had already lost the family's grand piano when he was fourteen: I will never forget the astonishment on my parents' faces when a Bekins van moved up to the house and the movers announced they were taking it away.) But gambling is not the only way of escaping through the back door of our psyche, there are endless ways of downward transcendence and dark dissolution. Murder, conspiracy, drugs, the orgy: we have only to read the daily newspaper to see such collapse all around us. And there will be more. I do not think I am stretching a point when I say that all of these are ways to effect the release our psyche periodically needs. There are various kinds of transcendence. Some lead to God and others to the Reign of Hell on earth.

But golf is still our business. For on the links there are ways to give way gracefully, to collapse with grace under that pressure from within. With Shivas I did it and shot a 34 to boot. It can be done even while shooting your loveliest golf, especially if you follow true gravity's subtle leading.

"The Fall had its place and always will," might be a good line from the notes to end this section with, "for everything human has two sides."

Even Dualism is all right in his plural theology.

His Ideal

A few of my friends have asked me to explain in some clear and fundamental way just what it was that Shivas Irons was finally hoping for. What is his *ideal?* they sometimes ask. George Leonard, with whom I share leadings like these more than I do with any other living person, has asked me time and again to characterize the goal my golfing teacher held up for us. It has been a difficult question to answer, for there is a certain amorphous and undefinable quality to his teaching. When I come to putting it down on paper, I have a feeling that I am forcing his vision; that no matter how I state the goal he would set, there is something left over that words will always leave out. So having warned you that this is the case, I will now proceed to lay out some first thoughts about the High Ideal of Shivas Irons (with all credit to Seamus Mac-Duff) concerning the Way We Should and Someday Will Be in This Fallen but All-Promising World of Ours.

"The world's a koan," he assured me just before I left, "a koan from the very beginnin' and gettin' worse day by day." A koan, as you probably know, is the paradox-invoking question Zen masters give their students to open up their minds; a famous one asks, "Before your parents were, what is your original face?" It is intended to reveal the Buddha-Mind underlying all the seeming paradoxes of our ordinary existence. Shivas believed that life presented us with koans every day, that if we approached them with an open, ready spirit the whole world turned to Zen training and successive revelation, that if we turned away they reappeared like Hydra heads. There is no escaping the paradoxes life presents us with; we can only choose whether to embrace or escape them.

The sense of paradox is growing more intense as human awareness develops and people crowd together around the globe; that is what he was referring to when he said it was "getting worse day by day."

"So many Gods and moralities now, so many logics and geometries, so many ways to see the world, so many ideas about running a family," his notes lament, "the Twentieth Century itself is a *koan.*"

The twentieth century as *koan!* The thought has obsessed me ever since I read it there, in Burningbush, fifteen years ago. It has set me thinking about the way our knowledge and art have turned the world into a roller coaster and a prism: how anthropology has revealed a thousand ethical codes and endless variety of sexual practice, how the study of families all over the earth has given support to a thousand deviant experiments in the U.S.A.; how Freud has shown us as much deviance and urge to break free in the psyche of the solid American citizen; how while this undermining of taboo is taking place, the intellect's certainties are giving way —to endless systems of logic and geometry, to playful models of the nature of matter, to the strong solvent of linguistic and philosophic analysis, to theologies that God is dead; how, while our moral and philosophical certitudes are dissolving, the artist breaks our perceptions down—into cubes, circles, and squares, into points of light and toilet seats, into the very vibrations of our retinal nerves, showing us once and for all that distance is nowhere fundamentally proper, that there is no *right* place to stand any more (for a cup is a cup in its middle or its edge, from a foot away or underneath a garbage can—a cup and the moon can look the same once you look more closely), even sound fragments as melody and harmony go into microscopes and magnifications of sense and come out like Stockhausen; how, while our morals and beliefs and perceptions proliferate, the commonalities of a given day take on a melting surrealistic uncertainty and our trusted friends and lovers are filled with sudden new intensities and challenge us in the middle of the night (the newspapers are full of it, so are the movies and the books and conspiracies all around); everywhere our certainties, our ideals and beliefs and most familiar perceptions are ripped away like our very own flesh, as if our souls were being skinned alive. Yes, there is no denying it, the twentieth century is a koan, pressing us to paradox until we cry uncle. When I hear *Hare Krishna* on the streets of the city I hear my own impulse to surrender forever to the One beyond all these incertitudes. At times I imagine our entire nation breaking into such a cry, going back to Jesus or Buddha or Muhammad—or finding a center in violence or oblivion self-induced. For there is no escaping the growing pressure. The koan is upon us with a vise-like grip and it is squeezing harder every day.

"A chameleon on a tartan plaid, that was the way it felt," said Shivas, describing his own early state. He was turning seventeen ways at once until the spirit broke through with an image of epilepsy and his body dismembered. His painful yet joyous reconstruction of character began that summer in Burningbush after the koan had finally exploded—I have already told you the story as I know it. Through primitive group therapy with members of the club, through years of study, meditation, golf in true gravity, and countless good deeds to his friends he had come to the glowing ever-adventurous state I found him in. He was well beyond despair and fragmentation by then.

I open a consideration of his "ideal" with these reflections because I think they point to the state and attitude he would bring us to. For, as the journal says, "there is always a Body beyond our little body, arms to hold us, new eyes to see, a larger being waiting here closer than our physical skin." There is a deeper self that thrives on the craziness of this teeming world, that "sees every breakdown as an opening to the original crazy shimmering dance, to the eternal explosion of the sun in the night, to the floating worlds all around."

His ideal would have us know this Body and this Dance, would have us live in it while playing golf and singing ballads and talking to our friends; yes, and even while we are trying to pass it on to others.

A Postscript:
The Dance of Shiva

In South India, not far from Madras and Pondicherry, lies the Temple of Chidambaram, known to many as the original home of Natarajan, the dancing Shiva. The temple there is like a canyon-fort, with great walls enclosing smaller temples of varying shapes and sizes, all of them passageways to different parts of Shiva's body. One without windows is black as night and houses the God's *akashic*, or etheric *Lingam*: in its dark recess Hindu women cover the black and tapering stone with melted butter, stroking it slowly until its shape is worn smooth. Another houses the great bell, which is struck to announce disappearances and renewals of the God. Around the compound there is a corridor with a thousand pillars, and near its southern gate there stands the pavilion with the famous figure. When the pavilion doors are open you can see the King of Dancers from any point—dancing on a pyramid of gods and demons in a prefiguration of His dance to bring the world down and end the cosmic cycle.

I visited the temple while I was at the Aurobindo ashram near the end of my journey around the world, passing through the outer gates in the wake of an American sadhu with orange robes and a devastating smile who said it had come to him in a dream that he should bring me here. The moment I crossed the threshold I felt the presence of the God. Not the excitement of anticipation merely or the strangeness of the place, but the overwhelming presence of

Shiva, as tangible as the drum rolls and basso chanting one heard in the distance.

We walked in silence around the temple compound, past the candelit cave which housed the *Lingam* (women chanting as they rubbed its sides, being entered by its etheric substance for ether is the medium of sound, and this is its *Lingam*), past the temple bell, and smaller passages that showed you Shiva's many faces, down the thousand-pillared corridor to the edge of a crowd pressing round the dancing figure. Its flying arms and legs were perfect poise. It was glowing as if lit from within.

Ceremonies were beginning and the Brahmin priests of Tamilnad were seated around the statue in ascending banks, chanting Sanskrit mantras with a ringing power and hard, insistent beat—a beat to open nerveways of the densest mind, no one, no part to be left behind in this culminating act of worship. Then the sliding doors slammed shut. The God had disappeared.

The crowd pressed closer, and for a moment I was lost in the wavering space. Then the doors slid back. The God was covered high with flowers, a mountain of petals and blossoms where the statue had been, and the Sanskrit chant began to swell, hint of frenzy ordered by the mantra-beat, every white-robed figure bobbing now with growing passion.

They began to stroke the flowers away, unveil the Natarajan, the King of Dancers. Then the doors slammed shut.

Then opened to show a pile of rice, Shiva in the food of India.

Seven times the God was covered and revealed—Natarajan at the center of all the elements, dancing even in glowing stone. Each time the doors swung open the great bell rang and those hundreds in the pressing crowd saw Shiva at the heart of things.

In flowers, rice, bread, and stone; the Dance. His arms and legs the tendrils of exploding worlds, his eyes eternal stillness, his smile the ecstasy. The Dance was at the heart of every atom.

A Bibliography for the Reconstructed Golfer

Assagioli, Roberto. *Psychosynthesis: A Manual of Principles and Techniques*. New York: The Viking Press, Compass Books, 1971.

Aurobindo, Sri. *The Life Divine*. New York: India Library Society, 1949.

———. *The Synthesis of Yoga*. Pondicherry: Sri Aurobindo Ashram Press, 1955.

Satprem. *Sri Aurobindo or The Adventure of Consciousness*. New York: India Library Society, 1964.

Carlyle, Thomas. *Sartor Resartus, The Life and Opinions of Herr Teufelsdröckh*. New York: The Odyssey Press, 1937.

Gurney, Edmund. *Phantasms of the Living*. Gainesville, Fla: Scholars' Facsimiles & Reprints. (In two volumes). 1886 & 1970.

Kirkaldy, Andra. *My Fifty Years of Golf: Memories*. London: T. Fisher Unwin Ltd., 1921.

Leonard, George B. *The Transformation*. Los Angeles: Jeremy P. Tarcher. 1986.

Myers, Frederic. *Human Personality and Its Survival of Bodily Death*. New York: Longmans, Green & Co. (In two volumes). 1903 & 1954.

MacDuff, Seamus. *The Logarithms of the Just, Being First Notes for a Physics of the Spirit*. (Unpublished manuscript.)

About the Author

Michael Murphy, a native Californian, founded the Esalen Institute (with Richard Price) in 1962. A graduate of Stanford University, he did further work there in philosophy and spent a year and a half at the Sri Aurobindo Ashram in Pondicherry, India. He is also the author of *Jacob Atabet* and *An End to Ordinary History*.

Enrollment Form

☐ *Yes!* I WANT TO BE A *Privileged Woman*.

Enclosed is one *PAGES & PRIVILEGES*™ Proof of
Purchase from any Harlequin or Silhouette book currently for
sale in stores (Proofs of Purchase are found on the back pages
of books) and the store cash register receipt. Please enroll me
in *PAGES & PRIVILEGES*™. Send my Welcome Kit and FREE
Gifts -- and activate my FREE benefits -- immediately.

More great gifts and benefits to come.

NAME (please print)

ADDRESS   APT. NO

CITY   STATE   ZIP/POSTAL CODE

 PROOF OF PURCHASE

**NO CLUB!
NO COMMITMENT!**
*Just one purchase brings
you great Free Gifts and
Benefits!*

Please allow 6-8 weeks for delivery. Quantities are limited. We reserve the right to
substitute items. Enroll before October 31, 1995 and receive one full year of benefits.

Name of store where this book was purchased_____

Date of purchase_____

Type of store:

☐ Bookstore   ☐ Supermarket   ☐ Drugstore
☐ Dept. or discount store (e.g. K-Mart or Walmart)
☐ Other (specify)_____

Which Harlequin or Silhouette series do you usually read?

Complete and mail with one Proof of Purchase and store receipt to:

U.S.: *PAGES & PRIVILEGES*™, P.O. Box 1960, Danbury, CT 06813-1960

Canada: *PAGES & PRIVILEGES*™, 49-6A The Donway West, P.O. 813,
North York, ON M3C 2E8

SIM-PP6B

▶ DETACH HERE AND MAIL TODAY! ▶

How to solve the riddle of Jessica Gavornée?

A frown furrowed Mitch's brow. The more he thought he was on the verge of understanding her, the more he realized he didn't know her at all.

The riddle had to do with a woman who had no record of existence until she was sixteen. A woman with no known parents, friends or past.

It had to do with a woman who looked like winter yet smelled like summer. A woman who kissed with lush innocence…then retaliated with bitter anger.

Mitch whistled softly to himself.

He had only a week left. But, if need be, he would use every last one of those seven days to unlock the mysterious Ice Angel.

He had to be right. He was Mitch Guiness.

And he could make magic….

Dear Reader,

This is another spectacular month here at Silhouette Intimate Moments. You'll realize that the moment you pick up our Intimate Moments Extra title. *Her Secret, His Child,* by Paula Detmer Riggs, is exactly the sort of tour de force you've come to expect from this award-winning writer. It's far more than the story of a child whose father has never known of her existence. It's the story of a night long ago that changed the courses of three lives, leading to hard lessons about responsibility and blame, and—ultimately— to the sort of love that knows no bounds, no limitations, and will last a lifetime.

Three miniseries are on tap this month, as well. Alicia Scott's *Hiding Jessica* is the latest entrant in "The Guiness Gang," as well as a Romantic Traditions title featuring the popular story line in which the hero and heroine have to go into hiding together—where of course they find love! Merline Lovelace continues "Code Name: Danger" with *Undercover Man,* a sizzling tale proving that appearances can indeed be deceiving. Beverly Barton begins "The Protectors" with *Defending His Own,* in which the deeds of the past come back to haunt the present in unpredictable—and irresistibly romantic—ways.

In addition, Sally Tyler Hayes returns with *Our Child?* Next year look for this book's exciting sequel. Finally, welcome our Premiere author, Suzanne Sanders, with *One Forgotten Night.*

Sincerely,

Leslie Wainger
Senior Editor and Editorial Coordinator

Please address questions and book requests to:
Silhouette Reader Service
U.S.: 3010 Walden Ave., P.O. Box 1325, Buffalo, NY 14269
Canadian: P.O. Box 609, Fort Erie, Ont. L2A 5X3

Mev

HIDING JESSICA

ALICIA SCOTT

Published by Silhouette Books

America's Publisher of Contemporary Romance

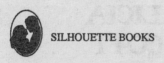

SILHOUETTE BOOKS

ISBN 0-373-07668-1

HIDING JESSICA

Copyright © 1995 by Lisa Baumgartner

This edition published by arrangement with Harlequin Books S.A.

Printed in U.S.A.

Books by Alicia Scott

Silhouette Intimate Moments

Walking After Midnight #466
Shadow's Flame #546
Waking Nightmare #586
*At the Midnight Hour #658
*Hiding Jessica #668

*The Guiness Gang

ALICIA SCOTT

is thrilled that her dream of being published has finally come true. Born in Hawaii but a resident of the Boston area, she recently graduated from college and is now working for a management consulting firm.

She has a deep appreciation for different peoples and cultures. And while reading and writing romances is one of her favorite hobbies, she also enjoys traveling and just talking to people—so much so that in her junior year of high school she entered a contest for impromptu speaking and won eighth in the nation!

Lucky enough to have journeyed to exotic locales such as Venezuela, Ecuador and Mexico, she intends to use them all in future books. Alicia brings her natural enthusiasm for life to her stories, and believes that the power of love can conquer *anything* as long as one's faith is strong enough.

To my oldest brother, Rob—
because you have always been my hero.

Special Acknowledgments:
Special thanks to Bill Lorenz for providing gun expertise and to Andrew Atkins for enabling Mitch to do magic.

Prologue

First he had to show ID, then walk through a metal detector. And then, just to prove they were learning from past mistakes, they took his gun from him anyway as he was not officially on duty.

If Mitchell Guiness hadn't known of the incidents that led to such precautions, he would have been impressed. Instead, he simply felt tense by the time he discreetly tucked himself into the courtroom and slid into his customary aisle seat in the back row. As usual, no one spared a glance for him. Everyone's eyes were still focused on the witness stand.

After a quick look, he couldn't blame them; the Ice Angel looked particularly lovely today. Blond hair back in an elegant French twist, sparing but effective use of makeup to highlight her arctic blue eyes. Not to mention a white designer suit that had cost someone more than a few pennies.

He wondered if that someone had been Les, and found himself shaking his head.

In his business, it paid to be cautious and cynical. But even he wasn't sure what to make of Jessica Gavornée, high-fashion model, Mafia mistress and now, federal witness.

In the beginning, everyone had thought she would play the victim: the naive woman who had fallen unwittingly in love, only realizing too late what kind of man Les Capruccio really was. The attorney general had even set her up for the role, wanting to increase the jury's sympathy for her. Yet yesterday, she'd sidestepped every question with blunt evasion.

"Miss Gavornée, could you please describe to the court your relationship with Mr. Capruccio?"

"I was his companion."

"Companion? Don't you mean mistress?"

"You could call it that."

"Then I think we'll call it that, Miss Gavornée. Exactly how long have you know the defendant?"

"Two years."

"And you lived with him for part of this time?"

"Yes."

"How long, Miss Gavornée?"

"Seven months."

"You know him well?"

Slight hesitation—Mitch still wondered about the hesitation. *"As well as I suppose you ever know someone."*

"Fine. If you could tell the court, Miss Gavornée, what kind of man was Mr. Capruccio?"

"Kind of man?"

"Yes. Was he a patient man, a tender man? Tolerant, perhaps?"

"He could be."

"Come on, Miss Gavornée. Isn't it true that he often flew into violent rages? That in fact, he used to beat you? People have already mentioned seeing the bruises."

"Perhaps I'm just clumsy, Mr. Douglass. And I don't see how you can hold Les accountable for that."

And so it had gone on for the afternoon. Miss Gavornée playing the role of the most reluctant prosecution's witness. Mitch could understand that if she was trying to protect her lover. But in fact, Jessica Gavornée was the one who had walked into the attorney general's office nearly five months ago and handed them Les Capruccio on a silver platter.

Hell, they'd been after the man since 1989, when the federal government had begun its crackdown on the various connections between the mob and the teamster's union. With the teamsters' help, most of the cleanup had gone pretty quickly. By 1991, the teamsters had even elected in their first "outsider" president, showing that the metal cuffs of corruption had finally been broken. But even then the attorney general's office hadn't been able to get its hands on Les Capruccio. They only had common knowledge of his crimes, not the hard evidence.

Until the day Jessica Gavornée had walked in with a stack of developed photographs, offering them Les Capruccio in return for enrolling her in the Witness Protection Program. Now they were about to nail the man on various charges of extortion, fraud and money laundering.

All because of this one woman who now sat on the stand without a flicker of emotion running across her face: no guilt, no remorse, no love, no agony—nothing.

He didn't like the coldness. Dispassion led to trouble.

As independent specialist to the Witness Protection Program, Mitch knew a lot about trouble. As of two weeks ago, Jessica Gavornée had become his assignment. He'd laughed at this one. The woman had only been one of the top models for the past eight years. And now they were simply supposed to make her disappear?

They'd already had two attempts on her life, one killing an agent.

And the more he researched the subject, the more Mitch wondered what was really going on. In his five years as part of the federal Witness Protection Program, he'd helped hide a lot of people. Some of them he'd trusted only as far as he could spit; they were low-down scums themselves who had only gotten off by nailing bigger fish. Others—the scared accountants, nervous fathers, terrified wives—he could sympathize with. All of them he at least understood. They had motives, and their motives were clearly outlined, recognizable.

Except for Jessica Gavornée.

What type of woman turned in her lover without any kind of remorse? What kind of woman gave up a life of international superstardom to nail a Mafia boss and didn't appear anxious or scared?

Eight years as one of the hottest models in the business, and still no one knew anything about her. According to the federal files, Jessica Gavornée was the elaborated version of Jessica Govern, but Jessica Govern didn't even exist before the age of sixteen.

Whatever her real name and identity had once been, Jessica Gavornée hid it very well. Certainly his own diggings hadn't been able to uncover anything, and he was willing to bet serious money that the defense attorney had invested quite a bit of time and resources trying to uncover her past, as well.

But, of course, they'd found nothing.

All Mitch had was a million photographs of a woman who had been jetting around the world since she was a teenager. According to the press she did not go out to wild parties. She was religious about exercise and privacy. She didn't own any pets and she didn't have close friends. Her only public appearances were generally at high-profile events where she would be expected to appear. She always had an escort, but she was never linked with anyone.

Had she hated Capruccio that much? If she had, it certainly didn't show on her face when she looked at the man. Did she love him? There was no indication of that, either.

Whatever went on behind those cool blue eyes didn't seem to be known by anyone but herself.

The prosecutor held up the first photographs of Les's records, and Mitch leaned forward to hear.

"If you would tell the court, Miss Gavornée, how did you come by prosecution exhibits G and H?"

"I removed them from Les's safe in his study."

"You removed these documents, detailing a list of artificial pension funds, from Mr. Capruccio's own safe?"

"Yes."

"How did you do that, Miss Gavornée?"

"I waited one night until he was asleep. Then I went downstairs to the study and removed the documents from his safe. I took pictures of the documents, replaced the originals and returned upstairs."

"And these pictures were the ones you submitted to the attorney general's office on August 14?"

"Yes."

"Thank you, Miss Gavornée. That will be all. You may step down."

Jessica Gavornée rose gracefully, murmurs filtering through the audience. She truly was stunning, all that cool blond beauty combined with full lips and thickly lashed eyes. She looked hot enough to burn a man, and cold enough not to care.

Mitch watched her step down carefully, and noted she did not look at Capruccio at all. She simply walked to her seat behind the prosecutor's bench. Hell, not even her hands were shaking.

As she sat down, the two FBI agents in attendance took their posts. Capruccio nudged the man sitting next to him, and nodded toward the two agents. Mitch didn't have to hear the words to feel his blood start to boil.

One agent was already dead, and the trial wasn't even over. There was not a good enough hell for a man like Capruccio.

He forced himself to take a deep breath. One more week, maybe two, and the trial would end. Then Mitch would take over things, meeting Jessica Gavornée in person at a remote cabin in New Hampshire. They'd wanted to move her to South Carolina to get her farther away from the area, but she'd refused. For now, they were humoring her. It was part of Mitch's job to make her realize the full implications of her new life. He had two weeks to orient her, to begin helping her select and build a new identity, then learn how to live with it. And he needed to understand her, needed to get under her skin to learn how to motivate her, how to change her.

But if there was one thing he had learned in the last few weeks of research, it was that no one had ever gotten under Jessica Gavornée's skin.

That would have to change, now, Mitch resolved. He had two weeks with the woman. Two weeks to turn her inside out and learn every nook and cranny of her existence. Then he would tear her down, and the rebuilding would begin. She would start her life over as somebody else.

That was the decision she had made.

And really, it was the only hope she had of surviving.

He made a few notes on his pad, and since her testimony was now complete, he slid back out of the room, retrieving his gun at the door.

Mitch returned three weeks later to hear the verdict, sitting once more in the back. As the judge took his seat, Mitch spared a glance over at the Ice Angel, looking composed and regal in pale blue.

The judge read off the verdicts. Guilty. Guilty. Guilty.

Cameras flashed, people erupting into a flood of clapping and clamoring. Jessica simply sat there, her hands folded on her lap, her eyes focused on the wall. Then Les Capruccio stood and turned right toward her.

Through the din of the confusion, he grinned at her, slowly raising one arm. He cocked his hand into an imaginary gun and pointing right at her head, he pulled the trigger.

Even as Mitch was leaping to his feet, the nearby FBI agents began pulling Jessica from the room. Stumbling slightly, she followed.

And this time, Mitch noted, her hands *were* shaking.

Chapter 1

The cold January morning dawned the same as any other. If she'd been allowed to look out the window, she was sure she would see a bright winter sun sparkling over soft white fields and trees.

Of course she wasn't allowed to look out the windows.

In the past five months, she'd learned plenty of things she was no longer allowed to do. Such as stand in front of windows. Answer doors. Be alone.

Her life now was carefully controlled and monitored by a bunch of men in stiff blue suits who continuously said, "It's for your own good, Miss Gavornée. Trust us on this one."

After the first few weeks, she'd stopped trying to argue with them. And she stopped trying to make them understand that Jessica Gavornée simply didn't trust anyone.

Once, in the very beginning of all this, she'd honestly believed it would work out. The Witness Protection Program would take care of her, and she would start over again as someone else. If anything, she was looking forward to the clean break. After all these years, the modeling was too draining for her and at twenty-four, she was past her peak in the profession; she wouldn't have minded a new life at all.

But those thoughts were before the late-fall afternoon when a sniper had taken a shot at her while the blue-suited men had been packing her into one of their dark sedans. That was before she'd seen a man abruptly arch, then drop into the bright gold leaves, taking the bullet meant for her. That was before the mid-December snow, and the Connecticut "room service" waiter had pulled out a semiautomatic with the entrée, only to be shot apart by four different blue suits.

That was before she'd learned how to watch men die and know it was all because of her.

Of course, she reminded herself now as she finished the last of her packing, it wasn't really because of her. It was because of Les Capruccio and the type of man he was. It was because of greed and corruption and violence. The only thing she had to do with any of this current mayhem was her arctic blond looks.

Les had taken one look at her, and decided he'd had to own her. What she hated to remember was the fact that in the end, he had. She'd underestimated him from the very start, thinking he'd accept no as all other men had accepted no. Then he'd appeared in her dressing room one day with the answer to the riddle she thought no one would ever solve.

Suddenly she had no choice in the matter.

Her hands tightened instinctively on the blouse she was holding and it took effort to make them relax. She hated Les Capruccio. Hated him in ways and depths no one would ever know. She hated his silk suits, his smirking face, his bloated hands. She hated the way he looked at her, and she *abhorred* the way he'd touched her.

One late night, six months ago, she'd realized that she just couldn't take it anymore. The pent-up anger was beyond even her control. If he touched her one more time, she would kill him. *And the blood would flow again, staining white hands, soaking into the carpet. The silent scream would sound, echoing remorselessly down shuttered corri-*

dors. And the man would fall, down, down onto the gold-patterned carpet—

The plan had come to her.

She didn't try to explain these things to the attorney general, and she certainly didn't explain them to the jury or to the blue-suited men. Her reasons were her own, and she was careful to keep them that way. All they ever needed to know was the evidence that put Les Capruccio away once and for all. The rest, she would guard as she had guarded it for the past eight years.

She was the Ice Angel, and she knew it.

Even now, nothing showed on her face as she folded the last of her blouses and carefully tucked it into the suitcase, smoothing the surface once, then closing the lid. As usual, two of the blue suits were playing cards at the small table. They were careful to try and give her an illusion of privacy, but it was only an illusion. She hadn't been left alone in over five months. In the beginning, she'd tried to learn their names and had gone along with the awkward attempts at small talk. It seemed a minor concession to make if they were all more comfortable.

But after Darold had been shot, she'd stopped learning their names. Now she considered their presence purely a business arrangement. She'd made her choice and that was why she was here. They had made their choices and that was why they were here.

She owed them nothing; they owed her nothing. She clung to that one thought more than she would ever admit.

"I'm ready to go now," she said quietly, breaking the silence. The two men looked up, their eyes resting on her briefly, then abruptly skittering away. She was used to it by now. Most men usually gawked the first time they saw her. Afterward, they tried so hard not to stare, they could barely look at her at all. These days, she found her face to be just one more of the grim ironies of life. Eight years ago, her blond looks had been her salvation. Now, they would probably put her in the grave.

How did you hide a cover girl? The blue suits really didn't know, though they were careful not to tell her that. But she already knew the fact well enough. She'd heard the bullets that had fired the point home. And she'd seen their impact.

Now the two men stood, nodding at each other in the kind of silent conversation they learned at FBI school. One came wordlessly forward and took her small leather suitcase and matching garment bag. Knowing the drill by now, Jessica stepped forward until she was between the two men. The front man—was his name Bill? Bob? she didn't remember and she didn't care—rapped on the inside of the door three times. After a minute, an answering rap came back, signaling the car was ready and all was clear. Only then did the man unlock and open the door. In a controlled rush, they moved her to the sedan.

Minutes later, they were pulling away, a small three-vehicle convoy. Keeping to her side of the plush leather seats, and protected now by the dark-tinted, bulletproof glass, Jessica could finally gaze out at the white-blanketed hills of Western Massachusetts. It was really a beautiful winter's day, she thought vaguely. Much too beautiful for blue suits that concealed black guns and dark sedans that carried grim arsenals.

After all these exhausting months of jumping from hotel to hotel, they were now taking her to some remote New Hampshire hideout, where some hotshot man would begin training her on her new identity. They trusted this man so much, only a few of the blue suits would remain behind, and they would serve only as lookouts. Mostly, she would deal with just this man.

She didn't really care, she decided. One man, three men, it didn't matter. They were only people doing their jobs, and no matter how good they were, sooner or later they would move on to other assignments. Then it would be just her, living some lie built upon another lie. Until some day she did walk in front of her new windows, until some day she did answer the front door by herself. The newspapers would carry the final headline. Quiet Schoolteacher Senselessly Shot Down On Her Own Doorstep.

Jessica looked down and realized for the first time that her hands were shaking. She focused on them, her blue eyes narrowing slightly in concentration as abruptly, the shaking stopped. Now her hands lay quiet and still on her lap. Better.

She was a survivor, she reminded herself now as she looked at her smooth, white hands. More so than anyone would ever know. She'd started over before, she'd start over again. Probably someday, Les would find her, simply because he wouldn't rest until he did. But she wouldn't go down without a fight. If anything else, she'd learned that lesson in the past year and a half. This time, she would not be intimidated. Why should she? she thought grimly. She'd beat the mobster on his very own game, and made him pay a far bigger price than he'd ever imagined.

She didn't need these men in their look-alike suits. And she certainly didn't need any hotshot in New Hampshire. She didn't really trust any of them anyway. She knew what greed could do to men, knew how easy it was to corrupt. She even knew the effect her looks had on men. She would be better off on her own.

Soon. She didn't have to trust the man in New Hampshire—just knowing she would finally be allowed a room to herself was enough. A little time on her own was all she needed. One night with no one watching.

Soon. Very soon.

Once more her eyes turned to the window, once more they settled on the white winter hills, rolling so smoothly by. And once more, not a single expression on her beautifully sculpted face gave her away.

Mitch had been waiting nearly half an hour by the time the sedans finally pulled up. He looked at them with something akin to disgust. He believed very strongly in the Witness Protection Program, and he believed very strongly in the men and women who worked so hard to keep the witnesses safe. But for crying out loud, who drove three dark sedans to a remote wilderness retreat in New Hampshire? They might as well stamp FBI in a huge target on the trunk.

This, of course, was why they used him so much. While he'd once been an agent, he'd never been good at conforming. Now, as an independent specialist to the Witness Protection Program, he was free from all the ''procedures'' he often considered more of a liability than a help to participants.

Soon the sedans would be gone, and he would pull out the four-wheel-drive Blazer that was much more appropriate for the situation. Of course he'd still have to convince the remaining two agents to give up their suits. What could be more conspicuous than tailored suits in the middle of nowhere?

He shook his head as the sedan doors finally opened. The team leader stepped out first, walking over to Mitch. Each nodded at each other in greeting, reciting their appropriate sentences for identity clearance. Mitch signaled that the location was secured and the agent then returned to the first sedan. At his indication, the other agents piled out of the cars. When everyone was in place, they opened the door for the woman.

She stepped out of the sedan gracefully, though she declined the agent's offered hand. With the white silk scarf wrapped around her head, it was impossible to see her features. But he had only to watch her walk to know that she was a model.

Today she was wearing a white traveling suit. As she stepped forward, the thin fabric moved with her, revealing the long, lean lines of a model's legs before falling back into place. In the thin fabric, she should be freezing. But she didn't even tremble as she moved forward.

Behind her sunglasses, he could feel her eyes raking him up and down. With an almost imperceptible move of her head, she glanced away, dismissing him as sharply as with a slap. He couldn't quite stop himself from raising a sharp eyebrow. So she was still the Ice Angel, was she? They would see about that.

Walking around in a small circle, as if to take in her surroundings, Jessica worked on controlling her breathing. That man, that man. Surely he wasn't the hotshot everyone had been talking about? Surely they weren't going to leave her alone for two weeks with him?

He dressed wrong, she thought abruptly. He was supposed to be wearing a generic blue suit—didn't he know that? Not some lumberjack green plaid under a sheepskin coat, and faded jeans that clung to his form. And he was too big besides. At least six-four, but even worse, he looked strong, powerful. The dark hair didn't help, either, and he wore it too long, the back brushing the top of his shoulders.

He looked too much like a man. A very strong man. She didn't like it. She wanted the generic suits back.

Abruptly she froze the thought, focusing on a tree just three feet away. There, the faint form of a gray squirrel nibbled on some small nut it had the rare privilege of finding this time of year. Jessica focused on the squirrel, spiraling her concentration inward until she found the control she was known for. Only then did she turn around.

Moving back to the circle of blue suits, she took off her sunglasses and unwrapped the scarf from her head, letting it settle on her shoulders instead. Vaguely, she was aware of the men's sharp glances. They should look, she thought intently. The white of the suit accentuated the pale gold highlights of her hair, which was pulled back into an elegant French twist. And her mascara, sparingly applied this morning, was still enough to frame the brilliant blue depths of her eyes. The suit, of course, with its exquisitely tailored lines, followed the flow of her long lean body to perfection. She knew the picture she presented, all right, and she used it. The more men were enraptured with the package, the less they asked about the contents.

She strolled leisurely forward, putting on her best presence.

"It certainly is beautiful here," she remarked, a rare comment that startled at least two of the men. Unfortunately, it was *that* man who chose to reply.

"Yes," Mitch answered in a deep, husky voice that sounded faintly amused, "and you can be sure it's safe, as well." He'd been watching her sudden unveiling before the gathered group, and it had struck him at once what she was doing. Something was on the Ice Angel's mind. In a minute, he figured they would all find out just what.

She turned to him, and even he had to admit she was beautiful. But there was a coldness to her looks, a tight control that kept them from impacting him. He much preferred the small, laughing faces of easygoing brunettes.

"And you are...?" she asked in a slightly imperious voice.

"Mitchell Guiness," he replied easily. He held out his hand, but she refused it.

"And you are the one that will be in charge of this area?"

He nodded.

She peered at him intently, and he could almost see the wheels turning in her mind. Abruptly it hit him. She didn't like him. For whatever reason, she did not like him. Slightly surprised, he found that it bothered him.

"How long have you been doing this, Mr. Guiness?" she asked now.

"Five years," he responded levelly. He gave her a wry smile. "Would you like to see a copy of my résumé?"

She ignored the last retort, focusing instead on the first. "And before those five years?"

"I was an agent."

"What made you quit being an agent?"

His face tightened slightly, the question hitting sensitive ground. Not that she could know that, he reminded himself.

"I wanted to expand my horizons," he said coolly.

She turned away. "This won't work," she said abruptly to Bill, who was the team leader. "Given the last two attempts on my life, I don't feel sequestering me in one place for two weeks with only this man and two other agents will be adequate protection. I would like a new plan, please."

Bill opened his mouth to reply, but Mitch cut him off before he had a chance.

"This isn't a vacation package," Mitch informed her tightly. "You can't simply pick and choose different options. While I appreciate your concerns, they're unfounded. I happen to be an expert in this area, sweetheart. If anyone can keep you alive, it's me. Trust me."

For one small instant, her features froze. Then she looked back at Bill, who was standing stiffly at attention.

"I want a second opinion," she said pointedly.

"Mitchell Guiness is the best," Bill said clearly. "You will be safe here."

She almost laughed at that, but after all these years her control was much too good. *"Trust us. You will be safe. Trust us."*

"Don't you trust me, sweetheart? Come on, trust—"

The words came out of nowhere, fragments of a memory that abruptly penetrated her mind. She couldn't help herself; she had to close her eyes. Then the memory was gone, safely tucked back away in the deep dark place she never allowed herself to go. Her eyes opened, and once more she was standing in the middle of a white forest with men in blue suits and one man who even now was watching her.

"I'll get my bags, then," she said quietly. They weren't going to change their minds, and she had no good grounds for argument that she cared to share. Her earlier thought returned to her. It didn't matter if she trusted the man, just as long as she finally got one night alone.

Moving as sure and controlled as before, she went to the trunk and withdrew her two bags. Two blue suits moved to help her, but she turned them away with the tight look on her face.

"If you could show me my room, then," she said, keeping her eyes away from the one man, "I would like to freshen up now."

Mitch nodded. There was a slight delay while he conferred with the other agents. Then, four of the blue suits returned to two sedans and drove off. That just left her, Mitch, the team leader Bill, and one more man who'd probably been introduced to her but whose name she didn't remember. Mitch said a few more things to the men, gesturing at the sedan, then their suits. Abruptly he walked back over to her.

"I'll show you around now," he said evenly.

She put her sunglasses back on before she nodded, wanting the dark cover more than she cared to admit. He stood too close, she thought angrily. The other men were careful to give her plenty of room, at least a respectful distance. But not this man. He stood so close, she could smell the spicy scent of after-shave. And she could see the faint stubble on his cheeks of a late-afternoon beard. Worse, she could feel the heat radiating from his large frame, feel the tightly restrained power.

She drew herself up carefully, keeping her own control tightly in place. His dark eyes moved over her speculatively, but she gave nothing away. After a moment, he reached over and took the bags from her. She relinquished them wordlessly, careful to keep her hands from contacting his. He turned and walked to a two-story log cabin; she followed.

Walking through the door, she was struck at once by the blaze of heat. For the first time she shivered, only now realizing how cold it had been outside. The man in front of her, of course, noticed the shudder.

"I hope you brought warmer clothes than what you're wearing," he remarked in that low voice of his. "Because this isn't exactly a resort here. In the next two weeks, you'll be outside a great deal, I promise you."

She removed her sunglasses once more, looking at him with her dispassionate blue eyes. "I'm sure I'll survive just fine," she informed him coolly.

He arched a black eyebrow. "Wearing silk in snow?"

"Mr. Guiness, I've worn bathing suits in snow, not that it's any of your concern. My room, please?"

He ignored her reminder. "Tough life being a fashion model, huh?" he asked, openly amused.

Rather than becoming defensive as he may have hoped, she simply shrugged a dismissive shoulder. "A job is a job," she said expressionlessly. "I'm sure there are parts of yours that aren't exactly 'heavenly,' either."

In his mind, he could practically fill in the blanks. Like baby-sitting a fashion model. He ignored the thought completely. Oh, but she was a cool one. Even in person she could keep that tight air of hot-cold sensuality. Her body practically begged for a man's touch. Her face said she would freeze the first man who tried. He himself wasn't sure which one to believe, but for now he was going with the message in her eyes.

Still, he wished more things about the woman would check out. It was the fundamental question he'd faced watching her at the trial. What kind of woman turned in her lover without any kind of emotion? What kind of woman could creep around a mobster's house at night without the slightest fear?

What did go on behind those cool blue eyes of hers?

All he knew was that she looked as beautiful in person as she did in the magazines, and she was perfectly aware of that fact. He also knew she didn't like him.

For now, that both amused and irritated him.

She was still looking at him with dispassionate eyes. With a mental start, he turned to their surroundings.

He gestured around the room. "As you can see, we walked right into the living room. The fireplace there gives off plenty of heat so the nights aren't quite so cold. Over to the right is the kitchen and dining room. The kitchen isn't that big but everything works and there are only four of us. It's also fully stocked, so food shouldn't be a problem. We can all take turns cooking. Tonight I'll draw up the schedule. Can you cook, Jessica?"

It was the first time he'd spoken her name, and it seemed to almost whisper in the air. Unexpectedly, she felt a small shiver creep up her back at the low utterance. With quick control she squashed the reaction.

"Passably," she said out loud, the words still expressionless. Mitch nodded, pointing out the staircase next. But before they started up it, he set down the bags as he shrugged off his thick coat to hang on one of the wooden pegs by the door. While she waited, Jessica's own eyes took in the area.

The lower level certainly seemed small and quaint. Everything was in earth tones, with a large brown leather couch in front of the huge fireplace. She could see a thick blanket thrown over the back of the easy chair, lending a homey touch. The red-and-brown Indian-print rug thrown over the wooden floors looked thick and sturdy. To her right, the dining room was an open expanse raised two steps from the living room. In the middle sat a huge pine table with benches on either side serving as the seats. Off the dining room, the kitchen was indeed tiny looking. All in all, the surroundings looked very cozy and comfortable. If she'd been vacationing by herself, she probably would have liked the cabin very much. But sharing it with three other people, one of them being the man in front of her... She wasn't sure she liked it at all.

She wanted more space. Lots more space.

The man in front of her seemed oblivious, picking her bags back up and now approaching the stairs at their immediate right. Wordlessly, she followed.

Even without his coat, he still seemed large. The wide expanse of his shoulders brushed against the sides of the narrow staircase, until he seemed to fill the entire void. The green plaid shirt he wore looked worn and comfortable on his shoulders, while his faded jeans clearly outlined his legs and hips.

She was careful to keep several steps between them as they went up the stairs. But even then, she could feel his presence in the nervous clenching and unclenching of her stomach. It was the strain of the last five months, she figured. She really did need some time to herself.

The stairs peaked at the wide open expanse of a loft. The front of the loft was finished by a wooden railing, which allowed a person to look down into the living room. Behind the loft were three doorways, each apparently leading to a bedroom. Between two of the bedrooms was a small bathroom. Mitch went straight to the last doorway and motioned her inside.

Maintaining as much distance as possible, she pushed by him into the room. It was a large room, simply furnished. In the center was a queen-size bed, framed by a simple wooden headboard and footboard. A matching nightstand was on one side, while a five-drawer dresser graced the wall. A thick, off-white shag rug had been thrown over most of the floor, and the winter sun streamed in through a triangular window set high in the vaulted ceiling. After months in tiny hotel rooms with tightly drawn curtains, it was a refreshing change of pace. Wordlessly, she walked over to the closet, throwing open the doors.

Mitch watched her every move from the doorway, saw her survey the room, saw her cross the floor with her graceful model's steps. But not a single expression filtered across her face the entire time. Not disgust, joy, contentment, disappointment. Nothing. Her pale skin remained smooth, her blue eyes dispassionate.

The woman must be hell to play poker with.

From the doorway, he shook his head. Why the need for such control? For such restraint she didn't even allow for reaction to a room? What went on in that head of hers?

She was crossing back to him, her cool eyes indicating the bags he still held in his hands. In silent acquiescence, he walked a few steps forward and placed the bags on the bed.

"And the bathroom?" she asked quietly, the words sounding abrupt after the long silence.

"Unfortunately, there are only two bathrooms—one upstairs, one downstairs," Mitch replied. "But as the two agents will be staggering their sleep schedules, it shouldn't be too hard to coordinate."

If the arrangement displeased her, none of it showed on her face. Instead, she looked at him with speculative eyes. "Why only two agents? Why send the rest away?"

"The more there are, the harder it is to hide," he said in his low voice. "A party of eight would be conspicuous. It would require a larger house, more vehicles, more supplies. Smaller numbers make for simplicity."

"How many times have you done this before?"

"Fifteen or sixteen," he said, counting forward from when he'd become an independent specialist and had started this program.

"And did it always work?"

"So far, yes."

"So far? What about now, Mr. Guiness? What do you think will happen this time?"

He looked at her, spearing her with his dark brown gaze until she had to consciously force herself not to turn away. "That'll depend on you. And by all means, call me Mitch. We're going to get to know each other real well in the coming weeks."

Once again her stomach clenched and unclenched. Once again she felt the faint shudder in her spine. Oh, but that was exactly what she was afraid of.

"I'm feeling tired," she announced abruptly. "I would like to rest now."

He nodded, his eyes never leaving her face. She could feel the focus like a probe, and it made her breath want to come out in restless gasps. Instead, she simply stood, willing her eyes to appear uncaring as she waited for him to leave.

At long last he turned toward the door. But at the doorway he abruptly stopped. His eyes were on her neck, then her hair, then finally on her face.

"Why did you do it?" he asked softly, the question that had been puzzling him for weeks finally pushing forth. "Why did you turn Capruccio in?"

She was silent for a moment, her face carefully turned from his. Then she glanced up, looking at him with the same cool blue eyes she'd had on the witness stand.

"Les broke the law," she said out loud. "Wasn't that enough?"

Slowly Mitch shook his head.

"He was your lover. People don't just hand over their lovers for illegal activities. If that was the case, you should have turned him in years ago."

"Maybe I didn't know about it then."

He raised a cynical eyebrow. "Sweetheart, everyone knew what kind of man Les Capruccio was. And you didn't exactly roll out of the cornfields of Kansas yesterday."

For a moment, he saw a faint tugging at her lips, like a small smile trying to break through. But what kind of smile? Sad, bitter, humorous, sweet? There was nothing in her eyes to give it away.

"If you know so much about Les," she said out loud, "then surely you know he's not an easy man to defy."

For the first time he nodded. And for the first time she thought she saw a glimmer of something besides the speculative disdain in his eyes. Maybe respect. It was hard to be sure.

"Was it worth it?" Mitch asked abruptly. "Was putting him away worth all this?" He gestured to the room with his large hands.

This time she did smile, a small smile of satisfaction. "Oh, yes," she told him with conviction. "It definitely was."

He digested this. So whatever sentiments she had toward Capruccio, they weren't affectionate ones. But why hadn't she admitted to it on the stand?

He looked at her long and hard.

"And if it does cost you your life?" he asked loudly in the quiet of the house, "will it still be worth it?"

She looked at him almost impatiently. "Come now, Mr. Guiness. Do you honestly believe that it won't?"

"Won't be worth it?"

"No, won't cost me my life."

He paused for a long moment, and when he finally spoke, his eyes were intensely serious. "Not as long as you're here it won't," he told her evenly.

She looked him over once again, her cool eyes appraising this time. He could almost see the struggle in her face, her assessment warring with her obvious dislike of him.

Abruptly she turned away with a small shrug.

"Perhaps" was all she was willing to concede. "But the problem is," she continued levelly, "sooner or later I will leave here. And what then, Mr. Guiness? What then?"

"In the next two weeks you'll find out," he told her.

She shook her head, moving over to her bags.

"I already know," she said softly. "You do, too. But it will be interesting to see how long it takes Les to find me. And it will be even more interesting to see how much it will cost him. Because I won't go down without a fight. Not this time, Mr. Guiness."

The very dispassionate nature of her voice seemed to lend the words credibility. He felt it again, the glimmer of emotion he didn't want to feel toward this arctic supermodel: respect.

"Mitch," he found himself saying. "Call me Mitch."

She gave him a sideways glance, then shook her head. "It won't do you any good to tell me your name," she informed him coolly as she unzipped the first bag. ''I don't bother to learn names.''

The words were so arrogant, so completely cold, they practically begged to be challenged. And Mitch Guiness was not a man who passed up challenges.

He found himself moving forward before he formed a conscious plan. He didn't stop until he was a mere six inches from her, the movement bringing her head up.

This close, he could see the faint filter of emotions flickering across her eyes. Only one could he pinpoint directly: wariness. Her chin came up, and she looked ready to meet his challenge head-on.

He raked her up and down, his eyes penetrating and intense. Leaning even closer, he caught the faint hint of a light fragrance. Peaches, he thought abruptly. He smelled peaches. And damned if it wasn't the sexiest thing he'd ever smelled.

''By the end of this week,'' he uttered softly, ''you'll know my name, Jessica Gavornée. And you'll know it well.''

Her chin came up even higher.

''You may leave now,'' she informed him coldly, her eyes not giving any ground at all. ''I have things to do.''

Oh, he wanted to press her further, he realized suddenly. He wanted to take another step forward until his face was inches from hers. He wanted to push her until the arctic control gave way, and he was looking at the woman instead of the carefully constructed Ice Angel.

He wanted to kiss her until the ice melted into passion, until she clung to him and whispered his name in fiery heat.

The thought came out of nowhere, and slammed into his gut with a fierceness that almost staggered him. What was he doing, having such thoughts about a witness?

Stunned at his own reaction, he took a step back instead. She watched him move back, and once again nothing flickered in her eyes.

The woman would drive even a saint to madness, he rationalized to himself, shaking his head like a man just emerging from a stupor. He moved back to the relative sanity of the doorway.

"Dinner will be in two hours," he informed her over his shoulder as he left. He didn't bother to see if she agreed or not.

Somehow she thought that might be a sign of things to come.

Chapter 2

"**Y**ou realize, of course, that if you ever reveal your true identity, you will be eliminated from the Witness Protection Program," Mitch was saying in clipped tones. For the last hour and a half he'd been going over all the guidelines of the program, guidelines she'd heard enough times in the past five months to recite in her sleep.

She didn't bother to hide her impatience as she nodded yet again.

"I've been over all this before," she pointed out coolly. "Since it's getting late, I'd just as soon cover new ground or no ground at all."

Mitch frowned at her. "I know you've heard it before," he replied firmly. Fifteen years of Northeast living had eliminated most of his North Carolina drawl, making his words curt and fast enough to match her own. "But the point is, do you absolutely understand? Because up until now it's just been talk. Here is where the rubber hits the road. We're talking about a new name, a new identity. We're talking about cutting all your ties with the past. Your family, friends, lovers—they don't exist for you anymore. Can you do that? Are you truly committed to that process?"

Her blue eyes remained emotionless. "I'm committed to staying alive," she informed him levelly. "As for friends, family and lovers, you ought to know as well as I do how few of those there are."

This was true, and he was aware of it. What amazed him was that not only was she aware of it, but it didn't seem to bother her at all. Then again, if dinner had been anything to go by, she certainly wasn't a social creature.

She'd come down when he'd requested her for dinner. By then she'd changed into a pair of designer jeans, covered by a long, thickly woven sweater. She'd accented the off-white sweater with a crimson-and-blue scarf draped artfully around her neck. She looked at once earthy and elegant, a look he was sure only someone like herself could ever completely pull off. And whereas the sweater should have made her look shapeless and bulky, it had a habit of moving with her, offering short, tantalizing glimpses of curved hips and rounded breasts before it swung back into place. He realized he was much more aware of these things than he really should be.

On the other hand, she seemed totally oblivious to him. She'd hardly spared him a glance upon sitting at the table. She'd simply passed around the food, eating in complete silence that was only occasionally interrupted by a polite "Please pass the rice."

She'd eaten her small, sparrow-size servings of everything. Then she'd sat back and, with her cool, expressionless features, patiently waited for everyone to finish.

The only redeeming quality he could find was that once everyone had finished, she'd risen silently and begun doing the dishes without discussion. At least the supermodel wasn't spoiled.

She seemed determined to make up for that in stubbornness, however.

"What about family?" he pressed on now. From all his research, he'd never come up with anyone. But then again, he knew nothing of the woman before age sixteen. "Is there anyone that can be held against you? Anyone Les can use to manipulate you?"

"No," she informed him coolly, her chin coming up defensively. This, of course, was a blatant lie, but she had no intention of telling him that.

"What about other lovers? Friends?"

"Look," she stated flatly, her patience clearly running out as her blue eyes darkened. She didn't want to be pressed and quizzed. Despite the long years of practice, lying disturbed her. Deep down inside, she knew it wasn't right, even as she knew wrong could become right, and right become wrong, all depending on the circumstances. "I have no ties, no commitments," she said out loud, keeping her eyes focused on the tabletop in front of her. "Which was one of the reasons I considered the Witness Protection Program such a viable solution," she continued. "Now let's move on."

"Fine," he answered curtly. He should be glad she didn't have any family or friends left. That simplified matters considerably. But for some reason he didn't feel comfortable about the subject yet. Still, it was getting late and they did have a lot of ground to cover.

"I want to start training you on your new life in the morning," he informed her bluntly. "Tonight we'll go briefly over the profile so you know what it is. Tomorrow the drilling will begin. At the end of the two weeks, you will be your new identity. Is that clear?"

"I'm not an idiot," she said in clipped tones, her eyes flashing arctic fire.

Her rest certainly hadn't improved her mood at all, Mitch thought dryly. At least she wasn't as dispassionate as before. Instead, she seemed to be driven by some icy anger he did not understand any more than he could avoid. Funny, the way she was acting, one would have thought he was her enemy, rather than the man working to save her beautiful blond life. At least public relations wasn't a required part of the job.

Keeping his own mood curt enough to match hers, he tossed her a manila file.

"There you go, Jessica," he informed her. "Meet the new you."

The expression in her eyes was wary as she picked up the folder. She looked at him once, but he merely sat there at the kitchen table, arms folded across his broad chest. The other agents had gone out on rounds, leaving the two of them alone in the kitchen.

She didn't like just the two of them, Jessica thought as she opened the file. She didn't like sitting with this man a scant two feet away. He was too big, too powerful. His presence filled the tiny space, crowding her. The effort at maintaining her control was beginning to drain her, and that made her even more resentful.

Why did he have to keep staring at her with such all-knowing eyes? Why couldn't he just do his job and leave her in peace?

She needed some time to herself, desperately. Some time away from this man. Besides, she had business to attend to.

Very soon, she promised herself.

She scanned the file.

"Jessie McMoran," she read aloud. "Isn't that name too close to Jessica?"

"Has anyone ever called you Jessie?" he quizzed.

Silently she shook her head.

"Good," he told her. "And actually, we didn't want to change your name too much. It makes slipups less probable. This way, no one can try to trap you by calling you Jessica. Though, by the end of the two weeks, you'll be polished enough not to automatically respond to anything other than Jessie."

She nodded, though her eyes remained critical. "How about Jess? I'm not so sure I like Jessie. No one calls me Jess, either, for that matter."

With a shrug of his broad shoulders, Mitch agreed.

"Saleswoman," Jessica read under the occupation title. "No," she said abruptly, "that won't do. I want to be a schoolteacher."

"What?"

"You heard me. I want to be a schoolteacher."

"Sweetheart," he drawled once more, his voice definitely impatient, "this isn't fantasy life. You can't just choose whatever occupation you've ever dreamed about.

You have to actually do it, which means you have to be qualified. And considering the fact you never went to college, you're not in the position to be a teacher.''

"I know this isn't a fantasy life—that's exactly my point. Whatever this occupation is, I'll be living it day in and day out. Which means I want something I would enjoy doing. Schoolteacher. Second grade would be nice. But I'm willing to teach anything in grade school. As for qualifications, I happened to have taken a number of classes by mail during my career.'' He nodded, having discovered that himself. "While none of them add up to a degree,'' she continued, "I believe that's beside the point. It doesn't matter what Jessica Gavornée has, only what Jess McMoran does. I presume that proper credentials will be provided as part of the new ID package.''

He nodded slowly, reluctant admiration filling him. She certainly caught on to the game quick enough. Still, she wasn't convinced.

"But you've never actually taught a class,'' he pointed out. "And taking classes doesn't equal teaching classes.''

"I taught adult literacy,'' she responded smoothly, "once a week for two years. While it was more of a one-on-one interaction, it taught me a lot of the principles of teaching. Besides, at the age of twenty-four, people would expect me to be inexperienced.''

"What if you're not twenty-four?''

"Pardon?''

"Look,'' Mitch said, leaning forward in earnest now, "everyone knows you're in the Witness Protection Program. So they won't be looking for you. They'll be looking for someone that fits the general characteristics of you. For example, someone with your height and build. Someone with your mannerisms and your age.''

There was a long period of silence. She sat there, her blue eyes giving nothing away, as she appeared to be considering what he had said. She shifted once, bringing her hands down to her lap.

Her hands were trembling—she could feel the tiny tremors—but she didn't have the concentration just now to make them stop. There were so many things to think about, so many changes to be made if she was going to pull this off. It would be easier to handle if he wouldn't keep looking at her, easier to take if he would stop leaning forward like that.

She could see the stubble on his cheeks once more. It would feel rough and raspy to the touch. Really, he had a strong face. As a model, she could appreciate that. The cheekbones were well sculpted, his jaw square. His black eyebrows and black, glossy hair added to his masculinity, while definitely giving him an untamed edge. Women probably found him very appealing.

But not her, she reminded herself squarely. He was much too large for her tastes, too powerful looking. And his eyes were much too intelligent when they skimmed over her. He seemed to understand her tricks better than she did, and she couldn't afford that right now. Earlier today, when she had pulled back her scarf, she'd gotten the impression he'd known exactly what she was doing. Even worse, he'd found it amusing.

This man was much too dangerous.

And he made it very hard for her to think.

She composed herself once again.

"So what do you propose?" she asked as calmly as possible.

"We want to make you a thirty-year-old," he told her evenly, watching her carefully for her response. "With cosmetic surgery, we can add some wrinkles around your face and mouth, perhaps a few lines in your forehead. Nothing drastic, but enough to alter your current, smooth-skinned appearance."

He waited for her to protest. Surely a woman that made her living off her looks would resent deliberately destroying them.

But instead she nodded. "Good," she said. "My looks must definitely be altered. They are entirely too well-known."

He nodded, trying to keep the surprise off his face. Where was the anger, or even the fear? He was used to dealing with people who logically accepted the program, but were still emotionally fighting the change. This kind of deep-rooted transformation was very traumatic. Yet the woman across from him examined it with the same logical scrutiny she'd displayed on the witness stand.

He wasn't sure if he should be grateful or worried.

"Then," she was continuing out loud, "we can simply have Jess graduate from college later than most. Of course. We'll incorporate both ideas. Graduated from high school, worked as a salesperson and then, at twenty-five, went back to college to become a teacher. Thus, I can be older and still be inexperienced."

Damn, the woman was amazing. Slowly he nodded his head. "That will work, then, if you are sure you have the ability to teach. I'll make the arrangement for the teacher's license in your new state."

"Perfect," she said evenly.

"Well, then," Mitch continued, "about further changes to your appearance. We'll dye your hair, of course—probably dark brown—and give you brown eyes."

"The hair should be very dark," she told him, "almost black. That way it will look natural with my fair complexion. We'll have to do my eyebrows, as well. I can also wear darker, richer colors in clothing. Given my traditional choice of pastels, that will further enhance the difference."

"You've given this a lot of thought," he observed dryly. Indeed, in all his years he'd never quite met anyone like her.

"It's my life," she informed him simply. "Of course I've given it a great deal of thought. Besides—" she shrugged "—when you're shut up in a hotel for five months, it's not like you have anything else to do."

"Was it that boring?" he asked softly, watching her intently for her response.

But once again she seemed determined to keep her distance. "It's over" was all she said.

He didn't push this time. Really, his only concern was acclimatizing her to her new life. The past was irrelevant to that. He continued. "You'll also need to gain weight," he told her. He gave her a critical glance, even though she was seated. "Probably a good fifteen or twenty pounds. It will add to the image of your new age, as well as soften the lines of your face and body. Right now, anyone could spot you as a model a million miles away."

She looked more reluctant this time. "Fifteen to twenty pounds?" she quizzed.

He nodded relentlessly.

"I don't gain weight very well," she told him.

"Judging by how much you ate tonight, I can believe it," he replied dryly. "Surely after all the years of being on a restricted diet, there are some things you'd like to indulge in."

This statement seemed to confuse her. Finally she shook her head. "Not really."

He looked at her skeptically. "Come on, now. What about a hot fudge sundae? What about brownies or croissants? There's got to be something. Something sweet, something forbidden."

Abruptly she felt that shiver fizzle up her spine again. *Something forbidden.* She wanted to shut out the words, but they kept echoing in her mind, and every time they did, she could feel her stomach clench and unclench.

What was wrong with her? She didn't feel these things. But as she looked down at her lap, she could see her hands still trembling.

When she looked up again, he was watching her, and it seemed to her suddenly that he knew exactly what was going on in her mind. Damn his brown eyes.

She drew herself up straight, summoning her years' worth of training.

"What about simply wearing padded clothing?" she queried, her eyes ruthlessly dispassionate. "Wouldn't that accomplish the same effect?"

"Not for your face," he replied quietly. She was starting to get tired, he realized. More and more, he was beginning to see the distant flickers of emotion in her face. Still, she did not give much away. But the icy control of this afternoon was starting to become strained. He wondered how far he should push her. He wondered what was really going on behind those icy blue eyes of hers. But even as he watched, he could see her eyes darken, gaining new strength from her growing frustration and anger.

"Fine," she bit out curtly. "I'll gain fifteen pounds. What else?"

"Oh, there are a lot of other things," he told her seriously. "We will work on everything from how you walk to how you talk. Do you understand yet how dramatic the change needs to be for you? If you weren't a celebrity, it would be one thing. But everyone knows you. They've seen you walk down runways, they've seen you on limited interviews and unlimited magazine covers. You probably don't even realize just how 'you' you are. You have a way of moving, a way of gesturing, a way of carrying yourself. It's distinct, you know. And things like a new hairdo and lines on your face won't cover it for long. Any familiarities will tug on people's memories. And they'll keep trying to place why you seem so familiar until they do recognize you. The changes then, must be beyond skin-deep."

This time he could see the strain on her face, but there was also grudging acceptance.

"Fine," she agreed smoothly enough. "If it will save my life, I will do it. Now, then, what about protection?"

"Protection?" he echoed.

"Absolutely," she said firmly. "You, Mr. Guiness, will work with me for two weeks. But as I pointed out earlier, what then? You move on, but I have to live my new life. I want a backup plan. If . . . when . . . Les finds me, I will not be some sitting duck. Do you understand?"

Her eyes had gone dark again, and her chin had taken on its now-familiar determined pose.

"Of course," Mitch replied easily. He understood her concern, in fact, he shared it. Never had he dealt with a witness who was so recognizable, nor a prisoner who was so relentless. It was not a good combination.

"The FBI will keep tabs on Les's activities even within the prison," he told her. "While Capruccio has his network, so do we have ours. As I'm sure you know, a contract has already been put out for you. However, as of yet, no one seems to have taken up the offer. From past dealings, we know who the common Mafia hit men are, and you can be sure we'll be keeping our eyes open. At the first sign of trouble, discreet agents will be posted nearby for your protection. They, of course, will be undercover, and at no time should you ever reveal your past identity.''

But Jessica was shaking her head. "And if something escapes your network? I won't live my whole life depending on some agent to show up in time to save the day. I want to know how to protect myself. I want to know how to shoot a gun, I want to know how to tell if I'm being followed. Things like that.''

He looked at her for a long moment, choosing his words carefully. "While I understand your concern,'' he started out slowly, "what you're asking can't be accomplished overnight. It takes years of schooling to develop those kinds of skills in an agent.''

"I don't care,'' she informed him flatly.

"I do,'' he told her honestly. "It's my job to train you for your safety, not to give you just enough information to be dangerous to yourself.'' Her eyes darkened once more to an icy blue, and he could practically feel the beginnings of the storm.

"Look,'' he said, seeing clearly where her thoughts were headed, "I know what I'm talking about. I've seen men who think they know how to take care of themselves become cocky, when in fact they know almost nothing. Instead of protecting them, their limited knowledge endangers them. Trust me on this one.''

It was the worst possible thing he could have said.

"No.''

The word fell like ice in the kitchen, and though her face never changed, he could see the black rage in her eyes. She leaned forward, and once again he could catch the faint scent of peaches. But mostly he could see the true coldness of her anger.

"I don't trust you,'' she iterated clearly. "Is that understood? I don't trust you, I don't trust the men outside that door and I don't trust anyone in the FBI, nor out of the FBI. I want to learn how to take care of myself, and if you can't teach me everything, then at least teach me something. I demand it.''

It was the worst possible thing she could have said.

His own eyes grew dark, but they also grew deceptively calm. While her voice dripped icicles, his became hauntingly soft.

"Well, you'd better trust me," he drawled slowly, "because for the next two weeks, Ice Angel, your life is in my hands. And even more to the point, my life and the life of those two men out there are in your hands. Do you get that? We are all in this together. You don't obey the rules, and we all pay with our lives."

She wanted to retort, she wanted to reply with anger if only to exorcise the relentless nervousness she felt in his presence. But all of a sudden she could see Darold again, his back arching as the bullet hit home. So much blood on the fall leaves.

Had he had a wife, a family? She didn't even know, and she didn't want to know.

God, she felt tired. Tired from the stress and the strain. She had never asked these men to protect her, never wanted these men to give up their lives. All these years she'd existed on her own, relying on herself, trusting only herself.

She didn't like how complicated it had all become since then.

It was their choice, she reminded herself firmly, searching for equilibrium once more. They had willfully chosen to become agents, to risk their lives for the law. Just as she had chosen to risk hers.

She had to keep it that simple, for her own sake.

Mitch's eyes were still on her, practically burning a hole through her head. She forced her eyes up, even if she couldn't quite muster the cold dispassion of before.

"Will you teach me how to shoot a gun?" she asked quietly.

He stared at her for a long moment. The ice was cracking. He could practically make out the spidery lines in her control, and he found himself leaning forward as if then he would see everything inside of her. All of a sudden, the shadows under her eyes were darker, the lines in the corners harsher. She looked worn, but still she didn't back down.

He swore. "I can show you the rudiments," he relented at last, leaning back with a sigh. "But damn it, you'll need to keep practicing once you get settled. All right?"

"Where will that be?" she asked, not pushing the matter any further.

"Given this new slant of being a schoolteacher, we'll have to work on that. I should have an answer for you in a couple of days."

She nodded. "New England, maybe? I like the area."

"Yeah, well, the scenery won't mean much if Les is on your doorstep by morning. New England's just too close."

"Perhaps," she said simply.

"Washington—start thinking Washington state or other places on the West Coast. We look for a good-size city, a place where a new person would attract little notice. We can discuss it when we know for sure." He threw in the last statement because he had the distinct feeling they were going to discuss it. He had only to look at the determined slant of her chin to know that for whatever reason, she wasn't keen on leaving the area. Rather strange, he thought, for someone who said she had no friends or family around.

And all of a sudden, he realized why he still wasn't feeling comfortable about all of this. As agreeable and intelligent as she seemed, Mitch was willing to bet money she had other ideas on her mind. It was the only explanation he could find.

So then the question became what were those ideas, and how much would it cost him to find out? He wasn't joking when he told her they would all bear the price of her mistakes. He'd seen it happen too many times before.

Someone made a mistake, but somebody else died.

Somebody close, somebody you cared for.

He pushed the thought away.

"Do you understand what our agenda will be?" he asked now, his voice curt as he once more scrutinized her with his eyes.

She nodded.

"I want to get an early start tomorrow. Let's say 7:00 a.m. Meet me downstairs. And dress warm—we'll be outside for part of the day. Do you have a proper coat?"

"No."

He frowned. "I'll have to see what I can do about that." He glanced at his watch. "It's midnight now. You should probably get some sleep."

You? What was he planning on doing? She didn't feel like asking, though. It had been a long day. There was just one thing she needed to get settled.

"How much freedom do I have here?" she asked, doing her best to sound casual.

"What do you mean?"

"Before, I was never allowed near windows, never allowed outside by myself. I'm assuming this location is safer than the hotels. Can I go outside by myself?"

He considered the matter for a moment. "You can probably have more freedom," he conceded, understanding how hard it must have been to be cooped up like that. "However, we need to know your whereabouts at all times. If you go out, find myself, Bill or Jamie. Tell us exactly where you're going and when you'll be back. And never wander off the perimeters of this site. You can tell that by the yellow property markers on the trees. That is the safe zone. Beyond that, we can't cover you if there's trouble. In all honesty, there is no reason for you to have to go farther. All supplies have been provided, and even then, the nearest town is a good twenty miles from here. Other than the occasional stray hunter, this area is completely isolated."

She nodded, her face expressionless even as she felt her heart sink in her chest. The nearest town was twenty miles from here? How would she ever make that? Especially considering the only vehicle she knew of was the sedan, and that would be easy to track. She would have to give this more thought.

If she could even just call.

It would make such a difference.

"I think I'll go upstairs now," she said abruptly. "I could use a good night's sleep."

He nodded, rising from the table. She watched him with wary eyes.

He truly was such a large man. Irritated that he loomed so far above her now, she also rose from the table. But her five-ten height still only reached his shoulder. After all those years of towering over men—even Les—to find herself still having to look up was disconcerting. He gestured with his hand for her to go first. Reluctantly she began walking.

She could feel him behind her as she approached the stairs. She could feel the strength of his presence, the scent of his after-shave. And once again her stomach tightened with a myriad of sensations. She forced herself to walk in even steps, forced herself to keep her head up as if nothing at all was amiss.

Now if only she could get her hands to stop shaking.

At the top of the stairs, she turned, facing him as nonchalantly as possible.

"Good night, Mr. Guiness," she said coolly.

He arched his eyebrow at her insistent use of his last name. God, but she was stubborn. He folded his arms across his chest, leaning casually against the railing.

She was standing just two feet from him, looking as cool as a cucumber. But he could still catch the faint scent of freshly washed peaches, and it was driving him half-crazy.

What was the Ice Angel doing smelling like peaches? How could one woman possibly be so sexy and so cold all at once? It really did play havoc with a man's senses.

And he wondered then if that wasn't exactly why she did it. This evening she had displayed a keen, impressive intellect. Coupled with her uncanny ability to remain in control, he had a feeling there was very little she did that wasn't carefully thought out ahead of time. But even now, he had no insight to her motives. What logic was driving her? And where would it all end?

Oh, she was up to something. But he didn't press just yet. He had a feeling Jessica Gavornée was used to having her own way and used to manipulating men, when necessary, to accomplish that. She would learn in time, Mitch promised himself, that this was one man she couldn't play her little games with.

The next two weeks were going to be very interesting.

She was still watching him with her cool blue eyes and that faint hint of wariness. He pushed away from the railing, and she moved closer to her own doorway. He nodded to her, resting his hand on the doorknob of the second room.

"Good night, Jess," he drawled, putting emphasis on her new name.

She had frozen in the doorway though, his words falling on deaf ears.

"Where are you going?" she demanded suddenly, the suspicion obvious in her voice.

"To my own room, of course."

He had the delight of watching her whole face freeze over, and he was beginning to learn about her well enough to understand the darkening of her eyes. Oh, the Ice Angel was mad. In fact, she was furious!

"Aren't there bedrooms downstairs?" she pointed out frigidly.

He shrugged his shoulders. " 'Fraid they're for Bill and Jamie. But don't worry," he said gallantly, not quite able to keep the teasing tone out of his voice, "you may use the bathroom first."

The look she gave him would have dropped another man dead in his tracks. But Mitch returned her icy blue anger with his own velvety grin.

"Sweet dreams," he told her, and disappeared into his room.

From his room, he heard her shut her door with emphasis. Not quite slamming—she had too much self-control for that. But a definite, firm closure. The woman did know how to make a statement.

He found himself grinning once more, but then abruptly his face sobered. He'd wanted her to know he was in the room next to hers, because he wanted her to know he was watching. Mitch was the best in his job because he knew people. And after just five minutes he could usually size up and relate to anyone he'd ever met. Jessica Gavornée was definitely more difficult; he'd never met another individual—man or woman—with more control than she had.

But he was starting to catch on, starting to see the little signs. And right now, all the signs told him this woman was not as she seemed. People learned to control their emotions for a reason, and generally that reason was to hide something.

He would be watching her very closely the next couple of days. Hell, by the time he was done, she'd think she had a shadow, because he had no intention of letting her out of his sight.

What he'd told her earlier was the truth. If she made a mistake, broke the rules, they would all pay for it.

And Mitch Guiness knew just how dear that price could be.

Chapter 3

She jerked awake with the scream still ripe in her throat. She lay there for a long, tortured moment, her fingers dug into the mattress, her eyes wide with terror. Then slowly, with more control than any one person really should possess, she forced herself to exhale.

It was all right now. Les was locked up and could never hurt her again.

His fists couldn't pummel her face. His legs couldn't kick her ribs.

It was all over.

But as she pulled herself out of bed, she felt sick. For a moment she pressed her hand to her stomach and willed the images to pass.

She really did just want to believe it was over. But sometimes, in the twisted workings of her unconscious, Les was no longer Les, but Harry. And even as she fought to escape the raining blows, she could hear the sound of her mother crying in the kitchen.

Wrapping the quilted comforter around herself for warmth, she began pacing the room.

The nightmares were a fairly new phenomena, she forced herself to acknowledge. Before, her body had simply slept when she told it to sleep. Indeed, it had been one of her greatest strengths as a model. She could keep the erratic hours and exhausting schedules simply by dictating her body's performance.

But in the last year, that kind of absolute control had begun to slip away from her. She hadn't functioned well anymore at work. The black smudges under her eyes had taken more makeup to conceal, an unwilling testimony to just how her life was catching up with her.

And sometimes the nightmare returned, and she would bolt awake at 3:00 a.m., her body shivering with a light sheen of sweat while the image hovered just beyond the reaches of her mind.

Luckily, Les was a heavy sleeper. The few times she'd awakened him, he'd merely grunted with impatience and rolled back over to oblivion. He wasn't a man who liked to be disturbed by other people's problems.

It was never a coincidence that those nights followed the times he gave in to his own ugliness and hit her.

In the darkness of the night, Jess allowed herself a bitter smile. Funny how life seemed to go in circles. And the very act of trying to escape the loop sent you back into it, curving around another spiraling cycle.

She started walking again, holding the comforter closer as if it could actually warm the chill that resonated so deeply inside of her. The cycle was over, she reminded herself. This time she'd broken it for good. And in a matter of days, she would be by herself again. A new name, a new person.

A stronger person.

And she would live alone forever, build a sweet, isolated life where no one could hurt her, and she could hurt no one. The violence would at long last end, and maybe, with enough time, the blood on her hands would fade.

It would work out. She swore it. She'd come too far, borne too much, risked too much, to fail now.

Still, it would not be easy.

Unbidden, another picture rose to her mind, but it wasn't of the grasping Les Capruccio. It was the dark, powerfully muscled Mitchell Guiness.

She found herself shivering, and tightened her grip on the blanket once more.

He was such a large man, large and powerful and magnetic. He filled the room with his presence, and it made her at once nervous and angry. If he'd been petty or bullish or stupid, he would have simply been a source of uneasiness. But his brown eyes reflected sharp intelligence, and his face a slow, easy smile.

That made him terrifying.

She knew what he was trying to do, she thought abruptly, drawing on the anger. That little display of his to let her know he slept in the room right next to hers. He wanted her to understand that he was in charge, that he was watching her.

Well, she'd just have to show him, she decided resolutely, walking now with quick steps back and forth at the foot of the bed. Les had also thought he controlled her, but she'd shown him. When push came to shove, she was not a woman to be trifled with.

She just needed the new identity, she reminded herself. She'd get her appearance altered, master her new mannerisms, learn how to shoot, and then she'd be out of here. Away from all the blue suits and the one dark man with his knowing brown eyes.

Her steps slowed, the exhaustion catching her all at once. And maybe, maybe in time the nightmares would leave her again. Living alone, the pictures would fade, and this new life built on the ruins of old lives would finally bring her the peace she'd been trying to find.

And in the dark of the night, she wouldn't have to remember the sound of her own silent screams, nor the color of the blood soaking into the gold-patterned carpet.

She shook her head against it, but it didn't do any good. And she knew if she looked in the mirror right now, the Ice Angel would be gone, and there would only be the large haunted eyes of a sixteen-year-old girl who was still running away.

She turned back to the bed. Sleep restored the body, sleep rejuvenated the mind. In the morning her control would be back, her face once more the smooth, expressionless slate she'd perfected so long ago. And she would need it, she thought, remembering once more the feel of Mitch Guiness's penetrating gaze upon her.

She would need it dearly.

For even as she slept, her dreams were filled with the visions of a large, dark man whose brown eyes knew all her secrets.

"I should have known you were a morning person." The deep voice came from behind her, only slightly out of breath from running. Identifying the voice immediately, she felt her face automatically freeze up. Unconsciously, she began to jog a little faster. He caught up without any effort at all.

"Do you always jog at 6:00 a.m.?" he asked, looking over at her as he easily kept pace with her long, lean legs. She still looked like a model, he thought abruptly. She was wearing some all-white, fancy jogging suit that probably cost more than a piece of fine jewelry. No worn-out sweats and baggy socks for her. He found himself smiling beside her, half shaking his head.

He could tell she was mad that he'd caught up with her. Her blue eyes were dark and determined as she stared straight ahead, refusing to acknowledge him with even a glance. He smiled a little wider.

"I imagine this is the first time you've been out in a while," he continued conversationally, unperturbed by her behavior. "You've got to admit, the air here is beautiful."

It was, Jess thought to herself as she struggled to draw in another lungful. It was crisp and clean and perfect for running. Except that she hadn't jogged in over five months, and was beginning to feel it in every aching muscle in her body. It hurt to move, it hurt to breathe.

But she'd be damned before she'd show any signs of weakness in front of him. Keeping her head forward, she continued running. Maybe if she just ignored him long enough, he would go away. And then she could walk. Or collapse. Whichever came first.

"I love the snow," Mitch was saying, trotting right along. He jogged six miles a day, so this morning stint was nothing new to him. In fact, he was rather glad to find she jogged, as well. If he had to stay cooped up all morning just to keep an eye on her, it would have been rough. But instead, he'd heard her up and moving a little after five. At five-thirty, her door had creaked open, and he'd heard her wander downstairs. Apparently, after a glass of orange juice, she'd journeyed outside. Coming downstairs, he'd seen her begin jogging and decided he would take advantage of the situation himself. "There's just enough moisture on the trees to keep the snow sticking to the branches," he continued cheerfully. "Really, this is as close to a New England postcard as you can get."

She seemed to nod slightly as he looked back over at her. Despite her steady pace, he could see the strain in her face. Her eyes looked grim, her hands balled into fists in front of her. It occurred to him that for someone who probably hadn't jogged in a while, she was going pretty fast. Almost imperceptibly, he slowed. She slowed with him, but did not relent.

"I grew up in North Carolina," he said out loud, not really noticing the words as his attention focused on her instead. "Every now and then we got ice, and maybe a little snow. But nothing as beautiful as this."

He eased back a little more, and she adjusted accordingly. Her breath was coming out harder now, in fast, frosty puffs, and he found himself frowning. Would she really run herself into the ground rather than stop in his presence? He would've tested the theory, but he figured he already knew the answer. Damn, but he had never met anyone so stubborn in his entire life.

He suddenly broke into a walk, and after a few more jogging steps, she slowed into walking, as well.

"Are you ever going to speak?" he asked, pretending to be winded, though why he was trying to protect the pride of such an arrogant woman was beyond him.

Speak? Jess's mind registered. Speak? Hell, she didn't have the breath left to sneeze. She didn't want to speak. She wanted to collapse on the ground and drag in huge gulps of air like a dying fish. As it was, she could barely restrain herself from hanging her head between her knees to gasp for air. Turning all her concentration inward, she forced herself to take two deep breaths. She could feel her pulse pounding away, but slowly it began to cool down. She took another steadying breath.

"You're sweating," Mitch said. She gave him a cool look, but he merely shrugged his shoulders like some innocent kid. "I didn't realize the Ice Angel sweats," he told her, then flashed his easy grin.

"I sweat," she said levelly, her blue eyes icy. "The only difference is that I look better doing it than you."

He arched a black eyebrow, clearly amused by this line. He halted, crossing his arms in front of him. "I don't know," he told her. "Most women don't complain when they see me sweat."

"Most women," she informed him, "are too polite."

He chuckled, a deep sound that seemed to reverberate through her own nerve endings. "And you're not afflicted with that state, are you now?" he said.

"What state?"

"Politeness."

She had to bite back another retort. It was clear he found her amusing, and that only grated on her nerves more. She didn't want to be amusing. She wanted to be cold and aloof. It was much more effective.

Abruptly she pivoted, and without giving him a second glance, walked gracefully back toward the house, her head high.

"Perfect," Mitch said, falling in step beside her even as she turned her head pointedly away. "I was getting hungry. What do you say? French toast? Or maybe blueberry pancakes with fresh maple syrup?"

He was walking so close, she could feel the heat radiating from him, a small envelope of warmth amid the frosty winter's day. And she could see the sheen of his perspiration when she glanced over. In spite of what she'd said, it wasn't disgusting at all. In fact, it was a whole host of things she refused to consider.

"I don't eat breakfast," she found herself saying coolly, taking longer steps as if she could honestly put distance between them.

"From what I observed," Mitch replied dryly, "you don't eat much for dinner, either."

She refused to reply, but it seemed she didn't have to. "You'll eat breakfast today," the man beside her said, and there was no more teasing in his voice. "You agreed to gain at least fifteen pounds and that's never going to happen with you picking at food like a small bird." His voice relented a bit, and he looked over at her once more, noting that her face was remote and controlled even at 7:00 a.m. "Come on," he said. "I'll make you chocolate-chip pancakes. I have a sister who's a chocoholic and she will tell you that I absolutely, positively make the best chocolate-chip pancakes in the whole wide world."

"Do I have a choice?" she replied stiffly.

He frowned next to her, and before she knew it, he'd grabbed her arm and jerked them both to a halt. He spun her around before she had time to react, forcing her to look at him. "Look," he said clearly, his dark brown eyes intent in the early-morning light. "I am not your enemy here, Jess McMoran. I am not the one out to get you. In fact, I'm trying to save your precious blond hide. So why the hell do you insist on acting like some arrogant martyr around me?"

Because you're large and strong and powerful, her mind registered as her pulse suddenly soared and her heart leapt to a frantic beat. Because your grip on my arm could snap the bone in two and there would be nothing I could do but bite back the scream.

She met his gaze fiercely, but at the last moment just had to look away.

"Let go of my arm," she said, as if her heart weren't pounding in her chest.

He swore, but released her arm. His eyes darkened with frustration as he ran a hand through his hair. "I'm telling you to gain weight for your own good," he said finally.

She turned back around and continued walking to the house. His impulse said to stop her, but what else could he say to her? When push came to shove, this was going to be a battle of brute will. And he would simply have to emerge victorious. It was the only way to keep all of them safe.

He folded his arms, a frown on his face as he watched her near the door. With her white designer jogging suit, she almost blended into the snowy surroundings, her pale flaxen hair all that gave her away. This evening they would dye and cut that hair. And definitely give her the contact lenses, as well. Perhaps, the sooner he started changing the outside, the sooner he would gain access to the inside. It was a small and feeble hope, but all that he had.

"Oh, Jessica," he called out abruptly, his deep voice carrying easily across the winter sky. She pivoted, her face already frozen into an expressionless slate.

But he simply shook his finger at her mistake of responding to her real name.

"Gotcha," he said. She froze, then turned sharply back around. This time, she did slam the door behind her. And standing out in the cold, Mitch found himself grinning once more. Oh, he would win this battle all right. Simply because whether she liked it or not, she needed him. He was the best there was.

Whistling slightly to himself now, he went back to the house.

When Jess came down after showering, she found that Mitch had indeed made chocolate-chip pancakes. At least some had chocolate chips, while others looked plain. Having regained some of her composure while showering, she did her best to appear unconcerned while she took one of the small unadorned ones, poured herself another glass of orange juice and sat down at the table.

Not, of course, that Mitch Guiness could leave well enough alone. Already seated, he took in her meager breakfast with a shaking head.

"You're missing the point," he told her sternly. Then, before she could stop him, he placed a pat of butter on the pancake and drizzled syrup on it. "Now eat," he said.

Meeting his eyes with her cool, expressionless gaze, she picked up her fork and took the first bite, chewing mechanically as she stared at him. It was sweet and warm and rich in her mouth, things she wasn't suppose to dwell on. Life was a matter of control. If you liked things, then you would want them. That led to problems. But feeling the butter melt on her tongue, thick and creamy, it was hard to remember all that. Which was why she rarely ate anything sweet or rich. It merely reminded her of all the denial a model's life entailed.

Then again, she wasn't a model anymore.

She took the second bite, still meeting his eyes with her own defiantly uncaring stare. But she cut the third bite even faster than the second.

Behind her, the front door opened.

"Good morning, Miss Gavornée," Bill called out. This time, she didn't respond, and Mitch smiled at her approvingly. It was that simple easy smile again, and she could feel its impact all the way to the tips of her toes. Who told this man he could smile so charmingly? What in the world was there to be so charming about? Her hands were suddenly shaking, and she set down the fork to take a long drink of the orange juice, tart and fresh on her tongue.

Mitch hadn't showered yet, but his black hair was still damp from jogging. She could see the way it faintly curled on his neck, and smell once more the compelling mix of sweat and soap. Her appetite left her completely, her stomach suddenly churning with a desperate sort of restlessness.

Summoning control from deep inside, she forced her breath out in a steady sigh. Picking up the fork, she took another bite. But this time, the pancake tasted like ashes on her tongue.

"You should really try a chocolate-chip one," Mitch said idly, his attention caught up by the barest flicker of emotions passing across her face. Bill had just stepped into the kitchen and was pouring himself a glass of orange juice, but Mitch hardly glanced at him at all. He was much more interested in the tightly controlled woman in front of him.

"I'm fine," Jess managed to reply, keeping her eyes slightly away from his steady gaze.

"They're very good," Mitch continued. "I used to make them all the time for my sister, Liz. When she was little, she would follow me around the house on Sunday mornings and beg for chocolate-chip pancakes."

"How nice," Jess answered emotionlessly.

But he ignored her tone, his fingers tapping mindlessly on the tabletop as he continued to watch her. "It's a shame you don't have brothers or sisters. I have three younger brothers and, of course, Liz, and it made all the difference growing up."

Jess took the last bite of the pancake, washing it down with the orange juice. Her hands were trembling, and her stomach kept clenching and unclenching. She had never felt this nervous in her entire life, as if she wanted to run, but didn't know where to run to. As if she were hungry, ravenously hungry, but no food sounded appealing. She slipped her hands under the table to hide the shaking, and it seemed to her that he saw her do it and knew exactly why.

"Where is your family now?" she found herself asking, seeking desperately for a normal, casual tone.

"Oh, scattered about I imagine," he said with a shrug. "Garret's a Navy SEAL, so we never know where he is. Last I heard, Jake was in Eastern Europe looking at some possible investments in manufacturing. Cagney's now a police detective in D.C. Then Liz—" He paused, and Jess risked a glance long enough to see the sadness abruptly wash over his face. In surprise, she didn't look away. "Liz's husband was killed two and a half years ago," he said quietly. "They'd known each other all their lives, and it was very hard for her. So she took a job as a nanny in Connecticut, working for some genius recluse named Richard Keaton. I was pretty suspicious in the beginning—some strange things were certainly happening. But last time I talked to her, she was positively glowing. They've been married a year and I've never seen her happier." His little sister was lucky—she'd found love twice in one lifetime. Himself... He didn't dwell on it. Things happened in their own good time.

He shrugged now, his face once more returning to normal, and Jess found herself nodding.

He seemed to really care about his sister. Truly and genuinely care. And suddenly the emptiness yawned in her so huge, she had to look away. Her whole life had been alone, and she would continue it alone. Alone meant safety and security, and finally after all these years, peace. By herself, she didn't have to mask every emotion or fear. And by herself, she didn't have to wonder when the other person's true colors would emerge, and the violent cycle would set in once more.

Because no one had ever talked about her with the caring emotion Mitch Guiness showed for his sister. And no one ever would.

It was better that way.

She stood, picking up the plates as she fought back the unexpected tightness in her throat.

"I'll help with that," Mitch said, watching her closely. He could see a tightness in her features, watch her Adam's apple work in her throat. Her eyes no longer met his, and though her facial expression hadn't changed, he suddenly detected a different mood about her. A strange mix of sadness, anger and bitterness.

He rose, reaching for the plate of pancakes and taking it easily from her hands. She didn't say anything, didn't even give him a cold scathing glance. Instead, she turned away completely and walked back into the kitchen, not even sparing a glance for Bill who was leaning against the doorframe, orange juice still in hand.

Given the smallness of the kitchen, they stood nearly shoulder to shoulder in front of the sink. Jess promptly offered to do all the dishes herself; the sooner he was away from her, the better. But Mitch insisted on drying, and after a long mutinous look, she gave in with a cool shrug. After that, she worked with quick, expedient moves. The sooner the dishes were done and she was out of the kitchen, the better.

"I imagine there's a lot to do this afternoon," she said at last, rinsing the soap off the last plate.

Next to her, Mitch nodded. "There's a lot of ground to be covered," he said. "From here on out, the learning never really stops. Bill, Jamie and myself will be testing you nonstop. At any given time, we may call you by your old name or your new name. It'll be up to you to learn to stop reacting."

She nodded, understanding. "And what's on this afternoon's agenda?"

"A beautician will be here around four. He'll cut and dye your hair, go over your new contact lenses with you and show you how to use makeup to further alter your appearance. Some of that, of course, will be review for you."

"Hey, Jessica." Bill's voice came from behind her. "Could you rinse this glass for me?"

She didn't turn around, merely glancing over at Mitch with cool eyes. He grinned back at her.

"If you're as good a teacher as you are a pupil, you'll do great," he said.

For some reason, the compliment inordinately pleased her. She did her best to suppress the emotion. After all, what this man thought was irrelevant. And she ought to be a good student—her life depended upon it.

Behind her, Bill congratulated her, and she took his glass.

"I'm going back out on watch," he told Mitch. "Jamie's been on shift since 2:00 a.m., so I imagine he's ready for some sleep."

Mitch nodded curtly, his face all business as he wiped his hands on the towel. "We'll have a small meeting at three, just to go over the schedules. See you then."

"Can I sit in?" Jess asked as Bill walked out.

Mitch gave her a penetrating glance. "Why?"

"It's my life," she replied evenly. "Maybe I want to know how it's being handled."

His face was set and he walked toward the doorway, putting more distance between them. "We're experts, Jess," he said in a shuttered voice. "And we haven't done so badly after all."

In fact, he had no intention of letting her sit in on the meeting. He'd had enough of her distrust. Sooner or later she needed to put some faith in him, just as he and two other men were putting their faith in her. They were all in this together. If any one of them slipped, they all paid the price.

She didn't relent, however, following him back to the sitting area. "If you were in my shoes," she replied shrewdly, "wouldn't you do the same?"

He didn't answer. Instead, he picked up a pack of cards sitting on the edge of the table, sat down and began to shuffle them. "When my sister first lost her husband," he said slowly, his eyes on the shuffling red deck, "she wouldn't eat, or sleep, or talk. We all worried about her, you know. I used to go up to her room, and play these little games for her. Magic tricks. Liz always liked magic tricks." He looked up, pinning Jess with his unfathomable dark eyes. "I bet you don't believe in magic," he said softly.

Slowly, not quite able to take her eyes off him, feeling that restlessness suddenly spark and smolder in her stomach, she nodded. In response, he fanned out the deck before her.

"Pick a card, any card. Look at it, then put it back in the deck. And no matter what, don't tell me the card you selected."

"I want to sit in on the meeting," she said.

"All in good time, Jess. Now humor me. Pick a card."

Reluctantly, she did, her features already freezing over as she drew out and then replaced the three of diamonds. He continued looking at her, his brown eyes boring into hers as he shuffled the deck over and over again with long, capable fingers. Abruptly he stopped the movement and the red cards fell silent. He clapped the deck onto the table.

"Cut the deck into three even piles," he instructed her.

Her eyes sharp and wary, she did as she was instructed, separating the one deck into three even stacks.

He held up the last stack, showing her the bottom card. It was the eight of spades.

She suddenly released the breath she hadn't even been aware she was holding, feeling the scorn settle comfortably on her shoulders.

"This is not your card," he whispered with his unreadable eyes. She felt the tension return, and watched unmoving as his lean fingers peeled the eight of spades off the bottom of the deck and set it aside. He moved to the second stack. Flipping it up, he revealed the queen of hearts.

"This is not your card," he repeated, and once more she nodded, feeling almost impatient now. Once more he peeled off the bottom card, setting it aside with the down-turned eight of spades. The remaining cards he piled back onto the first stack. Now there was just one last section of the previously cut cards. He flipped it up.

The three of diamonds.

Her stomach clenched, but she willed her eyes to remain unreadable. It was merely a sleight of hand she told herself, a con man's petty trick.

"This is not your card," the man before her said, and the triumph flared through her, suddenly hot. But it was followed by something else, not quite so comfortable, as she watched him set aside the card she had selected. A slight feeling of . . . disappointment. Quickly she shook the feeling away.

He was shuffling the remaining cards again, his eyes once more watching hers and giving nothing away. This was no longer the easy grinning man of the kitchen. This man appeared sterner, darker and much more powerful.

"Give me any number one through ten," he instructed softly.

He'd already set aside her selected card, the trick had already failed. But with a small shrug she went along with it.

"Eight," she said.

He nodded, his steady brown eyes boring into hers once more.

"I will bet you anything," he said, "that the eighth card I count out will be yours."

Her eyes narrowed shrewdly at this, her sharp mind quickly running over the possibilities. He'd already cast aside her true choice—it was sitting on the corner with the other two discards.

"What will you bet?" she asked cleverly.

"If I select incorrectly," he said evenly, "you can attend this afternoon's meeting."

"And if you're correct?" she quizzed, not wanting to give herself away by appearing overly confident.

"You have to trust me."

She balked at this, even though she knew she would win, and never have to pay such a forfeit. "That is a ridiculous bet," she informed him curtly.

He arched a dark brow. "You're so determined not to trust, Ice Angel," he whispered softly. "It almost makes me wonder what you fear."

Her back stiffened immediately, her eyes growing cold.

"If I lose," she clipped out slowly, each word dripping frost, "I promise not to question your methods again."

"Fair enough," he concurred, his face not giving her much ground. His gaze fell to the red deck, his hands deftly counting out cards from the bottom of the deck. At the eighth card, his hand froze. Abruptly he flipped it up to face her.

And she was staring at the three of diamonds.

She could not stop the flood of outrage that seized her.

"That's impossible," she snapped, and promptly reached for the three cards on the corner of the table, turning them up. Her eyes scanned over them. But what had once been the eight of spades, queen of hearts and three of diamonds was now the eight of spades, queen of hearts and nine of clubs. "You tricked me," she accused. "You cheated somehow; kept the card up your sleeve—something like that."

He took the cards from her without replying, shuffling them easily back into the deck.

"Maybe I didn't cheat," he told her evenly, setting the deck down on the corner of the table. "Maybe it was magic."

He brushed by her, feeling the anger that radiated from her like icy heat even as her face remained frozen.

"There's no such thing," she said tersely, her hands balling at her sides in her effort at control. He had bested her in a way she had not been bested in years, and even now her mind rebelled against accepting it. There was no such thing as magic.

He stepped down into the living room, glancing at her over his shoulder. And his eyes fell almost casually to her balled fists, then smoothed back up to meet her eyes with his own level gaze.

"Maybe," he told her, "you should believe in magic. Maybe you should believe in me."

He could already see the retort forming on her lips, and he didn't feel compelled to await its arrival. He calmly walked away even as he felt her eyes throw icy daggers into his back.

Behind him, he heard a dull thud, like a fist pounding a table, and as he walked up the stairs he began to grin.

Chapter 4

For the rest of the morning, Jess did her best to ignore Mitch. This wasn't easily accomplished. When she went outside for a walk, it was only to hear cries of "Jessica" behind her. Already duped once, she refused to take the bait the second time. However, she also forgot to turn when Bill called out Miss McMoran, earning another knowing grin from Mitch. Still, by midafternoon she was doing better. To help herself, she trained her mind to think of herself only as Jess McMoran, thirty-year-old schoolteacher. She daydreamed possible memories of college and early aspirations of becoming a teacher while she walked through the freezing January afternoon.

It was like an actress preparing for a role, she told herself. For a few days, she would immerse herself in the other person. And then she would simply be Jess McMoran. Except this role entailed a lifetime job.

Did a lie built upon a lie become a truth?

It would, she told herself fiercely, as she huddled under the thick warmth of Jamie's borrowed jacket. By sheer force of will, she would make it.

Mitch, Bill and Jamie had their meeting at three. True to her word, she did not attend, merely walking gracefully by on her way up to her room to read. Mitch had won the bet, though she'd be wary about being taken in again.

Her blue eyes narrowed as she topped the stairs. Magic was simply a trick, a sleight of hand. She hadn't caught it this time because she hadn't been looking closely enough. But next time, next time she would keep her eyes sharp. She didn't believe in magic, only mankind's knack for deception—something Mitch Guiness had apparently mastered.

At four, a pickup truck pulled up outside. From the upstairs loft, she could look out a window and watch as Mitch strode out to meet the vehicle. It was probably just the beautician Mitch had spoken of earlier, but that didn't quite stop her tension from building. Abruptly, she remembered a not-so-distant fall day. A car driving up, herself trying to get in. And then the cracking sound of rifle fire, the man beside her arching, falling down from the force of the armor-piercing bullet. They hastily shoved her inside the sedan and raced off, leaving her to look through the back window as three remaining agents picked up the lifeless body and bundled it into the last car.

The blood fell upon the crimson leaves and the dull black of the smoky sedan.

She shook the image away abruptly, the scenery before her registering once more the startling white of a snowy January. And Mitch was still standing there, in the wide open like a fool, she told herself vehemently. But her heart pounded in her chest and she could feel the light moisture of sweat on her palms.

Why did he stand there like that?

Suddenly the pickup door swung open. Mitch was already walking toward it, his arms wide in welcome while in her mind she could see the easy grin on his face. Such a powerful body, she thought vaguely. Dark and strong and brimming with vitality.

And absolutely mortal under the impact of a bullet.

She suddenly couldn't take it and turned away. Looking down, she could see her hands shaking while her body trembled with nervousness and dread. What was wrong with her? She didn't think of these things, right? It was all a business arrangement. He took his risk like she took hers, and if it didn't turn out, so be it. It wasn't her fault, damn it. It wasn't.

But for some reason, the thought of that large body suddenly arching under the impact of ferocious lead was too much to take. The past five months were catching up with her, she thought dully. And, of course, people could only take so much blood on their hands.

With a deep breath, she searched for her control. Only then did she become aware of the sound of footsteps on the stairs. She looked up in time to see Mitch emerging onto the loft, tall, commanding and very much alive.

He seemed to freeze halfway across the loft, his eyes suddenly sharpening and looking at her with keen interest. Did the strain show in her face? She couldn't be sure, but years of training enabled her not to fidget. Instead, she steadied her gaze and looked him straight in the eye, defying him to question her mood.

He arched a black brow as if he knew exactly what she was doing.

"Dan is here," he said. "If you'll come to the kitchen, he's ready to start work."

She turned away from the window completely and brushed by him without saying a word. She felt him fall into step behind her, the warmth and vitality reaching out to her once more. And deep in her stomach she felt the restlessness stir even as she fought it back bitterly.

She would not be affected by this man. She would not, she would not, she would not.

"Ready to become a brunette?" he asked, his voice low and close in her ear. "Or do blondes really have more fun?"

"Define 'fun,'" she replied coolly, descending the last few stairs without even a backward glance. She practically sailed into the kitchen, her head held so high and gracefully, she could pass as a queen. And behind her, she could hear Mitch's throaty laugh as he watched.

She still didn't turn around, but her eyes turned a crystalline blue that flashed with inner fire. She focused on the smaller man in front of her.

Dressed in faded Levi's and a brown plaid shirt, he looked more like a hunter than beautician. But when he held up his kit, she could see his eyes were serious and professional. Indeed, he was already raking her over with a critical gaze.

"Yes," he said shortly, his brow crinkled. "You're definitely a model. How challenging." He reached up a brisk hand, grabbing her chin and turning her head from side to side. "What cheeks. I have to say, most snitches don't have your bone structure."

He released her chin and turned immediately to his kit while she looked at Mitch with startled eyes. Mitch grinned at her.

"Meet Dan. He works for the Bureau, does all the important witnesses. Consider yourself in good hands."

"She's having wrinkles, correct?" Dan spoke up crisply. He was perusing the widest assortment of hair dyes Jess had ever seen.

"Yes. Next week, I think."

"Fine, fine. I can see your point now. Hair and eyes will help, but oh, that face. Truly remarkable. Black hair?"

"Dark brown," Jess amended.

He looked at her sharply, scrutinizing her skin once more. "Quite right. Sit. We have a lot of work to do."

It was the last thing he said to her for the next four hours. Mostly he mused to himself, evaluating her hair and face with critical eyes. When he did have a comment or suggestion, he posed it to Mitch who sat on a nearby chair, cutting Jess out of the process completely. She didn't question it because the interaction mirrored the modeling world and thus she was accustomed to it. A model was nothing more than a blank canvas, a passive receiver that came to life on demand. The beauticians and fashion designers were the true artists.

"What about a perm?" Mitch asked shortly. "Something soft and curly to round out her face. At least until she puts on more weight."

Jess glanced over at him coolly, as if the words didn't bother her at all. She'd be damned before she'd give the man any more ground.

"Yes, curls," Dan concurred. "That will help. And shorter, too, I think. It must be a totally new look."

And so it was, four hours later when he was done. Jess stared into the mirror at a dark-haired woman with pale, magnolia skin. Even her eyebrows and lashes had been dyed, accentuating new doe eyes of liquid brown. With a flare of rich, bold colors sweeping across her eyelids, her eyes looked huge in her face.

Huge and . . . soft.

Try as she might, they didn't quite harden the way her natural eyes had. The icy edge seemed suddenly gone, tamed by richer, softer colors. She wasn't sure she liked the change. On their own volition, her eyes swept up to find Mitch.

He was staring at her, a frown apparent on his face as his gaze raked her up and down with critical fervor. He looked uncomfortable for a moment, as if he, too, wasn't sure of this new woman. But then he gave a short, curt nod.

"The contacts bring it all together," Dan commented. For the first time, he addressed her in the mirror, holding up a small box. "You wear them twenty-four hours a day, then toss them at the end of two weeks. In here are enough pairs to last you the first four months. We'll automatically send you a new supply once you're settled."

"Are they hard to get?" she asked, hoping her voice sounded casual.

Dan shook his head, already packing up supplies. "Not at all. Standard disposable soft lenses in brown. Ever miss a shipment, just go to your optometrist. 'Bout fifteen dollars a pair. Just don't let anyone see you without them."

The front door opened, all eyes turning as Bill entered. He stopped upon seeing Jess's new look, then turned to Mitch. "Very good," he said approvingly. "She looks much different than before. At the end of two weeks, you'll have her completely ready for the world."

"Why, thank you," Jess cut in, giving them all a pointed look for excluding her from the conversation.

"We still have to work on that," Mitch abruptly said to Bill, and the other man nodded as if he understood completely.

"Work on what?" Jess demanded coolly, turning to Mitch.

"Your mannerisms," he said curtly. "You look like someone else, but the minute you open your mouth you ruin it."

From the corners of her gaze, she could see both Jamie and Dan suppress smiles. Her outrage was immediate and not quite controllable. Drawing herself up carefully, she pinned Mitch with her new, cold brown gaze. "I see," she said in a voice so smooth, it should have warned him, "so my talking gives me away. Why is that?"

"You're too damn cold," he told her bluntly, even as an inner instinct warned him he was going to pay for the comment.

"Cold?" Jess reiterated, rising slowly from her seat at the kitchen table. Mitch had a brief flash of insight on what was about to happen. But he'd already set the wheels in motion and now he could merely go along with the ride.

She took a step toward him. But this wasn't a Jessica Gavornée step. This was a hip-swinging, Marilyn Monroe style step that had three pairs of eyes suddenly looking at the long lean lines of a perfectly shaped leg. She took another luxurious step, her hands coming up to run carelessly through her new short hair. She shook her head, as if reveling in the freedom of cropped, curly hair. Her lips formed a small, teasing pout, while her brown eyes swept down to his lips, pausing one long, tantalizing second before brushing back up to his eyes.

"Cold?" she whispered this time, taking the last step toward him. She could feel Bill and Dan watching her, but her attention was only for Mitch. That tall powerful man just twelve inches away. Her hands came down to land lightly on his shoulders, like the gentle wings of a butterfly. And all the more maddening for the lightness of touch.

She leaned closer, until she could catch the faint scent of soap and feel the soft whisper of his suddenly indrawn breath. Once more her gaze came down, lingering on his lips. They were full and sensual—strong lips for a strong man. And she bet when he kissed a woman, he kissed her completely until there was no room for any other thought, any other sensation.

Her eyes came back to meet his own, and were rewarded by the low burning of reluctantly sparked desire. His breathing wasn't so steady, either. She leaned in just a tad more, as if she might caress his lips with her own. But at the last minute she veered to the left suddenly, like a mischievous lover who decided to whisper in his ear instead.

"Cold?" she whispered in a throaty voice so close, his hair fluttered from the caress. "Why, Mr. Guiness." Her voice suddenly hardened. "I'm the coldest thing this side of hell."

She pushed herself abruptly away with elegant hands that had turned to fists, all signs of seductive teasing suddenly gone as her face froze into the familiar angles of the Ice Angel. Her new brown eyes were hard with her anger and outrage, looking him over now as if he weren't even worth kicking.

And at that minute, he wasn't sure whether to curse her for her duplicity, or admire her for her control. Because God knows his own pulse rate had nearly tripled, and when she'd bent so close to him, with that maddening scent of peaches, it had been all he could do not to abandon logic and grab her.

In the challenge of wills with this woman, the winner would never be clear.

He released his pent-up breath slowly, willing his pulse rate to ease as he looked at her with openly amused eyes that admitted their own hunger.

"Well, we can't ever accuse you of having no talent, can we?" he said softly, crossing his arms in front of him nonchalantly.

The gesture also made him seem larger and more intimidating. She wasn't sure whether she should back up or arch one hand of carefully manicured nails across his challenging face. Never had any man treated her like he did, as if every move she made was for his personal enjoyment. The insufferable son of a bitch.

A tense silence stretched across the room, neither moving, neither giving in. At long last, Bill cleared his throat in the doorway.

"Excuse me," he said politely, suddenly resuming the mantle of blue-suited FBI agent. "But I believe it's my turn to cook dinner." Not waiting for their reply, he passed between them on his way to the tiny kitchen, giving Jess the excuse she needed to step back. She turned, still dignified and cool, and picked up the mirror. She took in her new self with one last critical look.

"Very good," she said at last, turning to Dan. "You did excellent work. The only real trouble should be keeping the roots up."

He nodded briskly, clearly relieved to be back on the subject at hand. "Yes, your hair was very light. Touch up at least every two, three weeks, definitely. Can you dye?"

She nodded.

"Good, good. Do it yourself then for the first six months or so. Mitch will agree it's the best for security. Don't want everyone to know right away you're not a natural brunette. Questions?"

"Not at all," she replied levelly. The brunette hair did make her look different, especially with the shorter, softer cut. The investment in time was well worth the gain in security. God knows Les was so caught up with blondes, he'd never imagine one voluntarily turning brunette.

Her reply seemed enough for Dan, because he was already closing his case. Mitch invited him to stay for the late dinner, but the man didn't seem interested. In a blink of the eye, he was out the door again, apparently with a long drive to his next appointment.

With him gone, there was only Bill to referee the silence at dinner. Mitch seemed to have relaxed to his normal self, but Jess refused to be drawn in. She was angry with the man. Angry because he didn't give her the distance most men gave her. And angrier still that no matter what she said or did to retaliate, he never seemed to mind. Most other men who tried to intrude were easily repelled, their fragile male egos squashed at her first coolly uttered comment. But this man seemed completely insufferable.

And the more she thought about it, the more it angered her.

After dinner, she once more did the dishes. She hadn't had to cook yet, so it was the least she could do. Bill excused himself immediately to catch some sleep before his 2:00 a.m. shift began. It was already nearly ten, the makeover having consumed most of the evening.

"Tomorrow will be a busy day," Mitch said from the table. He'd pushed back on the bench, stretching his long legs out before him. He seemed to fill the entire dining area, the soft plaid of his blue shirt shifting as he rolled a tired shoulder.

"What time do you want to begin?" she asked from the kitchen, her tone neutral.

He frowned as he contemplated this. "Probably 8:00 a.m.," he said finally. "That way you can get in another jog if you'd like."

Considering how tight her leg muscles were already beginning to feel, she highly doubted that. "Eight will be fine," she said. "And what will we be working on?"

"Tomorrow's the big day. We'll start with poise and walking. Then work on resting posture, hand motions, facial expressions. Everything that makes you, you."

She nodded from the kitchen, and the motion suddenly made him smile. Watching her now, he wondered if she even realized the extent of what he was talking about. She was a carefully controlled person, and tomorrow she would have to give that up. It was too distinguishing. Like now, for instance. No random splashing or crashing when she did the dishes. Instead, she took each plate, one by one, and wiped it clockwise three to four times. If there was one trouble spot, it received an independent scrub. Then the plate was run delicately under the water, first the front, then the back. Finally, she laid it carefully upside down on the towel to dry. Every motion was smooth and precise, like watching a well-oiled clock.

He could remember his own sister, Liz, doing the dishes. She liked to sing while she did them, and every now and then throw in little dancing steps, as well. She'd whirl plates, dash them under the water, stick them in the drying rack, then decide suddenly they weren't so clean after all and jerk them back out—until the entire sink area—and generally part of her, as well—was covered in soapy water. But she had fun doing it. Somehow he couldn't picture Jess ever describing anything as fun.

Strange, he thought suddenly. The woman before him was twenty-four, actually a few years younger than Liz. But watching her, the control of her expressions, the poise of her movements, she didn't seem twenty-four at all. In terms of manners and sophistication, she could pass for twice her years.

What aged a woman so quickly? He had a feeling she would never tell him. She didn't even like him. Then again, he baited her enough, he acknowledged to himself. He preferred her quietly simmering to coldly composed. At least simmering, she seemed close to human. And sooner or later he just might provoke her enough to actually give something away.

She finished the last dish now, setting it next to the other dishes to dry. She replaced the towel then turned, startling slightly at his intent gaze.

"I look that different, don't I?" she said, halting in the middle of the kitchen as her head came up.

He nodded, his gaze raking her up and down. She did look different. The shorter haircut accentuated the clean lines of her face, and her soft brown eyes looked huge. Combined with her dark hair and pale skin, she looked somehow fresher, and well, more vulnerable.

"Do you miss being the supermodel?" he asked quietly. She shook her head.

"Schoolteachers don't get to fly to Paris," he said. "And I don't suppose you'll get to wear designer gowns again, or stare people down with frosty blue eyes. Now you'll just live in suburbia with the rest of the masses. One more little fish in a big pond."

"Little fishes in big ponds attract less notice from sharks," she replied softly. "That's all I want."

He narrowed his eyes suddenly, looking at her with his keen gaze. "Why did you live with such a man? The more

I get to know you, the more I can't see you putting up with a man like Les."

"It's getting late," she said, turning her face slightly away. "I should be going to bed."

"Coward's way out, huh?" he prodded. "All these months, and you're still avoiding everyone's questions."

Her head came back around, her eyes meeting his squarely now.

"It's no one's business," she told him evenly. "No one's business but mine. It's not even your business, though I'm sure you hate to admit that."

He shrugged, acknowledging her point. "It's not my business," he admitted. "But I am curious. After all, I'm risking my neck to save yours. Maybe I just want to know how it all got started."

"I was born blond," she told him flippantly. "That's how it started."

He smiled at her, a sudden slow smile that disarmed her completely, which was probably exactly what it was meant to do. "Well, we fixed that now, didn't we?" he drawled.

She didn't trust herself to answer. When he looked at her like that, with that easy grin and those bright eyes, her stomach did things it wasn't supposed to do. Didn't he realize he was supposed to be menacing and cold? Or egotistical and stupid? Not this strange combination of ease and strength she couldn't quite figure out nor trust. Her hands came up to her hair. He was right—she was no longer blond. Now she had dark, curly hair and big brown eyes.

If you looked different long enough, did you become different, too? Would she go to sleep one night and dream Jess McMoran dreams, the nightmares of Jessica Gavornée long gone? Would there be a time when her instincts and impulses would no longer be her own, but belong to this new face and new name?

She imagined this man before her would tell her no, and she couldn't bear to hear that right now. This man appeared to be one of those tough, honor-bound, black is black, white is white type of guys, which was easy enough for men. They were stronger, so they could set the rules. Les Capruccio had also espoused strong sentiments of loyalty and honor. Of course, those had applied to his interactions with other men and associates, and certainly were no barrier to beating the woman he considered his property.

It was easy for this man here to look at her and want to know the truth, because how would the truth ever hurt him? He was strong and powerful and could probably knock a woman out with one negligent, drunken fist.

Of course, the lies could hurt him well enough, a small voice intruded. He told her she had to give up all claim to the past. That she had to trust him, because he was trusting her. That her mistakes could cost them all.

Like a bullet through the back, like blood on fall leaves.

She shook the thought away, her fists unconsciously bunching at her sides. She wouldn't be taken in by those lines. This man was the supposed hotshot; he ought to be able to take care of himself. It wasn't her responsibility; she refused for it to be her responsibility. In a matter of days she would be gone, and then her lies would be her own, and her mistakes, as well.

From the table, Mitch watched her. She seemed to have slipped away to unknown thoughts that darkened her brown eyes and clenched her hands into fists. He could see her stiffen, her face looking suddenly stark, then slowly she relaxed once more. Her expression melted back into its passive, neutral state, the control once more covering the dark sparks of her inner thoughts. He was left wanting more.

Her control wasn't as good by the end of day, he observed to himself. Both last night and tonight, things started seeping through. It appeared Cinderella began to waver as the clock neared midnight. If he kept her up late enough, exhausted her enough, would her secrets suddenly appear as blatantly as Cinderella's true rags? It was an intriguing thought.

"It's been a long day," he observed quietly, watching her intently. She merely nodded, still standing in the middle of the kitchen.

"Feeling sore from the jog yet?" he inquired, trying a new tactic.

"A little" was all she'd admit.

"There's a hot tub on the deck in the back," he suggested mildly. She immediately stiffened, though, her eyes growing wary.

"I believe I will be going to bed now," she said. And this time she no longer wavered but moved out of the kitchen. He noticed she kept close to the wall as she crossed the dining area, where he sat, into the living room. Oh, the hot tub suggestion had certainly spooked her. Did she think he had lecherous intents? He remembered his earlier reaction to her little act, and smiled wryly to himself. All right, so he couldn't blame her.

Still, he wasn't quite ready to let her go, either. He pushed himself off the bench, rising to his full height. She hesitated in the living room, then quickly went up the stairs. Almost leisurely he followed.

His longer legs took him up the stairs faster and he caught her still in the loft. Her hands began fidgeting, and her wariness was clear now.

"Isn't this a little early for you?" she asked sharply. "I thought you hotshot types stayed up half the night because you're so great you don't even need sleep."

He arched a black brow. "You've been watching too many movies," he told her calmly. "I personally enjoy sleeping very much. However, if memory serves, you were the one who got very little sleep last night."

"How do you know that?" she demanded at once, edging closer to her door. He was playing with her—her instincts told her that. But it was late and she was tired, and suddenly she hadn't any composure left for games. He was too tall and powerful and she wished he would have just stayed downstairs. Left her alone. She really just wanted to be left alone.

"The walls here are thin," Mitch replied. "And you're a restless sleeper."

That he knew so much about her stung. That even here she had so little privacy hurt. She was tired of all the protection, tired of the blue suits and all the things she had to do because they said it was for her own good.

"My sleeping habits are my own concern," she said tautly. "Don't you have better things to be observing or analyzing? At this point, dying in my sleep is the least of my worries.''

He chuckled, a low easy sound that reverberated all the way to her toes. ''You're quite right about that.''

He leaned against the wall, and the more relaxed stance took some of the edge off her nerves. He noticed her posture relent slightly, and stored that observation away for future reference.

''Don't worry,'' he told her now. ''You're quite safe here. Only myself and a handful of men know of this place.''

''It only takes one,'' she pointed out coolly.

He shook his head, marveling once more at her suspicious mind. ''You are so determined not to trust any of us, aren't you?'' he said, though it was really a rhetorical question.

She nodded, challenging him with her brown gaze.

''We haven't done so badly,'' he pointed out reasonably, not sure why he was trying to argue with someone who had such a reputation for being stubborn. Except that all his life, Mitch had been the trustworthy one. People always looked up to him, relied on him, and he'd always come through. From the child who had brought abandoned kittens home to the adult who had held his sister while she cried out her grief at her young husband's tragic death, he'd been the responsible one. Yet this woman seemed determined to think badly of him, and he didn't deserve it. ''We saved your life twice,'' he continued now. ''One of our agents even died for you. Yet you still scorn us. Pretty ungrateful, if you ask me.''

She stiffened, and he could tell he'd struck a nerve. ''From my perspective,'' she said frostily, ''two attempts were made on my life when I had been promised that I was safe, that no one would find me. So how did those two hit men find me, Mitch? If the Witness Protection Program is so good and you guys so reliable, why were there even two attempts?''

''Because Les is good, as well,'' he said levelly, acknowledging her point. ''And he has the money and the resources to hire the best.''

"That statement doesn't inspire confidence in my continued well-being," she said scornfully, her gaze raking him up and down as if he were nothing.

He didn't take offense, though. In fact, he winked at her, then grinned.

"You forget," he told her. "I'm a magician."

"Too bad I'm not a white bunny rabbit, then," she retorted smartly. He could grin all he wanted. She'd seen the true impact of bullets, and no sleight of hand could save him from that. Nor herself for that matter.

In front of her, Mitch had abruptly sobered and was looking at her once more with his penetrating brown eyes.

"'Oh, ye of little faith,'" he quoted softly. "You're so determined to keep the world at bay, Jess McMoran. But the truth of the matter is, you need me right now. And I don't care what you think, or what you say. I won't let you down. No matter what other men may have done to you in your life, I'm not them. I'm the man you can trust. And face it, sweetheart, you don't have any other choice."

Her posture abruptly relaxed, but this time he didn't find it reassuring. She suddenly smiled, an expressionless smile that worried him.

"So you say," she said quietly. "Good night, Mr. Guiness. You were right downstairs—tomorrow is going to be a long day. We both need our rest."

She ducked into her room before he could reply, closing the door calmly behind herself. He didn't move right away, though, but remained leaning against the wall, contemplating her door. He didn't like her sudden acceptance of his last statement. And he didn't trust it.

Something was up in Ice Angel's mind. His brown eyes narrowed, his sharp mind kicking into place. Oh, she was a challenge all right. But he meant what he said. He'd keep her safe.

Even in spite of herself.

Chapter 5

"No, no, no. You still look like you're on some damn runway. Slouch, I said. Slouch!"

Jess's brown eyes looked slightly mutinous, but she tried to do as Mitch instructed. Unfortunately, eight years of training to stand straight were hard to undo. Frowning, Mitch crossed the snowy distance to stand over her.

They'd been out in the cold for a half hour already. Jess had actually requested that they work outside. After being cooped up for five long months, she still savored the feeling of the icy January wind mixing with the crisp winter sun on her face. Mitch had her walking back and forth so much, she really didn't notice the chill much anyway.

"Here," Mitch was saying. Abruptly his hands landed on her shoulders and she stiffened immediately. He frowned again, peering at her with intense eyes. "Relax, for crying out loud," he said impatiently. "I'm trying to help you, not eat you for breakfast."

She wasn't sure whether she trusted that last statement or not, but she had little choice in the matter. As she'd already figured out, he wasn't put off by her glacial looks or frosty stares. Even now as she went rigid at his touch, he simply pushed on her shoulders harder, ignoring her reaction completely. If only she could ignore him, as well. But she could smell the faint scent of his after-shave and feel the strong pressure of his touch. And this close, she had to look up at his strong, dark features, leaning much too close to her own.

"Look," he was saying again. "Get this through your head. You are no longer a model, and life is not a runway. Okay? Now, five-foot-ten females who are not models are usually self-conscious about their height. Don't you remember being taller than all the boys in your class? Don't you remember any feelings of awkwardness at all?"

She merely looked at him with her cool brown eyes. He shook his head in exasperation and tried a new tact. "Remember the first night you were here," he said, "and you said you would do whatever was necessary to keep yourself safe?"

She nodded, and he threw up his hands in mock triumph.

"Well, here you go, sweetheart. This is what we're talking about. Now stop fighting me and start putting that considerable talent to work."

"I am trying," she said tightly, her eyes growing more mutinous. "It's not as easy as you think."

"Yes, it is," he told her. "You simply have to relax and stop walking like you have a ruler belted to your back. Think of it as a special show, I don't know. But do something to enable yourself to relax."

Relax? She certainly couldn't relax with him just eight inches away and peering at her with such intense brown eyes, she could feel her stomach clench and unclench with every breath. But then, she didn't seem to have any choice in the matter. Taking another deep breath, she turned her concentration inward. What he'd said from the beginning was correct. She needed a new identity, which meant new mannerisms and new attitudes. This would keep her safe, and if it meant dealing with the devil himself, then she would do it.

Turning away from Mitch, she walked four steps back to get the distance she needed. Then she closed her eyes and considered his goal. Slouching, relaxing, rolling the shoulders inward. She pictured the way she'd seen other people walk on the street, latching on to one example in particular. Then she forced her muscles into imitation, a skill she'd mastered long ago. It took a few more tries, but finally Mitch nodded approvingly.

"Better," he said, his gaze still critical as he watched her pivot and cross back in the other direction. "Now we're making progress."

In actuality, Jess caught on fast. But he knew her capabilities, and pushed her to meet them. A woman of her control and intelligence ought to learn fast. In fact, he'd expected her to adapt even faster than she was. But the woman seemed to fight anything that involved giving up control. Even now, her shoulders slightly forward, her steps shorter and easier, she still didn't look quite right. He walked over to where she was standing, looking at her intently once more.

"What are we doing wrong?" he demanded to know, his eyes sweeping her up and down. This close he could catch the faint scent of peaches, something he was trying very hard to ignore. But the scent was so fresh and subtle, as if she delicately dabbed a scented oil to each pulse point in turn, never overdoing, just the right touch. And now the fragrance mingled with the fresh New Hampshire air until peaches and pine and snow all tangled his senses and left him a little bit dazed. "The peaches will have to go," he found himself saying.

Immediately she stiffened up to her normal rigid stance, one newly brown eyebrow arching. "Excuse me?" she asked coolly.

"Your fragrance," he said, his voice tighter than it needed to be. Damn, she could play havoc with a man's senses. Looking like ice, smelling like summer. "It's too distinguishable."

Slowly she shook her head. "I never wore this for Les," she said evenly. "He was a Chanel man."

For some reason, that statement inordinately pleased him. Les had never gotten to smell the ripe scent of peaches of her soft, pale skin. Only he had.

He had to forcefully shake the thought away. It was none of his business. None of his business at all.

"All right, then," he said, but he didn't quite trust himself to meet her eyes. "The fragrance can stay. What else shall we change, then? You are still too you."

She shrugged a delicate shoulder. "I can slouch more if you like. Walk slower, walk faster. Perhaps a habit would be good. Some people twist their rings, chew their nails, that sort of thing."

He nodded, his mind considering the possibilities. "Yes, that would be good. You're still too controlled. Some sort of nervous habit would be an improvement. What do you think—a ring twister? Maybe you could chew on your lower lip."

She gave him a cool look at his last suggestion. "I will twist my ring," she said pointedly. He shrugged and had her practice it a few times. But even with the toned-down walk and rounded resting posture, it still wasn't right. It took him a moment to hit on it, but then it came to him.

"A smile," he said suddenly. "You need to smile."

She cocked her head to the side, considering this. "A simple smile?"

"Exactly. A simple smile. See, you're still too controlled. You maintain this certain air and poise of untouchability. It may be perfect for a supermodel, but how many grade school teachers have you ever encountered that looked distant? You need to relax, sweetheart. Smile a little, loosen those shoulders. When you look people in the eye, really look at them as if you're listening. As if you care."

The last statement came out matter-of-factly, but she could feel its sting. Jessica Gavornée never looked at people like that. Jessica Gavornée never really looked at people at all. She hadn't been known for being cruel or petty or mean. But Mitch was right. Jessica was definitely cold.

And now, according to him, she would have to give that up.

She would have to look at people as if she cared.

A ripple fizzled through her, a ripple of nervousness and fear and unease. She felt it and tried to fight it down but it wasn't that easy. And suddenly the implications of all he'd told her became clear. A new identity didn't mean learning a new name, it meant becoming a new person. All the way deep down in places she didn't really want to change.

In places she was too afraid to ever truly explore.

Jessica Gavornée had very good reasons for her control.

Mitch watched her stiffen, and in a matter of moments all his work of the morning dissolved before his eyes. The new posture was lost and her face stiffened to the remote neutrality he'd come to know too well. The only redeeming aspect he could find was that her left hand suddenly began twisting the simple silver band on her right hand.

He walked back over until he was close enough to catch the scent of peaches.

"Smile for me," he commanded softly. "Just one simple smile."

She looked up, and in her brown eyes he saw a myriad of flickering emotions. Then ever so slowly, her lips curved upward. But it wasn't the gentle, easy smile he'd been expecting. Instead, it was the stiff cold smile of a painted marionette.

He shook his head.

"Come on, Jess," he cajoled intensely. "Don't play hard to get like this. All we want is a smile. One smile. Remember, this is your life we're talking about here."

She nodded, and he saw something new glisten in her eyes. It seemed suspiciously close to torment.

Once again her lips curved, once again the smile strained against her face like an alien creature, uncomfortable and unsure.

Frowning, he reached up and traced the smile with his hands.

She recoiled as if slapped, her face resorting immediately to fierce closure.

Mitch shook his head, turning away with a small curse in the bright winter's day.

"You have to give it up," he told her finally, running a frustrated hand through his shiny black hair.

"Give what up?" she asked suspiciously. Her lips still seemed to burn from the sudden touch, and she was stepping back as she spoke. She didn't want him that close. She didn't want him to touch her like that. For anyone to touch her like that. But especially him, a man that made her stomach flutter when her stomach never fluttered.

"Whatever makes you so damn angry," he retorted sharply, turning enough to pin her with commanding eyes. "You're starting a new life, damn it. You are a new person. The past injustices don't matter anymore. They're gone, too. Now focus on that. Let all that icy control of yours go. Jess McMoran doesn't have any need for it."

Her face never changed, her hand remaining protectively in front of her. "I will work on it," she said finally.

He shook his head, swearing under his breath. "We're back to the basics, Jess. This is what I told you in the beginning. Your new identity has to be more than skin-deep. Which means you don't just work on it, you let it go. You are no longer Jessica Gavornée. Jessica Gavornée's problems do not affect you. I'm telling you now, that's what you have to do. I will not settle for anything less."

"Take me shooting," she said abruptly, her brown eyes narrowing.

"What?"

"Take me shooting," she repeated again, her voice level and her eyes cool. Suddenly she saw an opening, and she seized it with a calmness that belied the desperate beating of her frantic heart. "Take me shooting and I promise I will smile for you."

Mitch could only look at her incredulously. Never in all his days had he met such an infuriating creature. But the challenge of getting her to smile was too much to pass up. She promised him a smile. He would have it.

"Deal," he said.

She nodded curtly, sealing the pact. "What time?"

"Tomorrow morning. I'll set up the targets. Smile is deliverable upon end of session."

She nodded again, her face serious. "It has to be a real lesson. I want to know about the type of gun, how to shoot it, how to take care of it. Safety tips. Everything."

He nodded back, his face as serious as her own. "Believe me, Jess. I won't be the one to cop out of the agreement. You'll have a good, solid lesson."

"Fine, then." She looked away, her brown eyes focusing on the distance. She could still feel the nervousness and tension rivet through her. Funny, she'd thought this new deal would take care of all that. After all, it was one step closer to her freedom. She had her new look, except for the wrinkles, which were scheduled for next week. She had her new name and she at least understood how she was supposed to act. After tomorrow's lesson in defense, she'd be all set. She could devise a plan tonight and hit the road the day after tomorrow.

Then she'd be free of the FBI and programs, and most particularly, this man standing just a few feet away. They might try to find her, but she would have broken the Witness Protection Program pact, and thus they would have no obligations toward her. They would leave her alone, renouncing her altogether, and she could live with her new identity in peace. While the FBI would have no reason to protect her, they certainly wouldn't give her away, either. She'd simply be written off with a bureaucratic shrug.

They would get on with their business, and she would get on with hers. She'd take classes on her own, living off the money from her Swiss bank account. In time, she'd earn her teacher's license, since she wouldn't be sticking around long enough to receive one from the Feds. She would take care of herself, build a new life as Jess McMoran.

So the shooting lesson was the final step, and having secured it, she should feel relieved. In forty-eight hours, she would be gone.

But the frisson of fear and nerves snaked through her once more. Mitch said she needed to relax in order to pull off the new identity. He wanted Jess McMoran to let go of Jessica Gavornée's troubles. And she wanted to, she desperately did. But the smile wouldn't come to her face, nor the relief to her muscles. Because if the last two nights had been any indication, Jess McMoran still dreamed Jessica Gavornée's nightmares—and, under all the carefully developed control, dwelled the same dark pits she never allowed herself to explore.

And she wished this man wouldn't stand so close nor look so strong nor smell so good. She wished he'd simply go away, and yet when she'd bolted awake from the nightmares, his face was the first picture to come to mind, his easy grin the first grip on her salvation.

With a deep shuddering breath, she drew herself up once more, reclaiming her control. Sooner or later she would learn to at least fake the smile, as she had learned how to act so many other things in her life. If it meant her life, it was worth the effort. She would make herself Jess McMoran, and she would shut this man out of her mind once and for all.

"We should practice more," she said tightly, her eyes still focused far away where they wouldn't have to see his.

"Yeah," Mitch said. "We should."

He worked her the rest of the day. As he'd promised in the beginning, it was drill after drill after drill. Jamie and Bill constantly referred to her by changing names, anything from Jessica to Ms. McMoran to Jess Gavornée. But Jess adapted with shrewd swiftness that easily mastered the game. Never had Mitch worked with someone who could change so fast and learn so quickly. By dinnertime she'd relaxed her walk into an easy, rounded stride, mastered the art of carelessly toying with her ring and learned to look at people sideways through her soft, curly hair, making her appear more flirtatious. Or so she was told.

But with all that she still couldn't seem to relax her facial muscles, and she still wasn't close to a smile. It was a source of constant torment from Mitch, and by the end of the evening, a thorn in her side. She wanted to be able to smile, damn it, and she would. She swore it.

Yet, as she tried the motion time and time again in front of the privacy of her bedroom mirror, it still looked forced and artificial on her face. She had smiled for hundreds of magazines. Pouting smiles, sexy smiles and once, even a wistful smile. But here, even in the cover of the night, she could not find one natural smile.

You've got to leave Jessica Gavornée behind.

She truly wished she could. She wished life could be that simple, and new identities a simple process of erasing the old and sketching in the new. She wished she could will a smile as she willed everything else in her life. But the very control that had been her salvation was her nemesis now. And the control had begun so long ago and was ingrained so deep, she didn't even know how to begin to change it.

"If you're just quiet, sugar, he won't even notice you. He'll go away and you'll be okay. You just gotta learn to be quiet."

The memory came from nowhere, but suddenly she could see herself sitting on the edge of her mother's bed, watching her mother in the mirror. Seated at the vanity, her mother had a pot of makeup in hand. Slowly, with practiced strokes, she covered up the bruise on her cheek.

"There now, sweetheart. Good as new. Don't your mama look beautiful? Come along, now. We'd better get the roast in the oven. And remember, sugar, don't make a fuss tonight. For Mama, okay? Just be quiet for mama?"

But she could still hear the sound of her mother crying in the kitchen, still feel the sharp sting of the descending belt. Somehow, quiet had never been quiet enough. At least her mother kept a lot of makeup in that vanity.

She looked in her own mirror and tried one last smile. The movement just didn't match with her years. She found herself smiling cynically instead. Oh, but her mama could be proud now. Her daughter had learned to be quiet. She'd learned not to fuss, or talk back, or move at the wrong time. And she'd learned more tricks with makeup than her own mother had known.

So here was Jessica. One giant, controlled glacier that had made all her mother's mistakes. One incredibly smart, capable, strong woman who didn't even know how to smile.

You've got to leave Jessica Gavornée behind.

She couldn't. The ties were beyond skin-deep, and drew her to the past as surely as they ever had. She would become a new name, but she would never truly escape. Her only hope was simply for respite. She just wanted a quiet, steady existence in which nightmares remained nightmares and could never come true. Her mother had married a loser who'd beaten them both until that last fateful day. Jess had gotten entangled with Les.

If you learned lessons from the past, then family history dictated that having no man was better than having one.

And if Mitch Guiness even suspected the secrets she still kept...

She looked at the mirror one last time, willing a smile onto her new face. But once more, the twist of her lips refused to match the look in her eyes.

She shook her head and moved at long last to her bed. Tomorrow was going to be a big day. And the day after that, even bigger. She willed herself to sleep.

But not even her willpower could keep the nightmares at bay.

She was already waiting in the entryway when Mitch came downstairs. She was practicing her loose-shouldered stance and twisting the ring on her right hand with far more nervousness that she would ever admit to. He arched a dark brow, glancing her up and down as he observed her new stance combined with her new look.

"We're getting there," he said, and she didn't have to ask what he meant. In fact, Mitch was pleased by the progress they'd made. Compared to the first day when she'd stepped out of the dark sedan with her sleek blond hair and tailored white silk suit, the woman in front of him was different.

She kept her short, dark hair down, the left side tucked behind her ear while the rest of the chin-length waves swept forward. Her jeans and the thickly corded sweater completed the picture of a young, girl-next-door appearance. At least, until you looked at her face. Her eyes were still much too wary, her expression too settled. But they would work on that, he assured himself as he shrugged into his own coat. After all, today she owed him a smile. He picked up a small bag with the necessary equipment and headed for the door.

She followed him wordlessly outside, bundled up in Bill's jacket. From what she could tell, Jamie and Bill worked eight-hour revolving shifts. So Jamie was on watch now, working the 2:00 a.m. to 10:00 a.m. shift. Bill would then work ten to six, with Jamie then covering from six to two. She would have thought the schedule would totally ruin their body clocks, but they seemed to handle it. And it made it easier for her to figure out who was watching when. Her project for this afternoon was to determine their watch posts, or any walking patterns they made. Then she would be all set.

"Here, this ought to be far enough out," Mitch said. Jess came to a sudden halt to find herself standing in a small clearing beyond the edges of the property markers. Mitch opened up the plastic bag and took out two empty two-liter bottles. Then he withdrew two sets of headsets and finally, a small leather holster containing a gun. He handed her one headset, and she draped it around her neck like he did. Finally he turned toward her, his face serious.

"Now remember what I said earlier," he told her evenly. "Today's lesson should be used as a starting point, not an instant license to shoot to kill. It takes years of practice and training to become a good shot. Plus, guns are not an immediate problem solver, and really should be used only as a last resort when facing immediate physical threat."

She looked at him impatiently. "I'm not going to sue you," she said pointedly. "And I'm not in the FBI, so you don't need to quote me the official party line."

"I'm quoting you common sense," he corrected sharply, his brown eyes narrowing. "Now we do this my way, or we don't do it at all."

Her lips thinned, but she gave in with a curt nod.

"Now, then," he continued. He held out the leather holster and unsnapped it to reveal a decent-size gun. "This is a Smith & Wesson Chief's Special, your basic .38 revolver. You will find a lot of people running around today with semiautomatic guns, but this is still the best gun for a beginner. It has solid firepower and five chambers. Considering the fact that most gunfights occur with people just seven yards apart, you don't need a huge weapon, just control. It doesn't matter how big a gun you carry nor how many bullets if you still can't aim. The gun supplies the firepower, but you must supply the brains."

She nodded, looking at the form in his hands. It looked solid and heavy. Unexpectedly, she felt a strange achy feeling open in her stomach. She tried to swallow it back down and focus on Mitch instead.

"First, I want you to just get familiar with the weapon. There aren't any bullets in it now. Just hold it, become accustomed to the weight and the trigger. This is a double-action gun, so you can cock it for a shorter trigger, or after the first full pull back, the trigger will remain set for short, rapid follow-up fire. Here, you take it."

He handed her the gun, and for the first time, saw that her hands were shaking. He looked at her sharply, but she didn't say anything as she accepted the pistol. Her eyes were once more distant as she looked at the weapon, and her face remained expressionless.

"Never point the gun at a person," he said, his voice quieter now. "Even when you think the gun is empty."

She nodded, but he could see her hands were still trembling.

"Jess," he said softly. "You really don't need to know how to shoot."

"I want to," she said, but the words were unexpectedly low. She turned slightly away, raising her arms to point the gun toward the trees. The weapon felt unexpectedly heavy in her hands, and the shaky feeling wouldn't leave her stomach. Fear. She could taste it in her mouth, feel it in each light tremble rippling through her.

A gun is just a tool, she reminded herself. The only true evil is the person who carries it.

The gold carpet, the pattern of red and brown leaves. The distant thud of footsteps, drawing nearer, nearer, nearer...

"Pull the trigger." Mitch's voice came true and deep. "Feel the weight of the trigger. The first pull won't be easy."

She nodded, narrowing her eyes as she focused her attention on pulling back the trigger. It was tight and hard. Then abruptly, the trigger came back with the echoing click of an empty chamber.

"Come on, baby. Where are you hiding? Come say hi to your—"

She pulled the trigger again, hearing the empty click register in the silence. She turned back to Mitch, who took the gun from her nerveless hands with intense eyes.

"A gun is a serious weapon," he said quietly, "and is nothing to be taken lightly."

"Bullets, please," she said.

He showed her how to load the gun, inserting five .38 special bullets into the chamber. Then he had her put on the earphones. The outside world was abruptly muzzled, leaving her feeling suddenly alone in the clearing, too aware of her own solitude. Mitch gestured her to stand aside, and she mutely obeyed, her stomach hopelessly empty.

She suddenly thought she might vomit.

The first crack of the gun made her jump, even with the earphones on. The sound ricocheted through the silence like a boom of thunder, loud and abrupt. One of the two-liter bottles jumped back like a man possessed. A second shot cracked and the last empty bottle sprayed backwards. She could smell the acrid odor of gunpowder.

And the man falling, down down down onto the gold-patterned carpet. The soundless scream, echoing down the hall. The burning smell, the taste of bile—

"You try." Mitch's words penetrated abruptly, startling her. Slowly her new brown eyes turned to the gun, held out to her with its barrel pointed so carefully at the trees. "There are three shots left," he said, his voice muffled by the earphones. "Aim for the fallen bottles."

She looked up wordlessly, registering both plastic bottles now on their sides, several feet back. She could see the holes, jagged mortal wounds in the bottles' sides. She accepted the gun.

He got behind her, using his hands to guide her into the proper stance. Her muscles were rigid to the touch, her body strung so tight, he wondered how she didn't snap in half. "Arms straight," he told her, his voice whispering lightly against her neck. "There you go." He could smell the scent of peaches again, light and fresh like a rainstorm. And he could feel her tremble as he guided her arms up.

Suddenly the Ice Angel didn't seem so controlled. He was struck by the urge to step closer, to embrace her own trembling form with his solid warmth. If she needed his strength, he would give it to her. He was that kind of man.

But then, she wasn't the type of woman ever to ask for his help. He stepped back just a few feet, watching as she adjusted the gun in front of her. She sited one of the bottles, leveling the gun in front of her. For a long moment she just stood there, the gun frozen out in front of her. Then abruptly her arms dropped down, her body trembling harshly.

He felt something wash through her, something dark and anguished. But even as he stepped forward, her arms came back up and she fired the gun three rapid times. One bottle leapt to sudden life, exploding plastic fragments as it plummeted back down.

She remained staring at it, the bulletless gun still poised before her.

He wanted to see her face, Mitch realized suddenly. He wanted to see what horrors had flashed through her eyes in that one instant when her arms had come down. For one moment her control had been gone. For one moment he had sensed the torture of the woman beneath.

But now her arms slowly returned to her sides, and she looked at him without a single expression on her pale, blank face. He didn't know whether to admire her or shake her.

Or hold her close.

"You owe me a smile," he said instead.

She nodded a slow emotionless nod, then turned away. He saw her inhale, then exhale slowly. Abruptly she turned back around and smiled. But it wasn't the natural, simple smile he'd been seeking. It was the full sensual smile of her cover pages, slamming him straight in the gut. He felt his breath catch in his throat, while his body went immediately hard. He had to clench his fists against the fire, wanting to curse her even as he wanted to pull her into his arms and show her just what that smile did to a man. His eyes darkened, his feet stepping forward on their own accord.

Abruptly he saw something else flash across her cool arctic face: fear.

He brought himself up shortly, cursing her for looking at him like that after smiling such a smile, and cursing himself for having all the self-control of a rutting boar. To make matters even, he also cursed Les Capruccio for instilling the fear in her to begin with.

Angry and disgusted, he retaliated curtly.

"Too bad that smile isn't real," he told her. He stormed past her to the two-liter bottles before he could see the sliver of pain slash unexpectedly across her eyes.

Her gaze fell to the metal gun, hanging so limply at her side, while his words echoed in her head. He was right, after all. The smile wasn't real. It was merely part of the package meant to hide the contents. Meant to hide the sharp blades of fear slashing through her stomach, the persistent taste of rust and bile in her mouth.

She looked at the gun dully. She'd made the two-liter bottle explode. She had accomplished her goal.

And the man had fallen, fallen, fallen. Down on the gold-patterned carpet, while the soundless scream had echoed through the hall.

Oh, she was capable all right. She could kill a bottle while her insides screamed and the pain raked through her like heated coals. And she could smile a sensual smile, when she wanted to break down in the snow and cry.

And she could look at the tall dark man coming toward her and feel the fear even as her mouth opened with the empty plea of his name.

Why couldn't she call him back?

The confusion wracked her, but then she slowly stiffened her spine. This was her choice, and this is what she wanted. The gun was merely a tool.

"Are you ready to go?" Mitch said, his voice still cool as he raked her up and down with impatient brown eyes.

She raised her head, keeping her eyes carefully averted. Unconsciously, one hand pressed against her stomach.

"No," she said at last. "I would like to practice a few more times."

He paused, his eyes narrowing. He wouldn't have imagined that. But then, with a shrug, he reached for the gun and reloaded it. He was tired of trying to understand her.

"Fine," he said curtly. "Five more rounds. Go."

And she took the gun from him, held it smoothly in front of her and fired five more shots in the brisk New England air.

Chapter 6

But in the dark of night, the control was hard to find.

Every time Jess closed her eyes, she could feel the nightmare hovering just beyond consciousness. And her eyes would pop open again, only to find visions of a tall, dark-haired man haunting her waking moments. She thought she could smell his after-shave, feel the warmth radiating from his powerful frame.

And then her stomach would tighten, and her nerves would tense with a confused mass of overloaded sensations. That tight, restless gnawing in her stomach, those spine-tingling ripples of old fear mixing with new demons. She wanted at once to sink down into the oblivion of sleep and to jerk awake, her hand reaching out to the vision of a man who called her back.

She bolted upright in her bed, feeling her breath coming in gasps while her hands trembled like leaves in the dim moonlight. Too much, her mind thought. It was too much.

Her life had come full circle, moments in time paralleling each other so closely, it was hard to keep the past the past, and the present the present.

She kept seeing his face, Harry's fat, red-flushed face. All the times she'd looked at him with hopeful eyes. All the times she'd held out her little arms, so happy to see him come home. And then the sudden cracking snap of his palm across her cheek.

Always followed by the tears and the apologies. Never again. He'd never hurt her again. If she'd just behave better, be a little more patient, he wouldn't lose his temper like that. If she and Mama would just understand...

But each time, the slaps came a little faster, a little harder.

She never knew whether to love him, or to hate him.

Even now she didn't know.

She swung her feet over the edge of the bed, taking in deep gulps of air. Eventually, her breathing started to slow, but the aching restlessness wouldn't quite leave her stomach. She hurt, she thought dully. She hurt way down deep in places she wasn't supposed to hurt anymore. In places so old and dark, it was better not to remember them at all. But the persistent throb was there, the ten-year-old pain refusing to go away.

And in that moment she cursed Les Capruccio and Mitch Guiness and all other men who had ever walked the earth. And she damned them all for interfering with her life, when all she'd ever wanted was to live in solitude—cold and alone, but at least able to sleep at night.

If she closed her eyes now, she would sink into the black pit that had slowly been dragging her back down since the first moment Les Capruccio had walked into her dressing room with his slick smile and damning envelope.

She got out of bed altogether and, without really thinking about it, slowly began to dress. The clock glowed midnight as she crept out of her room. Downstairs she took Bill's thick jacket off the peg, throwing it over her shoulders. Bill wasn't due to relieve Jamie until 2:00 a.m., giving her over an hour to collect herself. It seemed tonight was as good a night as any for a little research.

The front door squeaked as she closed it, and she held her breath for a moment. Given the supposed security of the location, she was afraid she'd suddenly look up to find three FBI guns pointed at her. But nothing moved in the house, and after a long moment, she released her pent-up breath.

"Going somewhere?" a distinctly male voice said behind her.

She stiffened immediately, even as she felt her stomach plummet to her toes. Slowly, she half turned to find herself face-to-face with one Mitch Guiness.

"Shouldn't you be sleeping?" she asked darkly, her own voice not quite able to hide her weariness.

"I could ask you the same," Mitch replied, sweeping her up and down with his gaze. He'd been listening to her toss and turn for at least an hour from the room next to hers. Then abruptly, there had been the creak of her feet on the floorboards. He knew her well enough to guess what she'd do next. After her five months of hotel captivity, she practically spent all day outside as it was.

"Schoolteachers don't need beauty sleep," she answered him, and he grinned his response in the darkness.

"Nice night for a walk," he said casually. "Damn cold, but at least the sky is clear."

She nodded, taking a tentative step forward. The dim glow of the half-moon swept over her features, at once illuminating her features and plunging them into darkness. Her dark hair was tousled around her face, softening her finely boned silhouette. And it seemed to him that her eyes looked huge and luminescent, no longer cold but full of haunting shadows and swirling emotions.

His imagination was probably getting the better of him.

Still, his sharp eyes could detect the subtle signs of strain. The burdens of her secrets were catching up with her, he observed. The hour was past midnight, and Cinderella was dangerously close to turning into the ragged housemaid. The gun today had disturbed her. She'd refused to talk about it for the rest of the day, but at dinner he'd seen her hand shake when she'd tried to eat. She'd caught him watching her and had set down the fork with a brittle clank, yet her gaze still hadn't been able to meet his with its usually cool equanimity.

He should push her now, use his interrogation skills to wrench some of those secrets away from her while he had the chance. But as he watched her peer out into the clear night, shivering against the bitter cold, he couldn't quite find the desire to push his advantage.

"Trouble sleeping?" he found himself saying softly, his eyes watching her.

Slowly she nodded.

"My mother used to make warm milk with vanilla and nutmeg," he continued quietly. "Of course, a good glass of cognac works just as well."

"Did you learn that from your mother, too?" she whispered, her eyes still out on the stars. The emptiness was back, raking through her, and she could feel each tremble in her body. Funny, she was standing a good five feet from the man, yet it seemed she could feel his warmth, smell the faint scent of soap and shampoo. And she wanted to take a step closer, even as she wanted to rail at him for being out here, too, when she just wanted to get away. It seemed the man was everywhere, including the traitorous corridors of her own mind.

"Some talents," Mitch said with a grin, "I picked up on my own."

She nodded and the night fell silent. He could practically see the heaviness of her thoughts on her shoulders. And even as he watched, a faint shudder rippled through her.

"It's too cold to be outside," he told her gently. "Come on, let's go on in and I'll see if I can't find some cognac."

She nodded once more, but still didn't move. He walked toward her, reaching out his arm to her, then froze. Perhaps it was just a trick of light, perhaps the funny effects of a half-moon, but from this angle, her dark eyes sparkled with the suspicious moisture of suppressed tears. And the set of her lips didn't look so cold anymore, but rather like the tight lips of a woman fighting a huge battle.

He didn't question what he did, reacting instead on instinct. The arm that had meant to lead her inside turned her against him instead. Before she could utter a word of protest, he drew her against his powerful frame. She went rigid at the first contact, but he soothed her with a small hush.

"You're just cold," he whispered. "Stand here just for a moment and I'll warm you up."

She should fight him, she thought dully. She should push him away and hit him for daring to touch her so. But instead, his words echoed through her emptiness. She was cold. Cold, so deep down, she thought she might never be warm again. And yet even the warmth scared her, for the ice enclosed things better left entombed. Until she hated the cold but couldn't risk the warmth. So instead, she stood in Mitch's arms like a child, not quite able to move, and feeling only the relentless ache that wouldn't go away or give her peace.

And he was warm. Warm and spicy and soapy. And she suddenly wanted to uncurl her fists against his chest, burying her hands against the solid strength. Slowly she rested her head down against his chest. She could feel the reassuring thunder of a pounding heart, the rich leather of his coat soft against her cheek. He didn't move, and slowly she relaxed another fraction. He was tall and powerful. She could feel the whisper of his warm breath in her hair, and the ache within her grew.

Her head moved on its own accord, not knowing what it wanted but driven by the mixture of emptiness and fear. Until she shivered even harder, though this time not from the cold at all. And the fear raced down her spine even as she raised her eyes to find his own, dark and soft in the freezing night.

Her lips parted, her breath catching as her gaze came down to settle on his lips, full and sensual. He had a strong jaw, stubbornly set like she knew he could be. And there was the faint shadow of midnight whiskers. They would feel raspy and rough to the touch. Would he press them against her hard, until her soft skin scraped and bruised from the fierceness? Or would they brush against her gently, a tingling and tantalizing blend of rough against smooth, sandpaper against silk?

She parted her lips a little farther and unconsciously arched her neck back. The fear reared harder and she closed her eyes against the intensity.

Mitch saw the lips presented to him so openly, and even as his mind told him this definitely wasn't right, his head moved of its own volition. He could sense once more that flood of emotions sweeping through her. But the deep blend of shivering confusion and dark pain lent her a mysterious softness that drew him in as surely as a drug.

Gently, tentatively, his lips brushed over hers. She stiffened in his arms, her spine jerking straight. Soothingly, his hands smoothed down her back, willing her to relax. Murmuring soft words of nonsense, his lips swept over hers once more. This time he was rewarded by the soft sigh of her previously pent-up breath. One more time he brushed over her lips, and this time her lips followed his, seeking more. He responded by coming back to the fullness, deepening the kiss ever so lightly.

He felt her tremble, a deep shiver that filled him with need. He arched her neck back a little more, outlining her lips with the gentle teasing of his tongue. Another soft sigh and her lips parted, sending a surging rush of warmth to his groin. This time he did press the advantage, his tongue plunging in to find her sweetness. Far off he heard a soft moan, and he pressed her more tightly against him, fitting the warm curve of her hips more intimately against his own.

Then suddenly she wasn't pressing against him anymore. The same hands that had flattened against his chest abruptly balled into fists and hit him. With a sharp jerk, she pulled away, practically falling down in her haste.

"No," she gasped out, her chest heaving in the night. Her eyes were round and huge, the fear engulfing her in waves. "I don't want this! I don't want you, I don't want any man!"

His own breathing was sharp, his blood still thundering in his ears. His eyes narrowed, and he looked at her darkly.

"Sweetheart," he drawled thickly. "That wasn't what your lips were telling me just thirty seconds ago."

She scrambled farther back, wiping the back of her hand across her mouth as if trying to rid herself of his taste. "Get away from me," she warned.

He didn't move, but nor did his eyes relent. "If you will recall," he said tightly, "I didn't start this little interaction."

"You took advantage of me," she accused. In some small corner of her mind, she knew what he was saying was true. But the fear and confusion were racing through her now, consuming her blood as she shook with tremor after tremor. Visions and sensations warred within her mind until she wanted to cover her eyes with her hands and will nothingness to descend. Already she felt the sharp chill of the night, the warmth suddenly torn from her until she was lost and cold and filled with uncertainty. "You said you were just going to keep me warm," she found herself saying. "But you're like all men. That was just an excuse for one thing, and one thing only."

She knew she shouldn't have said the words, and the minute she did, she saw him stiffen dangerously. Slowly he took one step forward.

"I'm going to say this only once," he told her, his voice as smooth and low as velvet. "Whatever emotional baggage you got from Les Capruccio is between you and him. You want to talk about it, I'll listen, sweetheart. But don't you go accusing me of being like other men. All men didn't just kiss you. I did."

She looked at him dully, the bitterness washing over her sharply, cleansing her of all else. "A woman is raped every five minutes," she declared slowly. "Every sixty seconds a child is physically abused. You don't have to be all men. Just being male is dangerous enough."

He swore something low and dark in the night. Looking at her now, he shook his head. "I'm not sure I didn't like you better as the Ice Angel," he told her. "And I certainly don't consider you some helpless victim. Whatever Capruccio did to you, you made him pay for it, sweetheart. In that courtroom you made him pay for it dearly."

He stepped back, looking at her one last time. "For the record, you kissed me. When you're ready to deal with that, you know where to find me. I'm not Les Capruccio, Jess. I'm the man risking his life for you. And if you will recall, one of our agents already lost his life trying to protect you.

You can't look at the evil men do without seeing the good, as well.'' He looked her up and down with scornful eyes. "Then again, maybe *you* can.''

He walked back into the house before she could say anything else. In truth, she had nothing to retort, just the emptiness swirling inside of her.

Once more, the images flooded her mind. The gold-patterned carpet. Blue-suited Darold arching back as the bullet hit home. Les's face contorted as he stretched his hand back for another blow.

And a powerful dark-haired man drawing her close, the scent of his after-shave, the touch of his lips, the soft rasp of his beard on her cheeks.

Her hand came up and rubbed across her cheek in the night. No bruises, no scratches.

And she decided then that she hated Mitch Guiness as she'd never hated anyone before. Because she knew how to deal with Les, and she had indeed made him pay.

But she had absolutely no defense against tenderness. Les had never lied about who he was and what he wanted. Far more dangerous was the man that led you in, the man you wanted to love, the man you wanted to trust.

Far more dangerous was the man you needed.

She shivered in the night, the thick wool jacket worthless against a chill reverberating from the inside.

The next morning, the Ice Angel was back. He could tell simply by the way she walked back into the house from her early-morning jog. Sure, her hair was now brown and colored contact lenses camouflaged the true frost in her eyes, but the rigid bearing of her spine and haughty expressionless face was pure Jessica Gavornée. Mentally, Mitch cursed himself. Last night his behavior had been beyond unprofessional. You did not get involved with people in the Witness Protection Program. One, it was a very vulnerable time for people as they were asked to give up everything they'd ever known. Two, it was precisely the point that they had to give up all ties to the past. Which in roughly a week and a half would include Mitch Guiness.

Had Jess not pulled away last night, he would have. Or so he liked to tell his pricked conscience. And he certainly would have handled the whole thing better if she simply hadn't compared him to all men. That rankled. Mitch Guiness lived his own life by his own standards. And he had no intention of paying for other men's crimes. Not even for a fresh brunette beauty.

But last night was last night, and no matter how he looked at it, he was still a man with a job to do. As much as she might want to ignore him, that certainly would not be happening.

He pushed himself off the bench in the kitchen to stroll toward the entryway. She didn't even bother to glance up as she finished stretching out her tired legs. He could see a light sheen of sweat on her forehead, and her chest was still heaving from her exertions. He had a feeling that if he got any closer, he would also catch the faint scent of peaches.

He remained several feet away.

"Good morning, Jessica," he said casually. She ignored him and moved toward the stairs.

"It doesn't matter if you don't respond to the name," he called out after her. "Every step you take, every expressionless muscle in your face gives you away. You've worked hard the last few days. Don't lose all the progress simply because of one midnight walk."

She turned finally, her brown eyes as cool as only she could make them. "Duly noted," she said evenly. And then even as he watched, her shoulders curved in, her face muscles relented and her left hand began to fidget with her right-hand ring.

He grinned at her, half in jest and half true admiration. "That's my girl," he said. She stiffened abruptly, her face taking on an instantly wary stance. But before he could probe it any further, she whirled away from him and pounded up the stairs.

He watched her go without saying anything, a frown furrowing his brow. Funny, the more he thought he was on the verge of understanding her, the more he realized he didn't know her at all. He thought she was gun-shy from Les Capruccio, but was there anything else in her past to make her so cold? And then something hit him on the head so hard he couldn't believe he'd never considered it sooner. Les Capruccio hadn't been the new variable in Jessica Gavornée's life. She'd become the Ice Angel six years before meeting him, and her life had been suspiciously absent of all men, even back then.

No, the riddle had far more to do with Jessica Gavornée. It had to do with a woman that had no record of existence until she was sixteen. A woman with no known parents, friends or past.

It had to do with a woman that smelled like summer and looked like winter, a woman that kissed with a lush innocence and retaliated with bitter anger.

Slowly he began to whistle to himself as the wheel turned in his mind. He had over a week left. And if need be, he would use every last one of those days to unlock the woman upstairs. He'd been right last night. He wasn't other men. He was Mitch Guiness, and he could do magic.

He found her an hour later in the kitchen. Much to his surprise, she was cooking, and the warm scent of French toast wafted through the air.

"A late breakfast," he breathed, inhaling deeply. "I like it."

She barely glanced at him, but at least she was standing in her new, relaxed posture. "I figured it was my turn to cook by now," she said neutrally.

"By all means," he agreed. He looked over her shoulder enough to make out the fresh stack of warm French toast. "Are these ready?" He couldn't quite keep the eagerness out of his voice.

She nodded, doing her best to keep her back to him. But it was hard to ignore a man when he practically filled the kitchen, and even now was reaching over her shoulder with one strong arm to grab the plate. She moved to the side the best she could, but in the small confines of the kitchen that didn't stop his arm from brushing against her shoulder. She felt goose bumps creep up her neck, and did her best to ignore that, too.

She'd lost too much control, she'd concluded late last night. Mitch had told her to leave Jessica Gavornée behind, and now she saw the truth. She could leave Jessica behind because Jessica had never been more than an act, like Jess McMoran would be yet another act. Deep down, the nightmares and the control were simply hers. She would keep both, even as she adapted to her new role. And she would shut this large dark man out of her mind once and for all because she had the control to do so.

She swore it.

"These are very good," Mitch said from the table.

"Save some for Bill," she said. "He should be in soon."

"Sure thing. So is cooking French toast a common modeling skill?" His voice was still casual, and she remained neutral.

"Models don't eat French toast," she replied. "But I imagined schoolteachers do." She didn't have to turn around to know he would be grinning at her.

"You are a fast study," he told her, the approval plain in his voice. "A real natural for adopting assumed identities."

Did she hear a faint edge in the last statement? She couldn't be sure, and so she did her best to ignore him completely. She flipped the last piece of thick bread, nodding approvingly at its golden tone.

"If models don't make French toast," Mitch was saying from the table, "did you learn it from your mother? My mom makes amazing French toast."

This time she did tense. Mitch could sound as casual as he wanted, but she knew better by now. Already she could sense his sharp eyes probing her back. The man was on a fishing trip, but she wouldn't be the one to take the bait. Let him wonder all he wanted. By midnight she would be out of here.

She turned around as if she hadn't heard his last statement at all, bringing the final plate of French toast to the table. Slowly, almost leisurely, she sat down and helped herself to one steaming piece. She drizzled the fresh maple syrup over it, admitting only to herself that she actually liked not having to worry about what she ate anymore. She did like French toast, not to mention thick maple syrup.

"Do you know where I'll be living yet?" she inquired casually, taking a bite of the new treat.

Mitch watched her with an arched eyebrow. He'd never seen her show so much interest in a meal before. Probably figured between it and him, the French toast was the lesser evil.

"Actually," he said now, prompted by her question, "we're looking at Portland, Oregon. Good size, reasonable distance away."

He watched her closely, wondering how she'd respond to this after her previous insistence at staying in the Northeast area. But she simply nodded, swallowing her bite of toast.

"And ID?" she inquired. "I haven't seen anything to go with my new identity yet."

"It's in the file," he told her. "Social Security card and birth certificate. Once Oregon is official, I'll have the driver's license and the teacher's license for you, as well. It'll all be taken care of."

She nodded, her brown eyes neutral as she absorbed this bit of news. She would have preferred having all the ID, now, but the Social Security card and birth certificate would do. With those she could get anything else she needed.

She polished off the last of her toast in silence, the wheels in her mind spinning rapidly. Another afternoon walk would give her the last of the information she would need. By midnight. It could all be done by midnight.

She stood, looking down at her empty plate now smeared with syrup. Then her gaze swept up to find Mitch once more watching her with intent brown eyes.

"I believe it's your turn to do the dishes," she said simply. And without waiting for a reply, she walked over to the entryway, grabbed *his* coat and was out the door.

He watched the closed door a little longer. Strange she would take his own coat when she never had before. Unless, of course, she'd taken his coat precisely so he couldn't. He got up from the table, leaving the dishes behind. Grabbing Jamie's smaller jacket, he threw it over his shoulders and left, as well.

If she didn't want him outside, it was all the more reason to go.

She retired early that night, excusing herself at nine, just after dinner. She had a big night ahead of her, and it wouldn't hurt to get a couple hours' sleep before it all began. Her nerves were tense, her face slightly flushed from the adrenaline pounding through her veins. She took off some of the edge by packing a small bag with enough clothes to get her through the next two days. She'd taken the Social Security card and birth certificate from the file, so now she was all set. She looked one last time in the mirror.

The hair was different, the eyes, the face. And Mitch was right. If she slouched forward just a little, she lost that smooth, model's grace. Whatever else she thought of the man, he was good at his job. Hopefully so good that Jess McMoran could fade off into never-never land without any problems at all. Or so she hoped.

Through sheer force of willpower she slept for two hours. At eleven-thirty she was up again, the adrenaline easily banishing the sleep. She picked up the bag and took a deep breath.

Not having her own coat was going to pose a problem. Mitch's was definitely the warmest, but it also retained that hint of spicy soapiness that she associated so strongly with him; she didn't really want to spend more time in that coat. She would take Jamie's instead, at least until she got to town. Then she'd definitely have to buy a new one as Jamie's was too easy to recognize.

They'd told her it was a good twenty miles to town. After giving it a bit of thought, she decided she really had to take the car. And a casual conversation with Bill this afternoon had told her exactly where to find it. The keys were conveniently located in the kitchen drawer.

Starting the car would alert everyone that she was leaving. She hadn't been able to think of a way around this. At least they could only follow her on foot, giving her the distinct advantage. She'd leave the car in town, of course. She wasn't a thief, only a woman who wanted her privacy back.

She looked inside her bag, thumbing the thick stacks of cash she'd withdrawn from her account six months ago, when she'd first set all the wheels in motion. Twenty thousand dollars. That ought to help her with some nice relocation funds. Not to mention all the money she'd been secretly stashing in a Swiss bank account for six years now. It was as if even back then, she'd known this day would come. Her life had been a cycle of violence and running. At least with age she was learning to do it in style.

The last thought brought a bitter smile to her lips, but she banished it with a firm squaring of her shoulders. This was the last time. She would keep Jess McMoran, go back to school for her teaching license and live out her days as a brunette schoolteacher in a small town somewhere. She would buy a modest country house, grow a garden. Maybe she'd get a couple of cats, a dog and a goat. Her life would be nice and simple and free of complications.

Just her and her mother.

Picking up the bag, she crept quietly to the door. No floorboards creaked this time, and she eased down the stairs. A brief foray to the kitchen, and the car keys were hers. She grabbed Jamie's jacket from the peg, and slid outside the house.

Her watch glowed 12:15 in the dim moonlight. If she understood Bill's comment earlier, he and Jamie ran a strange, rotating mix of walking patterns, designed by Mitch. To an outside observer, the scheme appeared completely random, making it hard to sneak in under the watch's guard. There was an underlying order, however. Jess just hoped she understood the concept well enough to use it.

If memory served, Bill would be behind the house now, leaving the front right corner unattended. Exactly where the car was camouflaged. She crossed over, keeping low in the night. There, that large pile of brush in the corner.

Her heart pounded, but her lips thinned into a grim smile of determination. She fingered the heavy metal of the keys in her hands. Almost there, Jess. Almost.

She quietly pulled the first dry brush away, illuminating the pale glow of a metal door handle. Quick glance at the watch. She had only five more minutes before Bill would round the corner. It was time to move faster.

But just as she reached over to pull off the leaf-encrusted net, a shadow shifted and solidified to her left. There was no time to move, no time to scream.

All of a sudden a man was before her, and the dull gleam of a 9-millimeter gun made his intentions all too clear.

Chapter 7

"You don't even use the limited sense God gave you." The black-clothed figure swore softly. "Just what the hell do you think you're doing?"

Jess felt a sharp spike of relief stab through her; it was only Mitch. As she watched, the gun dropped down, though the aggressive stance refused to relent.

"Start talking, Jess, or I might just change my mind and shoot you anyway. At this point, I think more lives might be saved that way."

Her chin came up, her face cool and expressionless in the dim moonlight. "How did you know?" she demanded.

"You asked Bill too many questions," he replied evenly. "And there's no reason for you to care about the car—unless, of course, you planned on going somewhere."

She nodded, acknowledging the mistake while the wheels turned round in her mind. He'd caught her red-handed. What to do now? How much to even say? Mitch took a step toward her, and she stiffened.

"Well?" he challenged, dark and low. "Are you going to start talking yet? I'm mighty curious why the woman I was hired to protect seems hell-bent on running away. That eager to get yourself killed, Jess?"

She said nothing, her brown gaze watching him warily as he took yet another step forward. In the dim moonlight, he loomed larger than ever. Big and strong and dangerously angry. She raised her chin a little higher, but her heart beat frantically in her chest.

Abruptly he stopped, his eyes narrowing as a thought struck him cold.

"Son of a bitch," he breathed softly, the realization washing over him with stunning sharpness. All the questions that had been puzzling him suddenly clicked together like a cruel jigsaw puzzle. "There's another man, isn't there?" he stated sharply. "That's why you turned on Les. After all, he'd never let you leave him for another man. And having gone through all that, you certainly don't want to give up your new lover now, do you?" His voice sunk an octave lower, the anger rising fierce and fast. *"Do you!"*

Her hands were beginning to shake lightly—she could feel each tremble in the hollowness of her stomach. But she kept her gaze level, willing the icy control to flow through her.

"No," she said at last, her voice quiet in the darkness. "There is no one . . ." she hesitated slightly. "No man involved."

But she could see Mitch shaking his head, hear the low stream of his angry curses. Before she could so much as react, he stormed past the car, bearing down upon her with two hundred muscled pounds of fury.

"Do you remember what I told you the first day?" he demanded fiercely, towering over her with his dark face. "Do you remember that small trivial point on how we're in this together? That while you might fear we'll betray you, in fact you can betray us, as well? What did you think I was talking about, Jess? What did you think I even meant?"

She couldn't quite stop herself from shrinking back this time. He was such a large man and so angry. On their own, her eyes glanced down at his fists. Large, powerful fists. They could probably knock her down with one blow, send her sprawling while her face exploded in nerve-popping pain. Her lip would split, her cheek bruise.

He whirled away from her abruptly, not noticing how she'd looked at him. He walked back two steps, feeling the adrenaline border overload. She had been about to betray them, and all for some man. He felt at once enraged and disappointed, and something else suspiciously close to hurt. Had she thought of this lover when she'd been kissing him? Had she planned this midnight rendezvous even as she'd pushed closer, angling back her head to deepen the passion? He shook his head in disgust at himself, the night and the situation. That little fool. He'd known all along she'd harbored a secret. But somehow he hadn't wanted to find out it was this.

He turned back around, willing his anger under brutal control. She was still looking at him, her face expressionless and waiting in the pale moonlight. He ran his hand through his hair, and shook his head again.

"You don't really understand, do you?" he found himself saying.

Ever so slowly, her eyes never leaving his, she shook her head.

"Six years ago," he said curtly, "there were two agents on assignment. Two of our best agents, I might add. An attempt had already been made on the witness, a sleazy accountant who'd agreed to turn over evidence against a big-time drug smuggler. It was a big case and a big bust. We just needed to keep the man alive. Of course he was terrified, especially after almost being shot into Swiss cheese. The two agents... They decided to disappear with the man. You know why they did that, Jess?"

Once again she shook her head.

"Because they suspected a leak inside the department," he informed her impatiently. "Because they thought someone might betray the accountant for the lure of easy money." He took a restless step forward, his eyes burning and intense as his voice dropped low. "And do you know how this man repaid them, Jess? Do you know what he did?"

Pinned by his gaze, she could only continue to shake her head.

"He violated the Witness Protection Program agreement, Jess. Rather than walk away from his old life, he skipped out on his two agents—sound familiar, Jess?—so he could show up at a bank and claim the small fortune he'd embezzled from Valéncia, the drug smuggler. Of course, the drug smuggler had found out about this embezzlement and had men watching the bank. The two agents showed up just in time for a dark sedan to drive by. A dark sedan with very big guns."

He ended flatly, his eyes grim with disgust and anger and pain. Jess found herself whispering the question, compelled to hear the ending she already knew.

"And the accountant died?"

Slowly, his brown eyes boring into hers, Mitch nodded.

"And the agents?" she whispered, autumn leaves and blue suits slashing through her mind. "They died, too?"

"One of them," Mitch said softly. "The other lived to be blamed for the incident. His renegade ways had made enough enemies as it was. They were only too happy to kick him out of the FBI as an example. They took away his badge, his gun. Everything he'd worked for, everything he'd ever wanted to be."

Slowly her brown eyes widened in the moonlight, the first flash of recognition sweeping over her.

"It was you," she stated dully. "All of this was about you."

Once again, that relentless nod.

"But you're back now," she stated, trying to fight the facts laid so baldly before her. "You work for the program now."

"Later," he said levelly, "they caught an agent redhanded, accepting money from Valéncia. There really had been a department leak. Had we stayed within the normal procedures, Ramos would have been killed, and probably Victor and myself, as well. Of course, Ramos's betrayal led to his and Victor's death anyway. At any rate, I was offered my job back. I wouldn't take it, though—the red tape is too dangerous. Instead, I worked out a deal to become an independent specialist, operating on my own terms."

"Then it worked out in the end," Jess said.

"Tell that to Victor," he replied coolly. "I became an independent specialist for one reason and one reason only, Jess. I am determined to keep my witnesses safe. In return, however, I expect them to play by my rules. You broke those rules, Jess. And it's not just my own life I'm worried about. It's Bill's and Jamie's, as well. Wasn't Darold's life enough, Jess? How much blood do you want on your hands?"

She felt her stomach fall out of her, the chills catching her quickly as the last statement rang through her head. *How much blood do you want on your hands? How much, how much?* He couldn't know, she reminded herself faintly, but that didn't stop her features from turning ashen.

For the first time, she wavered. For the first time her master plan ripped through her mind and she wondered if she might not be dreadfully, horribly mistaken. She'd thought to run away. She'd thought that if she lived by herself long enough, she would finally find peace and no longer be a threat to anyone.

But what if Mitch was right? What if her "escape" actually led to discovery? Les knew about her mother. Indeed, Les had blackmailed her with that information for a long year and a half. Somehow she'd figured she could slip in for just one crucial meeting under the cover of her new identity. But what if she was wrong? What did she really know about such things and such men? She'd just been a model, for crying out loud.

For the first time, she contemplated failing. And not just failing herself, but the large seemingly immortal man in front of her and the two other men she'd come to know. She couldn't take it. She had to look away.

Mitch's eyes narrowed as he watched her. Her face looked suddenly pale in the moonlight, and as she brought a hand to her throat, he could see it tremble in the chilly night. He'd struck a nerve, all right. The Ice Angel may have secrets, but at least she had a conscious, as well.

"Tell me about him, Jess," he prodded, moving closer. "Tell me about this man that you just can't leave behind. Surely the Ice Angel doesn't find any man worth dying for."

The last words were mocking, but she didn't respond. Instead her gaze remained focused far out into the night.

"There's no man," she said quietly at last, inhaling softly as if she might say more.

And for one tiny moment, the desire did tug at her. The desire to simply tell him everything: the smoking gun, the gold-patterned carpet, the nightmare she couldn't quite ever leave behind. And about her mother and the horrible bond that drew them together in a haze of guilt and pain and misery. She had left cities behind, past identities. But she would never turn her back on her mother. She owed her too much, even as she half hated her for the debt. Les had known that. Les had thought he could use it to torment her forever, until the one night she'd crept down to the library, intending only to remove the incriminating evidence against herself, and discovered as well all the information she'd needed for her vengeance.

Tell Mitch, a small corner of her mind whispered. Just tell him everything. Maybe Mitch, of all people, would understand.

"Come on, Jess," he breathed softly, reaching out one arm toward her. "Tell me what's going on. Trust me."

She stiffened abruptly, the moment of weakness washed bitterly away at his words. Trust him? *Trust him?* There was no such thing as trust, she thought vehemently. No such things as reliability and safety and security. There was only yourself, and she had gotten herself this far. She stiffened her spine, feeling the coldness fill her now, giving her strength. Slowly her eyes came up, the brown depths no longer shadowed, but frosted into a brittle hue.

"I trust no one," she told him coolly. "No one at all."

He watched her sudden transformation with a growing sense of helplessness. Once more he'd sensed the woman beneath, only to watch her retreat behind the prison of her control once more. He shook his head in the night, the frustration tearing at his gut.

"Damn you," he swore low. "You and all your control. Do you really think a frosty stare can stop a bullet, Jess?"

She didn't even blink, angering him all the more.

"Fine, then," he bit out. "Tell me how much you don't need anyone. I don't really care what you say. Facts are facts, and right now the fact is you do need me. And the fact is I can't trust you. No more outside privileges," he said curtly. "From here on out, you will have one of us in your presence at all times. And I will personally keep guard outside your door each and every night."

"You can't do that," she retaliated frostily. "I am not some prisoner here!"

He leaned forward, glaring at her with dark brown eyes. "You forget, Jess. I'm the boss around here, and I don't have to follow FBI procedures or PR. Welcome to the true meaning of 'independent specialist.' The way I see it, you're a threat to yourself and the rest of us. Therefore, you are unofficially under house arrest for the duration of this session. Now is that clear?"

She looked at him for a long moment, and he could practically see her bite back the retorts rising to her tongue.

He looked at her coldly. "Whoever he is, Jess," Mitch said slowly, "he's not worth it."

"I said," she bit out evenly, "there's no man involved."

"I think you're lying," he stated baldly. "And given that *you're* the one who made an agreement with the program you never had any intention of keeping, and that *you're* the one who's sneaking around after midnight to steal cars, I say *you're* the one who can't be trusted. Not me."

"Damn you to hell," she replied.

"Sweetheart," he drawled, "if this evening is anything to go by, I'm already there. Now back to the house."

She whirled away, her short hair whipping around to hide her face. And even as she cursed him a thousand times in her mind, she still felt the unexpected sting of unshed tears.

Because everything he'd said about her was true. Which meant he had every right to hate her. Every right to distrust her.

But no matter what, she vowed sharply as she marched to the house, she would never tell him the truth. She'd meant what she said. No one was worth trusting.

Not even the strong-armed, slow-kissing Mitch Guiness.

* * *

She awoke to the heart-stopping pressure of a black-gloved hand over her mouth. Automatically a scream rose to her lips, her eyes widening instinctively in fear.

"Shh," came the low familiar voice next to her ear. She was allowed to turn her head enough to make out the black-shadowed shape of Mitch, crouched next to her bed. He looked at her with steady, grim eyes.

"We got problems," he whispered quickly. "Now when I take away my hand, you're not going to make any noise at all, okay?"

Dutifully, she nodded, her heart still pounding in her chest as all her nerves came to frantic attention. Her gaze swept to the nearby nightstand where the clock glowed 2:35 a.m. She'd only been asleep for an hour.

Mitch followed her gaze to the clock. At least she had a cool head; tonight he had a feeling all that icy control he hated so much was going to come in handy.

"Remember when I won the bet with the cards?" he reminded her softly, easing his grip. "And you agreed not to question my methods anymore?" She nodded. "Well, here's the test, sweetheart. I want you to do exactly what I say when I say it. No questions, no complaints. I know you hate to trust, little Ice Angel, but this night you're going to have to."

His voice was so grim, she didn't dare retort. Instead, her brown eyes luminous in the darkness, she once more nodded. He released his grip completely, quickly drawing back the covers as he motioned her up out of the bed. At once she felt the chill of the cold night penetrating her thin satin pajamas. She shivered unconsciously, her arms wrapping around herself for warmth.

Belatedly, she became aware of his eyes sweeping down her long, slender frame. He turned abruptly away, but she could see the tightness of his jaw betraying his tension. It left her at once breathless and afraid. She scrambled quickly out of the bed, reaching for the relative safety of her robe.

He stopped her with one hand, though, signaling no with a faint shake of his head.

"Clothes," he breathed. "The warmest ones you can find."

She nodded, her eyes falling to his grip on her wrist. It was firm and powerful, but not bruising. And when he withdrew his hand, the cold air felt suddenly sharper and lonelier. She shook the sensations away.

Moving expediently to the dresser, she tried to ignore the fact her body was in full view. She was fully covered, she reminded herself. The satin top and bottoms certainly revealed less than all those swimming suits she'd once posed in. But somehow, with his brown gaze following her every movement, she felt abruptly exposed, the satin too cool and smooth against her skin. Every movement had the pajamas swinging against her, revealing each gentle curve of her long, limber body. When she turned, she held the clothes against her chest like a feeble shield.

"Change in the corner," he whispered curtly. "I'll pack your things."

She wanted to protest. Certainly she had no intention of undressing with this man just feet away. But the unrelenting set of his jaw told her words would be useless. And once again the sense of urgency washed through her. He'd said she couldn't question him, and looking at his grim face, she thought she'd better obey. She crept to the corner, instinctively avoiding the boards she knew creaked. He nodded approvingly.

True to his word, he turned and gave her his back. For the first time, she became aware of the small black duffel bag he held in his left hand. Even as she watched, he opened the first drawer and casually withdrew a thin lacy bra, which he threw in with hardly a second glance. Her cheeks burned and she looked away. Well, if he could be so damn casual, she thought determinedly, so could she. Hastily she began to dress.

Mitch knew he had only to look up, and he would be able to see everything in the mirror before him. But a man could only take so much, and now certainly wasn't the time to push his limits. Things were wrong, very wrong.

He'd only been asleep half an hour before the sensation had woken him. Four times before, he'd had the sensation, the spine-tingling, stomach-clenching certainty that something very bad was about to happen. The first time, he'd been a young boy climbing a tree. He'd been fighting the sensation when the tree branch broke, plunging him to the ground and breaking his arm and shoulder. The second time he'd paid more attention and walked out of an old barn right before the roof had collapsed.

Then, he'd had it fifteen minutes before he'd seen his partner shot down in cold blood, taking two hits himself. Finally, he'd had it when Liz's husband had been brutally slain in front of Maddensfield's tiny cinema. He'd found himself buying tickets and boarding a plane back home before he'd ever even heard the news.

He trusted his instincts, and tonight was no different. Especially when he'd checked Bill's room and found no one. If all was going according to plan, Jamie should have relieved Bill over half an hour ago, and Bill should have been back in the house. Instead, he was nowhere to be found.

He grabbed a last sweater and thrust it into the bag. That ought to get them through at least one day. Hopefully by then they'd be in a position to buy whatever else they needed. Or so he hoped.

He glanced up then, catching Jess pulling her sweater down over her jeans. They were all set. But then, looking down, his eyes fell on a small crystal bottle of oil. He didn't have to pick it up to know it probably smelled like peaches.

Did her lover like the smell? he found himself thinking savagely. She'd said she'd never worn it for Les. Maybe the unknown man had given it to her in some romantic tryst. So help him God, he wanted to hurt the man should they ever meet.

But even as he swore at himself and cursed Jess for her illicit lover that would probably kill them both, he found himself throwing the fragile bottle in the bag, as well. It would serve him right.

His face was dark and angry when he turned back around. He forced himself to take another calming breath. There would be plenty of time to be angry later. Now he had to get them out alive.

"Ready?" he asked. She nodded, and both their eyes moved in unison to the clock. It glowed 2:42. It had taken them seven minutes to become prepared, and in his mind, Mitch knew that was seven minutes too many.

"Follow me closely," he said curtly, his voice hushed. "And for God's sake, don't make a sound."

Once more she nodded, her face pale but set in the faint light. No screaming female here, he acknowledged grudgingly. There was something to be said for that.

Keeping her low and behind him, he crept from the room. The whole house was quiet, the deep abnormal type of quiet he'd learned to distrust. From far off came the faint click of the water heater turning on, and they both jumped. Mitch reached back a hand for her. Without questioning, Jess took it, folding her small, slightly trembling hand into his warm, solid grip. Down the stairs they went.

At the landing, he took out his gun and used it to lead them around the corner. But the entryway was empty, no sound giving anything away. Moving low and quickly, he half pulled her to a back door behind the stairs.

Jess shivered as the cold hit her, her hand tightening on Mitch's grip. Then dimly she became aware of the fact she was in a garage, a garage housing a big black Blazer. In the back of her mind, she registered surprise at seeing the vehicle. No one had said anything about there being another car present. But there was no time to contemplate it further. Next thing she knew, Mitch was urging her inside the driver's door. She clambered over to the passenger's seat and he unceremoniously dumped the duffel bag in her lap.

"Head down," he ordered. She ducked obediently.

Softly she could hear him counting under his breath.

"One, two, three." And then in a flash of an instant, the Blazer roared to life, thrust into Drive and tore through the garage doors. Jess covered her ears at the sound of the impact, her gaze coming up enough to see wood fly by the windows.

The crash was followed by thundering cracks, and in a thin moment of clarity, Jess realized someone was shooting at them. Mitch's head bounced down as a bullet slammed through the windshield, burying itself with a thud in the leather seat.

"Down," he commanded again, though Jess was already huddled as low as possible. She turned out of the seat altogether, crouching with her back under the dashboard. It seemed the whole world had exploded into roaring engines, screaming rubber and booming guns. With a small curse, Mitch slammed the vehicle into Reverse, ripping it through a 180-degree turn, then gunning it forward once more. The back window shattered as two shots found their mark, and he could feel the sudden rush of chilling wind ripping through the cab.

Now if only they didn't hit the fuel tank, he thought grimly, slamming the gas pedal to the floor. He practically flew over the bumpy gravel-encrusted road, the vehicle hitting eighty miles an hour before he threw it around a sharp turn. A straightaway opened up before him, and he throttled the Blazer to a hundred miles per hour, but not before seeing two gray sedans rip around the corner behind him.

He found himself smiling. Sedans. The damn fools.

He slowed slightly for the second corner, but even then the vehicle rocked briefly onto its side and he had to fight for control. At least there were chains on the tires or he most likely would have lost it altogether. He spared one glance for Jess, still hunkered down under the dashboard. Her face was pale, but composed. He nodded at her in grim admiration, and she silently nodded back.

Then he abruptly swung the wheel left, and swerved off the road altogether. The Blazer hit a solid bump, and for a brief moment was airborne, then landed with a jolting crash guaranteed to require ten years' worth of chiropractic. Jess was slammed against the right side from the impact and she winced. But she didn't cry out loud, realizing Mitch needed all his attention for the snowy, tree-studded terrain.

Glancing back, Mitch saw both of the vehicles make the turn. The first vehicle, however, wasn't so lucky in its landing. The lower-sitting sedan hit hard, the hood flying up from impact. Blinded, the driver swerved only to hit one of the numerous trees now surrounding them. The second car barely made it around the first, only to find itself zig-zagging through the forest to keep up with Mitch.

To his left, Mitch saw a sharp incline and, without a second thought, he drove straight for it. The Blazer's four-wheel drive could handle a lot more than some luxury sedan—he was willing to bet his life on it.

He slammed on the brakes abruptly, realizing if he hit the incline at this speed he'd simply roll the vehicle. Once more Jess slammed against the floor, and this time two more shots were fired as the sedan gained on them.

But then with a grim look of determination, Mitch plunged the Blazer up the hill, gunning the engine as he slammed it down into low gear. There was an agonizing moment as the wheels spun, searching for traction in the slick, winter snow. Then the chains dug in, and the Blazer surged upward.

More shots rang out, followed almost immediately by the sharp sound of crashing metal. Looking into the rearview mirror, Mitch caught the disappearing sight of the second sedan flipping over and rolling down the hill. He grinned an unpleasant grin.

Next time, they'd learn to adapt to their surroundings.

But then he instantly sobered. Of course, there would be a next time.

He slowed down as the Blazer crested the hill. He had only the faintest idea where they were, and it would take some doing before they hit a main road. Not to mention the fact that the Blazer left tracks as clear as a landing strip. They'd have to move fast to keep one step ahead.

They came out of the woods to what looked to be the local route. He angled the vehicle to the north, drove half a mile, then swung a careful 180-degree turn that headed them south without leaving any signs of tracks along the road. Satisfied now that all signs indicated they'd gone north, he drove them towards their true direction.

Glancing over, he watched Jess gingerly climb back onto the seat. Her face grimaced slightly as she moved, and he imagined she'd gotten more than a few bruises from the ride.

"First class just isn't what it used to be, is it?" he said wryly, weaving in and out of the trees.

She merely looked at him. "They're gone?"

"For now."

She nodded. The air was blowing like a fan through the holes in the front windshield and the missing back window. She could see her breath when she breathed, and already goose bumps were racing up and down her arms. She huddled, conserving what body heat she had.

"I think there's a blanket in the back," Mitch said softly. She glanced over the seat, and after a bit of exploring, pulled out a green army blanket. She spread it out over both of their laps, earning herself a sharp look.

"You can have it all," he told her curtly. "I'll be fine."

"I haven't argued with you all night," she pointed out levelly. "So maybe you could reward me by just giving me this one."

He grinned suddenly, liking her backbone. Even half-frozen, shot at and bruised, she remained thinking on her feet. She was definitely something else.

"All right," he conceded, and found he was honestly grateful for her thoughtfulness. "Just don't tell anyone."

Her features at once froze, her brown eyes sweeping up to find his with aching hauntingness.

"Bill and Jamie?" she asked softly. "What do you think happened to them?"

The grin vanished, and suddenly his face was tight.

"I don't know," he said flatly.

She looked down at her hands, suddenly twisting the blanket into fists.

"But it's probably not good," she said absently.

"These people play for keeps," Mitch said darkly. Abruptly he slammed his fist into the steering wheel, causing her to jump. A road miraculously appeared before him, but he turned the Blazer onto it without any real thought.

Her question conjured up images he'd pushed thus far from his mind. Like Victor, falling down as the shots rang out. Like his own startled cry as a bullet had ripped through his upper arm. And deep inside, he knew what had happened to Bill and Jamie. It filled him with anger, deep dark anger at himself because he was supposed to be the specialist. He was supposed to keep people safe. *He was supposed to be the strong, capable one*.

And with the anger came another dark thought and another low curse.

"Was he worth it?" he found himself asking, his voice so tight, he barely recognized it.

"Who?" Jess asked. The grinning Mitch was gone, and in his place was the formidable, furious man who had caught her trying to take the car just three hours earlier.

"Your lover," Mitch ground out.

She shook her head, looking away. "I told you," she said, "there is no other man."

"Then how did they find us, Jess?" he quizzed intently. "How did they know where we were?"

She hesitated, and for the first time the true implications of the last thirty minutes washed through her. All at once her heart was pounding again, and she didn't have to look down to know her hands were shaking.

"I don't know," she told him, a slight quiver in her voice. "I honestly don't know."

"You didn't tell him anything?" Mitch prodded brutally, not quite ready to relent. "You didn't contact him, leave some signal for Les's men to trace?"

She shook her head vehemently.

"Look," she said, willing the conviction into her voice. "I wanted to leave, Mitch. I wanted to leave because I was afraid of just this moment. Don't you understand? The violence follows me. It doesn't matter what I do, what I try. And I thought—" Her voice broke slightly, but she forced herself to continue. "I thought if I could just be by myself, live by myself, then finally everything would be all right."

He glanced over at her, and for the first time, her face was something other than an expressionless canvas. Instead, the worry and the fear etched lines in her forehead and shadows in her eyes.

"There's no one else?" he asked again, but this time his voice was softer.

She looked out at the white patterned landscape rippling on by. The lie stuck in her throat, and even as she cursed herself for the weakness, she couldn't summon the dispassion needed to look this man in the eye and lie.

"I don't have a lover," she said at last. That much was true.

The words took a weight off his shoulders that he hadn't realized had been there. The kernel of his anger dissolved, and at once he realized just how much he'd put her through this evening. He had condemned her for her inability to trust, but looking at events this far, he wondered if she hadn't been right.

Two attempts were made on her life during the trial, and now, in the place he'd told her was safe, the place he'd told her he was in charge of, yet another attempt.

The implications furrowed his brow and darkened his gaze. Because if Jess hadn't betrayed them by outside contact, *who had?*

Chapter 8

They traveled for one more hour in silence, both burdened by their own heavy thoughts and the numbing cold. Mitch would like to have put more distance between themselves and their pursuers, but the cold was becoming a serious safety factor. They'd long ago pulled on the additional clothes from the duffel bag, but even then, Mitch's fingers had gone numb on the wheel, and he'd lost all sensation in his face. He was more than willing to bet that the first stages of frostbite were setting in, and at this point, he and Jess couldn't afford the weakness.

At his suggestion, Jess once more huddled under the dashboard. At least it protected her from the frost-tinged wind blowing through the vehicle, though he could tell from her sporadic shivering that it wasn't adequate protection.

There was a town up ahead, not large, but at least he could already see the glowing red Vacancy sign for a small strip motel. He pulled in, and Jess roused herself enough to peer out.

"Here's the deal," he told her, the severity of the situation making him curt. "Sooner or later, Les's men are going to pass through looking for a man and woman traveling together. So we need to make it appear like I'm traveling by myself.''

Jess looked wary at this idea, but in her half-frozen, sleep-deprived state, she couldn't quite pinpoint why she should be concerned. Then, of course, he spelled it out for her.

"That means I'm going to go inside there and get one room for one person. You're going to sneak into the room later.''

He saw her half open her mouth and he cut her off before she had a chance to say anything. ''We're both exhausted,'' he said flatly. ''And we're both adults. And so help me God, we are going to share that room, and you're not going to argue with me. If you absolutely can't stand it, you can sleep in the tub for all I care. But we've got a big day ahead of us tomorrow, and we need our rest.''

Then before she could so much as muster a reply, he opened the door and climbed down from the Blazer, slamming the door firmly behind him. Alone now in the deep freeze of the cab, Jess let her head sink to her knees. She was truly exhausted and she was truly frozen. And her heart still beat painfully in her chest, her mind dull from the strain.

She was in no condition to share a room with a man like Mitch Guiness, yet in no condition to argue, either. Never in all her life did she crave solitude so badly, and fear it just as much. Because in the loneliness lay the nightmare waiting to find her.

The door opened again, abruptly penetrating her thoughts. She raised her head slightly, her eyes wary.

''Room 3B,'' Mitch said crisply. He drove them to the spot in front, climbed out with the bag and unlocked the door. He looked around, saw no one in sight and then motioned her in. She tried to obey as quickly as possible, but the long hour in a crouch had cut off too much blood in her legs. Pins and needles stabbed through her, and she would have cried out if she'd had the energy. She bit deep into her lower lip instead.

Mitch watched her, and the strain on her face filled him with guilt. Damn it, he'd told her to trust him. He'd told her he knew what he was doing. And here they were running like thieves in the night. Damn it all to hell.

"Stretch out slowly," he found himself saying. "And take a warm shower to heat up. But start with the temperature on the cool side. Your nerves are so numb, you can scald your skin if you're not careful."

She looked around the tiny, cramped room, her eyes making out the shadowed pocket of a bathroom. A shower sounded wonderful. Warmth sounded wonderful. She gave him a sideways glance.

"And you?" she asked carefully.

"I have to attend to the car," he said obliquely. "It could be a while before I'm back."

She froze, suddenly feeling another frisson of fear wash through her. He was leaving. She should want him to leave. She should want the solitude. But the trembles running through her belied the words. And suddenly, deep and heartrending inside of her, she didn't want him to go.

And knew no words to make him stay.

It was the shock of the last few hours, she told herself. The aftermath of the fear. But no matter what logic she used, she felt her heart thump painfully in her chest as he opened the front door. Images slashed across her mind, and at once she remembered the feel of his soft, urgent lips upon her own, his strong, solid arms wrapping her in a secure, warm embrace as he filled her with sensations she'd never felt.

Warmth. Strength. Heat.

She swallowed hard, closing her eyes. But even then, the yearning tore at her.

It's the fear that's causing it all. Because you don't care, you never care. You are the Ice Angel and all you need is to be alone.

He walked through the door, and she stood there in the middle of the room like a mannequin. Her insides screamed as she watched the door close. The click seemed to echo with finality. He was gone.

And suddenly she was all alone in the dingy motel room with a mind full of demons and heart filled with pain.

She didn't even understand why.

PLAY
SILHOUETTE'S

LUCKY HEARTS
GAME

AND YOU GET
- ★ FREE BOOKS
- ★ A FREE GIFT
- ★ AND MUCH MORE

TURN THE PAGE AND DEAL YOURSELF IN

PLAY "LUCKY HEARTS" AND GET . . .

★ **Exciting Silhouette Intimate Moments® novels — FREE**

★ **PLUS a lovely Pearl Drop Necklace — FREE**

THEN CONTINUE YOUR LUCKY STREAK WITH A SWEETHEART OF A DEAL

1. Play Lucky Hearts as instructed on the opposite page.

2. Send back this card and you'll receive brand-new Silhouette Intimate Moments® novels. These books have a cover price of $3.75 each, but they are yours to keep absolutely free.

3. There's no catch. You're under no obligation to buy anything. We charge nothing — ZERO — for your first shipment. And you don't have to make any minimum number of purchases — not even one!

4. The fact is thousands of readers enjoy receiving books by mail from the Silhouette Reader Service. They like the convenience of home delivery...they like getting the best new novels months before they're available in stores...and they love our discount prices!

5. We hope that after receiving your free books you'll want to remain a subscriber. But the choice is yours — to continue or cancel, anytime at all! So why not take us up on our invitation, with no risk of any kind. You'll be glad you did

* * *

Two hours passed. At first she pretended she didn't notice. She did some minor stretches, easing her tired muscles. She showered and pulled back on her jeans and a heavy knit blue sweater. She flipped through stations on the tiny, badly colored TV and told herself after the excitement of the evening, she just wasn't tired yet.

And even as she glanced at her watch for the fifth time in half an hour, she told herself she couldn't possibly be waiting.

She didn't wait. She didn't care about other people or their schedules. She took care of herself—that's the way it had always been. When she felt tired, she slept, regardless of anyone else's plans. And at any time now, she could take the brown-and-orange floral blanket and curl up safely in a corner of the floor to sleep. She could.

But as her eyelids drooped down, she didn't.

Two hours turned to two and a half, the sun beginning to lighten the sky. The entire night ended, leaving the dimlit dawning of an uncertain day.

Where was Mitch Guiness?

Sitting on the floor, her backside numb, she couldn't escape the growing apprehension. He could have left; it was possible. Just gotten into the Blazer and driven away.

She shook her head, trying to dispel the notion. She didn't care, she thought fiercely. She'd said she wanted to be on her own, and she would take care of herself. Though she hadn't had time to grab the twenty thousand from her room last night, she had five hundred dollars in cash in her purse, which would take care of a lot.

But a minute later she abandoned the idea altogether. Mitch wouldn't walk away like that. He just wouldn't.

Once more she remembered his kiss.

Warm, strong, compelling. She'd felt every muscle of his powerful body tense and bunch with the passion. His embrace had been firm, his chest hard and unyielding. Yet gentleness had tempered the strength, restraint easing the power.

Tonight, when Mitch had woken her, the fear had never reared very hard. He'd been with her, guiding her through the silent house with his sure steps and capable strength. He'd led her to the vehicle he'd sequestered, driven them through a rain of bullets and plunged them safely through a snowy forest. Somehow, hunched down beside him, she'd never doubted that they would escape. She only had to look at the grim expression on his dark face, the deft control of his large, callused hands, and she'd known it would be okay.

He'd even thought of ways to make her warmer while his own fingers had grown thick and sluggish with the biting chill.

He'd done all that he'd ever promised, and even now, two and a half hours later, she knew he would come back.

He was that kind of man.

She half shuddered, wrapping her arms around herself as she huddled on the floor. The exhaustion filled her, and her head slipped forward to rest on her knees. But she didn't close her eyes. She knew the minute she did, the nightmare would find her, plunging her down into the desperate blackness.

She wrapped her arms a little tighter, unconsciously rocking a bit. One more glance at the watch. Two hours and forty-four minutes since Mitch had left. Surely he would be back soon, filling the tiny motel room space as he filled everything with his presence. Her gaze crept slightly to the single bed, then skittered away with unstated apprehension.

She would sleep on the floor. She would take the top comforter, curl up on the floor and abandon her fearful vigil. Mitch would be here, and even as he filled her with uncertainty, she knew he would take care of things. As long as he was nearby, Les's men wouldn't get her.

Mitch would be standing guard.

A noise sounded at the door, and she jerked, her head popping up. Her spine instantly stiffened, all expression leaving her face as her control slid unconsciously into place. The telltale scratching of a warped key in a rusty lock penetrated the silence, followed by a low, familiar stream of curses.

Mitch returned. Whatever relief that brought her, none showed on her face.

He opened the door only enough to let himself in, closing it quickly behind himself. He looked haggard and worn, the lower half of his jeans encrusted with mud as if he'd made a long journey.

Seeing her sitting there on the floor, he gave her a small grin, lopsided with the exhaustion.

"Waiting up for me?"

"You were gone?" she returned, feigning ignorance, her eyes habitually cool.

"At least you missed me," he said wryly, leaning back against the wall with obvious weariness. For a moment, she felt a strong stab of guilt. He'd had a long night, and all because of her.

"Where did you go?" she asked quietly.

"I dumped the Blazer in a nearby river," he said. "It's too easy to trace back to us. Tomorrow we'll rent a new vehicle."

She nodded. "You think of everything."

He glanced up sharply, but there was no trace of sarcasm in her voice. Did the Ice Angel just compliment him? He wasn't sure he dared dream so big. Finally he gave a small shrug, leaning down to work on his mud-encrusted boots.

"It's my job," he said casually.

She watched him attempt to untie his shoelaces. Funny, now that he was back, she wasn't tired at all. Instead, her nerves surged with a new kind of restlessness. He filled the room and the one bed loomed like a billboard. She found she couldn't quite meet his eyes.

Mitch was back. Large, strong and vital.

Her stomach clenched again, and the memory of the kiss threatened to overwhelm her brain.

She looked away altogether.

"Damn it." Mitch swore again, penetrating her thoughts. She glanced over through shuttered eyes to see his hands plucking ineffectually at the water-swollen laces. Without thinking, she rose.

"Let me," she found herself saying, easily crossing the few steps between them. Before he could reply, she was on one knee before him, reaching for the laces.

Her own nimble fingers undid the mud-entangled knots easily, and she loosened the laces all the way down.

"There," she said. She kept her eyes on his boots, knowing if she looked up, she would find his warm brown eyes and strong, unrelenting jaw just inches from her own face.

"Your hands are dirty," Mitch said. His voice sounded unexpectedly gruff to his own ears. He could see the silky sheen of her wavy brown hair. It looked so soft, he wondered how it would feel to the touch. It had been a long night, and the morning was still far from certain. And all of a sudden, he just wanted to pull this woman into his arms, bury his face in her neck and breathe in the warm, beguiling scent of fresh summer peaches.

"My hands can be washed," Jess replied. Her heart thundered a maddening beat in her chest. She wanted to look up. She really did. She wanted to see his warm eyes, soft with exhaustion, and she wanted to trace the line of his unshaven jaw with her own slender hand.

She wanted to bury herself against his chest and see if he felt as warm and comforting as she'd felt last night when he'd stolen a kiss from her lips.

Her breathing increased and she felt a small shudder ripple down her back as her stomach filled with that heady combination of want and fear.

Slowly, of its own volition, her head came up.

His breath froze in his chest. Her eyes were dark and luminous as they fell upon his lips. There was no mistaking that look. And even as he told himself he was asking for trouble, his large hands reached down to find her shoulders and drag her up against him. She came against his chest hard, but neither protested. Mitch's gaze settled on her lips, pink and swollen, waiting for him. His gaze swept up one last time to find her eyes still mesmerized by the desire.

"Is this what you want?" he found himself whispering thickly.

She nodded, leaning her lips slightly closer. But he refused to comply so easily. Last time he'd been taken in by the invitation, only to be held as the guilty party when it was through. He would not be accused of taking advantage of her twice.

Her eyes darkened further, her mouth pouting slightly with the frustration. His large hands slid up her back, drawing her in farther. He could feel the long, graceful lines of her body, soft and pliable against him. His hands slid more to the side, and discovered the tantalizing swells of her breasts. She shivered, her own hand coming up to rest on the shadowed line of his jaw. Softly her long index finger discovered the rough feel of twenty-four-hour whiskers.

She drew his head forward, and this time, he gave in to her unspoken demand. His lips found hers warm and inviting. There was no need for careful exploration. Her lips parted willingly, inviting him in as she pressed closer. He felt the first rush of shudders as he found her tongue and sucked lightly. Her hands were suddenly on his shoulders, pulling at him as she moaned lightly.

The sensations were warm and wonderful and pushed all the apprehension from her mind. He filled her senses, and willingly she gave herself over to the onslaught. There were no more sinister shadows or waiting nightmares. Just this strong man with his warm lips that moved on hers knowingly. Just this one man with his maddening scent of soap and spices that left her dazed and wanting.

His lips snuck away from hers, but before she could whimper her protest, they soothed their way to her ear. She felt the warm whisper of his breath against her sensitive neck, and a small gasp escaped from her lips. She arched back, and he seized the opportunity to explore her delicate ear with his tongue, then blazed a tantalizing trail to the seductive curve of her shoulders. The bulk of her sweater got in his way, and he seized it with impatient hands. She stiffened slightly in his arms, but he relaxed her again with reassuring murmurs. The next thing she knew, her sweater was being swept over her head until cold air struck her tender flesh.

She drew back slightly, the cold penetrating the spell. For one moment she tensed with the fear, and her hands balled on his shoulders.

She shouldn't be doing this; she shouldn't be letting any of this happen. But his lips returned to hers, softer this time, cajoling. His hands splayed carefully across her back, replacing the air with sure fingers. They swept up to trace the straps of her bra, but did not remove it.

He felt her relax a fraction more, but she was still tense and uncertain in his arms. He frowned unconsciously, deepening his kiss, and he sought her earlier pliability. Instinct told him she was on the verge of pulling away, and his own red-hot senses told him he would possibly explode if she left him now. He wanted her with an intensity that was new and startling for him.

Her hands flattened on his shoulders once more, the deep stroking of his tongue in her mouth filling her stomach with unknown yearning. She could feel his heartbeat, fast and strong, and she reveled in the sensation. For one tantalizing instant, she wondered what it would be like to feel skin against skin, heat against heat. Her hands paused at the edge of a button.

The desire to tear it away mixed once again with the fear, and abruptly she became conscious of his hands moving along her back, sliding forward, cupping a lace-covered breast.

The fear reared hard and she couldn't stop herself. She pushed away with a violent oath, her own desire and insanity ringing in her ears.

"Stop," she cried, whirling away. Her hands crossed in front of her in a feeble attempt to cover herself, and in that instant she suddenly looked like a small, vulnerable child.

He looked at her heavily, his hands balling at his sides as he fought against his own raging passion. Deep inside, he realized he'd been waiting for this moment. All along, he'd known she'd pull away. And then he abruptly became aware of something else.

Like the way she was hunched forward and the way her eyes were watching him warily under the cover of her brown hair. Her gaze swept down to his hands, and in that moment he understood. She was waiting for him to hit her.

He wanted to swear, low and violent and ugly. He wanted to shake her for thinking so little of him. And he wanted to reach out and draw her back into his arms until she understood not all men were cruel and abusive.

Not all men were like Les Capruccio.

Slowly he reached down and picked up her sweater. Without saying a word, he held it out to her. She took it carefully, her eyes still alert. Then, as if she thought he might change his mind, she turned quickly and yanked it on.

"Do you want to talk about it?" he asked quietly.

"About what?" she said in a muffled voice, not turning around.

"About Les and how he treated you."

Her back went rigid, her shoulders squaring, and she slowly turned around. Her face was once more controlled, but he could see the wariness in her eyes.

"There's nothing to talk about," she said stiffly.

He shook his head. "You are the most stubborn creature I've ever encountered," he told her bluntly. "Why are you so determined to protect the man? Everyone knows what Les was like. And enough people testified on how he treated you. What not just get it out, Jess? Why not just admit the man was an abusive bastard who hit you."

"It's no one's business," she said slowly, but he could see the hurt in her eyes. His voice gentled.

"It's not your fault," he said softly. "Surely you understand that."

She shivered, her arms unconsciously wrapping around her. The defensive move made him wince, and at that moment he would have liked nothing better than to slam a concrete fist through Les's smirking face.

"You should have left him sooner," he said quietly. His voice was gruff. "God knows you deserve better than the likes of Capruccio."

Slowly she nodded. "I hate him," she said suddenly, the words toneless. "I hate him more than I've ever hated anyone."

"How did you even hook up with such a man?" Mitch said, running his hand through his hair as the tiredness once more began to sink in. In the beginning, he'd been prepared to dislike Jessica Gavornée because of her association with Les Capruccio. Because she'd remained the mistress of a cruel and abusive man. But now, having seen her intelligence and her strength, the whole thing seemed suddenly like a huge waste to him. That such an ugly man would claim such a beautiful woman, and lock her life onto a violent, unending path.

"He introduced himself to me," Jess replied. She hesitated, feeling suddenly torn. She shouldn't speak about it, she understood that. There were too many pieces of the puzzle she couldn't reveal, and Mitch was the type of man who would spot the holes. But at the same time, a part of her wanted him to understand. She shouldn't care what Mitch thought of her, but standing in this tiny room, the taste of him on her lips, she did.

"Wined you and dined you," Mitch filled in. "Sounds like Capruccio."

She looked at him sharply. "I refused Les's offer for dinner," she said levelly. "Unfortunately, Raphael, the designer, didn't agree with my decision. It seemed Les had given Raphael a bit of money for the show. Well, it's not so unusual to dine with major backers. I went."

Mitch watched her carefully, the questions burning in his mind, and he worked to hold them back. So dining was common. How far did that "professionalism" extend? a small voice whispered. Was she supposed to sleep with him, too? He looked away, his muscle working furiously in his jaw.

"One thing just led to another," he said finally, his voice deliberately neutral.

Jess smiled, a bitter smile Mitch didn't see. Yes, one thing had led to another. One week later Les had walked into her dressing room, asking her to join him at a charity ball. When she'd told him no, he'd produced a file filled with black-and-white photographs of her visiting a woman in a prison's uniform. She'd tensed then, but her face hadn't given anything away. She'd visited the Women's

Correctional Institute just three days before. Apparently, Les had had her followed. Still, there was nothing wrong with a charitable visit.

Of course she'd underestimated the matter and Les's resources. In the next fifteen minutes, he'd laid out to her just how much he knew about the other woman in the photograph. And he'd called her by a name no one had used since she was sixteen years old.

"Did you fall in love with him?" Mitch asked suddenly. He could at least understand that even if it did turn his stomach. Women had fallen in love with scum before.

"Love him?" She practically spat the words out, rubbing her arms in agitation. "I hated him. I hated the way he smiled, the way he dressed. I hated the way he ate, and I hated the way he would caress my cheek right before he hit me. Les Capruccio is a low and vile man who deserves to rot away in jail for the rest of his godforsaken life!"

"There!" Mitch said, taking a step forward as he pinned her with intense brown eyes. "You admit how he treated you. So why did you stay, Jess? Why spend a year and a half with the monster?"

Her mouth opened, then abruptly snapped shut. She felt his eyes burning into her and stiffened her resolve against it. She couldn't tell him. It didn't matter that he'd saved her from Les's men, and it didn't matter that his kisses made her feel things she wasn't supposed to feel. She'd already given him too much of herself, when deep inside she knew it would only come back to haunt her.

People could be good, but they were also capable of the most horrendous actions on earth. The only way to truly be safe was to depend upon yourself.

"I was weak," she said simply, willing herself not to turn away from his gaze. She gave a small shrug, but it didn't fool him.

His eyes turned black, and he shook his head with frustration.

"You're lying," he said flatly. "You're the strongest person I've ever known, and I've seen for myself that you don't do anything you don't want to do." His voice low-

ered. "You're still hiding something, Jess. And I'm get
ting mighty tired of waiting for the truth."

She faltered momentarily, looking at him with uncertain
eyes. Her gaze fell unconsciously to his hands, large and
waiting by his sides. He followed her gaze and issued a
dark, low oath.

"Don't look at me like that," he warned ominously.
"Don't you even begin to compare me with the likes of Les
Capruccio. I've never hit a woman before in my life and
certainly don't plan on starting now—though there are
times you frustrate me to the brink of violence."

Her gaze swept up once more, searching his eyes with
open suspicion.

*"I'm so sorry, baby. Daddy didn't mean to hurt you.
Damn, I'm so sorry. It won't happen again, sugar, I swear
it won't happen again. If you would just do what I told
you... I'm sorry. I'm so, so sorry."*

She turned away, feeling the unexpected tightness of a
lump in her throat. And for a moment, she hated Mitch
Guiness simply because he could stand there and tell her he
would never hit her, never be like Les Capruccio. And she
hated herself because she wanted to believe him, wanted to
think that he was somehow different.

Just like all those years when she'd believed her father
wouldn't hit her again. And each time he had. Until she'd
learned to hate him, but even then she'd wanted to believe.

Because she'd wanted so desperately to have someone to
believe in.

*Even as the blow had landed across her mouth, sending
her flying across the cracked linoleum floor while her
mother had screamed in the background, and the sick
stench of cheap whiskey had filled the air.*

"I need to go to sleep," she said quietly, but her voice
didn't sound quite right. She took another deep breath. Oh,
what was wrong with her? She never thought of these
things. Her father was long gone and she was no longer a
child. She'd grown into a woman who knew how to take
care of herself. She did.

"Fine," Mitch said, his own voice curt as he watched her
pull away from him. He half wanted to strangle her for be

ng so damn stubborn and for keeping secrets that would
probably cost him his life. And once more he wondered if
there wasn't some man after all. Then again, given how
skittish she was around him, the logical part of his brain
dismissed it.

Then who was she protecting? And why wouldn't she just
tell him? He'd done everything in the world to deserve her
trust. But no matter how much he'd worked on her identity, Jess McMoran was still the Ice Angel.

And no matter how much she'd wanted his kiss earlier,
she still locked him out of her thoughts now.

He was the fool to even let her get to him.

"I'm going to shower," he said flatly. His watch told him
it was already nearly seven, and they had a long day ahead.
"You can have the bed."

"I'll be fine on the floor," Jess returned. She took two
steps away, but in the small room, that still didn't put much
space between them. She turned, willing her face to be
neutral. "You need the sleep worse than me, I got to nap
earlier." It was a small lie, but for a good cause.

"Whatever," Mitch said finally. The sleeplessness was
catching up with him, and he certainly had no intention of
wasting precious time arguing with her. "We have until
nine. Then we need to get a car."

She nodded. That meant only two hours of sleep, but she
didn't complain. She stepped back to let him pass, but even
then, his shoulder brushed her. Then he disappeared into
the bathroom, the sound of running water penetrating the
silence.

She was left alone in the tiny space, pulling the cheap
floral comforter off the bed to wrap herself up with on the
floor.

Her eyes closed wearily, and she used her iron control to
will herself to sleep.

She didn't wake when the sound of running water shut
off. And she didn't wake when the large man emerged from
the bathroom to contemplate her sleeping form on the
floor. Her face remained expressionless even in slumber, the
smooth, soft skin not giving anything away.

Briefly, Mitch imagined Les Capruccio bringing back a powerful arm and hitting that smooth skin. He could almost see the bruise, and it filled him with a rusty rage. So help him God, if he ever met Les in person he'd teach that man what it meant to feel pain.

Forcing the thought away, he bent down and easily lifted her up into his arms. She mumbled once, but remained soft and relaxed in his arms. He could feel the curve of her breast against his chest, and his body reacted accordingly.

"Rutting bastard," he murmured to himself. He deposited her gently onto the bed; she rewarded him with a soft sigh, stretching out like a languorous cat without ever waking. He had to forcefully turn away.

With a grim expression of control, Mitch laid his own large frame down in front of the door. In a matter of minutes, he, too, was asleep.

And for Jess, the nightmare stayed away. Instead, slumberland stirred with the faint heat of a faraway kiss, and the gentle warmth of a strong embrace. She slept well.

Mitch slept, too, but one thought remained solid in his unconscious state: How had Les known about the retreat? Where had it all gone wrong? And in the darkness of his mind, a blond woman appeared with icy blue eyes and a perfect porcelain face. She turned to point a carefully manicured finger at him, and even as he watched, her hair abruptly turned brown and short, though her eyes remained blue as they bore into his own.

For one moment, the ice relented and the blue depths grew shiny with yearning. He reached out to her, discovering for the first time that his legs were shackled.

She remained captive beyond his reach, and as if she realized it herself, tears began to softly roll from those blue blue eyes.

He reached down, grabbing the iron shackles with mighty hands. But they wouldn't budge and he looked up in time to see the dark shadows rolling in, threatening to take her from him.

He held out his hand, but it was too late. Suddenly she was gone, and only her cries still rang in the corridors of his mind.

Chapter 9

Mitch awoke in approximately one hour and forty-five minutes, his internal alarm clock performing well. A quick glance at his watch told him it was five minutes after nine, and more than time to get ready. Slowly he sat up, wringing the last of the sleep from his sore and tired body.

He could feel the strains of last night every time he moved, and the exhaustion hovered like a shadow behind his mind. Dim images of a forgotten nightmare floated just beyond his reach, leaving him feeling muddy and apprehensive.

Unbidden, his gaze swept up to the bed. Jess still slept soundly, rolled up like a caterpillar in a floral cocoon. Only the top of her hair was visible, shining in the dim light of the shaded room.

He should wake her. The day before them would be long.

He took a deep breath and swept away the last of the sleep. He'd operated on little sleep before, and knew that adrenaline could keep a man moving long after normal physical endurance. Already his mind began to race with the multitude of unanswered questions.

Something had gone wrong, something that now put his and Jess's lives in immediate danger. He could handle that—it was his job and he'd been through the drill, time and time again. At the beginning of the assignment, he'd made plans just for nights like last night. In his wallet, he already had a driver's license and credit cards for a whole new identity, while the duffel bag held two thousand dollars in cash. In two other cities, he'd opened safe-deposit boxes, all in different names, that held yet two more sets of new identities and more than an ample supply of cash.

He could keep them going for a long time without leaving a plastic trail. And he could incorporate enough identities to further complicate the chase.

The question was, Who were they running from?

He frowned, running a large hand through his hair. He stretched once more, wincing at the tight muscles in his back. Hell, what he'd give for a hot Jacuzzi and a cold beer. He stood.

He didn't know what had happened to Jamie or Bill. One of them could have been the leak. Not Bill—he'd worked with Bill before. Unless something had happened in the meantime...

Men like Les Capruccio had a lot of levers at their disposal, and not all of them were money.

Still, Mitch shook his head. He trusted his instincts with people, and his instincts had told him Jamie and Bill were the right choice. And God knows, there were other ways Les could have learned about the retreat: Dan, the other agents who'd come to the retreat, Mitch's boss...

His gaze went to Jess. How much did he know about this woman? She'd told him she'd hated Les, and yet she wouldn't say why she'd stayed with the man for a year and a half. Just nine hours earlier, she'd tried to sneak out of the retreat, though she claimed there was no man involved.

Hell, the woman kissed like a yes and pulled away like a no. Nothing about her made sense. Could she have intentionally betrayed them? He thought of how she'd acted last night. The surprise had at least seemed genuine, and the shudders of her frame had seemed real enough. No, she'd been scared last night. If she'd given away their location, at least it hadn't been intentionally.

But that didn't matter, Mitch thought grimly. The results remained the same. The woman hoarded her secrets, and those secrets might very well become deadly.

And he'd done this job long enough to know paranoia was the best policy. When all else failed, the answer was the one that had been before you all along.

He walked the two steps over to the bed.

Her eyes opened the minute he approached. He could see the top of her lashes as they fluttered up.

"Is it time?" she asked quietly. He could hear the thickness of exhaustion in her tone and he nodded.

"It's after nine," he said.

She sat up, the comforter still wrapped around her shoulders. Her hair fluffed out around her, mussed and rearranged by her two-hour nap. Dark rings rimmed her eyes with strain, and he knew she was tired even as he knew she'd never admit to it.

"You should shower," he said, "Get cleaned up the best you can, do your hair. There's nothing so obvious as people who look like they're on the run."

She half grimaced, then nodded. "I've known photographers less demanding," she informed him wryly.

He spared her a grin, but motioned her out of the bed. They really didn't have much time to waste. He noticed she climbed out on the far side of the bed, and shook his head.

The woman didn't give an inch.

Soon he heard the rhythmic sound of running water. Then he put his plan into action.

Jess emerged just twenty minutes later. With no blow dryer, she'd pulled her shorter hair back into a tentative French braid. The loose braiding gave her a soft, romantic look that went well with her dark rose sweater. Mitch's hands paused on the table, his gaze momentarily caught.

She didn't look the same anymore, he thought, telling himself he was making the suitable observations of the official trainer. The darker hair and brows gave her skin a vulnerable translucence, a girl-next-door image that belied her frigid reputation. Maybe it was the coaching, but now she did stand looser, her shoulders curled enough to look relaxed. And her face looked soft, her dark eyes beguiling with the faint smudges of a long night.

As he watched, one hand came up and she began to slowly twist her ring.

He looked away, feeling a sudden, unfamiliar hollowness. Was he watching one more act, one stage of Jessica Gavornée's metamorphosis into a new and elusive identity? Or was he seeing the woman beneath the ice, the possible Jess McMoran?

He wanted to believe in the act, he realized suddenly, even as he knew he'd helped create the illusion. And magicians knew better than to be swept up by their own tricks.

He looked up, keeping his brown gaze hard.

"You do that very well now," he said levelly. "Your new identity is coming along well."

She faltered for just a moment, and something like a shadow swept behind her eyes. A flash of pain? He knew better than to think such things. But then she stepped forward, the faint scent of peaches wafting in, and he felt himself lose his mind all over again. God help him, this job would kill him yet.

"What's all this?" Jess asked softly, uncertainty edging the words.

Mitch had pulled the night table away from the wall, and was sitting behind it in the feeble desk chair that would most likely crash from the burden of his weight. His hands rested on the bare wood of the table, and from the few feet that separated them, she could see the dull gleam of silver coins.

"Have a seat," Mitch said, and gestured to the bed. She hesitated, feeling the beginnings of apprehension. He looked so intent sitting there, and obviously this had all been set up with a purpose.

"Sit, Jess," Mitch said flatly. She slowly crossed to the bed.

"Do we really have time for this?" she prodded, her voice wary.

"You don't even know what this is," Mitch replied curtly. His grin was gone, and at once she recognized this was the strong, relentless Mitch before her. Her apprehension doubled as she sat down gingerly on the very edge of the bed.

"You look like you're on the verge of flight," Mitch commented, looking at her intensely now with his piercing brown eyes.

"Should I be?" she returned levelly, summoning her control to return his gaze. Her shoulders and back were ramrod straight, and her hands rested calm and controlled on her lap. Nothing at all gave her away.

Mitch shook his head, his eyes never leaving hers. "Here's the deal," he said briskly. He spread out his hands to reveal four silver dollars lying on the table. "I'm going to make these silver dollars go through the table, one by one," he told her.

"Is this another bet?" she asked sharply.

"Not at all," he replied levelly. "I know you don't believe in magic. I know you believe it's just a bunch of con man high jinks. So this time—" he paused meaningfully "—this time I'm going to tell you how it's done."

She remained suspicious. "Surely we don't have time for a brief magic-trick interlude. Didn't you say something about renting a car this morning?"

"Absolutely. But this isn't just a brief 'interlude' as you said. See, knowledge isn't for free, Jess. I'm going to show you how right you think you are, but I want something in return."

"What?"

"Nothing you can't refuse to give to me," he said obliquely. He held up the coins. "Four silver dollars." He handed one across the table to her. Her gaze remained skeptical and impatient, but she took the coin.

"It's a real silver dollar. Correct?"

She nodded, and he took the coin back and handed her the other three. "All solid. Correct?"

Once more she nodded.

"And the table, Jess?" He rapped it lightly with his knuckles. "Solid, as well. Correct?"

"Yes, yes," she agreed, with an impatient wave of her hand. "Everything is solid. You shouldn't possibly be able to do what you're going to do, et cetera, et cetera."

He grinned at her this time, some of the old Mitch back in his eyes. "It's good to know you believe," he said wryly.

He placed the four coins on his open palm, then curled his fist around them. He rested the fist on the table, showing her his other empty hand. "I'm going to rap on the table," he said evenly. "And when I do, one coin will pass from this fist, through the table, to my waiting hand."

She looked openly skeptical. The table and the coins were solid, so what he was saying was indeed physically impossible. Which meant, of course, she reminded herself, that it wasn't actually going to happen. It would just appear as if it happened.

"Four coins. See?" he prompted her, showing her the coins in his one hand again. She nodded, watching his empty fist go under the table. His closed fist abruptly knocked on the table. There was a small pause and a look of concentration on Mitch's face. Abruptly, she heard a small metal clink.

Mitch brought out his one fist from under the table and opened it for her to see. One shiny silver dollar gleamed on his palm.

"Not all things are impossible," he told her.

She didn't bother with a reply, though one hand crept out to rest on the edge of the table. It certainly felt solid.

Her eyes narrowed and she looked at him more intently.

"Three coins in this hand," he told her, and showed her his left hand again with indeed three coins. "One coin in this hand," he held it up, "which will act as bait—silver attracting silver through the wood. Three here. One here."

She nodded, and his right hand with its one coin disappeared under the table. His left hand knocked on the wood; she felt the faint vibration of the impact. Then the metal clink sounded again. His hand came out with two coins.

He grinned. "Not bad, is it?"

This time she could only nod.

"Two in this hand," he said, holding up his left hand. "Two in this hand. Once more, the silver will act as bait, drawing one more coin through the table."

She watched carefully this time. His right fist closed over the two coins, disappearing under the table. Two coins were under the table; she'd seen them go there. She scrutinized his left hand.

It knocked on the table, and sure enough, a metal clink. But she wasn't so hasty this time. Instead, she watched him draw out his right fist. Surely the trade-off was really occurring here, the left hand somehow sneaking a coin to the right hand. But his left hand never moved, remaining passive on the tabletop.

His right hand opened. Three gleaming coins winked at her. Only then did he turn over his left hand, exposing one lonely silver dollar.

She frowned, clearly perplexed.

"It's not possible," she said flatly.

"Observe," he told her quietly, his brown eyes once more serious. He leaned slightly forward, and she felt the intensity crackle in the air around him. Her stomach unexpectedly tightened, and for no good reason, her gaze fell to his lips.

"One last coin," he whispered. "I'm going to pass it through the table, as well, solid silver through solid wood. Watch closely, Jess. Maybe you'll see a bit of magic."

He held out the one going, silver and gleaming. His right fist closed around the other three. As she watched, his left fist closed around the last coin and rested on the table. His right fist slipped under the table.

"The last coin is a little harder," he said. "You'll have to bear with me." Once more his face tightened with concentration. Then, rap, rap, clink. He suddenly smiled, but it didn't dim the intensity of his gaze.

His right hand came out, and revealed four silver dollars.

"That's impossible," she blurted out, but the frown was etched between her eyes. She'd watched carefully, very carefully. Of course, there had to be some explanation. Without asking, she reached out and took the coins from his warm and callused hand. The silver dollars felt solid and heavy in her hands. Frowning again, she wiped one hand over the top of the table, then beneath it, as well, for good measure. It all felt obscenely solid to her.

A strange, exotic sensation gripped her: amazement. She pushed it away.

"Maybe it's magic," Mitch said softly, his brown eyes searching hers.

She shook her head.

"Why not?" he prompted, leaning over once again. "You watched it with your own two eyes. No sleight of hand. I saw you looking for it. The coins are real, the table is real. Why can't it be magic, Jess?"

"Because there's no such thing," she replied curtly, sitting up rigidly. Her eyes narrowed. "You told me you would show me how it's done."

He paused for a minute, then slowly nodded. Was it her imagination, or was there a flash of disappointment in his eyes?

"I'm going to do it slower this time," he said quietly, settling back into the chair. "If you watch closely, you'll see how it's done. Stand up, though, so you can look down on the process."

She did, bending closer as he once more showed her four coins in one hand, no coins in the other. His right hand once more went under the table. This time, however, just as he was closing his fist around the four coins, she saw one suddenly shoot back to fall off the edge of the table onto his lap. It happened in a fraction of an instant, and would not have been visible from her previous sitting position. His left fist was now closed around three coins, and he rapped it on the table, the other coin safely gripped in his right hand.

"And that's how it's done," he said, looking up into her watchful gaze. "So you were right, Jess. It never was magic, just a sleight of hand. Do you feel vindicated now?"

She shifted, feeling suddenly uncomfortable and not wanting him to know. The trick was just a trick, as she'd known all along. Yet, somehow, having seen it actually done, it took something away. She felt all at once . . . disappointed.

The silver dollars were just silver dollars, the wood just wood and Mitch just a man with crafty hands.

"Shall I do the trick again?" he asked quietly.

"No," she said.

"Why not, Jess?"

"I already know how it's done."

He nodded, and she understood that she was being led along some path. He'd set this all up, and as he'd said, nothing was free.

"So you're going to ask me a question now?" she said, stiffening her back once more.

But Mitch shook his head. "No. Do you like the trick, Jess? Do you like knowing how it was done?"

All at once she had to look away, the words suddenly homing in with stunning clarity. No, she didn't like knowing. To actually see the switch of the silver dollar, it had killed everything somehow. Slowly, unconsciously, she found herself shaking her head.

"No," she said softly.

Mitch nodded, leaning forward until his arms rested on the flimsy weight of the cheap table. He caught and held her gaze with his own. "It's the magic, Jess," he told her seriously. "It's the mystery of belief. Even though you knew silver shouldn't be able to go through wood, even though you knew I shouldn't be able to make silver go through wood, a part of you wanted to believe. A part of you liked the believing."

She wanted to tell him no. She wanted to point out with cool logic and clean rationality that intelligence and knowledge were better than illusions. But somehow she couldn't look at him and say the words. Because in that one moment, when he'd held up the silver dollar that had passed through the table, she had felt amazement.

She'd wanted to believe.

"Are we done now?" she said, trying to look away while a million thoughts began to claw and crowd in her mind. But Mitch refused to relent.

"You keep pushing me away. You keep telling me only fragments of the truth, when I've never done anything to deserve your lies. Why do you do that, Jess? Why do you push me away when you need to believe in me and I need to believe in you? There are men out there trying to kill us, and at this moment I don't think I can trust you, and I know you're determined not to trust me. So where does that leave us, Jess? Do we fight each other, or them? Because we can't do both. And I saw your eyes when I held up that first coin, Jess. I know at least a little part of you still wants to believe, still wants to trust."

"There's a big difference between a magic trick and escaping hit men," she said, but her voice lacked spirit.

He looked at her levelly, his voice strong and unrelenting when he finally spoke. "Did you tell anyone where the retreat was, Jess? Did you violate the rules of the Witness Protection Program?"

She suddenly smiled, a wry, bitter smile. "Is that what this was all about?" Her new brown gaze swept up to meet his. "You could have just asked. No, Mitch, I didn't tell anyone about the retreat."

"Who were you going to see last night?" he pressed, the intensity back in full force. "Why were you running away?"

She shook her head, not giving in. "No one," she said stiffly.

The next thing she knew, Mitch had risen so fast, the chair fell back with a crash onto the floor. He grabbed her arm, his grip firm while his eyes grew hard.

"You're lying."

She stiffened her spine, but under the intensity of his gaze, she faltered. Her control suddenly didn't seem too strong, and instead her mind was seeing his hand holding up that silver dollar. Damn him, she had wanted to believe.

Damn him to hell.

"Talk to me," he commanded, and she could hear the urgency in his voice. "I can help you, Jess. You know I can. And I want to." His voice abruptly softened, and on their own volition his eyes came down to rest on the lush promise of her lips. His hand suddenly moved up to cup her cheek, and with infinite carefulness his thumb traced her lips, feeling each small tremble. "Talk to me, Jess. Believe in me."

Her shoulders came slightly forward, the strain almost agonizing. For just one moment, the words hovered on her lips. After eight long years of silence, she just wanted to blurt it all out. Maybe he was right, and maybe he could make it better. And maybe she could lean into the warm circle of his arms and rest her head against his shoulder.

She could feel the callused strength of his thumb, rough and capable and tender. She liked how he kissed her, and marveled at how he turned away when God knows she provoked him beyond all reason. But he hadn't hit her, not even when lesser men would have found an excuse. And last night, when all hell had broken loose, he'd been the one to get them out. He'd taken care of everything.

Her mouth opened, she felt the words squeeze her throat. But then abruptly her mother flashed before her eyes. A pale, fragile woman lowering the smoking gun as Harry fell down, down, down onto the gold-patterned carpet. And Jess could see the look of acceptance on her mother's bruised face as her husband sank down onto the carpet.

And Jess had looked up and met her mother's eyes, and in that moment everything passed between them. The relief, the shock, the guilt and most of all, the unrelenting pain. Because somewhere deep inside of them both, even after all the drunken rages and explosive blows, they'd still loved him. Even as they'd hated him, they'd loved him.

And now the violence was at long last over. All that remained was the guilt.

Jess looked away.

"I can't," she said, and for the first time Mitch heard the anguish in her voice. It filled him with frustration as he looked at her with waiting eyes. He just wanted her to reach out to him, he just wanted her to finally let him in. And though at least it pained her, she still held him at bay. He couldn't take it.

As if it might make a difference, his head suddenly swooped down to claim her lips with his own. There was no gentleness to this kiss, but a wealth of frustrated demand. She surrendered to it easily, letting his lips plunder her own with unspoken need while the unexpected burn of tears clogged her throat.

And the gun smoked, and she screamed, and looked at her mother as they both realized it had been done. The blood seeped into the cheap, golden carpet, and she cried his name. But her father never moved again, and a bruised battered part of her felt the relief. Because, as her gaze lifted to meet her mother's once more, both knew what he had been about to do. And though they never ever spoke it out loud, they knew.

Her throat thickened, the first unshed tear threatening the corner of her eyes. The desperation overwhelmed her, and she pressed herself against Mitch, willing him to drown out the memories, to make her feel anything other than the horrible coldness so deep down inside. She wound her arms around his neck, pressing herself along the entire burning length of his hard, muscled body. He responded by deepening the kiss, burying his large hands in her carefully coifed braid until loose strands and hairpins spilled down in a tumbling heap.

It wasn't enough, would never be enough. She pressed closer, reveling in the strength and the heat. He was too warm and capable and hard, and even now he dizzied her senses.

And he'd been right all along. She did want to believe. She wanted so badly to believe that this one man would finally be the one she could turn to, even as she knew deep inside she could never turn to anyone.

"I'm so sorry, baby. I won't hit you ever again, I promise. I promise...."

"No!" she cried suddenly, tearing herself away as the memory rocketed through her tormented mind. Unconsciously her hands went to her forehead, pressing against her temples as she sought sanity.

"Just leave me alone," she whispered brokenly, unable to meet his eyes. Because surely it all showed in her eyes, and the minute he looked at her with concern, it would all tumble out in a giant, muddled heap. She couldn't handle his tenderness. She had no defenses for such caring.

Mitch shook his head, swearing softly under his breath. His blood was pounding full speed, though he knew it had been stupid to kiss her and knew she would pull away sooner or later. She always did.

Face it. The woman didn't believe in magic, and she certainly didn't believe in him. The frustration darkened his eyes and furrowed his brow.

"You'll be the death of us yet," he finally said darkly, one hand running through his hair.

She gave him her back, one hand pressed against her mouth, and she struggled for control. After the heat of his arms, the room seemed so cold. And suddenly, despite all her best intentions, she wanted nothing more than to turn back around and throw herself into his embrace.

Let his arms enfold her. Let his lips descend and chase away the darkness with the most tantalizing sensations she'd ever felt. *Let her believe in him.*

She felt a moment of raw bitterness. As if he would have anything more to do with her, a woman so cold, the whole world called her the Ice Angel.

She straightened her shoulders, and from somewhere deep inside, she drew up all the strength and courage that had gotten her this far.

"I swear, Mitch," she said evenly, her back still turned, "I swear to you that I didn't...haven't done anything to let Les know where we are. I swear."

Mitch stared at the vulnerable curve of her back for a long time. So here they were again. She was still running hot and cold, kissing him passionately, then shutting him out completely. Yet he was supposed to believe her. He shook his head. How the hell had he gotten into this mess? If he lived through this experience, he was going to demand a raise.

Then slowly he released a deep, pent-up sigh. He was three times the fool but, in fact, he believed her.

He glanced at his watch. Ten o'clock. They'd already been here far too long.

"Come on," he said finally, resting a light hand on her shoulder. She stiffened at the first contact, then relented. "We have to go get a car," he reminded her.

Jess nodded. Her brown eyes fixed on the wall as she allowed herself one shuddering breath. Then the control locked into place, the memories pushing down, down, down to where they belonged. Her face became composed, her shoulders straight. She picked up the duffel bag, turning back to Mitch.

"I'm ready," she said, still not quite able to meet his eyes. He merely nodded, moving ahead of her to peer out the door. At least he opened it and motioned her through. This time she was the one who noticed how he kept himself carefully back, putting plenty of distance between them.

And even as she stuck out her chin in nonchalance, the pain rifled through her.

In his arms, she'd found the only limited comfort she'd ever known. But she'd even pushed him away. Because ultimately, Mitch Guiness wanted her to believe, when she knew perfectly well there was nothing you could believe in.

Not even magic.

Chapter 10

After consulting the local Yellow Pages, Mitch led them to a nearby car-rental agency. The outfit was small, carrying a limited number of choices. Mitch surveyed his options carefully, already missing the Blazer. In the end, he settled for a Taurus, though it hardly qualified as an all-terrain vehicle. He rented it under the name Mike Cohen, showing the fake ID without batting an eye. He put it on a new MasterCard, and then they were all set.

His face grim, he took the keys and led Jess out to the car. Her own face was serious, her brown eyes dark with exhaustion and strain.

"So what do we do now?" she asked quietly as they climbed into the vehicle. Mitch paused, then adjusted the seat to allow for his longer legs.

"We get more information," he stated, checking all the mirrors.

"Information on what?" she persisted. The feeling of foreboding was growing stronger with each waking hour. Now she had to consciously fight the desire to look over her shoulder and see if anyone was following.

"We need to know where the leak is," Mitch explained calmly. Familiar now with the car, he started the engine.

"Look, Jess. I have enough cash and fake identities to keep us running for a long time. But we have to know who we're running from. Can we call in to the program? Can we trust the Bureau? I don't have these answers, and until I do, it's hard to know when we're actually going to be safe."

She nodded, the words making sense to her even as they deepened her apprehension. She risked a sideways glance at the large man beside her. His hands looked strong and capable on the wheel. She could still picture them guiding the Blazer over the thick snow, dodging trees and bullets with breakneck speed. He'd gotten them out of trouble before. He'd gotten them this far, and already had contingency plans in place.

She relaxed slightly, easing back against the seat without realizing she was doing so. As the car sped back along the interstate, the lethargy set in. She'd only slept two hours the night before and her eyes felt scratchy and dry beneath the new contact lenses. They'd left the pack of contact lenses back at the retreat, so she'd have to make sure she took good care of these. She had how many days left before she took them out . . . ten, twelve? It seemed so long already since she'd first gotten them.

Her eyes drifted shut.

"Where are we going?" she managed to mumble, her head tilting toward him. He spared her a glance from the road, taking in her tousled hair and soft cheeks. Damn, she was beautiful. His grip tightened on the wheel, his face becoming even more serious.

"Mitch?" she prodded again, her voice falling husky and deep from her lips as her eyes drifted closed.

"Back to the retreat," he admitted levelly from the wheel, though the calmness of his voice did little to minimize her reaction. Jess's eyes suddenly popped open, her back becoming ramrod straight with the shock.

"You can't be serious," she exclaimed, her senses on full, spine-tingling alert. "That's where Les's men are. What if they're waiting for us?"

"Chances are they consider us long gone from there," he replied evenly. His voice relented a bit, and he looked away from the road long enough to give her a reassuring glance.

"I have to find out how they knew about the retreat when only a select group of people had access to that knowledge. You say you didn't give us away. Well, then, is there a leak in the Bureau? Maybe Bill or Jamie? Dan? Or did I just make some stupid mistake along the way that allowed Les to find us? We have to know."

Jess felt her heart thunder in her chest and she didn't have to look down to know her hands would be shaking. Once more the foreboding hit her dead-on. How had Les known? And even now, if she glanced in the rearview mirror, would she see a dark sedan pulling in behind them? Unconsciously, she shivered.

Mitch caught the motion, and his jaw clenched. Of course she was scared; hell, she ought to be. He'd told her that first day she would be safe at the retreat, and here they were, creeping through New Hampshire on two hours' sleep in a damn rental car. So much for his promises.

"Go to sleep, Jess," he told her curtly. "We've still got a good hours' drive to go, and you can use the rest. No sense in both of us becoming exhausted."

She nodded slowly, her gaze sweeping carefully to the side mirror. Long, empty stretches of the highway reflected back. But it didn't ease the tightness in her chest.

"Wake up, Jess," Mitch called softly. He shook her shoulder lightly, and her brown eyes fluttered open. For a moment, he could see the blind exhaustion in her gaze; then her control slowly slid into place.

"We're here," she stated quietly. He nodded. She sat up straight, looking out the window at the endless snow and trees surrounding them. She looked over at him sharply, and he understood her confusion.

"We're a few miles back," he explained, "basically parked behind the retreat."

"Why?" she quizzed intensely. "I thought you said Les's men would be gone."

"It's better to be safe than sorry, Jess."

She wanted to protest. If he was that uncertain, then they shouldn't be going back at all. But she could tell by the firm set of his jaw, Mitch's mind was made up.

"You wait here," he was saying now. "I'll go scout out the place, see what I can learn." He reached into the duffel bag, and before she could react, pulled out the Chief's Special she'd practiced with before. "You know how to use this," he stated matter-of-factly. "If anything goes wrong, don't hesitate."

She simply stared at the gun, laying so peaceful and dull in his outstretched hand. She shook her head.

"You keep it," she said softly. "And I'll stick with you."

"Not an option," Mitch informed her flatly.

Her eyes narrowed, and she looked at him intensely. His jaw was set, his gaze clearly telling her he had no intention of yielding. It only made her more determined. If he thought she would simply wait passively in the rental car, watching the hours roll by, wondering what horrible thing may have gone wrong, he had another think coming.

"You go, I go," she stated clearly.

"I'll lock you in the trunk if I have to," he replied.

"I don't think so," she countered. At least that much about him she understood. "Look, Mitch," she said impatiently, her brown eyes piercing, "if you were me, would you just want to sit in the car, waiting and wondering? Like you said, I know how to use the gun. If I go, I can cover your back. Two is certainly safer than one."

He shook his head. "This isn't a Boy Scout trip," he said with deadly seriousness. "This is creeping up on an area, realizing that being discovered could cost you your life. I've been trained for these situations—you haven't. Besides," he finished gruffly, "it's not safe for you. I won't put you in that much danger."

His gaze caught her own, his brown eyes so intense, her heart beat faster in her chest. He was looking out for her. He cared.

It was only his job, she reminded herself forcefully. But somehow that didn't stop her gaze from falling subtly to his lips. She licked her own lips nervously and had to suddenly turn away. The flutters in her stomach now had nothing to do with fear.

Mitch watched her tongue come out, lightly flicking across her lips. His body reacted immediately with a fierceness and intensity that took his breath away. So help him God, he wanted nothing more at that moment than to drag her onto his lap and kiss her thoroughly and utterly into submission. He wanted to show her with each heart-stopping sensation just what a fool she was being, and just how much he suddenly wanted to keep her safe.

He took a deep, shuddering breath. What was he even thinking? When had Mitch Guiness become such a rutting fool over a woman?

His jaw clenched tighter, the effort beginning to hurt his teeth. "You're going to stay in the car," he said flatly. "Allow me, just this once, to actually do my job."

The words tore through her. She could feel each and every syllable cutting like a knife through her own stomach. It was his job, after all. Nothing more, nothing less. He took care of her because he had to. And she would take care of herself, she thought fiercely, because she had to.

"No," she replied coolly. And when she turned around this time, Mitch found himself confronted once more by the Ice Angel. "You have your job to do, but I'm in this mess, as well. Now you can sit here and waste precious time arguing with me, or you can realize that either way, I'm going to follow you back to that house. The choice is yours."

For one dark moment, she saw his fist clench with the frustration. A tiny frisson of fear quivered up her spine, but she didn't relent. Then slowly, very slowly, Mitch let out his breath. He knew her well enough by now to acknowledge that she wouldn't back down. And the truth of the matter was he couldn't afford to waste time arguing with her.

He forced himself to relax, nodding his head in curt agreement. At least this way he could keep his eye on her, as well. And if anything did go wrong... Well, he'd be there to handle it.

He handed her the gun, and she took it with hands that trembled only slightly. "It's loaded," he told her curtly, his brown eyes boring the seriousness of the situation into her own. "Please don't be a fool and shoot us both."

Her back stiffened, his words chasing away the last of her fear, exactly as he'd intended them to. "Don't worry about me," she said frostily. "I can take care of myself."

He nodded, opening the car door. Oh, Jess was back full swing to being the Ice Angel. But given the situation, that's exactly who he wanted her to be. God knows the Ice Angel could probably stare down Death itself. That might come in handy in the next few hours.

It took them twenty-five minutes to reach the perimeter of the retreat. Sheltered by the trees, Mitch could make out the gleaming wooden roof of the two-story cabin just a hundred yards away. He gestured for Jess to keep down low and behind him. Intent now, his eyes scanned the premises.

At first glance, the place appeared abandoned. No black sedans were in sight, and no signs of life were coming from the cabin. But then, that's exactly how Mitch would have wanted the place to appear if he was the one waiting inside. Rather than going forward, he directed Jess to follow him around the tree-covered outskirts. From this angle, he could make out a faint gleam coming from around the back of the house. Perhaps a car roof, poorly concealed by brush. Just as he was about to angle toward it to find out, he felt Jess's hand capture and squeeze his own.

He ducked down in time to see a gray-suited man appear on the left. The black shape of a semiautomatic pistol rested in the man's hand.

So Les's men hadn't left the area after all. Mitch turned, and keeping half an eye on the approaching man, he indicated for Jess to fade back more into the brush. She nodded, her face tight but her eyes clear as she inched backward. Her heel caught a pinecone, emitting a faint crunch in the snowy silence. Immediately, they both froze, their eyes riveting back to the gun-toting guard.

His eyes swiveled over to their hiding place, and it seemed to Jess they ought to stand out as clear as day. Her pulse was beating so fast, she thought her chest might explode from the pressure, and she could feel the blood drain from her face. She tensed, waiting for the sound of a gunshot, waiting for the violence to boom through the quiet afternoon.

But then the man's head turned back, and he once more resumed his pacing. Mitch's hand caught and squeezed hers in silent reassurance; she thought she might faint from the relief. She left her hand lying on his own strong palm and he made no move to let it go.

With subtle pressure, Mitch led her once more around the outside of the camp. His senses were on full alert. One man had obviously been left behind. They must have guessed Mitch would want to come back. The question now became, Were there more? Or perhaps even Bill or Jamie were with the men, sitting at the kitchen table at this very moment, laughing and drinking orange juice as they contemplated their newfound fortunes of blood money.

At that moment, however, Mitch's sharp eyes caught a sight that tossed the idea out the door once and for all. He turned to catch Jess before she saw it, as well, but he was too late.

Already her eyes were fixated on the tree up ahead and slightly left. Sitting at the base were Jamie and Bill, their sightless eyes still horribly rounded with that last instant of surprise. The small holes in their forehead told the story. From all appearances, they had been ambushed when changing their watch shift.

Jess's face went pale, all blood draining from her face as her eyes registered the terrible shock. At that moment, Mitch wanted to kick himself for his stupidity in allowing her to come along. He should have seen this coming. He should have trusted his instinct that Jamie and Bill never would have betrayed them. And he felt the crushing weight of guilt descend upon his shoulders.

They had been two damn fine men. The best. And no one had even had the decency to close their eyelids.

Where the hell had it all gone wrong?

Before him, Jess began to shake, her eyes still glued to the men that had volunteered their lives to protect her own. Hadn't she had breakfast with Bill just the other day? Hadn't she borrowed Jamie's jacket just yesterday afternoon for a long walk?

And now they were dead. *And the blood was all on her hands!*

"Don't, sweetheart," came Mitch's low voice. "Don't even think like that."

He saw the guilt and the horror so clear on her face, felt the reflection of his own regrets in her vivid brown eyes. Softly he drew her into his arms. She did not protest.

He could feel each shudder in her tormented frame. Feel her disintegrate in his very arms, the cool control of the Ice Angel shattering in the warm comfort of his embrace. He leaned his cheek against the top of her head, stroking her back as he absorbed every heart-wrenching shudder of her delicate frame. He eased them back behind a tree, seeking cover as he held her close.

God, he had not wanted it to be like this. He had not wanted it to be like this at all.

Then suddenly, before he could react, Jess was pushing herself away from his chest. He looked at her with sharp concern, seeing a sudden fierce intensity in her eyes.

"I didn't want this," she gasped out, her hands curling into desperate fists on his chest. "Please believe I didn't want this."

"I know," he told her, trying to soothe her agitation. "I know. It's not your fault, Jess. It's not your fault."

But she didn't seem to be hearing him. Instead, her eyes were ablaze with dark shadows of stark horror and pain that took his breath away.

"I just wanted to get away from the violence," she said desolately. "I wanted it all to end, I wanted to be free. And now..." Her tortured eyes fell to his chest, the look of despair on her face so crushing. "There's so much blood, Mitch," she whispered. "So much blood on a single pair of hands. And I never wanted any of it. I always hated the violence. I just wanted it to go away. To just go away."

He didn't know what to tell her anymore. The stark admission tore at his own gut, until her pain knifed through him like his own. Looking at her now, seeing the torment in her face, he didn't know how he could have ever thought she was cold. And he didn't know how he could have ever wondered if she'd betrayed them. He drew her once more into his arms, willing her burden onto his own strong shoulders.

But his guilt was overwhelming. He should have seen this coming. He should have kept them all safe. Somehow he should have made sure that everything turned out all right.

And he knew that this moment would haunt him, like the death of Victor haunted him. In his job, his decisions didn't mean whether or not some boss was happy. They didn't mean a company made money, or even that someone kept a job. His decisions, from where to take the witness, to who should be the guards, to what type of backup plans should be made, were life-and-death decisions. And when he failed . . .

When he failed, the cost was simply too damn high.

Abruptly he felt a surge of intense anger. Someone had betrayed them. Someone had let Les know how to find them. Someone had sold them out, trading lives for cash. And if Mitch ever found that person, that person would plead for death before Mitch was done with him.

Even if it was this woman in his arms?

The thought came from nowhere, and he hated himself the minute it slashed like neon across his brain. He could still feel the heartbreaking trembles of her shock-filled frame. Her horror and anguish were too real to be faked. Certainly she hadn't sold them out.

Then again, it didn't have to be intentional. She'd tried to leave last night. She said there was no man involved, but she'd been creeping out somewhere. He knew her too well to believe it was impulsive. Whatever she'd been trying to do, it was according to some plan, some motive, she refused to tell him about. And perhaps in that plan, she had unwittingly tipped off Les Capruccio.

What had she meant when she'd said, "I didn't want this. I just wanted to get away from the violence"?

He didn't know. So help him God, he didn't know.

Suddenly, almost violently, he swore at himself. Since when did Mitch Guiness become so emotionally involved in his work? Once boiled down, decisions were remarkably clear. Fact: Someone had betrayed them and it wasn't Jamie or Bill. Fact: Jessica Govern, a.k.a. Jessica Gavornée, a.k.a. Jess McMoran, had been sneaking away from the retreat twenty-four hours before, a clear violation of the

Witness Protection Program. Fact: This same woman kept secrets, including the small matter that Jessica Govern didn't appear in records until age sixteen.

His instinct told him she hated the violence, and she hated Les Capruccio. But she still had a hidden agenda that could have accidentally given them away. Mitch's frame stilled, his dark eyes becoming stark and clear. When all boiled down, he couldn't trust this beautiful woman tucked in his arms.

Until she trusted him and started revealing those secrets buried under the Ice Angel's rigid control, he had to consider her a liability to them both.

It was the only way to be safe.

Jess felt Mitch's hand suddenly still on her back. She felt his body stiffen, and all at once a sharp pang of loss cut through her. She didn't question the instinct that drove her. Instead, her head raised up to find his eyes.

And the emptiness within her was complete.

She didn't say anything, she simply stepped away. And by the way Mitch's brown eyes followed her, her suspicions were confirmed. Oh, they weren't hateful eyes, nor condemning. Instead, they were simply alert and carefully shuttered. Whatever caring she'd seen just sixty minutes before in the car was gone. Mitch had abruptly removed himself from her, effectively breaking the fragile emotional bond that might have once existed.

It hurt more than she would have thought. Instinctively, her hand came up to her throat. She could feel it trembling. Mitch suspected her. It was the only explanation. And as her brown eyes swept unbidden to the two men dead at the base of the tree, she realized deep down inside she couldn't blame him.

All this time she'd tried to outrun the violence. And now three men were dead because of her. Had living with Les been that bad? Had enduring his touch and his blows truly been so horrible? Were the lives of three men truly worth her escape?

And once more she could see her father's shocked eyes as the gun exploded, and he fell, down, down, down, onto the gold-patterned carpet. Her mother's face, so starkly resigned as she lowered the shotgun. The blood pooling into the cheap carpet as Jessica began to scream, the long silent scream that had never quite ended.

She would never have to fear his drunken rages anymore. She would never have to wonder what he had wanted that night, when he'd come to her room with his breath stinking of cheap whiskey. It was over, all over.

But at what price?

Her gaze swept up to the large dark man standing before her, watching her with his intense brown eyes, and she wondered what he would think if he knew the thoughts running through her mind. She wondered what he would do, if he knew all the things she had seen in her lifetime.

She wondered if maybe then he would understand.

And she knew, in that instant, that she would never tell him. Because she'd sworn to her mother she would never tell, and because she was afraid. Afraid that this man would look at her with disgust or even pity. Afraid that this one strong man, would turn away from her altogether.

"We've been here too long," Mitch said under his breath, breaking the silence. Jess nodded. And then she did something he never would have imagined.

She crossed right to Bill and Jamie, and with a hand that only trembled slightly, reached out and closed both of their eyelids.

"You were the bravest men," she whispered. "I will not forget you."

The gesture touched Mitch, and once more his suspicions filled him with guilt. The more he learned about her, the less he understood.

"I want to finish scouting the area," he said gruffly, his brown eyes not quite meeting her own. "Stay behind me."

She fell in step behind him without saying a word. Squaring her shoulders, she followed him through the woods.

In the end, Mitch determined that two men had stayed behind. They seemed to be firmly ensconced in the house, probably keeping watch in the event that Mitch returned. That finding left him with little knowledge, however.

If anything, his mind now blazed with more questions than before, and the snowy silence offered few answers. Jamie and Bill were dead, and it appeared he and Jess would be on their own a bit longer. Given the uncertainty, he couldn't risk a call into the program. There was no telling who might be listening.

He vented some of his frustration by slashing the tires of the ill-concealed vehicle. That would slow down the two men left behind, and give them something to ponder. He would have liked to do more damage than that; he'd like to burn the whole place down to the ground to avenge Bill and Jamie.

But such actions weren't prudent, and he still had Jess to consider.

They went back to the car in silence, two shuttered people lost in their own thoughts and suspicions. The exhaustion was nagging, but the sense of danger kept them moving.

This time, Mitch turned the car southward. They drove to a little town on the New Hampshire-Massachusetts border, where Mitch had set up one of his three contingency plans. As Jess waited in the car, Mitch went into the bank, produced a second set of fake ID and received access to a prearranged safe-deposit box filled with more cash and another set of ID. As he'd told Jess, he could keep them running for a while.

It was now late afternoon, but that didn't matter to Mitch. Both he and Jess were exhausted, however, and exhausted people made mistakes. He drove to a small, roadside motel.

"Six hours," he informed her curtly as he shut off the engine. Jess stared back at him with confused eyes.

"Six hours of what?"

"Sleep. Then we hit the road again. Probably with another car."

She nodded, turning away from Mitch so he wouldn't see the shadows she knew were in her eyes. They'd driven the entire distance in silence, and now that he was finally speaking to her, his voice was so curt, she didn't know which hurt her more.

And she hated herself for feeling the pain at all.

"Fine," she said out loud. "We leave at ten."

But as she watched him climb out of the car, she allowed herself to acknowledge the truth once and for all. She wouldn't be leaving with Mitch Guiness at ten. No, she intended to do what she should have done a long time ago.

She was getting out on her own.

Because as she watched the strong, dark man beside her stand, she knew there was one man's death not even the Ice Angel would be able to handle.

Chapter 11

When Mitch came back from the reservations desk, he carried with him only one key. Jess looked at it immediately with wary eyes.

"Where's my key?" she asked more sharply than intended.

He merely glanced at her. "Same deal as last night," he said crisply, "though this room happens to have two beds."

"Unacceptable," she bit out, her brown eyes unrelenting. The certainty of her word was probably too strong, however, for Mitch instantly stiffened. His jaw became grim.

"We are both adults, Jess," he reminded her with edged softness. "We can handle this." His eyes bore into hers, clearly telling her the matter was resolved. She refused to back down, though. How could she? There would be no chance of creeping out on her own if they were both in the same room.

"I need time to myself," she managed to say. "I sleep better alone."

Mitch took a deep, steadying breath. He was tired and short-tempered. His doubts about this woman sickened him, just as the gravity of their situation refused to allow him to relent. Damn it, he had a job to do.

His voice dropped to an octave she'd never heard before, and when he spoke, he spelled out each word with such precision, she felt every syllable in the hollow ache of her stomach.

"We *will* share a room tonight. You *will* sleep in one bed. I *will* sleep in the other. You *will* do exactly as I say, or so help me God *I* will wring your neck right here and now and save Capruccio the trouble. Now is that clear, Ms. Mc-Moran, or shall I carry you up to the room myself?"

He took one step forward and it was all the encouragement she needed. Looking into the dark seriousness of his eyes, she had no doubt that he would in fact lift her up before a lobby full of people and manually cart her off to the room. No doubt at all.

"Fine," she managed to say, trying to inject enough curtness in the word to salvage her pride. But instead, the word came out rather breathless, and a faint blush crept up her cheeks. Mitch's gaze followed the coloring like a magnet, and the responding tightness of his body was unmistakable.

The next six hours would most likely kill them both.

"Fourth floor," he practically growled.

Jess nodded and turned away to punch the upward arrow button for the elevators, grateful for the cover.

The elevator arrived with a ding, and she walked through the doors without looking back. She didn't have to; she could feel Mitch's presence in every shivering flash of awareness whispering down her spine.

They traveled up in silence, both looking at everything but each other. Then they were on the fourth floor, Mitch leading the way down the dimly lit hall. After a bit of jiggling, he opened the door. They both walked in, took one look around and tried to keep the tension from showing on their faces.

The room did contain two beds. However, they were crammed so close together in the tiny confines of the room, it hardly seemed to matter. Between the dresser, TV and nightstand, the room offered little spare space and even less privacy. Jess felt like screaming, even as the tightness within her stomach grew.

"It will have to do," Mitch said at last, trying to keep the wariness out of his own voice. He'd been hoping for more space. A lot more space. His nerves were on edge and his body seemed to be in a constant state of half arousal. She thought she'd sleep better in her own room. Hell, he knew he would.

But, he reminded himself grimly, this was the safest course given the situation, and he was a man whose primary concern was safety. He walked over to the first bed and sat down.

The mattress sagged so damn much, he practically reached the floor. This time, he couldn't quite keep the frustration from flickering across his face.

Jess saw the look, and tried to give him a narrow berth as she crossed to the other bed. Given the tight quarters, however, she brushed past his legs, causing him to stiffen so fast, she was surprised he didn't snap in half from the motion. Her own jaw clenched and her nerves tightened to near breaking point. She pretended nonchalance while pressing down on her bed with a tentative hand. It was at least a little better.

"I hope you didn't pay too much for the room," she said at last.

"A dollar would be too much for this," Mitch grumbled back. He stood wearily. "We have five and half hours left before ten. I'm getting some sleep."

Jess nodded, watching him behind shuttered eyes as he turned once more to the bed. With a sigh, he sat down again and began taking off his boots. Jess watched that, as well, her nerves slowly stretching tighter.

Would he sleep in all his clothes? Or maybe just take off his shirt? Surely it couldn't be comfortable to sleep in jeans. She imagined he slept in the buff most of the time. Totally and completely naked.

Her head pivoted sharply toward the wall, but she still had to take a deep, shuddering breath. Behind her she could hear the complaining creak as Mitch lowered all two hundred pounds of himself onto the bed. She risked another glance to see him sprawled on his back, fully clothed, on top of the covers. Within minutes, his breathing had evened out to the smooth, low tones of sleep.

Now why did she feel so disappointed?

Trying to move quietly so she wouldn't disturb him, she tentatively stretched out on her own bed, also fully clothed. But while her muscles protested their exhaustion, her mind refused to shut down. Never in her life had she felt so tired. And never had sleep seemed so far away.

Staring at the water-stained ceiling above her, she could still see the bodies of Jamie and Bill, propped up so coldly against the base of the tree. And she could see Darold, falling down into the crimson-colored leaves. And the sound of the shotgun, her father's own surprised face as he stumbled suddenly forward, the dim comprehension that never fully materialized as he died in an instant at her feet.

She shivered, unable to block out the image, and rolled onto her side. But the curtains of the room were gold-and-orange patterned, seeming to mock her until, once more, she felt the anger and pain.

She'd hated the violence. Hated her father for coming home late at night and beating her poor mother even after he'd sworn just that morning that he would never hurt them again. And she'd hated him for always crying afterward, for begging their forgiveness and swearing that he'd quit the booze and he'd control his temper and somehow they'd all be a family again. Because he never quit. And even as her cheek had bruised and the blood had dripped from her cut lip, she'd known he would come home drunk again.

At times, she had hated her mother for shooting him. More than that, however, she hated herself and that one small flash of relief she'd felt as her father had fallen once and for all at her feet. No more fear. No more pain. No more promises of the good life that had never come.

The terror was gone, but it had only been replaced by the nightmares. Because she had loved him. He'd never been a good father, he'd never been anything other than a drunken, violent man, railing at the world and his wife and his daughter for his own failings. But he'd been the only father she had. And even at that last bitter moment, the bile rising in her throat, the tears stinging her eyes, a part of her had still loved him.

And had still wanted to believe that someday he would be the father and husband he'd always promised he would be.

She curled up tighter, feeling the burning in her eyes and refusing to give in. It had all been so long ago. A horrible, awful past she'd spent her whole life shutting out. When they'd taken her mother away to prison and pawned Jess off onto the Social Services system, she'd made her vow. She would walk away, and she would walk proud. She knew never to trust, because even those who were supposed to love you were weak and petty and violent. And the only person you could ever believe was yourself. Promises were too easy to make, and even easier to break.

She'd thought she'd done so well, too. Until Les Capruccio had started the cycle all over again, blackmailing her with his knowledge of her mother. Even then, she'd thought she'd found a way out. She wasn't going to be the victim anymore. It had all seemed so simple.

Until Darold fell into the fall leaves. Until she looked into the shocked eyes of Jamie and Bill, and realized that ten years later, the blood was still flowing and it was all on her hands.

No matter how far she ran, she never escaped.

She was shivering; she could feel each violent tremble as she curled up tighter. Control, she reminded herself, control. But all she could see was Jamie and Bill sitting at the base of the tree. Dead because of her. Because of her.

And the gold-patterned carpet turned red while the sound of her own silent scream echoed down the hall.

"Jess?" Mitch's voice cut through. "Jess, are you all right?"

She didn't trust herself to speak, didn't even trust herself to move. There was one horrible moment when she was flooded by the panic. He couldn't know, he couldn't know. She just wanted to be left alone. Very, very alone. Because then the nightmare would fade, leaving her in a solitude where no one could hurt her, and she could hurt no one.

But through the stomach-hollowing panic, another emotion cut through: relief. *Because this man knew how to hold her. This man could do magic....*

She heard a groan as the bed behind her protested Mitch's departure. Then abruptly her own bed sagged as Mitch sat down. It rolled her half toward him, but she couldn't stop the trembling. Softly he placed his warm hand on her shoulder.

"It's okay, Jess," he told her in his low, strong voice. "Death isn't an easy thing to deal with. It's better if you just let it all out."

She half nodded, concentrating on the feel of his hand on her shoulder. Firm and warm and gentle. Like an anchor back to the present, something to cling to. But it wasn't enough, she realized dully. She didn't want just his hand on her shoulder. She wanted all of him, warm and solid, pressed next to her. She wanted to bury her head against the strength of his shoulder while her body shuddered away the last of the aftershock. She wanted to feel him against every inch of her, solid and giving.

And she wanted his lips hard upon her own, chasing away all the shadows from her mind until she wasn't Jess McMoran or the Ice Angel or anyone else. Until she was just a woman with a man. Nothing more, nothing less.

She didn't know exactly when she rolled over. She never met his eye, never gestured with a coy glance. She simply found him in a blaze of movement, sitting up and claiming his lips all in one smooth blur that left no doubt in his mind what she wanted. He could taste the desperation in her lips. Taste the salt of unshed tears, the earnestness of unfinished pain. She hurt, and the pain moved him.

In this one moment he didn't care what his training told him. He didn't care he had every right to be suspicious, that indeed she was a woman with secrets. In her kiss, she was a woman who needed him, and he knew at this moment he needed her, as well.

His hands buried themselves in the thick silk of her hair, drawing her closer to deepen the kiss. She responded immediately, pressing against him urgently as her arms clung to his neck and her breasts flattened against his chest. She was a tormented woman, and he could feel that torment in each raging kiss, her lips slanting savagely across his own as her hands clutched fiercely at his shirt. The wildness called upon something deep within him, as well, until his normally restrained desire was gone, leaving just the urgency and fire.

She bit his lower lip, a light nip that made him growl and press her closer. His fists closed around her sweater, and without ceremony dragged it over her head. Far from protesting, she tugged his own shirt from him with quick vigor, then pulled his head down for another deep and hungry kiss. Her bare skin pressed hotly against his own, and the contact was electric.

He felt like a man on fire, wanting and desiring and hungering beyond all sanity. He wanted to tame this wild woman. He wanted to absorb all the rage and torment inside himself until she shuddered and sighed and gasped with the relief. He wanted to hear his name drawn like a prayer from her lips. And he wanted to bury himself deep inside her until the fury left even himself, and they could lie like exhausted children in the aftermath.

His hands traced the lace outline of her bra on her back, searching for the clasp while she arched and rubbed against him. With something akin to savagery, his deft hands twisted the clasp free and quickly tore the bra from between them.

His hands slid forward and found her breasts.

The sigh escaped her in a tiny rush, fueling them both. She could feel the rough calluses of his thumbs, rasping over her tender skin until her nipples puckered with sharp intensity. Each sensation coiled down to her stomach, feeding a deep and growing ache.

There was no room for darkness here. No room for bitter memories of Les's clutching hands, no room for the hatred and the pain. Just this one man whose touch lit her aflame until she hungered for things she knew too little about to hunger more. She wanted this man and she wanted this moment. She welcomed the intensity of his touch, the way it chased all the thoughts from her mind until she was

simply a wild and sensual creature searching for the release he could provide.

His lips returned to hers, blazing away the unshed tears
while his hands curved around her breasts. She shuddered,
a low shudder that had nothing at all to do with fear. Her
own hands grew bold with the urgency, splaying themselves flat against the muscled contours of his chest. She
could feel his heart beating, powerful and true. It acceler-
ated at her touch, and for the first time she realized her own
ability to impact him. Emboldened, she trailed kisses along
his jaw before dipping her head down to find his corded
neck. He tasted of salt when she nipped his neck, and this
time, he was the one who gasped.

He pushed her back farther onto the bed. She did not
protest, but dragged him down on top of her, not wanting
to let him go even for an instant. His chest pressed against
her breasts, and she could feel the prickling sensation of his
sparse black chest hair tickling her nipples. Instinctively,
she rubbed herself against him, firing them both with desire. Her jean-clad legs instinctively wrapped themselves
around his hips, seductively pressing herself against the hot,
rigid heat of his desire.

He growled low in his throat, his hands reaching instantly for the clasp of her jeans before he completely lost
all control. He pulled away long enough to tug at her jeans,
pulling them down and off her long slender legs. She shivered slightly from the impact of the cold, her eyes growing
rounded and suddenly unsure. But then Mitch was there,
his lips upon her own, returning her to the world of his
touch. He blazed his own trail to her ear, wanting to learn
every nuance and intrigue of her body. He found her ear-
lobe, sucking it gently between his teeth. The arching response of her hips told him she liked it. Then there was the
spot above her elbow he discovered with his tongue, the
dipping hollow of her throat. And finally the taut bud of
her nipple, which he gently rolled into his mouth.

Her body tensed, every muscle responding as the bolt of
desire shot fiercely through her. Her hands tangled in his
hair, holding him close, because surely if he left now she
would die. Her body seemed on fire, raging and coiling

with sensations and energy she'd never felt before. She
wanted him, needed him.

"Please," she gasped, unaware of the sound.

But Mitch heard and understood. Oh, the Ice Angel
might have done her best to appear cold. But he was learning quickly enough there was a wealth of woman underneath all that control. A woman capable of great pain and
great passion.

He rose, his hands falling to the waistband of his jeans.
For a moment, she opened her mouth to protest his leaving. But then she watched him roll down his jeans, and her
eyes once more grew round. She tensed, the panic hovering around the edges. He was such a large and powerful
man. Surely such a man would most likely hurt her. How
could he not?

Mitch saw the uncertainty penetrate her eyes once again,
and at that moment he would cheerfully have liked to kill
Les Capruccio. To fill such a beautiful woman with fear...

He rolled on a condom and came back to her on the bed
more gently this time, his passion tempered by her gaze.

"Let me please you," he whispered. "Trust me, Jess.
Just this once, trust me."

She closed her eyes, her body still half on fire, and nodded.

He lay down fully beside her, gently bringing her body
against his own until flesh pressed against flesh. His lips
found hers once more, teasing and beguiling this time as he
allowed her to become fully accustomed to him. Then, in a
quick and fluid motion, he rolled her on top of him, legs
intermingling with legs, skin pressed against skin.

For one moment she tensed, but as his hands smoothed
sexily down the curve of her back, she relaxed once more,
marveling in the feel. He was so strong and hard, a distinct
and tantalizing difference from her own rounded softness.
Experimentally, she rubbed one leg against his own, unconsciously positioning her hips more comfortably against
his rigid hardness.

Mitch had to clench his fists to keep from taking her then
and there. He could feel the moist softness of her so incredibly close. An easy twist of his hips and he could sink

into the softness, bury himself in her femininity. His eyes darkened to near black with the erotic strain.

Her head came down, and this time she kissed him, long and slow. Her tongue traced the outline of his lips, experimenting and tasting as the nervousness subsided and her passion returned ten-fold. Her hips rotated against his, brushing against his rigid length until they both gasped.

There was one last moment of hesitation, one last moment of doubt. But then she let the raging fire guide her, and ever so slowly, slid down onto him.

Mitch's jaw clenched, his breath torn from him as he slid inside. He felt at once as if he wanted to plunge fiercely inside her, ending it all in a mind-splintering explosion, and also wanted the moment to stretch out forever, easing in, gentle and sure. He watched her own brown eyes darken with the pleasure, and was filled with blatant masculine satisfaction.

She whispered his name softly, biting her lower lip as the sensations rocked through her. The tension kept building, the ache so fierce, she thought it might consume her.

"Easy," Mitch said, his hands coming to her hips to guide her. Slowly he eased his hips in and out, prolonging the pleasure until beads of sweat appeared on her brow and her eyes burned with the need.

"It's okay," he assured her, watching her tremble with glittering eyes. "Take it, Jess. Allow yourself this pleasure."

Her eyes closed, her head falling back and before she could think again, he suddenly changed the pace entirely, plunging into her with a passionate savagery that threw her over the edge. Her back arched, his name wrung from her lips as the fire convulsed and exploded through her veins. And his own hoarse cry told her she was not alone. He followed her over the edge, joining with her in joy and ecstasy.

She collapsed on top of him, her body still shivering from the aftermath. She could feel the light sheen of sweat covering his body, and knew it covered her, as well. She would have moved, but all motion seemed much too difficult, and the feel of her cheek pressed against his pounding heart-beat much too comfortable.

Slowly, leisurely, his hand caressed her back, then came up to cup her cheek.

He didn't say anything, just listened to the sound of her breathing ease back down to lethargy. His own body felt suddenly exhausted, all the tension and strain of the past few days blazed fiercely away. The release went beyond muscle and bone, until even his mind seemed suddenly cleansed and at peace.

At this one moment, nothing at all mattered but this woman lying so relaxed and quiet above him. It occurred to him that nothing at all had ever felt so right. Ever so gently, his thumb brushed her cheek, coming away with a tinge of moisture.

Sweat? Tears? He didn't know and simply held her closer. Content and worn, his eyes slowly drifted down. With his arms wrapped around her, he slipped into slumber.

Jess knew the minute he fell asleep. She could hear it in the soothing rhythm of his heartbeat, in the low easy tones of his breathing. Her own body felt the exhaustion. Her muscles seemed to have turned to Jell-O, her bones to have melted into nothing. It would be so easy to just lie in the warmth of his arms and listen to his heartbeat.

In all of her life, she'd never felt what she felt now.

And it scared her more than she'd ever been scared before.

Slowly her eyes opened to stare starkly at the opposite wall. She'd wanted him. She'd needed him. And he'd given her things she wasn't supposed to have, made her feel things she wasn't supposed to feel. In this one instant she felt safe. In this one instant she felt comfortable.

She felt . . .

She shut the thought away, blocking it out completely. It didn't matter, she reminded herself. This man, this moment—none of it mattered. She knew what she had to do. She'd known it from the beginning.

Slowly, before she could lose her courage, she slipped out of the warmth of his arms. Mitch stirred, his eyes drifting slowly open.

"I'm just going to the bathroom," she whispered, having to bite her cheek to keep from protesting her own lie. He nodded, his eyes lowering once more as his powerful body returned to much-needed rest. She hung her head, and for one awful moment she thought she might not be able to go through with it.

She bit her lip, hating herself for her own weakness. When had she let him get to her like this? Her life had been laid out long ago, her decisions clear from the very beginning. If she stayed with this man, he would only get hurt as everyone else had been hurt. Bitterly, she forced the images of Bill and Jamie into her mind once more. Too many people had paid the price; she could not let it happen again.

She picked up her clothes on her way to the bathroom, careful not to make a sound. Her hands slid into the duffel bag, finding a thick wad of cash, and she took a handful without bothering to count. She disappeared into the bathroom.

She took a quick shower, wishing the water could cleanse her mind as easily as it did her body. She would be sore tomorrow, and the ache would only be a painful reminder of the things she shouldn't have done. She flushed against the stinging spray. Had she really been that wanton? Had she really touched him like that, bit him like that? And how in the world had he ever made her feel so good?

She shivered slightly and stepped out of the shower without turning off the spray. Slower than was necessary, she pulled on her clothes. She left her wet hair down, not bothering with another attempt at a braid; she could still remember the feel of his hands tangling in her hair the last time when he'd kissed her.

The small bathroom was thick with the steam by the time she was done, her heavy sweater damp and clinging. Even then she paused with her hand on the doorknob.

Once more she could remember the feel of him sliding slowly into her. Once more she could remember the sound of her name, low and hoarse on his lips.

"Let me please you, Jess. Trust me, Jess. Just this once, trust me."

She opened the bathroom door and stepped out. She risked one glance at the bed. Mitch was still sleeping, sprawled out across the bed with the comforter half thrown over himself as if he'd awoken just enough to realize he was cold. The shower still sounded steady and calm in the background. She counted on it to deceive his normally uncanny instincts.

Her hand went to the doorknob; she was surprised to see it shaking so much. Once more she hesitated.

But it wasn't worth it anymore, she thought suddenly, vehemently. She'd lost sight of her vision somewhere along the way. She was supposed to use her new identity to get out and live on her own. All by herself, where no one could hurt her, where she could hurt no one.

Especially not the strong, capable man sleeping so soundly on the bed.

She squared her shoulders, her eyes becoming cool and controlled while all expression left her face. Jessica Gavornée be damned. Jess McMoran be damned. When it all boiled down, she was simply the Ice Angel, and she could do anything.

Minutes later, she was in the parking lot, opening the rental-car door. Even if Mitch woke up now, he wouldn't have any instant means of following her.

She had the car, and only she knew where she was going.

After all, she had a very important meeting to make.

But as she slipped the car into Reverse, and drove out to the interstate, she could suddenly see in her mind Mitch coming awake, reaching out a large hand for her, discovering himself suddenly alone. She could see the darkening of his eyes, the clenching of his jaw, when he found how she duped him.

Somewhere along the four-hour drive to eastern Connecticut, the Ice Angel learned to cry.

Chapter 12

He awoke abruptly, his heart thundering in his chest as his sixth sense blazed with sudden urgency. On instinct he rolled for his gun, only to discover himself naked and weaponless on the bed. His body stilled entirely, his mind spiraling inward as all senses came alive.

He was completely naked, his legs still tangled in the comforter as his eyes spied his jeans piled up on the floor. His gun remained in the duffel bag, a good five steps away. His head arched up toward the bathroom. The sound of running water. Jess was showering. But immediately he frowned, that idea sparking his mind with jagged inconsistency. And then it came to him: her clothes were no longer on the floor and his subconscious said the shower had been running a long, long time.

In one fluid motion he rolled out of the bed. He dragged on his jeans while trying to cross the room, one hand still working the button fly while the other threw open the bathroom door. The thick steam choked him; he had to wave his arm to penetrate. Almost viciously he yanked back the shower curtain. The sharp clenching of his jaw was all the emotion he allowed.

Working in overdrive, he grabbed his gun from the bag as he ran out the door. A woman gasped as he pounded down the hall, clad only in half-buttoned jeans, armed with a gun. He ignored her, his bare feet pummeling down the stairs as he flew out to the parking lot. Gravel dug into the unprotected skin as he hit the pavement, but he barely noticed.

He had eyes only for the empty parking space that confirmed what he already knew. And then he did allow himself emotion—one dark, savage oath that didn't even come close to summing up how he felt.

She was gone. *Damn it, she was gone!*

Hotel security scurried out, clearly alarmed to see a half-naked man standing wild and armed in the parking lot. One look at Mitch's dark face and the barely restrained fury there, and the plump uniformed officer dropped back a step. Mitch saw the motion, and it pulled him back to reality. Forcing his shoulders to relax, he tucked the gun into his jeans, muttering he was a police officer under his breath and passing by without giving the man enough time to question it.

He returned to the room, scowling down at his bloody feet, gauged and scratched by the gravel. He grabbed a wet washcloth to clean them, and sat down hard on the bed.

Damn it all to hell.

His heart slowed some, the immediate urgency passing to leave him only with a strange tightness in his chest. Almost absently, he placed the washcloth on his right foot and found that he was grateful for the pain. It gave him something to focus on. Something concrete, something real. Something other than the horrible feeling of dread building in the pit of his stomach.

Some part of him had known this would happen. Hell, just two nights ago he'd caught her trying to sneak away. He'd demanded then to know why, and she'd never given him a satisfactory answer. Jessica Gavornée had been a riddle from the very beginning, the carefully constructed Ice Angel who never gave any of her secrets away. But he'd tried, God knows he'd tried. And today...

He shook his head. God, he truly was the fool. He'd told her he would keep her safe. He'd sworn to himself that he would save her in spite of herself. Yet, in the end, she'd shown far greater control than he. Hell, she'd come to him in a blaze of passion, then left his bed without so much as a backward glance.

He forced himself to take a deep breath. He hated the feeling, the tight unbearable feeling in his chest as if a part deep inside truly hurt. Nothing hurt, damn it, except his pride. All along, his interest had been professional. And while sleeping with her had hardly been the best thing to do, she'd needed him and he'd needed her. He still believed that. And so they'd come together, offering each other very elemental comfort.

He'd been in such situations before; he knew how they worked. While hardly a man for the meaningless flings so many of his cohorts enjoyed, Mitch had known his fair share of women. He'd cared about them all in one form or another. He was the kind of man who cared about everyone. But then the need had passed and everyone moved on—no need for hysterics or hurt feelings. It was simply the way things worked.

So there was no reason to feel as though he'd suddenly been kicked in the gut. He'd been duped and made out to be a fool, but only because after one week of being with the Ice Angel, he should have known her better. He should have solved her riddles and unburied her secrets. He should have gained her trust.

Yet, somehow, some way, he'd thought he'd touched her. He'd thought...

He shook the notion away, feeling all at once uncomfortable and not himself. His interest in Jess was purely professional. Always had been. And damn it, he needed that professionalism back. Jess was out there somewhere alone. And he had to find her before Capruccio did.

After one week with the woman, he still had no idea what her true agenda was. She'd run, but where was she running to? Or who was she running from?

But then another thought struck him and he smiled a grim smile. He knew how to find her, all right.

Because while he didn't know all of the Ice Angel's secrets, he knew the man who did.

She drove like a bat out of hell, averaging a good eighty miles per hour. And every fifteen minutes her eyes would pop to the rearview mirror as if suddenly Mitch would swoop down upon her bumper, his brown eyes black with the rage of betrayal. And then her foot would flatten out on the gas pedal, as if somehow she could outdrive his presence, outdrive her own guilt.

It was for the best, she reminded herself. She was back to her original plan, out on her own. And no one would get hurt anymore. No one, at least, except herself as the horrible, jagged pain knifing through her stomach could attest.

At eight, a little ways into Connecticut, the exhaustion overcame the panicked adrenaline and she almost drove off the road. Giving in, she took the next exit and drove a couple of miles to a cheap roadside motel. There she booked two rooms, refusing to look the huge, cigar-smoking hotel manager in the eyes. She paid in cash, having counted out the amount in the car so she wouldn't appear conspicuous by presenting an entire wad of money.

Her eyelids half-closed, she selected one of the rooms at random, shutting all the curtains tightly and double-checking the locks. Then, and only then, she lowered herself fully clothed onto the rickety bed.

She slept in a matter of minutes.

But with the sleep came the dreams; only, this time they were a confused mix-match of past and present. Her father loomed above, his face contorted in rage as one meaty fist drew back. Except suddenly it was Mitch, his dark eyes glittering black and his jaw tense. But then his face collapsed into a contortion of anguish, his arms reaching out to her until she felt the tears on her own cheeks.

"I'm so sorry, baby. It won't happen again, I swear it won't happen again. I don't want to hurt you. I truly don't. If you would just trust me..."

And she did; she wanted to. But when she tried to tell him yes, the words wouldn't come. Until she watched in grow-

ing horror as his face suddenly changed and he wasn't
Mitch at all anymore. He was Les Capruccio, staring at her
with oily black eyes and laughing.

Sometime in the course of the night, she crawled off the
bed until she was hunched into a ball in the corner between
the bed and wall, buried under the brown comforter.

She was up and running again with the dawn.

She drove fast and furious, her eyes grim upon the road
and nervous in the rearview mirror. But throughout the all-
day drive, no dark sedans appeared except in the overac-
tive depths of her mind.

At seven in the evening, she hit Ohio, and eased up her
frantic pace. She could be there in a matter of hours, and
with her destination finally so close, the exhaustion hit her
hard. She drove for one more hour, then once again sought
out a nondescript hotel.

This night, she didn't even try the bed. She grabbed the
comforter and rolled up in a little cocoon in a dark corner
of the room. But even then, the night offered no comfort.
With sleep came the dreams.

She showered briskly in the morning, taking more time
than was necessary with her appearance. Her hands were
shaking lightly, something that surprised her. But she ignored the nervousness of her stomach and the light, growing feeling of dread.

She was here, she'd made it. Step one of her new life was
about to be accomplished: she was back on plan.

At 8:00 a.m., she arrived at Ohio's Women's Correctional Institute. She got out of the car slowly, keeping her
face composed. Carefully, her eyes scanned the parking lot.
In the past week, she'd learned a thing or two from Mitch
Guiness, and that was never to underestimate your opponent. Les knew about her mother. He'd blackmailed her
with the information for the entire year and a half. Coming here was a huge risk on her part, but then, it was a risk
she had to take.

Taking a deep breath, Jess walked into the facilities. She
kept her shoulders rounded, her head down, her steps short
but easy. She wasn't Jessica Gavornée anymore, she was
Jess McMoran. And even if she saw Les's men she would

walk by them as if she'd never met them before in her life. On its own, her hand began to twist the simple ring on her finger.

It was still early for Sunday visiting hours. Then Jess realized it would look suspicious for Rebecca Morgan to have a social visitor anyway. After all, the only visitor Rebecca ever had was a scarved and sunglassed blonde who came approximately once a year. Reaching into her purse, Jess withdrew her identity with a hand that trembled only slightly.

She held her breath and approached the guard at the desk.

"Good morning," she whispered, then cleared her throat for a more commanding air. She squared her shoulders, summoning the control from deep inside. "I am Jess McMoran, attorney-at-law. I'm here to discuss some new legal developments with a Rebecca Morgan."

She didn't have a business card, something that became quickly apparent. She managed her way around it, however, with a good show of bravado. The business cards must have fallen out of her purse. They were more than welcome to call the office and verify her position, of course. Then again, no one worked on Sundays. She would come back later, but the matter truly was urgent. All she needed was half an hour. She promised to keep it short.

Rebecca Morgan was a model prisoner, after all. A worn shadow of a woman who'd done the laundry for eight years now without ever muttering a word of protest. She kept to herself and never caused trouble. In the end, the guard made Jess sign four forms in triplicate, then let her in. By the time the documents were traced and found to be false, she would be long gone.

She had ten minutes to compose herself; then her mother was led into the room. She was a tall woman, but her shoulders were frail and hunched as she walked. Her hair hung long and stringy by her face. Once it had been an exquisite ash blond. As a child, Jessica used to brush out that beautiful hair, sitting behind her mother on the bed. She would marvel at the pale beauty, and her mother would tease her and tell her that she would be even more beautiful one day.

Now, Jess looked at the long strands that had become muddy with time, and felt her heart constrict painfully in her chest. For one long moment, she had to look away.

In the doorway, Rebecca halted slightly upon seeing Jess. The hair was different, the eyes different. But a mother knew her daughter. Abruptly her head came down and she walked forward as if nothing else was amiss. She sat down on the other side of the table, the security guard standing a discreet distance away at the door.

"Jess McMoran," Jessica said, sticking out her hand as she forced her face to appear composed. Rebecca's eyes were wary but patient as she shook her daughter's hand with a watery grip. "I'm here to discuss some new legal developments in your case," Jessica continued smoothly.

"You shouldn't be here at all," Rebecca replied quietly, the midwestern drawl slow and soothing in her voice. Jessica had worked for one long year to eliminate that accent from her own voice. Her mother, however, would never be her mother without it.

Jess acknowledged Rebecca's statement with a small nod. "How are you doing?" she asked, her own voice dropping low. On her lap, her fingers continued to twist her ring.

"Fine," Rebecca replied. She always said fine. Every year for the last six years she'd said fine. And every year Jessica still asked. It was like a little ritual. The motions of talking, of communicating, without any of the actual connection.

"You're up for parole soon," Jess said softly. Her heart seemed tight in her throat. But she didn't know what words to say to ease the pressure, so she stuck to the pattern they both knew so well.

"Six months," Rebecca acknowledged.

"I'll have a place then," Jess rushed out. "A place in the countryside with a garden. Maybe even a goat or two and lots of fresh air."

Rebecca simply nodded. Jessica mentioned this house each time she came. And each time Rebecca nodded. As if someday she would be out of prison. As if someday she would be with her daughter again, and they would live out the future as if that one dark night never happened. They would carry on simple little conversations, never quite meeting each other's eyes. Never talking about all those years that had shaped them both, and the night that had changed it all forever.

"You shouldn't have come," Rebecca said again. "I follow the news, Jess McMoran. I know you shouldn't be here." She'd followed everything about Jessica Gavornée's life. She'd gotten every magazine cover, clipped every article. In the quiet solitude of her cell, she'd followed her daughter's life and never talked about it at all.

"I wouldn't leave you," Jessica said stubbornly. "You know that."

Rebecca shook her head. "I made my choice, and I've made my peace. You should get on with your life."

This was old ground, the discussion they always had without actually ever mentioning events. That ten years ago Rebecca had lifted a gun against the man about to rape her daughter. That she'd shot her husband. But they never talked about that one night, and they never spoke of the fourteen years leading up to that one violent moment of truth.

And then there were the times Rebecca had grabbed her daughter and fled into the darkness of the night. But by the light of day she always went back. In the sunlight she always believed Harry's sobbing claims that he would never hurt them again. And sometimes he wouldn't anymore. Sometimes it would be as long as months in a high-strung peace. But eventually the darkness fell once more. Each year spiraling deeper, bringing more drunken episodes.

Until that one night, he'd come home from a bar and gone to his daughter's room. Rebecca had come at her daughter's startled cry, and this time she'd brought the gun she'd been staring at night after night, wondering if she would ever have the courage.

That night she did. And Harry Morgan never beat anyone again.

But even after all these years, she could still see her daughter's huge blue eyes as her father had fallen before her. Rebecca never forgot the horror in those young, blue depths. And she never forgot the sight of her daughter's mouth opening into a long, silent scream.

She'd failed, as a wife and as a mother. And when they pronounced her guilty of manslaughter, she'd hardly protested the sentence. She served her time, knowing her hands were stained with the blood. Then, the horrible phone call had come, telling her that her sixteen-year-old daughter had run away from the foster home. For two years she'd despaired, feeling the hopelessness, certain that all her sacrifice had been in vain. On Mary Morgan's eighteenth birthday, however, a visitor had arrived at the prison. A tall, elegant blonde who looked far older than Mary's eighteen years and introduced herself as Jessica Govern. Her eyes, however, were Mary's eyes. Rebecca's daughter had returned, and she would have cried except she wasn't allowed to cry anymore. And looking at the controlled, empty depths of Mary Morgan's sophisticated eyes, Rebecca knew how much she'd failed her family and the beautiful daughter she'd loved so much.

"You should go," Rebecca said now, her faded blue eyes glancing down. "Don't put yourself at risk for me."

Jessica looked at the woman before her, and for the first time she felt the anger. The pattern, the six-year pattern said she should leave. Jessica Gavornée always had. Jessica had always pulled back on her silk scarf, like a priest donning the collar, and had walked out the door in a breathless rush of shimmering silk, never looking back.

But suddenly she didn't feel like leaving, and she didn't feel like playing the mystery woman in an overdone drama that never got any closer to happily ever after. She looked at the woman before her, the faded eyes, the limp hair, and she felt the anger build and build and build.

"What do you mean?" she demanded in a low voice, her new brown eyes dark. "If I don't put myself at risk for you, then who do I do it for? You're all I have left."

For one moment Rebecca looked so stricken, Jessica wished she could take the words back. But abruptly she could hear Mitch talking about his sister, the love and affection so clear in his voice. And she felt the frustration grow even more.

"You're my mother," Jessica found herself saying, leaning tightly forward while Rebecca's eyes darted nervously to the guard. "You're the only family I have. And—" her voice suddenly stumbled, the words choked and hoarse in her throat. "—I love you, Mama. I really do."

Rebecca looked stricken again, shaking her head at words so long unsaid. "You don't know what you're talking about, baby," she whispered. "You don't."

Jess's head slumped forward, bowing in defeat. Her life had fallen apart ten years ago. Her father had died before her eyes, her mother had been carted off to jail. And she'd been stuck in foster homes with people that could be just as quick with their fists as Harry had been. So she'd learned to be quiet and controlled. And all the while she'd plotted and schemed until at last she made her bid for freedom, running all the way to New York City where she'd started her new life.

But maybe she wanted part of her old life back. Maybe she wanted something besides the bitter memories and aching emptiness. It didn't matter. She'd vowed to always take care of Rebecca. But not just because of guilt, not just because this woman had killed for her, given up her own future so her daughter could escape the darkness. Maybe Jessica also wanted her mother back.

And suddenly she could see Mitch, tall and strong as he grinned down at her. And she could remember the taste of him on her lips, the feel of him driving the emptiness away with each heartfelt thrust. She wanted him. She wanted to climb into his arms and cling to him like a child. Because he could find her card in the deck and make coins go through tables and hold her like no one else ever had.

And no one else ever would.

She rose from the table, pushing back her chair as she looked at her mother with expressionless eyes.

"Sometimes," she whispered, "sometimes I hated you for that night. I hated you for killing him, for making him actually die after all those nights when I would lie in bed and wish it upon him. I hated you for not being strong enough to walk away, and I hated you for being too strong to take it a minute more. I hated the violence, you know. I always did.

"But I knew what he was going to do that night, Mama. We never talked about it, and you never said, but I knew. As I got older, I certainly knew. You stopped him with that gun, and maybe that was the only thing that was ever going to work. I don't know. We never will. And I remember all the times you stood before me, all the times you took his anger even if it simply meant he beat us both instead. And—" her voice broke, the tears suddenly welling up when she'd never allowed herself to cry much before "—and I remember the time we made blackberry pie and ate the whole thing, just you and I, laughing and giggling. And I remember brushing your hair and you reading me stories late at night. I remember you putting salve on our burns and makeup on the bruises. I remember so many things, Mama. And not all of them are so bad."

Her voice broke completely and she had to look away. She didn't know why she was saying all these things now, why she was breaking the covenant of silence they'd shared for so long. She couldn't quite seem to help herself.

And once more she found herself thinking of Mitch and longing for the warm comfort of his touch. Her arms wrapped themselves around her; the gesture was unconscious but Rebecca saw it, and it made her own worn-out eyes glitter with unshed moisture.

For one moment she almost spoke up. For one moment she almost reached out to the strong, beautiful woman her daughter had become. But she'd given up that privilege a long time ago, when she'd taken her child back to the man who beat them both. And she'd forfeited the claim altogether that night she'd picked up the gun, and shot her own husband before her daughter's bright blue eyes.

"When you're ready," Jess was saying, softly now, "go to the post office ten miles from here. Ask for post office box 7246. It will be in your name. I'll leave a letter for you there, telling you how to find me. Please." Her voice faltered once more, then she found her strength. "Please allow me to do this much."

She didn't turn around enough to see if her mother agreed or not. She wasn't sure she could take it if Rebecca rejected the offer. Instead, Jess headed straight for the door. At the last moment, however, she found herself compelled to hesitate. She could still see Mitch in her mind's eye. The question slipped out before she consciously willed it, but once spoken, even she understood why it was said.

"Did you love him?" she asked suddenly. "Tell me, Mama, did you love him?"

For a moment, Rebecca looked startled. Then slowly her eyes widened as comprehension dawned. "In all these years," she whispered softly, "you never asked me that. I always thought, someday, someday when you were old enough, you would. Who is he, Jess? Is he a good man?"

But Jessica shook her head stubbornly. "I asked first," she pointed out. "Please, I want to know."

Slowly Rebecca nodded her head. "Harry wasn't always a bad man. And sometimes, sometimes I did love him."

Jess nodded, but the knowledge only added to her confusion. "Is that why you stayed?" she asked finally. "Because you loved him that much?"

Rebecca shook her head. "I stayed because I was too afraid to leave. Because I didn't know how to support myself and I didn't know how to support you. And because I was too proud to ask for help and too afraid no one would give it to me."

Jess nodded, her throat momentarily tightening as she forced herself to swallow. She'd hated Harry for beating them and hated her mother for staying. And loved them both because they were her parents and she wanted to love them anyway.

"Baby," Rebecca said suddenly. Jessica's gaze swiveled up, her heart pounding from the unexpected use of the term of endearment she hadn't heard in ten years. "You're stronger than me, baby. You always were, even as a child. You don't have to make the same mistakes. Follow your own instincts. If he's a good man, he'll be worth it."

Slowly Jess shook her head. "There's no way to know, Mama. No way to be sure."

For one moment Rebecca Morgan straightened her shoulders and opened her mouth. But then, as quickly as it had come, the moment passed and she slumped back down to her shadowy self. She offered her daughter a weak smile, all she would allow herself to give. And even as she watched, the beautiful creature she and Harry had somehow created walked back out the door.

Jess was preoccupied going back out to the parking lot. Her throat still felt tight and she had the absurd desire to simply sit down and weep.

She never used to cry, she reminded herself fiercely. She never used to cry and she never used to care. She knew how things worked, and she was strong. She would live her life alone and she would be happy, damn it. She swore it.

She reached for her car door and found her hand swallowed by a firm, encompassing grip.

"Going someplace?"

Her heart jumped in her throat, her breath coming out in a tight gasp. But there was no mistaking it. As she turned around, Mitch Guiness stood right before her, and his eyes were practically black with rage.

"How did you find me?" she managed at last. Her heart still pounded in her chest as her brown eyes slowly swept up to see his face. His jaw was clenched, and she could see the tightly restrained anger in every line. This was no longer the grinning, mercurial man she'd met at the New England retreat.

This was the hunter. And that made her the prey.

"Doesn't matter," Mitch replied, now in clipped tones. "All that counts is that you have a lot of explaining to do."

She looked at him almost desperately. Her emotions felt too raw for this. She wanted at once to break down in his arms and also to flee.

"It doesn't matter," she found herself saying, the words whispery. "You don't have to follow me anymore. I violated the program, Mitch. I'm no longer your responsibility."

His eyes narrowed, searching her face intensely. If she even knew the worry she'd caused him. He'd had to risk a call to an old friend in the Bureau's Tech Services Division to find her. The Division had enough wire taps and surveillance on Les and his men to supply every movement. Most of their movements made sense, too, except the two men who were waiting for a "package" at the Ohio Women's Correctional Institute. Mitch had taken the gamble and driven like a banshee to get here. Now, here, was the long-lost Ice Angel, and every time he looked at her the exhaustion wreaked havoc on his mind. He wanted to sweep her up into his arms and kiss her savagely until she swore she would never run from him again. Until she broke down and told him all the secrets she still locked so tightly in her chest.

"What do you mean, you're no longer my responsibility?" he demanded instead, not trusting himself enough to even move.

She faltered for a moment. She had to tell him about her mother; then the FBI would no longer be obligated to look out for her. This man could go away and never be hurt because of her. He could walk away strong and vital, and she would never see him again.

For some reason, it physically hurt her to say the words. "I saw my mother. I violated the agreement."

Mitch couldn't quite stop the surprise that slashed through him. He hadn't understood why the Correctional Institute, but he'd never imagined that the Jessica Gavornée, who had no surviving relatives, had a mother in prison.

"Any more surprises I should be aware of?" he drawled finally.

Jess shook her head, but then her eyes widened abruptly. "Oh, no," she breathed.

Mitch's body went on instant alert, his sharp gaze sweeping around as she spoke. Then he saw them, too. Two gray-suited men walking toward the prison doors. And as they moved, their jackets flapped back in the wind to reveal the unmistakable black shape of guns.

Mitch had found the Ice Angel, all right. But he wasn't the only one.

Chapter 13

Mitch looked down sharply, his face pure business.

"Listen up," he said, low and deep. "They know who I am, but I don't believe they know the 'new' you yet. So I'm going to walk away from here, very casual, very quick. And you're going to get into your car as if you're just another visitor about to leave. If they look over at you, if they see you, remember everything we practiced. I'll keep an eye on you, and if anything goes wrong, I'll jump in. Otherwise you simply drive away from here, heading toward I-80. I'll follow you in my truck. Got it?"

Wordlessly she nodded, her gaze still riveted to the entrance through which the two men had disappeared. She'd seen one of them before. Vitola? Victorola? Something like that.

Mitch moved back a step, and she forced her shoulders to relax. This was just like they had practiced. Taking another reassuring breath, she slipped her key into the lock.

Mitch's hand on her shoulder momentarily stopped her. She turned enough to see him watching her with fathomless eyes. "And, Jess," he said softly, "don't even think about disappearing again. I don't make the same mistake twice."

Slowly she shook her head in agreement. And wasn't surprised at all that neither of them believed her.

Mitch glanced at the empty entranceway; then his gaze swiveled back to her for one dark, unreadable moment. Just as abruptly, his hand slipped off her shoulder, and he turned away without so much as a backward glance. She watched him go, realizing for the first time how much she'd lost. She'd betrayed him, and the grinning Mitch was gone. This was the agent, and he would always be on the alert around her.

Her throat tightened once more, but she forcefully ignored it. Life was full of choices, and she'd made hers. He would never understand all the reasons, but that didn't matter. She knew she would always walk away, always run to be alone, and that was all that counted. She slid her key in the ignition and turned.

The engine had just roared to life when the entryway doors came swinging open again. She did her best to appear unconcerned, sliding the car into Reverse. But she returned her gaze to the front in time to see the one man stopping and pointing straight at her. Over the buzz of the engine she heard a faint shout, and then both men began to run. She didn't hesitate anymore. The adrenaline took over and she slammed her foot on the gas. Too late she looked in the rearview mirror and saw the approaching car.

Even as she slammed on her brakes and heard the unmistakable warning of a horn, she smashed into the vehicle, the impact jolting her forward. For a split instant, she was conscious of nothing. Then abruptly, angry words penetrated her shock.

"What the hell!"

"The lady's very apologetic—here's some money."

"What the—"

Jess didn't hear the rest. Her car door was thrown open, Mitch's powerful arms reaching in and unfastening her seat belt while she looked at him with dazed eyes. Suddenly a cracking explosion ripped through the air and even as she was pushed down, the windshield in front of her exploded. Mitch swore low under his breath as tiny shards of glass drove into his skin, but there was no time for second glances.

He pulled Jess from the car onto the ground as a second shot penetrated the air.

"Keep down," he barked to both Jess and the unfortunate driver of the second vehicle. Sirens were beginning to sound, mayhem erupting from the impact of gunshots in the parking lot. The situation was quickly deteriorating beyond Mitch's wildest nightmare, and if he didn't get them out quick, they were all in for a pack of trouble. His sharp gaze darted to his rental truck just ten feet away. The engine was still running and the door was open from when he'd jumped down after seeing the accident. If he could just get them that far without getting them killed.

"Do exactly as I say," he whispered, sparing Jess a quick glance. Flattened against the pavement, she nodded at him with solemn brown eyes. Leave it to the Ice Angel not to become distressed by a few gunshots. He glanced back up, seeing the two men bearing down on them quite quickly now. Without a second thought, he rolled smoothly up, drawing the Chief's Special from the small of his back as he did so. He fired quickly and efficiently, both hands aiming and pointing with long-practiced precision. The blast threatened to deafen them all, but the shots were effective. One man dropped immediately, his run coming to an unnatural halt. The second man ducked behind a car.

"Into the truck, now!" Mitch roared. He didn't have to spare a glance; instead, he heard Jess scramble up and dart for the vehicle. He fired three more shots in the air, backing up as he did so. Then with quick urgency, he jumped into the truck, slamming the door shut even as another bullet cracked the air. "Head down," he commanded, shoving the truck into Reverse and hitting the gas.

The tires squealed as the truck responded. Mitch straightened, peering over his shoulder as he deftly raced the vehicle backward through the parking lot. Dimly he heard another shot and the glass in his window exploded. He flattened his foot on the gas pedal.

At the end of the row he slammed on the brakes and cranked the wheel, throwing them into a nice 180-degree spin. Then he shifted to Drive, and plunged them forward, roaring out of the parking lot while shots and sirens and mayhem erupted from behind.

"Are you all right?" he asked curtly as he fired down the two-lane road. He whipped past a car, then another, finally risking a brief glance over. Her face was pale, and he could see a faint trickle of red blood where one of the shards of glass had nicked her. But she nodded, turning enough to meet his gaze.

"They know now," she whispered softly. He nodded grimly, screaming past another car before slamming over into a side road.

"The one man can report back your new description," he agreed.

"The one man?"

His jaw clenched, and he wondered if he should have said anything. But then his shoulders settled rigidly. She said she hated the violence, so she might as well know the results of her little escapade.

"I believe the other's dead," he said bluntly, not trying to ease the words at all. He glanced in the rearview mirror, seeing empty space behind them. Another turnoff presented itself, and he took it, slowing down at last. There were few houses here, mostly just miles and miles of fields. He had no idea anymore where they were, and no idea of where they were going. He was just driving, the adrenaline racing too fast to stop.

"Mitch," Jess's voice penetrated, soft and low. "Mitch, you need a doctor."

Feeling almost dazed, he looked down at his left arm. The dark skin was so shredded and cut by glass, it looked like it had been through a blender. Shards of glass winked back at him, tiny and insidious as they lay embedded in his flesh. Judging by the abrupt sting in his cheek, his face suffered the same. He clenched his jaw in sudden anger, but it only made the pain worse.

More houses whizzed by, and for a moment the exhaustion almost overwhelmed him. Where the hell did they go now? How far to run, and just how many were at their heels? Grimly, he forced the thoughts down. He was Mitch

Guiness, the best in his field. He'd gotten through worse situations, he was sure, even if none now came to mind.

It was all a matter of one step at a time.

"Pull out the map from the glove compartment," he commanded softly, his face and arm feeling stiff and fiery now from the pain. He didn't dare turn to watch, but heard the click as she opened the compartment.

"Find where we are," he continued, "then find a small touristy-looking place. Someplace where we'll find a bed and breakfast. It's too easy for them to check out hotels."

In the meantime, he came to a more significant-looking road, and turned onto it.

Jess nodded, going over the midwest map with a careful eye. It simply wasn't detailed enough, however, to allow her to understand where they were. In the end, they simply continued to drive in tense silence.

Twenty minutes later, they came to a small pocket of civilization. Not giving it another thought, Mitch pulled into a gas station.

"Go get the key for the bathroom," he said tightly, his jaw rigid with the pain. Jess didn't dare question the command. She simply slid out of the truck and obeyed.

She came back with the key and Mitch took it from her for his own use. She waited only five seconds, then she followed. He hadn't quite shut the door all the way, and she didn't bother to knock. Instead, she strode straight in, her face blindly determined as she kicked the door shut behind her. The small room smelled of urine and sweat, the light dim and rusty from above. She refused to notice any of it.

"We should stop and get some hydrogen peroxide," she said. Mitch's gaze swept up to meet hers in the scratched glass that served as a mirror, his eyes dark and set. He had a fistful of wet paper towels in his hand and was doing the best he could to clean his arm.

"I'll be fine," he said through clenched teeth as his careless motions drove another shard of glass deeper into his skin. "They're just scratches."

Jess didn't say anything; she didn't quite trust herself to speak. His face and arm looked awful, and it was all because of her. He'd been keeping her safe. He'd been doing exactly what he'd promised.

She stepped forward and took the paper towels from his hand.

"Let me," she said.

He didn't stop her, though her actions placed her far closer to him than he would have liked. Now he could smell the faint remnants of peaches, see the shine of her brown hair in the badly lit room. Her hands were gentler than his own, and even as he watched, her careful fingernails sought out and removed the splinters from his arm.

"You weren't going to tell me, were you?" he said grimly, his eyes focused blackly on the top of her head.

She didn't have to ask to know he was talking about her mother. Instead, she simply shook her head without even glancing up.

"Was it worth all this?" he demanded harshly, the muscle jumping in his jaw filling him with more pain. "Was it?"

She glanced up. "I...I don't understand what you mean." She could feel the anger in him. This close it radiated out like a magnetic field.

"Like hell," Mitch ground out, the words flat and furious as his eyes narrowed in on hers. "Les knew about your mother. He's been staking the place out, just waiting for you to contact her so he could trace it back. How the hell did you think I found you?"

That answered one question, but somehow she'd never bothered to really wonder how he'd come to the prison. A part of her had always known he would find her. He was Mitch Guiness, the magician.

"But I didn't contact my mother," she replied coolly enough, focusing her attention on the matter at hand. She saw the open doubt in his eyes, and it struck her deeply. Her head bowed back down, her eyes and fingers returning to his injuries. "I swear, Mitch," she said softly as she found and unearthed another sliver of glass, "I swear I did not contact my mother while under protection. I figured Les probably had some men stationed there. That's why I waited for my new identity. And then I ran away on my own..." Her voice trailed off, then she forced herself to sound brisk. "That way... that way even if they did find me, at least it wouldn't harm anyone else."

Her hands trembled on his arm. She could still picture the shocked eyes of the unsuspecting driver when the shots had broken out. She was trying so hard to get away. Yet it seemed everything she did just sucked more people into the whirling darkness.

Mitch's right hand came down and tucked under her chin. Before she could react, he'd tilted back her head until she was forced to meet his intense eyes.

"You mean to tell me that you never contacted your mother from New Hampshire?" he demanded to know. In the tight quarters, her body practically pressed against his own, the low intensity of his voice sent tremors down her spine.

Slowly she shook her head.

"What about before that?" he snapped in rapid fire, his eyes boring into hers. "Or from the hotel?"

"Not at all," she replied, the words slightly breathless. "I just showed up."

"You just...showed up," he repeated. She nodded once more, and then inexplicably, Mitch swore. Before she had time to react, his right fist went flying immediately past her to slam into the wall. The rickety mirror trembled and Mitch winced instantly from the contact.

Jess couldn't help herself—she shrank back toward the sink, her eyes open and wary.

"Don't," Mitch warned, low and tired. "I'm ticked off but I'm still not a man who hits women."

"You're angry at me," she said, the words soft and hushed. She could no longer look at him, her gaze falling down to the bloody mess of his arm. The sight made her cringe, and the pain inside of herself was sharp and sudden.

Mitch stared down at her bowed head for a long minute, feeling the adrenaline finally slow in his system. At long last he raised her chin back up.

"Yeah," he told her. "Yeah, I'm angry at you. I'm angry at this whole damn mess and the fact two good men are dead. I'm angry that Les seems to be one step ahead of me, and I still don't know why. I thought maybe you'd tipped him off by calling your mother. But if you're telling the truth, then he couldn't have found out that way. There must be a leak. Or maybe you're not telling the truth. How should I know? Seems to me you don't trust me with a damn thing, let alone the truth."

His words hurt, mostly because she couldn't refute any of them. She could feel his eyes searching hers; they made her feel vulnerable and bare when she didn't want to feel either. Slowly she raised her hand and began to work on his cheek. She saw him flinch from her first touch, and that hurt, as well.

"I didn't want you to know," she said at last, the words soft and emotionless as she dabbed at the blood. "I didn't want anyone to know."

He looked at her with frustrated eyes. Her hand was so gentle on his cheek. He didn't know whether he wanted to walk away from her in frustration or pull her into his arms and hold her so tight, the last of the dread would leave them both.

Once more he became aware of their surroundings, the stench of urine and sweat and dirt. He laughed, but it wasn't a pleasant sound. Slowly her brown eyes swept over to meet his, and he thought he saw his own soul in her gaze. His right hand came to her waist, his body suddenly tight with need.

"I want you," he whispered hoarsely. "I want you naked and under me. I want to hear you cry my name, I want to watch the satisfaction darken your eyes, see the way you bite your lower lip as I plunge into you. I want your nails digging into my back, your teeth biting my shoulder. I want one hundred percent of you, all of you writhing and clinging and wanting me."

Her breath quickened, the pulse on her throat pounding rapidly as her eyes darkened. One part of her understood the words. She'd hurt him, and he needed to reclaim her. He needed to feel that she trusted him in the most elemental way, since she denied him that trust in every other.

The other part of her didn't care about logic or understanding at all. The other part of her could already taste him on her lips, feel him thrusting into her. The other part of her wanted him to reclaim her, because he could make the emptiness go away. In his arms she wasn't Mary Morgan or Jessica Govern/Gavornée or Jess McMoran. In his arms she was simply a woman, needy and passionate and sensual.

He made her feel like no one else ever had.

Her gaze swept down to his lips, her tongue darting out unconsciously. She could feel the cold porcelain of the sink pressed against her hip, and it contrasted dramatically with the thick heat radiating from his body. She leaned slightly closer.

Mitch saw the movement, and the surge of satisfaction that shot through him was purely male. The heat in his loins became unbearable, and he forgot about the pain in his face and arm.

She wanted him, too, and that was all that mattered.

His left hand reached out, the tightening of his jaw the only sign of the pain. He could feel her gasping intake of breath, and it fueled the fire. He took her lips with his own.

It wasn't gentle or beguiling or sweet. It was hot and angry and needful. His tongue plunged into her mouth without preamble, and she welcomed it without regret. His hands jerked her forward until every soft curve of her was pressed against every powerful muscle of him. She could feel his hard length, rigid and demanding against her own dampening need, and she pressed closer. But even that wasn't enough. He brought her left leg up and around his waist, pressing himself intimately against her until she moaned at the contact. His tongue plunged in once more while his right hand found her breast and the rigid nipple there.

She moaned again, the intensity of the passion sudden and consuming. Never had she wanted anyone like she wanted him right now; never had she needed anyone like she needed him. The need should have scared her, but there was no time for fear. His hand on her breast was demanding, his tongue skillful and the rhythm of his hips compelling. She wanted him inside her, hot and slick and strong. She wanted to rake his back with her fingernails, bite his shoulder with passion.

She wanted all of him, now.

The knock on the door threatened to kill them both. Mitch swore, low and vehement and not even a fraction of what he truly felt. He felt Jess go rigid in his arms, the sound crashing them back to reality while his raging hormones protested the trip. For one last moment, he clutched her to him, burying his groan of frustration in the thick beauty of her hair.

"I'm so sorry," he breathed. "Oh, sweet Jess, I'm sorry."

He felt her press against him in response, and if he could have seen her face at that moment, he would have seen tears.

The knock sounded again, loud and insistent. Mitch was half sure he would murder the bastard.

"Occupied," he managed to call out, his voice so hoarse, he barely recognized it. It took one more moment to collect himself, and even then his body felt pain.

"We have to go," he whispered to Jess, her body still pressed against his own.

She nodded her reply against his shirt, not trusting herself to speak. The frustration tangled with the pain and emptiness of earlier today, until she felt raw and vulnerable and totally exposed. She couldn't bear to meet his eyes, couldn't bear to see her own shattered face reflected there.

Slowly she drew in a deep breath, searching for the control that had been her mainstay. But the Ice Angel was growing tired, and the control was hard to find. At last she managed a low, shuddering sigh. She pulled away, patting his shirt and the faint dampness from her tears.

She still couldn't meet his eyes.

The truck driver was more than a little surprised when the door opened and a good-looking woman walked out, followed closely by a man. He might have said something, but the dark look on Mitch's face promised it would be the last words he ever said, and the truck driver had no desire to die young. He took the offered key, and hastened to his business.

Mitch paused long enough to ask the gas attendant a quick question about where they were and where they might go, then hoisted himself up into the truck. Jess was pressed far against the passenger side, her head resting against the door, her eyelids already shut. She looked exhausted and amazingly vulnerable to him.

He felt a pang cross his stomach, and once more that unbearable tightness in his chest. When he looked at her now, her pain and loneliness staggered him. There were so many things about her he still didn't know. Such as, why was her mom in prison? Why hadn't she told him about her? Did she have a father, too, then? Perhaps a brother or sister?

So many questions, and looking at her now, he wondered how painful the answers would be.

He started the engine as quietly as possible.

Darkness was beginning to fall as he drove. A light mist turned to rain, and the rhythm of the windshield wipers filled the cab. He looked over at Jess and saw that she was now completely asleep, slumped like a child against the window. She most likely needed the rest.

He reached for the radio, finding the tail end of a country-western song. He sat back again, satisfied with the choice. But what came on next made his spine snap to rigid attention, his knuckles whitening with the force of his grip on the wheel.

"In a surprising announcement earlier this morning, Mafia boss Les Capruccio's trial was ruled a mistrial. The federal court of appeals concurred that the jury had possibly been biased by the media surrounding the event. A new trial date has not yet been declared. In the meantime, Capruccio has been released on a million dollars bail."

Damn fast mistrial ruling, Mitch found himself thinking darkly. And how many palms had been crossed to accomplish this? He spared a swift glance over at Jess, but she slept on, peaceful and oblivious against the door. He reached over a hand to wake her, then realized there was little point. All that the information would do would be to add to her tension, and in fact, neither of them could do anything about Capruccio's release. It merely added one more dimension to a puzzle already far too complicated.

Mitch's gaze grew dark and hard in the rainy night. He'd been in tough spots before, but none quite like this one, he thought grimly. He was willing to bet right about now a good several hundred people were looking for him and the woman sleeping beside him. Les's men were probably flooding the area, coupled by any low-life street scum interested in the five-hundred-thousand-dollar bounty on Jessica Gavornée's head.

The FBI had most likely also tried to find them. Surely, by now, they knew something had gone wrong at the retreat. No doubt they were also aware of Les's sudden release.

All these bodies trying to find them, some definitely for bad, some ostensibly for good, and he had no clear way of telling the difference. Jess said she didn't call her mother from the retreat, which meant there had to be a leak somewhere.

Once more his gaze slid to the sleeping woman beside him. He'd told her he would keep her safe. Mostly because it was his job. And now, because looking down at her vulnerable features, soft with sleep, he knew he'd kill the man who tried to hurt her.

He eased his grip slightly on the wheel, concentrating on maneuvering through the dark, slick night. The soft sounds of Mary Chapin Carpenter filled the cab with stories of love and heartbreak. He drove on.

Through a series of twisted roads and byways, he came to the small lakeside community the gas station attendant had spoken of. Through the darkness and the rain, he could make out the glassy smoothness of a lake on one side, and the endless flow of fields on the other. Up ahead, he saw the first sign for a bed and breakfast, followed by others. He drove by all the inns once, then selected a smaller, white-washed old house that looked clean and trustworthy. He turned the truck around and drove back to it.

Jess woke as he killed the engine. She blinked several times, her face looking sleepy and disoriented.

"Where are we?" she managed at last.

"A small town," he replied with a slight shrug. "It's out of the way, and there's no logical reason for anyone to ask for us here. I think we'll be safe for the night."

She nodded, rolling her shoulders as she finished waking up. Mitch pulled out the duffel bag, their only luggage, and jumped out into the pouring night. He jogged lightly up the porch, hearing Jess's rapid footsteps behind him. The rain was cold and insistent, but felt somehow cleansing after a long day.

He'd killed a man today. It wasn't something he liked to dwell on.

The older couple at the makeshift front desk were midwestern friendly. They smiled a lot, looking at Mitch and Jess and already cooing romantic assumptions. Mitch didn't bother to clarify their relationship. He went along with their smiles, saying he and Jess were passing through from Connecticut, driving west. He paid for the room up front, learning a continental breakfast would be supplied in the morning.

He thanked the couple, and led Jess upstairs before too many more questions could be asked.

The room was almost too perfect, Jess thought. The hardwood floor shone with fresh wax and smelled of pine. The huge, four-poster bed wore a large, brightly colored blue-and-pink quilt, while dried flowers adorned the nightstand. The dresser looked antique and country, the drawers large enough for thick sweaters and warm flannel. Peering into the bathroom, Jess spotted an old, claw-foot bathtub that practically begged to be used for a long soak.

"You first, me first, or together?" Mitch asked behind her, easily following her thoughts. She turned with a small jump, only to find him grinning down at her. She hadn't seen that grin in a couple of days now, and its impact on the fluttering of her heart was unmistakable.

"You should go first," she said quite seriously, her gaze falling to his arm. "You must be exhausted, and tomorrow you'll be stiff."

He grimaced a little, recognizing the truth of her words. But as he went to push himself away from the doorframe, she startled him with a light touch.

"Mitch," she said softly. He stilled, looking at her hand so slender and white on his huge shoulder. "I've never thanked you for everything you've done." She paused for a moment, her eyes falling down to his chest. Her throat seemed to grow tight. It was the exhaustion. She really did need more sleep. "I...I want you to know," she said shortly, "I'm grateful for what you've done. And I'm glad...you've been there."

The words were hard for her to say, and they seemed to take a lot out of her. She wasn't used to thanking people. She wasn't used to needing anything from them to thank them for.

Slowly Mitch's large hand folded over her own.

"I told you in the beginning I'd keep you safe," he said simply.

She nodded and felt the unexpected burning of tears in her eyes. It was silly, this desire to cry. It was silly to want to bury her head against him, to throw herself in his arms. He was just doing his job, after all. And she was just passing through. It didn't matter what he'd done for her. In the end, she was putting him in danger by staying with him. In the end, she would leave once again.

It seemed to make her eyes burn even more.

Mitch saw the sudden softening of her face, the suspicious sheen in her gaze. Once again he could sense the pain inside her, and it drew him in. There were so many things about this woman he didn't know. And he did want to. He wanted to be the one she trusted. He wanted to be the one she turned to. He wanted to be the one to hold her.

His jaw clenched, but he forced himself not to move. She was like a skittish colt, his Ice Angel. If he pushed too hard, she would simply turn away, folding inside herself and shutting him out altogether. He was a patient man, and he knew what he wanted. He would succeed.

"Jess," he said softly, "why didn't you tell me about your mother sooner?"

She shook her head, the reference causing more pain when she already felt like an exposed wound.

"Honey," he persisted, his voice low and strong, "there's a lot worse sins in life than having a mother in prison."

She smiled, a wry, tremulous smile. "Even if she shot my father?"

She hadn't meant to say the words. They whispered out on their own, and she was rewarded by Mitch's shocked gaze.

"Maybe you'd better start at the beginning," Mitch said.

The funny thing was, she did want to start at the beginning. She wanted to start at the beginning and do her whole life over again. Maybe this time she'd do it better. Maybe this time fewer men would die.

"My father..." she said, the words flat and emotionless as she stared at her hand on Mitch's shoulder. "My father liked his fists. And his belt and hot water and cigarette butts and anything else that was handy. And my mother...my mother I guess just didn't know how to leave and stay away. So we took it, for fourteen years. Until this one night, you see." She paused. She couldn't say the words. She'd never spoken them out loud; she never would. Maybe if it was never said, then eventually it would be as if it was never done. It made her smile a wry, bitter smile that brought shivers to Mitch's spine. "This one night he really drank too much. And he came upstairs, but not to his room. And I woke up and screamed. My mother came, and she shot him."

And he fell, down down down onto the gold-patterned carpet, while her silent scream echoed down the long, long corridor.

There was silence in the room. Mitch looked at her, with her gaze fixated on his chest but not really seeing him at all. And he thought he'd never felt so inadequate since his little sister's husband had been shot, and all he could do was hold her while she cried.

"Jess," he said at last. She didn't look up, and finally he couldn't take it anymore. He didn't ask permission, and he wasn't even sure who exactly he was comforting. He simply reached down, and with one strong arm, he pulled her tightly into his embrace. She went rigid; he could feel her spine so stiff and straight, he was afraid she might snap. But he didn't move, didn't let her go. He simply held her, and after one long tense moment, she seemed to collapse suddenly in his arms.

He felt her sag against him, her face pressing tightly against his chest as if somehow that could press the memories away and the nightmares would be no more.

"It's all right," he whispered, his large callused hand stroking her hair. "It's all right now."

She didn't move, didn't respond other than to press herself more fully against him. As if his arms were suddenly essential, his embrace the only defense against the darkness she knew too well.

Then suddenly she was no longer passive. Her head came up, but not to speak or to cry. Instead, her lips found his, desperate and hungry and filled with an urgency that sparked the embers still glowing in his own blood. Her hands closed around his shirt, pulling him tight against her while her lips assaulted his.

She tasted wild but he tasted strong.

"Make love to me," she whispered, kissing him so thoroughly, he had no breath left to reply. "Make me feel so alive, Mitch. Make me feel so warm."

He groaned in the back of his throat, the low deep groan of a man's surrender. He wanted her as much as she wanted him, and though a part of his mind called him a fool, he couldn't say no. It might be another trap. Maybe once more she thought to seduce him to sleep so she could run off again. He couldn't be sure, but maybe at this moment he didn't care.

He scooped her up in his arms, ignoring the pain, and carried her to the four-poster bed.

Chapter 14

She was like wildfire in his arms, scorching his skin with searing kisses while her hands fought and tugged at his shirt. He would have calmed her, but her urgency inflamed his own blood, igniting his own passion. She wanted his shirt gone—he pulled it off in one fluid motion. She wanted bare skin against bare skin—he tossed her sweater to the floor. She wanted all of him, naked and hard—the remains of their clothes puddled on the floor in a flash.

She didn't wait for him to join her on the bed, but pulled him down hungrily. Her lips slanted across his with mad desperation, her legs entwining around his waist until she could feel him, hard and rigid against her own softness. She rotated her hips and his gasp was unmistakable.

"Now," she breathed against his lips. "I want you now."

He knew he shouldn't. It was much too fast and she was too much woman to be rushed. But then her hips moved and she took the matter out of his control.

She tensed at the first penetration. She hadn't allowed her body sufficient time to adjust, and she was still tight and uncomfortable. She could feel him draw back, trying to pull away. But her legs tightened, not letting him go. She needed him in ways she would never tell him. She needed him hard and hot and driving the emptiness away. She needed his lips on her breast, his hands on her skin. She needed to feel him, thrusting inside, filling the hollowness, taking her places where nightmares didn't exist and the fear wasn't real.

She drove him back inside, feeling the pain and welcoming it.

"No, Jess," Mitch managed to utter. "Slow down. Let me please you."

But she shook her head, feeling the prickle of tears behind her eyes. "Take me, Mitch," she whispered, pulling him tighter. "Please just take me."

He groaned, knowing it was wrong and helpless to slow down. His own body betrayed him, surging deep into her while his mouth found hers. He couldn't stop the thrust of his hips any more than he could keep her still under him. She wriggled and pushed against him, driving him deeper as his breath caught in his throat with the intensity.

He wanted to take her slowly; he wanted to show her the magic of a man's touch, the gentleness of control. He wanted to watch her eyes darken with wonder, he wanted to coax her over that cliff, reveling in her passion.

But instead, she drove his blood to boiling, until his body was no longer his but hers. And he let her use it, let her use him to fill an emptiness too deep for quiet comfort. She needed the intensity and she even needed the pain.

She felt him tense, knew he was on the verge of exploding, and her legs wrapped tighter, drawing him in so deeply, she lost even herself. She could feel his muscles bunch, could feel the sweat rolling slick and salty down his back. And it was strong and powerful and pure. Her eyes burned, the tears gathering behind her lashes.

And as his head came back, his teeth gritting with the passion, the tears rolled out, blind and heedless. She cried for the childhood that would never be hers. She cried for the father with whom she would never make peace, cried for the mother she'd lost along the way. And she cried for this man, because he was everything she'd always wanted and never hoped to find. And she would run from him anyway, because even as he filled the emptiness, he couldn't fight the shadows. He offered her warmth and comfort, but she could only reply with the death and destruction that encircled her life.

He climaxed, a giant muscular explosion she felt deep inside. She absorbed each shudder, clinging to his shoulders, and the tears mixed with the sweat.

He climaxed, and she relished it because she loved him.

He collapsed, and she cried silent tears against his shoulder because she would never stay.

"Damn you," he swore, the words exhausted and low. She quieted him with a long, slow hand down his back. The tears still flowed, and she didn't trust herself to speak. His weight was heavy and sure, but her body was still on fire, her hips moving helplessly of their own accord.

Suddenly he rolled off her, his gaze finding hers, dark and bleak. For the first time, he saw the tears on her cheeks and his jaw tightened. He bent down with stark eyes and captured her lips with his own.

She shuddered, low and deep, her body surging against his own in helpless desire. She didn't have to speak; he already knew her too well. His right hand cupped her breast, rolling her nipple with his thumb while his tongue dueled with hers. She shivered again, pressing needy and shamelessly against him. His hand feathered down, parting her legs and finding her.

She gasped at the first touch, her flesh so sensitized, she didn't know anymore if it was pleasure or pain. Her hands clutched his shoulders as he slid the first finger in, and he felt her tighten and tense around him. She was moist and hot, and his own exhausted body was already responding again. But this wasn't about him or his needs anymore.

It was about this beautiful woman and the tears on her cheeks.

He moved his hand slowly, half soothing, half arousing. He eased her back down to sanity, then drove her back up to passion. His hand moved against her flesh, his palm rubbing against her most sensitive areas until her head fell back and beads of sweat broke out on her lip. He kissed her again—her lips, her throat, her earlobes. And as he moved her over the top, he kissed the tears from her lashes and captured her shattered cry with his lips.

He rolled her over on her back, and before she could come down from the ecstasy, he plunged into her again, his hips thrusting strong and demanding into her. She cried out his name, and he took the sound as his right, his eyes black with need.

He claimed her secrets as he claimed her body, captured her need as he captured her tears. He drove into her again and again and again, until she was dizzy from the desire and helpless from the onslaught. And then he took her again, both of them imploding from the passion, dying from the ecstasy.

There was nothing left but the sweat and the tears and the thundering beat of two exhausted hearts. He rolled her into his arms, placing her head upon his shoulder, his legs entangled with her own, his hand caressing her hair.

Together they slept.

Mitch awoke first, his eyes flashing open in a moment of disoriented panic. He could feel his heart thundering abnormally in his chest, and instinct took over. His eyes darted around the room, seeking out every shadow, every darkened corner, every sunken nook. Nothing in the room stirred, no sign of disturbance, no sound of careful, monitored breathing.

Just him, and the woman in his arms.

He took a deep breath and released it slowly. Even then, the feeling of uneasiness didn't completely leave him. Then yesterday's news broadcast flashed across his mind, and he remembered. Les was free and the shoot-out at the Ohio Women's Correctional Institute had probably brought every cop and robber alive to the nearby vicinity.

Hell, and he wasn't even sure where they were. Just some small, innocuous town far from major interstates. It was the best chance they had.

He glanced down at the woman still sleeping so softly in his arms, her hair splashed across his chest like silk, and he wished he could offer her more.

Her words yesterday had chilled him to the bone. He had never imagined the true depths of her secrets, never imagined a life so patterned with violence. Of course she was slow to trust. All the men in her life had done nothing but exploit her. Yet she'd survived it all, even duping Capruccio at his own game.

Mitch had never met a woman like her. And he admired her more than he admired anyone, even as he wanted to hold and protect her from the shadows that had grown too real.

He wondered, though, looking down at her sleeping face, if she would ever let him be there for her. It had taken her so long to open up to him, and even then, he wondered what else was behind those eyes of hers. How had she ever become Jessica Gavornée? And how had she met Les? He could imagine now that Les had blackmailed her with the truth. She'd said before how much she hated the man, and Mitch didn't doubt it was true.

Still, she was a woman who had always lived alone, stood alone. Even upon seeing him at the prison, her first words to him had been that he could go, she was no longer his responsibility. While that might be technically true, Mitch had no intention of turning his back. No, he was in this with her, and he would fulfill his promise to her.

His hand began to absently stroke her hair, relishing the soft, silky feel. He felt her shift slightly, but she didn't waken and he didn't want to disturb her. His hands shifted down to his wrist and he glanced at his watch—8:00 a.m.

They'd gotten at least eight hours of sleep, enough for his body to know what it had been missing lately. In all honesty, they both could use more, but he didn't want to linger. The state of Ohio probably looked like an anthill right about now, swarming with conservative suits, dark sedans and semiautomatic weapons. Everyone looking for two people tucked away in a bed and breakfast, hoping the couple downstairs didn't watch the news much.

Mitch felt the tension in his shoulders and forced himself to relax. The odds didn't look good, but those were the situations on which he thrived. He just needed to break things down, step by step, and a plan would come to him.

The interstates were most likely out. Between FBI watch posts and Les's men at the rest stops, it would be like driving through a mine field, wondering which detonation he'd hit first. That left back roads, but going where?

That, of course, was the heart of the problem. Without knowing the source of the leak, they truly were running blind. He didn't know who they could contact, and when it would be safe to stop. And once the date for the new trial was set, Jessica Gavornée would be in demand again or, most likely, Les would walk.

After all the bloodshed, that was unacceptable.

They had to go back.

It was the first time he'd consciously thought it, but now that it revealed itself baldly in his mind, he knew it was true. They couldn't keep running from monsters in the closet, trying to outrace an evil they couldn't even identify. The best defense was a good offense, and it seemed that was the last option they had.

He could find a place to stash Jess, with people he trusted, people who would keep an eye on a woman just as likely to run as to wait. Then he'd go back to the program, and do a little digging on his own, undercover. Twenty people had known about the retreat, give or take a few. That gave him a clear starting point. Perhaps in a week or two, he could figure it all out.

If they had that much time.

His sixth sense was tweaking again, the sense of dread growing. He couldn't quite escape the notion they'd run out of places to hide, even as he couldn't accept it. There were always options. Fate was for people with no imaginations.

Liz, he thought instantly. He would take Jess to where Liz and her new husband lived. Richard Keaton was not only a reputed genius and an established millionaire, but according to Liz he was also the next best thing to sliced bread. Between Liz and Richard, surely they could keep Jess under control. God knew Liz was hardly a pushover. Growing up with four older brothers, she'd learned how to tame Satan himself. From what he originally knew of Richard, perhaps she had.

Great, Mitch thought. Now, he just had to figure out how to get them to Connecticut. Details, details.

The woman in his arms stirred again, and Mitch looked down in time to see Jess's eyes fluttering open. She stretched for a long, languorous moment, still half-lost in sleep. He could tell the moment she came fully awake because she went rigid against him.

"Good morning," he said softly.

Her eyes fluttered up, the brown depths still half-wary. He looked at them, and felt the frustration stab deep. None of it, however, showed on his face.

"How did you sleep?" he asked casually enough. His hand began to stroke her hair as if nothing was amiss. Very slowly, he felt her relax against him.

"Well," she said at last.

"Good sex will do that," he replied conversationally. He was rewarded with a slow blush that crept all the way up from her neck to her forehead. He would have liked to have seen where the blush started, but the quilt pulled up under her arms obstructed further view. Very gently he tucked a hand under her chin and tilted back her head. "It's okay," he told her with his most charming grin. "I don't turn into the big bad wolf the morning after."

She blushed again, disconcerted by just how well he followed her thoughts. That damn grin of his was almost too much. She felt it all the way down to her stomach, and then for no good reason at all she found herself smiling.

His own grin widened to a genuine smile. It softened his face, easing the tension around his eyes. "Hey," he said softly, "you finally did it. You finally smiled for me."

The smile froze for a moment, caught by self-consciousness. But then he grinned at her again, and the smile seemed to grow of its own volition. How did he do that? she wondered in half amazement. As if he knew exactly how to make her relax, exactly how to make her feel good?

And this magic trick didn't require any sleight of hand.

His callused fingers slipped down to caress her back, and she couldn't quite stop herself from snuggling closer. Her legs were entangled with his own—she could feel the tantalizing prickles of his hair against her own smooth skin. She could feel the powerful flex of his biceps against her cheek every time his arm moved, and hear the soft rhythm of a steady heart.

She felt warm and comfortable and good, and her breasts pressed against his side felt sexy, as well. She suddenly understood why people might like to wake up like this every morning. It certainly was a nice way to start the day.

But then her smile halted, her gaze sweeping back down until it was hidden by her lashes. She'd never known love, never thought to find it. But this morning, it was here in bed with her, and she finally understood why people might sacrifice so much, endure so much, for it. But also, she knew she would never sacrifice Mitch. Every moment she was with him put him in danger. He might think he could keep her safe, but she knew better.

She had to leave, and she would. She would run far away until she could find the little house of which she spoke to her mother. And she would buy the goat and chickens and maybe a horse or two. She could go back to school, get a teaching license and start a new life. And she imagined she might wake up each morning and remember this moment and the man she'd finally learned to love.

Her throat felt tight and she hated herself for the weakness. He continued to stroke her back with a soft caress, and she hated him for his kindness. She'd always known her choices, and it didn't matter what name or identity she assumed: the truth remained the same.

"We should go," she said softly.

He nodded, feeling the sudden heaviness in her shoulders. He'd lost her already to the darkness of her own thoughts, and the frustration struck again. Maybe he'd thought with her confession would come her trust, but that didn't seem to be the case. She'd told him the truth but still guarded her thoughts. She'd slept with him, used him to find comfort, but in the daylight, she clung to her shadows.

He wanted to hate her for it but found himself cursing them both instead. Funny—all the women he'd met over the years had come to him so easily, charmed by his grin and his easy affection. He'd cared for them all without feeling any intensity, something no doubt they knew. And everyone moved on without any traumatic scenes, just the way he wanted it.

Maybe deep inside he'd always viewed love as being what his parents had: Dotti and Henry Guiness had been hit by the thunderbolt during a chance trip to Las Vegas. They'd taken one look at each other and fallen hard. Four days later they were married. Forty years and five kids later, Mitch didn't think they regretted it at all.

So he'd waited, figuring one day he'd be struck, as well, or simply never struck at all. And he'd met and cared for his fair share of woman—simple, easy relationships. Until now, and the sudden tightness in his chest. Until he looked at this woman and felt the intensity all the way down to the deep clenching of his stomach.

The first woman who truly touched him, and he couldn't seem to affect her at all.

For a moment he almost told her. For a moment he found his mouth opening and his throat actually finding the words. Abruptly he snapped his mouth shut. He loved this woman—he would admit it to himself. But he knew her too well. She was not above using that weakness against him. And until she trusted him, until she loved him, too, his emotions were a weakness. Nothing more, nothing less.

His hand stilled on her back as he absorbed the truth.

"Yes," he said out loud, his voice quiet, "we should be going."

Jess felt the withdrawal within him as surely as if it were physical. One minute he'd been grinning and teasing her, now he was the somber agent.

It was better this way.

She showered quickly, then left the bathroom for him. They didn't speak anymore, but moved in a concise unison that didn't require words. The new day had dawned and the race began once more.

When he emerged from his own shower, towel wrapped around his waist, he found her sitting cool and composed on the edge of a rocking chair. Immediately he was wary.

"I think we should split up," she said without preamble.

He paused, then began to briskly dry his hair with a second towel.

"No" was all he said.

"The Witness Protection Program is no longer responsible for me," she persisted, each word so calm and rational, he wanted to strangle her. Last night she'd cried silent tears in his arms. Today the Ice Angel ruled once more.

"I don't think Capruccio appreciates that technicality," Mitch replied loosely. He pulled on his jeans, leaving the top button undone as he searched through the duffel bag for a clean shirt.

Jess swallowed and tried to keep her thoughts on track. She'd never tried to carry on a conversation with a man still getting dressed, particularly this man. Her hands were trembling so hard, she had to fight the urge to sit on them. She took another deep breath, then plunged on. This was for his own good—she had to remember that.

"What do you mean?" she asked, levelly.

"I mean Capruccio is looking for both of us. And if he finds us together, or separately, I don't think that stops his order to shoot. This isn't a school yard game, Jess. You can't hold up both hands and say, 'Time out, I'm switching sides.'"

He found the shirt he was looking for and pulled it on, the motion causing a nice rippling effect down his muscles. Jess bit down on her lower lip, but it didn't help.

"But if he finds you without me," she said bravely, "surely he'll have no reason to harm you. It's me he wants."

"Exactly," Mitch concurred. "Therefore he'll torture me until he learns where you are. And even if I don't honestly know, he has no reason to believe that."

This time the distress was evident on her face. She hadn't considered all this. Mitch was guilty by association, his fate irreparably tied to hers. No matter what she did, he would still pay the price.

She looked away, no longer able to bear the sight of the large, vital man in front of her. She could still remember the feel of him, plunging inside her. She could taste his kiss, see his grin, remember his touch.

She wasn't sure she'd ever hated herself more.

"Don't," Mitch said. The more he learned about her control, the more he understood the careful shimmerings in her eyes. "I'm not some fool dragged along for the ride, Jess," he told her with low and forceful words. "I'm a specialist in this type of situation. It's my job to keep people like you safe from men like Capruccio, and frankly, I'm the best there is. I'm going to get us both out of this yet. Believe in me."

But he could tell in her eyes that she didn't. She looked at him and she saw the blood of so many other men. He didn't know whether to understand or to shake her silly. Damn it, he wasn't other men.

"Tell me your name," he said abruptly. Her gaze swiveled up, startled.

"What do you mean?"

"What's your real name," he continued impatiently. "I know it's not Jessica Govern. She didn't even exist until you were sixteen. So tell me, who are you really?"

She hesitated only slightly, the name rusty and foreign on her lips. "Mary Morgan."

"Mary Morgan," he repeated. It sounded like a good, midwestern name. A wholesome match for a former blond-haired, blue-eyed girl. "So how did you become Jessica Govern?"

Once again she paused, but then she shrugged. He already knew so much about her, why not all the truth? No one else knew—not even Les Capruccio had managed to fill in all the details. "I used to ride my bike to a small town," she said. "There was this old church there, and it kept records in the basement. It took me six months, but then I found the birth certificate for Jessica Govern, born the same year as myself. She'd been a stillbirth, attended to by the local midwife. From what I'd read on getting new identities, it would work, so I took it. And then I ran away to New York. I'd just turned sixteen and didn't have many records anyway—no driver's license, voter's registration, et cetera. In New York, I lived in a teenage shelter as Jessica Govern and put my modeling career together. All things considered, I was very lucky."

Mitch nodded. She was more than lucky, given all the things that could happen to teen runaways. Then again, looking at the cool, composed woman before him, he wasn't at all surprised. He was beginning to think there was very little the Ice Angel couldn't do. Except, of course, trust.

"How much of this does Les know?" he asked.

She was quiet for a long moment, her brown gaze soft and serious. "He knows," she said finally. "I kept refusing his invitations, you see, and he began to obsess. So he had me followed and quite by chance learned about my mother." She smiled weakly. "Can you imagine? I visited Rebecca only once a year, and it just had to happen the one week I was followed. At any rate, Les threatened to expose her and myself, and well . . ." She shook her head, not sure how to explain the strange bond between her mother and herself. "When I first saw my mother six years ago as Jessica Gavornée, she made me swear I wouldn't go back. She told me I had built a new life now, and I deserved it. I wasn't to talk about her, I wasn't to tell anyone. It was what she wanted, so I agreed. But then Les had the photographs detailing my visit. I couldn't let him expose her or myself, so I did what he wanted. Until the one night I crept down to his study, took the evidence I needed against him and burned the negatives and the photos."

"What about the trial?" he asked at last. "Weren't you afraid all of this would come out then?"

She frowned slightly, cocking her head to the side as she turned it over in her mind.

"I was concerned," she said slowly, thinking out loud, "but I had a feeling it wouldn't. See, Les needed the threat of exposure to keep control over me. I realized one day, however, that the power lay solely in the threat. Once I walked away from him, exposing the information would also lead to the discovery he blackmailed me. Such a revelation would imply Les had to use blackmail to keep the blonde, that sort of thing. Think of it. That would mean Les was doubly incompetent. Not only had his 'girl' turned on him, but she'd beat him at his own game. Destroying his evidence against her while gaining her evidence against him. I gambled that given the nature of Les's ego, he would want to keep a lid on as many of the details as possible. And by never talking of our relationship, well, that was my way of not provoking him.''

Mitch nodded, the clarity of her plan once more earning his admiration.

"Then here's the deal," Mitch said softly, looking at her with his intense brown eyes. "I have a plan, Mary Morgan, but for it to work, you have to trust me. I'm going to take you to my sister and her husband. There you'll be called Sarah because everyone already knows about Jess and Les knows about Mary. What's your father's mother's maiden name?''

She was already following his line of thinking. "Brownstone. So I can be Sarah Brownstone.''

He nodded, appreciating once more her quick mind. "Exactly. Morgan's already known. Look, it's the same drill. From here on out, I'm only going to call you Sarah and you're only going to answer to Sarah. The first small town I can find, we'll pick up hair dye. If we drive straight through, we can hit Connecticut late tonight. You'll dye your hair then, and in the morning everyone will meet the black-haired, blue-eyed Sarah Brownstone. See how much fun this is?''

The last words were only slightly sarcastic, and she managed a small smile. For one moment, she allowed herself to believe in his plan. Mitch Guiness was at work, and one way or the other, he would get them through. He said so.

But then the vision of Jamie and Bill popped in her mind and her smile faltered on her face.

"And you?" she asked softly. "What will you do?''

As she watched, Mitch's face settled into a grim, dark look that sent shudders up her spine.

"I'm going to find the bastard that sold us out," he said quietly.

Looking at his face, she didn't doubt what would happen to the man he found.

Abruptly Mitch's face cleared, his eyes becoming the calm ones she knew so well. He reached out his hand. "Come on, Sarah," he said with his crooked grin. "We've got a lot of driving to do. It's time for a new vehicle, too. What do you say? How about a limo this time? Let's go out in style."

She almost smiled again—almost. But his words hit too near the fear inside her heart. This man could seem so invulnerable, and he did think of everything. But as he'd said before, Les seemed to be always one step ahead of them and neither one of them knew how.

"Sarah," Mitch said as she stood. She was a quick enough study to turn her head, and for the first time, she saw uncertainty on his face. "There's one last thing I should tell you," he said quietly. "Les was released yesterday. The federal court of appeals ruled it a mistrial."

For a long moment, all she could do was look at him. Then slowly, very slowly, she nodded her head. Les was free and there was nothing she could do about it. The dread was complete.

She took Mitch's offered hand and followed him downstairs without a word.

They paused long enough to grab two cups of coffee and a couple of muffins, then hit the road. Mitch stopped at the first pharmacy they came to, just a couple of miles away. He instructed Sarah to look for jet black hair dye while he used the pay phone. It took him a small fortune in change, but finally he connected with his sister in Connecticut.

"Mitch!" Liz exclaimed upon first hearing his voice. "I've been trying so hard to get a hold of you!"

Mitch frowned, instantly on alert. "What's up?" he found himself saying. Her voice was concerned, but not panicked. "Is everything okay with Richard and Andrew?"

"Oh, yes," she assured him. He could hear a smile in her voice—no doubt reflecting Liz's happiness with her husband and stepson. "It's Cagney, Mitch. There's been a shooting."

For a minute, Mitch didn't say anything at all. He forgot about Capruccio and all the impending danger. He could just see the solemn gray eyes of his youngest brother eight years his junior. Cagney—Cage—had always been the quiet one in the family. But then ten years ago he'd astounded them all by announcing he was going to follow in his big brother's footsteps and join the police force. Of course, Mitch had gone on to the National FBI Academy while Cage had remained in the force.

"Is he okay?" Mitch asked, the words harder to get out than he'd imagined.

"Yes," Liz replied, but the word was slow and dragged out. "His leg was hit, but not badly. He shot a kid, Mitch. A fourteen-year-old gang member."

For one moment, Mitch bowed his head. He never doubted for a minute that his brother hadn't shot in self defense. Cagney, with his serious gray eyes, was the last person in the world who would hurt a child. He'd coached a Little League baseball team as a senior in high school. But Cagney was also the last person in the world to forgive himself for such an act. And right now, when his brother needed him, there was nothing Mitch could do.

"He'll have to come to terms with it," he said out loud, the words inadequate in his own mind and completely uncharacteristic.

On the other end of the phone, there was silence. No doubt Liz wondered at her brother's callous response. Mitch was always the first one to offer support, the first one to be there. He was the consummate older brother, and she loved him for it.

"What's wrong, Mitch?" she asked quietly. "Why did you call?"

"Capruccio case," Mitch said curtly, his sharp eyes looking around for possible eavesdroppers. He wouldn't elaborate more, knowing his little sister could put the pieces together. "Late tonight, expect us."

"Of course," Liz agreed quickly. She knew better than to ask for details. Mitch knew she'd come to terms with his chosen profession long ago, though she worried about him constantly. All of his brothers seemed to be driven to danger like moths to the flame.

A recording came on, demanding more money, and Mitch knew it was time to go.

"Look," he added, one last bleak thought coming to him, "if we don't arrive, get your hands on Garret—no, wait, you'll never find him. Cagney. It has to be Cagney. I know the timing is horrible, but, Liz, if you don't hear from me, you have to call him. Tell him I'm working on the Capruccio case, and tell him there's no one else I can trust. He'll figure out what to do."

"Mitch—"

The operator's voice came back on, cutting Liz off.

"Take care, Liz," he said quickly, softly. "And tell that husband of yours he's got the best woman in the world. At least the second best. I love you, little sis."

He was gone before she could say another word. She put down the phone with a small frown furrowing her brow. Second best? Now what was that all about?

Suddenly she was very curious about her brother's newest assignment. She went to find her husband to tell him about their impending guests.

Liz and Richard stayed up all that night waiting for their visitors, Liz's head bowing against her husband's steady shoulder as the hour grew later and later and later.

But Mitch and Jess never did arrive.

At 3:00 a.m., Liz picked up the phone and called Cagney in D.C.

Chapter 15

Mitch knew they were in trouble after just four miles. At that point, their simple back road abruptly poured into a four-lane highway. He kept his eyes peeled for a place to turn in the truck for a less conspicuous vehicle. Every restaurant and gas station he passed, he expected to see a dark sedan pull out behind them. Damn it, they were too exposed on a well-traveled road in a known vehicle.

The small strip malls that dotted the roadside, however, hardly offered car-rental opportunities. On the other hand, he considered grimly, he could always pull into one of the restaurants and hot-wire someone else's car. Given all his other concerns, being chased by cops for grand theft auto hardly seemed relevant.

But just as he was about to resort to such actions, a dark gray Cadillac Eldorado abruptly pulled out from a gas station behind him. It might not have been worth noticing except it caused four cars to come to sudden, screeching halts. The action wasn't one of a prudent driver. More like a determined one.

Mitch stepped on the gas, shooting ahead in the light traffic as Jess identified the danger in her side mirror.

She looked at him for a long moment, her face composed but sober.

"I'll start looking for a turnoff," she said quietly.

Mitch nodded, watching the Cadillac accelerate to catch them. For once, Mitch wished there was more traffic. Anything to use as an obstacle. But instead, it was more like blatant speed against blatant speed. Given the Eldorado's two-hundred-and-twenty-horsepower engine, Mitch didn't have high hopes of their truck winning the race. To make matters worse, the guardrail alongside of the highway prevented him from going suddenly off the road and exploiting the truck's rough-terrain advantage.

He shot up to eighty miles per hour, and began to dash around the few cars he came upon. Eighty-two, Eighty-eight. They were flying by like thunderbolts, the strip malls and guardrails nothing but an indistinct gray blur. Ninety.

"On your left," Jessica warned.

Mitch looked up in time to see the sedan making a bid for the open lane. Without slowing, Mitch slammed the truck over, watching with some satisfaction as the driver of the vehicle was forced to slam on his brakes. But the Eldorado recovered quickly enough, its powerful engine bringing it back up to speed. This time it dodged right, and once more Mitch swerved to counteract.

A sign shot by. Jess's head swiveled back to try and catch the letters.

"An exit's coming up," she told him in a small rush. "On the right. Now!"

He swung the truck over at the last possible minute, slamming on the brakes, dashing across two lanes and running over bumpy embedded road lights. The sedan slammed on its brakes too late to react, missing the exit entirely.

Mitch was just about to congratulate himself when he heard Jess's sudden gasp.

Too late his eyes returned frontward, seeing the three cars waiting patiently for a green light at the top of the ramp. There was no time to come to a full stop, and at over forty miles per hour he didn't dare hit them. He slammed on the horn with one hand, cranking the wheel to a hard left with the other as he pumped the brakes.

They screeched around the last car so close, Jess could see the white-eyed horror in the driver's face. Then they were bouncing along the side of the road, skittering toward the intersection. Jess braced herself with a hand on the dash even as she heard the warning honk of the oncoming vehicle. Dimly she was aware that Mitch was no longer slamming on the brakes but actually accelerating in a mad-dashed attempt to beat the approaching car through the intersection.

For one moment Jess thought they might have made it. For one moment her muscles actually relaxed as a dreamlike quality took hold. Then abruptly the Volvo slammed through the back of the pickup truck, setting them into a hurtling cycle of spin after spin after spin. Abruptly the truck found the guardrail and the spinning stopped. She heard the sickening grind of metal against metal, heard a distant scream that might have been her own.

Then there was only darkness.

Mitch pulled himself back together slowly, each instinct kicking in one by one. He was sitting upright, his forehead flat against the wheel. He could feel the trickle of something warm and wet down his face, and when he tried to open his eyes, the world refused to come into focus. He heard the sound of running feet, the faint hiss of a broken radiator.

His door was thrown open, and for one clear moment he knew he should attack. But then he made out the shocked eyes of a truck driver staring down at him.

"Are you all right, mister?" the stranger asked.

Slowly Mitch tried to nod his head only to find out he couldn't quite move.

"The girl," he whispered. "How's the girl?"

The stranger looked beyond him, and his eyes grew wider.

"You have to get out," the man said. "We can't open her door. Can you do that?"

Mitch thought that might be a silly question. If Jess needed him to jump out of an airplane at one thousand feet, he would do it. That was love, right? That's what love was all about. He forced himself to sit up straight.

The world spun crazily, his face turning pale then green as he fought not to pass out. Slowly, ever so slowly, he managed this time to turn his head. Jess was slumped forward, her door caved in until that side of the truck didn't exist anymore at all. Her legs looked pinned by the wreckage, and for a moment, Mitch could no longer breathe. He'd killed her, or at the very least paralyzed her. The helplessness and horror that flowed through him was as numbing as it was foreign. Huge, capable Mitch, the oldest brother, the man who was always there to help everyone, had finally failed.

"You'll have to help me pull her out," he heard a voice say. After a minute, he realized it was his own.

The stranger spoke up. "Mister, if you don't mind me saying so, you're in no condition to do any such thing."

"I mind," Mitch heard the voice say again. "I have to help her, I have to."

The truck driver opened his mouth as if to persist, then perhaps realized the futility of arguing with a man who had blood down his forehead and stubbornness in his jaw.

"Can you undo your seat belt?" the man said instead. Mitch managed that after a bit, and the truck driver helped him down from the vehicle.

"I'll get her," the driver said. "You just sit here for a minute."

Mitch sat, much harder than necessary. He could still feel the warm wetness trickling down his forehead, and he had to squint his eyes against the abrupt glare of the day. Dimly he became aware of all the people milling around. He needed to look out for Les's men, he found himself thinking. He had to protect Jess from Les's men.

Two people were helping pull a woman from the Volvo and a jumpy-looking man was calling the whole thing in on his cellular phone, his hands waving in the air with his agitation.

He heard a soft moan, and turned to find the stranger laying Jess out on the hard asphalt.

"I think she's just unconscious," the man said, his voice concerned. "She hit her forehead on the dash, but at the least the seat belt kept her from going through the windshield. Her right leg's cut up. It may be broken. But then, I don't know much about these things."

Mitch forced himself to focus on the man. He saw the pulled-down cowboy hat, the scuffed-up toes of working boots. He saw a sprinkle of freckles and dust, and earnest blue eyes. He looked like home, and the sunny, hardworking days of raising hell with his brothers in Maddensfield, North Carolina. Mitch didn't question his instinct. He just knew he and Jess needed help, and this man was all he had to work with.

But before he could say anything, two dark shadows fell across the ground. The stranger's gaze shifted up, and Mitch followed it to find the very thing he'd been dreading. Les's men smiled down at him.

"FBI," one of the men said crisply. "We've been chasing these two through five states. If you don't mind, we'll take it from here."

The stranger looked uncertain, and Mitch opened his mouth to argue. But then a faint breeze rippled the first man's jacket back, revealing a 9-millimeter gun.

They would shoot the man, Mitch realized in the last sane corner of his mind. They would shoot the truck driver and anyone else they had to if he pushed it. He clamped down abruptly, the movement making his head swim. Like a drunkard, his head swiveled back to Jess, lying pale and unconscious on the ground. She was still alive, according to the stranger. But from here, even he could see the blood staining her jeans. He had to do something.

Think Mitch, think.

But abruptly the stranger was gone, and the second man was leaning down.

Move, just move, damn it.

For one fierce moment, he bit down hard on his own tongue. The shock of pain racked his overloaded system, clearing his head for one mind-splitting moment even as the taste of warm blood filled his mouth. He came up like an animal.

Two hundred raw pounds of anger and desperation surged to its feet. And the air filled with the low, savage cry of battle as Mitch's first fist flailed out. He felt the solid satisfaction of connection and watched the man collapse at his feet as the world around him suddenly exploded into screams of fear and shock. He didn't notice the yells, his fist merely balling at his side as his eyes narrowed. He had to fight, he had to kill.

He had to protect Jess. He had to protect . . .

The world suddenly spun, the warm wetness on his face trickling into his eyes. He lashed out again, as if he could conquer even the dizziness. But the momentum of the motion spun him slightly around, skewing the world even more.

He was going to pass out; he could see the black mist just beyond his sight. He howled, low and dark, the frustrated groan of an animal that sees its own trap.

One last time he tried to come around. One last time he fought for his life and the woman still unconscious at his feet. One last time his massive fists reared back.

And the second FBI impostor stepped forward with the deft agility of a healthy man, and slammed Mitch Guiness in the jaw.

Dotti and Henry's son crumpled to the hard asphalt, and knew no more.

Jess came awake to the persistent throbbing in her head. She groaned, the sound rousing her further. She hurt, she thought dimly. She hurt in every known muscle and then some she hadn't known about before.

She tried to open her eyes and bring the world into focus.

It took a while—much longer than it should have. And then she became aware of the fact she was in the back of a car, her face pressed down against the seat. She remembered the car crash, and with it came the horror.

In a sudden, swift movement, she tried to find Mitch. The pain rocketed through her like a knife, and she thought she might pass out again. But then she caught sight of his hair, to her left, and her muscles sagged with the relief.

He was here with her. He was here.

Dimly she heard the voices of two men talking. They were low and forward, muffled by the barrier of plush seats. She tried to move again, this time the motion subtle and slow. She didn't appear to be tied up, but her back hurt, and a low, consistent pain throbbed in her right leg. Face down on the seat, there was little she could do that wouldn't arouse immediate attention.

She tried to simply shift her head to see Mitch better. He appeared to be folded over somewhat, his body curled like a lifeless rag doll. The first pangs of dread clutched her chest.

"Mitch?" she whispered.

He didn't move.

"Mitch?"

Slowly, ever so slowly, his head bobbed. She waited a minute more, then whispered his name again. This time the movement was even more pronounced. As she watched, he pulled himself back from the unconsciousness.

"Jess?" he muttered at last, the word more a groan than a whisper.

"I'm here, Mitch," she managed to whisper, the string of three coherent words sending a needle of pain through her forehead.

"Give me a moment," he said at last. She waited, her dark eyes worried and tight as he propelled himself back into the land of the living.

They were in a car, his senses said. In a car. Which meant, of course, his muddled mind concluded, that they weren't dead. Why weren't they dead? His head protested the thinking, but he got the thought through. Witnesses. If Les's men had shot them in front of all those people, there would be too many witnesses.

And why risk the attention when Les's mistrial presented him with an opportunity to walk away altogether?

Especially when they could drive him and Jess to the middle of nowhere and kill them there. Nice and neat and no attachments. Maybe cement shoes and big-city bridge?

How sublimely cliché.

"Mitch?" Jess's whisper penetrated again. And for the first time that he could recall, he heard fear in the Ice Angel's voice.

It rallied him, giving him the focus he needed to clear the last of the pain and grogginess from his mind. The human body could withstand an amazing amount, as long as you didn't think about it.

"How bad?" he replied, keeping his voice low so not to attract attention to them.

She hesitated. "My back hurts," she said at last, the fear still there but controlled. "And my leg. You?" she said in a rush, the words more urgent than she'd intended. "Are you okay?"

"Of course," he told her, his voice so arrogant, she knew that if she could see his face, he would be grinning at her. "I'm the magician."

She smiled, recognizing his false bravado, but welcoming it nonetheless. Leave it to Mitch Guiness to try and make her feel better even when they were tossed like corn sacks in the back of a Cadillac, headed most likely for certain death.

"Can you make us disappear with a puff of smoke?" she whispered back. She found herself biting back the ridiculous desire to giggle, and one corner of her mind recognized the beginnings of hysteria. Funny, she thought. She'd never been hysterical before.

"Follow my lead, Jess," Mitch suddenly replied, his voice low and intense. He doubted she'd recognized it yet, but the car was slowing down. No doubt they were about to reach their destination. "No matter what happens," he told her, "just do as I say."

She tried to nod, and almost fell unconscious again for her efforts. The pain in her leg intensified, and she had to bite down on her lip to keep from groaning. Her hands were clammy, and she suddenly trembled with the cold. Shock. She was going into shock.

The passenger door was thrown open.

Mitch had to blink against the sudden infusion of bright light. He squinted and made out the face of the man he'd decked earlier. Upon seeing that Mitch was conscious, the man's face drew into an ugly scowl.

"Move, and I'll kill you," the man said without preamble.

Mitch acknowledged the statement with the slightest motion of his head. "Where are we?" he asked, the words thick and rough in his dry throat.

"Nowhere," the man replied. He smiled suddenly, the smile of a man who knew what he was about to do and was delighted by the opportunity.

"I need to speak to Les." Mitch worked to get the words out. His mouth was so dry, he thought he might kill for a glass of water. "I have information for him."

"Too late. Out of the car, Guiness. I've been looking forward to this all day."

"Sure. But when the D.A. calls up the surprise witness at Les's new trial, and the witness reveals I knew all about him, even helped him, Les is going to have a conversation with you. A very short conversation."

"You're bluffing," the man said, his face not taken in at all. But then Mitch became aware of a second voice.

"Wait a second, Charley. He may be bluffing, but he may not. And I know better than you what Les will do to us if we're wrong."

Charley's face scowled even deeper, and he turned away to address his companion. Mitch let out the breath he'd been holding. Seeds of dissension had been planted—now it was just a matter of watering the field. He risked a glance back over to Jess. Her eyes were closed once more, her face dangerously pale. His chest tightened, and for a long moment he thought she might be dead. But then he made out the slow motion of her rising chest. She was still alive, but she needed medical help, and fast.

"She's dying," he said out loud. Charley's gaze swiveled immediately back, his suspicious gaze focused on Mitch and Jess. "She's dying," Mitch repeated again. He didn't have to force the dread into his voice. "And if she does, I guarantee you Les will see you both to hell and back."

For the first time, Charley began to look uneasy. "It just saves us the bullet," Charley said, puffing out his chest in a display of false bravado.

"When Les hears who the witness is, he'll want her again," Mitch said. "He'll need her for bargaining power. But if she's already dead . . ."

"You're making this all up," Charley repeated again.

"It doesn't matter," the second voice said abruptly. "Look, Charley, it's our hides we're talking about. Why take the risk? Look at them. She's half-dead, and he's so banged up, he'll pass out again if you breathe too hard. Let's take 'em to Les, and let him decide. If he's lying, we'll shoot them there. If he's telling the truth, Les will be pleased with us. Don't be stupid, Charley."

Charley's face grew dark, but his eyes were uncertain. Finally he gave in with an ungraceful shrug. "But we tie up Guiness," Charley insisted, his hand unconsciously coming up to his sore jaw.

After further discussion, they did more than just tie Mitch up. They also split up him and Jess. She was moved to the front seat, while Charley joined Mitch in the back. The situation made it impossible for Mitch to communicate with Jess, but at least it bought them some time. And when the second man finally saw how bad Jess's leg was, it also earned her some medical attention. After all, they wouldn't gain anything by delivering her corpse to Capruccio.

The second man brought out a first-aid kit, and allowed Mitch to treat her the best he could. He had to cut off the leg of her jeans, the mangled mess of her thigh almost making him sick. He'd never sewed up a woman before, and every time he had to pass the needle through the rubbery texture of her smooth skin, another bead of sweat popped onto his brow. He hated himself for having hurt her, and he hated Capruccio even more. The first chance he got, Mitch would show Les Capruccio just what a Guiness could do.

The second man, still nameless, was humane enough to cover Jess with all their jackets, and blast the heater for extra warmth. He also pulled out three bottles of water from the trunk, allowing Mitch to drink a little, and administering the rest to Jess. Then Charley took over, binding Mitch's hands behind his back and shoving him into the back of the car.

Mitch's head swam once more, and with the loss of adrenaline, he became aware of his own aches and pains. There was nothing more he could do for Jess and himself but rest. He closed his eyes, and as the Cadillac turned onto I-76 heading east, he fell into exhausted slumber.

They drove nonstop. Charley and Neuman—as the other man was called—switched off the driving.

In the front of the car, Jess passed to easier breathing. Neuman kept her plied with water at least, and her body had stopped its shivering. She slept continuously.

They stopped at a rest area, and Mitch felt his hopes rise. If he could just get to a phone and tell Liz or Cagney or someone what had happened. And where they were going. Hell, where were they going?

But Charley escorted Mitch to the men's room, not allowing any openings even as he untied him briefly. The best Mitch could do was stretch out his muscles as much as possible and ease the circulation back into his fingers. The dull throbbing in his head had begun to ease, though he knew he looked like a fright with all the dried blood on the left side of his face. He could use that to his advantage.

They stopped again, and still Charley didn't let him out of his sight. The third time, however, Jess was conscious.

"Jeez, I can't take her to the ladies' room," Neuman was whispering to Charley under his breath. "I mean, there are people here. How would that look?"

"Well I can't take her, either."

The two men stared at each other.

"Maybe we don't let her go."

"Charley, if she's gotta go, she's gotta go. We got eight hours of driving left. Don't be stupid."

"Can she walk?"

They turned to Mitch and Jess, staring at them both hard. "Can you walk?" Neuman demanded to know.

Jess, leaning heavily against the car and pale as a sheet, shook her head.

"She don't look good."

"She don't look good."

"If we'd have shot 'em, we wouldn't have these problems."

"Charley, don't be stupid."

They continued to stare at Jess, who finally summoned a wan smile.

"Why can't Mitch at least walk me to the door?" she suggested weakly. "I can handle the rest on my own."

Charley puffed out his chest. "I'll walk you to the door. Then you take care of the rest."

Mitch looked at her sharply but couldn't catch her eye. Leaning heavily on Charley's arm, she began shuffling toward the bathroom. Few cars were around the rest stop, few people noticing as he pulled the heavy metal doors open for her, and using the wall for support, she struggled into the dark, dank interior. At the sink, however, a stooped-over woman with gray hair was washing her hands.

Jess went straight toward her.

"Ma'am," she whispered urgently, her voice cracking with the effort. The woman didn't look up, and finally Jess tapped her on the shoulder. The silvery head popped up, finding Jess's reflection in the mirror with startled, watery blue eyes.

Jess looked at the aging woman, and began picking her words carefully.

"Look," she said softly, leaning against the wall until her shredded thigh was apparent "I'm with the FBI, but I'm in trouble. There's a man standing outside this door, a very big man, who hurt my leg. I have to go back out there, and I think he may kill me. Do you understand?"

The woman blinked her watery blue eyes and said nothing. Jess felt her hopes sink.

"Please, I don't need you to do much. Just call the police. Tell them FBI agent Mitch Guiness of the Witness Protection Program needs assistance. We're on I-76, eastbound. I don't know where we're going. Maybe you could get the license plate number off the car when we leave. Please, anything."

Her voice cracked completely, and she slid down a little on the wall. Sweat began to bead on her forehead, and she felt suddenly nauseous. God, she was probably going to get this sweet old lady killed, as well.

Then the woman began to move her fingers in sign language, and Jess thought she was going to cry. She closed her eyes, the sweat rolling down her cheeks in silent desolation. She didn't know what else to do.

She was tired and scared and utterly defeated.

She turned, and crawled back toward the door. She was actually grateful for the support of Charley's arm, and that only made her feel worse.

They stopped twice more but never could get a moment alone.

Eight hours of hard driving later, they were in northern New Jersey.

Charley shoved Mitch out of the car when they finally pulled up to the back of the nondescript house. Mitch stumbled once, then regained his balance. He didn't say anything, didn't even bother with a dark glance. Let Charley play bully. Mitch was saving himself for the real opponent.

Jess was awake, her brown eyes dull and glazed. She leaned heavily on Neuman, obviously unable to walk on her injured leg. Mitch watched her in growing concern, his jaw muscle tightening unconsciously. But then for one fleeting instant, her gaze swept up to meet his. He was startled by the clarity he suddenly found there. Then her glazed look returned, and she moaned softly as she stepped.

Mitch looked away, the small communication clear in his mind. He wasn't the only one that knew how to play wounded sparrow. Damn, but she was impressive. He almost grinned, feeling suddenly rejuvenated.

The Ice Angel was back and in fine form. Now he just had to bail them both out of this mess.

The next thing he knew, they were face-to-face with Les Capruccio.

Les looked them both up and down as if dirt rags had suddenly been paraded into his living room.

"I don't like you bringing them here," he said flatly, addressing Charley and Neuman.

Neuman spoke up. "They said they had information for you."

"Most likely they were lying in a vain attempt to save their own skins, you idiot," Capruccio said, clearly bored. His gaze flickered to Jess, taking in her damaged leg and bruised face.

"You don't look so good, sugar," Les drawled. "But then I always told you you'd get what you deserved."

Jess didn't say anything, but looked at him with her glazed, expressionless eyes. This seemed to amuse Capruccio, and he rose from the sofa to walk toward her. Mitch had to consciously restrain himself as Capruccio reached up and caressed Jess's face with deceptive tenderness.

Mitch forced his attention back to the rope binding his hands. Each time they'd retied it, it had gotten looser. Now, while everyone was distracted by Jess, he had his perfect opportunity.

"Nice haircut," Les whispered silkily. "But then, I never much went for brunettes."

Jess didn't respond. If anything, she sagged heavier against Neuman, who had to shift suddenly under the change in weight.

"You lose, sugar," Les told her with one last Cheshire grin. "I go free, and you die. You weren't worth much anyway. Hell, you weren't even worth it in bed."

He turned sharply away, his dark eyes finding Mitch.

"Nice try," Capruccio said, buttoning up his silk suit as he straightened his shoulders. "But I have my own contacts, Mr. Guiness, and I probably know more about what's going on in the program right now than you do."

He turned away, already heading for the doorway.

"Kill them both," he called out casually behind him.

But just as he was about to step from the room, a bullhorn suddenly interrupted the silence.

"This is the police. Come out with your hands up."

Les pivoted sharply, his face turning a mottled red. "You fools," he hissed fiercely to his men. "You led us all into a trap."

With a roar of rage, he reached inside his jacket for his gun.

Mitch didn't wait. Giving his hands one last vehement tug, he barreled into Les.

"Run, Jess!" Mitch yelled. "Get out now!"

A shot exploded, both Mitch and Les crashing to the floor. Charley and Neuman danced at the edges, guns pulled but denied a clear target. Jess pushed herself forward, grabbed the nearest lamp and slammed it down on Charley's head. He crumpled to the floor, even as Neuman whirled and fired his gun. Her leg gave out, and she toppled off-balance in time to hear the bullet whiz by her ear.

Dimly, she heard the front door splinter open, then the sound of more gunfire. Neuman staggered back, red blooming across his chest. But then she caught sight of Charley's gun, sliding across the floor. She scampered toward it, clutching it desperately.

Another shot rang out, ceiling plaster collapsing upon them in a choking cloud of dust.

"Everyone freeze! Now!"

Jess came to a halt and Mitch instinctively paused. Les used the moment to abruptly catch the larger man with a clean uppercut. Mitch staggered back on his knees, Les coming up in time to find himself confronted with seven police officers bearing guns.

He froze, his beady eyes darting around the room in desperation. Quick as a whistle, he dropped back to his haunches.

"One move and she's dead," he announced abruptly.

Jess looked confused; then her eyes suddenly rounded as she caught sight of the small .22 caliber pistol now pinned on her from his ankle holster.

Without thinking, she pointed her own gun right back at him.

"One move, and you're dead," she said quite clearly. Behind her, she heard the police officers shift uncomfortably. She kept her gaze focused on Les.

Les laughed, but his own expression was no longer so sure as his eyes darted around the room. "Jessica, I'm serious." He cocked the gun.

She responded by cocking her own, and pinning him with her cold arctic eyes. Out of the corner of her eye, she could see Mitch slowly positioning for action. She held the gun steadier.

Les's smile began to look very forced, his eyes suddenly on the cops in line behind her. "I will kill her," he reiterated. Abruptly he smiled at her, a sickening sweet smile. "Come on, sugar," he cajoled. "Set the damn thing down before you hurt yourself. I know you never liked guns. Do they remind you of your father, little Mary Morgan? Do they remind you of when he fell dead at your feet?"

Oh, he was good, Mitch thought, balancing on the balls of his feet. Mitch had never wanted to hurt a man like he wanted to hurt Capruccio right now.

Jess, however, never wavered. No sign of emotion flickered across her face, no tremble in her arm gave away the strain.

"I'm going to count to three," she said calmly. "At the end of three, I'm going to shoot you, Les. One."

"Put it down," Les demanded again, but this time his voice wasn't so calm. He'd always hated how she could look at him like that, as if he wasn't anything but a cheap suit who could take her body and never possess the rest of her. "The minute you so much as flinch, you're dead."

"Two."

Les's eyes went wild. Mitch could feel the growing desperation in the man, and his own muscles grew tense with the strain. Any moment now, any moment.

Les stepped forward, the sweat now noticeable on his brow.

"Come on, sugar," he tried again. "You can't shoot me."

He took another step forward, and for just a moment, Jess hesitated.

And suddenly, little Mary Morgan did see her father, his eyes rounded in surprise as he dropped at her feet. And she saw Darold arching back, and Jamie and Bill sitting sightless at the base of the tree. She saw all the blood and destruction, and felt the cycle snap shut like a trap.

She leveled the gun, her finger pulling back on the trigger, and she understood her mother all those years ago. The only option left was death.

"No, Jess!" Mitch's voice cracked through, Les's head swiveling toward the sound even as her finger jumped on the trigger. The gun exploded in her hands, the acrid smell of gunpowder filling the air as the .357 Magnum jumped to life. She heard the dull ringing in her ears, and felt the dim sensation of tears sliding down her face.

Les crumpled to the floor, two blooms of crimson suddenly appearing on his chest. His gun dangled lifelessly from his fingers, and two police officers immediately stepped forward. Mitch waded through them easily, grabbing her up in his arms.

She clung to him, the tears flowing like a river, and felt another police officer remove the gun from her fingers. She cried harder.

"It's okay, it's okay," Mitch whispered against her hair. "Your bullet's in the floor, Jess. It's in the floor. The cops got him, okay? The cops."

She tightened her hold on his neck and wouldn't let him go.

Epilogue

"Approximately one hundred and ten people die a day in motor vehicle accidents."

"For the last time, Andrew, she's not going to die. She simply needs a lot of rest."

Jessica's eyes fluttered opened to find herself staring into the thick-lensed gaze of a little boy. His blue eyes blinked rapidly.

"You're alive," he declared.

"Oh, dear."

The boy was pushed aside, and a woman took his place. She had long, mahogany hair that swept forward when she bent down, and she possessed the most striking pair of midnight blue eyes that Jessica had ever seen.

"Don't mind Andy," the woman said, her voice soft with a Carolina drawl. "He just likes his statistics. How do you feel?"

Like hell, Jessica thought, but her mouth was too dry to form the words. The woman seemed to understand and held out a glass of water. She helped prop up Jessica's head so she could drink.

"Mitch?" she croaked out finally. The young boy was back, staring at her with inquisitive eyes.

"Mitch is asleep, too," Andy replied. "Liz chained him down so he couldn't bother you."

Jessica's eyes flew open, her gaze finding Liz in time to see the beautiful woman's face turn red. She laughed somewhat self-consciously.

"I didn't actually chain him down," she assured Jessica. "I just locked him in. Though knowing Mitch, he's probably found a way around that by now. But honestly, honey, he was pacing this room for three days straight, and it wasn't doing either of you a bit of good."

Jessica could only nod. Somehow the name Liz seemed familiar to her, but she couldn't quite place it. She took another drink of the water, on her own this time, and finished collecting her scattered thoughts.

"Where am I?" she asked at last.

"Oh, dear," Liz said, then laughed good-naturedly. "I forgot to introduce myself. Well, I'm Liz Keaton—used to be Guiness—Mitch's sister. And this little rascal is my stepson, Andrew. He likes to quote statistics, but don't let him fool you. He's a sucker for strawberry ice cream."

This time Andrew blushed, but he didn't refute the statement.

"You were in a shoot-out," he announced, this bit of information seeming to appeal to him tremendously. "Did you know firearms kill thirty-six thousand people a year?"

Weakly, Jessica shook her head. This didn't seem to phase him.

"My father says guns are bad, you shouldn't have to use violence to fight violence. A real hero uses his mind."

If only he knew, Jessica thought. She was saved from replying, however, by the door suddenly flying open. Judging by the sudden paling of Liz's face, Mitch had arrived.

"Liz," he practically roared. "What the hell did you think you were doing, locking me in like that?"

"Letting you sleep," she replied casually. Her brother towered over her, easily twice her size, but she didn't even flinch. "You're losing your touch, Mitch. It used to only take you fifteen minutes to break out of a room."

"This place is built like a damn stone prison," he informed her darkly. Then abruptly he noticed that Jessica's eyes were no longer closed but looking at him. The next words died completely in his throat, his entire face suddenly softening. "Hey," he said quietly. "You're awake."

Jessica could only nod, no longer trusting herself to speak. Mitch looked tall and powerful and vital, and she didn't think she'd ever seen anyone more beautiful in her life. He was alive. She hadn't killed him. He was alive, and he was here.

Liz saw the look pass between her brother and the mysterious woman on the bed. Being madly in love with her husband herself, she didn't require an interpreter to understand the sudden intensity.

"Andrew," she began tactfully, "why don't you help me go make brownies for Jessica?"

Andrew looked as if he would have argued, but Liz's hand was already firm on his shoulder, guiding him from the room.

"Remember, Mitch," she called out over her shoulder, "she's still weak and needs plenty of rest."

The closing of the door saved her from her brother's succinct reply.

"How are you doing?" Mitch asked as soon as they were alone.

"Tired," she admitted, her eyes still fastened to his face. He looked slightly paler and like he might have lost some weight. But then he grinned at her, and she felt her heart leap in her chest. She moved over slightly in the bed, and he took that as an invitation to sit down on the edge.

For a long while, neither of them said anything. They just drank in each other's presence, the fact they were here and alive and together.

Finally Mitch bent down and gently kissed her lips.

"I've been waiting a long time to do that," he said softly. Three days to be exact.

She nodded, her now-blue eyes growing dark.

"Kiss me again," she whispered. He complied, a slow leisurely kiss that made her feel at once warm and protected. She had to consciously fight the urge to wrap her arms around his neck and bury her head against his shoulder. For one intense moment she could see him fighting with Les and the fear rippled through her.

Mitch felt her shudder against him and understood. "It's okay now," he soothed. "It's all over, Jessica."

"Jessica?" she asked.

He looked at her with calm brown eyes. "Since Capruccio is dead now, there's no need for you to be Jess McMoran anymore. You can have your life back now. Go back to fashion shoots and international jaunts."

He said the words simply enough, not even aware he was holding his breath until she abruptly turned away, her blue eyes focusing starkly on the wall.

"But is it really over?" she asked softly.

He nodded. "I helped file the paperwork myself, sweetheart. Capruccio is as dead as dead gets, and without him the contract on your head is worthless. Les never acknowledged a successor and he didn't have any children, so the police are predicting an internal struggle for power, now. At any rate, no one really cares about Les or Jessica Gavornée anymore."

"Maybe I'm not really Jessica Gavornée," she said at last. "Maybe Les was right, and I'm still Mary Morgan." She turned abruptly, pinning him with her intense blue gaze. "I shot at him, Mitch. I was willing to kill to save you, to save myself. All my life I've hated the violence. Yet six men are dead because of me, and I would have taken Les's life myself if I'd aimed better."

"You can aim fine," Mitch told her abruptly, his brown eyes serious. "I saw you with those two-liter bottles. You have no problem at all hitting a target. However, you did miss Les and that's not unusual. There's a big difference between firing at plastic bottles and a human being. Agents have to learn how to shoot in the field, to overcome that resistance. Your heart knows the difference. If you truly hadn't cared, Jess, you would have hit him as easily as you did those bottles."

She was still quiet. "I wanted to hit him, though," she said softly. "At that moment I wanted him dead."

"You didn't kill him, Jess," Mitch repeated. "The cops did."

He could still see the guilt on her face, the torment in her eyes, and it tore at him. He just wanted the whole mess behind them. He wanted to hold her in his arms, and keep her safe. He wanted to look to the future, instead of drowning in the past. He wanted to wake up with this woman every morning of his life and gaze into her intelligent blue eyes. He wanted to be there for her when she needed him, in sickness and health and death do us part. He wanted the whole nine yards.

She turned in the bed, wincing a little as the movement pulled her leg.

"Why are we here?" she asked at last, changing topics altogether.

"I'm still working things out with the Office of Professional Relations," Mitch told her. "Remember, Capruccio had to get his information from somewhere. I didn't want to take any chances of bringing either of us in until the whole situation was resolved. I did call Merill, the case agent in charge, though, after I called the police. He has some ideas on who the person probably is. It seems one of our billing people has developed an expensive gambling problem. I guess in addition to processing the expenses, he decided to make a bit of money by selling the name of the retreat to Capruccio. While Merill takes care of him, I told him we would keep a low profile." And he'd tried talking to Cagney, but his brother seemed to have withdrawn completely after the shooting. His leg was healing, but the shadows in his eyes weren't.

Yesterday he'd called Mitch and announced he was quitting the force. Then, before Mitch could react, he'd simply hung up. Neither he nor Liz have been able to reach Cagney since.

Before him, Jessica nodded, her hand reaching out to lay next to his. Unconsciously, she began to doodle a little pattern on the back of his palm with her finger. He felt warm and strong. Her heart fluttered again, her stomach tightening.

"And the police?" she asked.

Abruptly he grinned at her. "I've been meaning to thank you," he said softly. She looked at him, not understanding. "It seems you told a Mrs. Abbott what was going on. She gave the license number of the car to her husband and he called it in. With my brother Cagney having already put an APB out on us, the police found the car pretty quickly. They followed us to Capruccio, not wanting to risk a confrontation with us still in the vehicle, then got into position. You did good, Jess. But then, that doesn't surprise me."

"I didn't think she understood."

"She reads lips."

"Oh."

She wanted him. She wanted him to lie down beside her so she could rest her head on his shoulder. She wanted to feel his arms around her, holding her, keeping her safe. He alone knew all her secrets, yet he'd never turned away from her. He alone had kept all his promises to her. He was her magician, and she wanted to keep him.

She just didn't know how to say the words.

"Are you all right?" Mitch asked finally. Her face looked peculiar, kind of tight. He thought for a moment she might cry, but then that passed, as well.

"Will...will you lie with me?" she said finally. Her gaze skittered up, and once more he was struck by her eyes. And then it hit him. She looked vulnerable and afraid.

"Of course," he said, his voice gruff. He lay down carefully, not wanting to hurt her. But she pushed herself into his arms the first moment she could, resting her head upon his shoulder as he drew his other arm around her. She was wearing just an old T-shirt of Liz's. He'd seen her in it before in the last couple of days when he'd cared for her. Now the picture was suddenly arousing in his mind, and he found his body responding.

Forcefully he reminded himself of Liz's parting words and settled for caressing Jess's bare arm instead. He could feel her relaxing against him, and he thought it might be the most perfect sensation in all the world.

"What are you thinking?" he asked at last.

Jessica didn't answer right away. Her throat was tight and her eyes once more burned with tears she didn't completely understand. It was too perfect in his arms, she thought thickly. She wanted and needed him so much, when she'd sworn never to want or need anyone.

"I don't want to be a model anymore," she said at last, the words husky. "I want to be a schoolteacher."

Mitch's hand stilled on her arm, then resumed its gentle strokes. "So be a schoolteacher," he told her.

She nodded against his chest, but the simplicity of the situation didn't ease the tightness in her throat. Suddenly unable to bear it, she raised her head and found his lips with her own.

He could taste the urgency in the kiss, taste the intensity and the pain. He half drowned in the onslaught, but he knew better than to give in this time. She'd turned to him like this in the past, only to shut him out again later. Gently he placed both his hands on her shoulders and drew her away.

Her eyes opened wide with confusion.

"You...you don't want to kiss me?" she asked. The broken woundedness of the words threatened to tear out his heart. Very slowly he shook his head.

"I love kissing you, Jess," he told her honestly, his brown eyes dark. "I could die a happy man, kissing you. But what is it *you* want?"

Her gaze slid down to his lips, her tongue darting out to lick her own in confusion. He felt the lightning rod of desire flash through his stomach. She'd be the death of him, yet.

"I want you," she whispered.

He nodded, not doubting her words. But he needed her to want him for more than just the moment, for more than just the pain. He needed her to want him forever.

"Jess," he said quietly, "why didn't you ever tell the program about your mother?"

She shook her head, looking confused by this sudden question. "I told you before," she said. "I promised my mother I wouldn't tell anyone."

"No," Mitch said. "Maybe that's what you tell your-self, but I don't believe you. We weren't just anyone, and the situation wasn't a cocktail party or a *Vogue* interview. We were the people trying to save your life, and you held back vital information. Be honest, Jessica. Admit why you didn't tell anyone. Admit that you didn't trust us."

Her gaze came down, unable to meet his eyes. Then suddenly, her head came up with a flare of intensity.

"Why should I have trusted you?" she demanded to know. "Because you told me to? My father used to tell me every day he'd never hit me again. And it didn't mean a thing, Mitch. It didn't mean one damn thing. And even you guys, swearing you could protect me when two attempts were made on my life in the first five months alone. People say things all the time. It doesn't mean anything."

"Are you safe right now?" Mitch countered calmly. She looked startled. Then slowly she nodded her head. "Then I fulfilled my promise, Jess. I can't vouch for other peo-ple, and I certainly can't change what your father did. But I can tell you about Mitch Guiness. When I make prom-ises, I intend to keep them. And I will fight with every-thing I have to do so."

Slowly her eyes melted in front of him. She looked at him, and she remembered her mother's words.

"I didn't know who to trust. So I went back to the evil I knew, hoping it wouldn't be as bad as before."

For the first time, Jessica Gavornée wondered if she'd done the right thing. Shutting everyone else out, had she in fact created the same cycle her mother had? By running from everyone, she'd limited her options by limiting her avenues of help. Until in that one final instant, she'd faced her mother's last choice and made the same decision.

Violence to end violence, blood flowing to blood.

Her head bowed down with the weight of the guilt. Mitch saw the gesture, and it broke his heart.

"Don't," he whispered, reaching down to catch her chin with his hand. "You can't change the past, Jess. You knew two real bastards, and they made your life hell. But it's not your fault. You survived. Now let it go, Jess. I told you in the beginning, you've got to learn just to let it go. Live in the darkness too long, and you'll forget how to see the light.''

"I don't know how," she admitted brokenly. "Oh, Mitch, I just don't know how."

"With love," he told her simply. "Mary Morgan/Jessica Gavornée/Jess McMoran, I love you."

She looked so startled, he held his breath in his chest. Then slowly, ever so slowly, her face became composed and serious.

"Mitch," she said, "I trust you."

He nodded, still holding his breath.

"And I think I love you, too."

He grinned, that wonderful magical grin that made her heart pitter-patter in her chest.

"I think it's time for one last name," he told her, stroking her arm leisurely. "Yes, I think Jessica Guiness would sound quite nice."

She pretended to consider it for a moment, then beamed at him with a precious, new smile. "Jessica Guiness, the schoolteacher," she told him.

"Quite nice," he concurred. "What about Jessica Guiness, the mother of three?"

"Mother of two," she determined.

"Deal," he conceded, then drew her deeper against his chest. His grin grew lazy, his darkening gaze fastening upon her lips. "And Jessica Guiness, the lover of Mitch?" he whispered huskily.

"Oh, yes," she agreed against his lips. "Quite nice."

Then he kissed her, and neither one spoke for a long, long time.

* * * * *

Take 4 bestselling love stories FREE

Plus get a FREE surprise gift!

Become a
Privileged Woman,
You'll be entitled to all
these *Free Benefits.*
And *Free Gifts,* too.

To thank you for buying our books, we've designed an exclusive FREE program called *PAGES & PRIVILEGES*™. You can enroll with just one Proof of Purchase, and get the kind of luxuries that, until now, you could only read about.

*B*IG HOTEL DISCOUNTS

A privileged woman stays in the finest hotels. And so can you—at up to 60% off! Imagine standing in a hotel check-in line and watching as the guest in front of you pays $150 for the same room that's only costing you $60. Your *Pages & Privileges* discounts are good at Sheraton, Marriott, Best Western, Hyatt and thousands of other fine hotels all over the U.S., Canada and Europe.

*F*REE DISCOUNT TRAVEL SERVICE

A privileged woman is always jetting to romantic places.

When <u>you</u> fly, just make one phone call for the lowest published airfare at time of booking— <u>or double the difference back!</u>

PLUS—you'll get a $25 voucher to use the first time you book a flight AND <u>5% cash back on every ticket you buy thereafter through the travel service!</u>

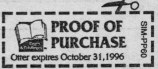

PROOF OF PURCHASE

Offer expires October 31, 1996

SIM-PP60